YEAR'S BEST
TRANSHUMAN SF
2017 ANTHOLOGY

Edited by C.P. Dunphey

Gehenna & Hinnom Books

ACKNOWLEDGMENTS

Thank you to all the fantastic authors who submitted to us, believing in our mission and trusting in us. We only opened our doors in April of 2017, and this anthology you are reading is our second major publication (aside from the bi-monthly *Hinnom Magazine*). We received so many fantastic stories and it truly moved us to see the amount of passion from these writers. We hope to release similar anthologies in the future, as the experience of this volume alone was filled with exciting and breathtakingly inspired works.

Special thanks to all the authors included in this volume, and to the many members of the professional science fiction community for their unwavering support.

Finally, thank you to everyone who decided to
Embrace the Unknown.

TABLE OF CONTENTS

THE VIVARIUM
By M. Lopes da Silva

The cities had shrugged off enough of their skylines to become wastelands, interconnected by swathes of desert aglow with fiery phosphorescent shrubbery. One of these forgotten cities used to exist beside a sea. The rubble crunched with shells underfoot. A group of people—dusty and raw—traveled in a loose group of six. They were wary, and swung their guns around with a swagger they did not feel.

One of them, a foot taller than the others, saw the dome first and called out. Immediately they began to chatter amongst themselves. As one, they headed towards the white structure, their wariness tempered by a sudden lightness of mood.

They knew everything, and they knew nothing.

The egg of the Vivarium was slightly larger than an ancient arena, squatting over the city in pearlescent white. Its shell was actually a network of windows, with solar shields that sucked power from the sun while filtering appropriate amounts of light through their intelligent plastic. Nanites crawled across the shell, invisible to the naked eye, busy with preprogrammed tasks.

Within the Vivarium a series of broad sculpted plains, each rich with different varieties of flora and fauna, encircled a mountain like a massive spiral staircase around a post. Each plain was at least a mile long, some longer, and threads of water trickled raucously, connecting many of the plains with foaming waterfalls.

The yolk of the Vivarium was lush with life. Peacocks screamed and elephants trumpeted. Wolves prowled through densely-planted woods while goats clambered up rocks and grazed on berries. The air was thick with flying creatures; birds and bats and droning bees. The flying beasts were always popular.

And among the living animals, a few mechanical ones roamed as well. Some of the androids were semi-realistic simulacra, imitating known species, but many of them were fantastic. Small dragons and alicorns tumbled through the air, while unicorns roamed among herds of organic horses below. And beneath the mountain, under the tiny sea set in motion by wave-generating hydraulics, automatic mermaids and mermen played among briny wonders of coral and seaweed.

Apart from the merpeople, the only robots that resembled humans physically were the fairies—tiny winged automatons that gamboled among the flowers—but neither of these machines could speak any sort of language out loud. The merpeople were programmed to emit a series of musical notes through their mouths when they crested the waves, and the fairies made a kind of tinkling sound, like bells, whenever they "spoke."

This apparent lack of humanity was deceptive.

C-23 was looking for 33 again.

33 liked to hide in herbivores, in particular. 33 identified as female, though gender was irrelevant for the constellations. Every day they could choose anew from the vast array of living and automatic phantasmagoria within the Vivarium; males and females and hermaphrodites and asexuals and everything betwixt and between existed. At the end of the day a series of preset alarms summoned the diurnal constellations away from their various hosts, and the sentient clouds of data would steam from the pores of creatures and robots and verdure, drifting to return to the nests along the walls. Conversely, the nocturnal constellations would leave their nests, collecting like shadows along the ceiling until they selected their hosts of choice for the evening, and floated down to slip into skins.

The nests were long, hollow tubes that connected to a vast

closed system. There, the resting residents could run a dream randomizer, or play in the digital world of the Vivarium. C-23 wanted to find 33 before the final alarm sounded. 33 always ran the dream randomizer, and never uploaded. She said she didn't need to run a human avatar around in a digital wonderland, that she preferred the things that the dream randomizer showed her instead.

C-23 drifted above one of the muggy lagoons in the body of a barn owl, and let out a screech. C-23 often chose to occupy the barn owl hosts, and 33 knew that. C-23 landed on a mossy branch overlooking the water, waiting for a ping on the innercom.

Every host in the Vivarium had an innercom, or a small, location-based communication device, surgically implanted and regularly maintained by nanites. The only problem with the innercom is that signals had to be directly sent to specific hosts, and couldn't be broadcast to general areas or zones. Visual confirmation was the most direct way to open up an innercom link with another person in the Vivarium.

C-23 fidgeted on the branch. He wondered if 33 had actually said that she'd meet him at the lagoon today, or if he'd misremembered her. A fish bubbled up from the lagoon and sent a friendly "hello" ping—not 33. C-23 broadcast a brief reply: "Sorry, waiting for a friend."

With a flop the fish sank down into the murk.

A distant chime and a mechanical voice rising from hidden speakers announced the hour: 6 P.M. Only two more hours left. Storybook-like, as the hour struck, they would have to leave their hosts and return to form vague nanite clouds flying in precise constellations of preferences, input, and operational heuristics; "Everything but the meat," as the old Vivarium advertising slogan had once cheekily put it. The barn owl's talons flexed nervously. C-23 preferred to be nocturnal, but had gone diurnal recently, since he'd met 33. There was something about 33 that was addictive to be around; after long contemplation he realized that it was her absolute engagement with whatever unfolded in front of her. There was no inner obfuscation, just naked raw focus and unchecked curiosity. Life lit her up; she never occupied the robots. She said that the organic interfacing tissue just wasn't enough. She wanted to feel pulses, and smell the foul reek of the dirt and shiver in the shallows of the icy pools.

Suddenly an alarm—far louder than the chime announcing the hour—gave a brief squawk. C-23 sat up alertly; the "C" referred to the command group of constellations that were in charge of all

Vivarium emergencies.

The mechanical voice spoke with bland equanimity: "Six unidentified organics, human, attempting to enter the shell. C staff requested at the front door."

Immediately C-23 thought of the exit password, and the barn owl spread its wings and shifted to keep its purchase on the branch as the particles that composed C-23 steamed from the bird's pores. C-23 rose as a cloud, speeding towards one of the blinking emergency access tubes in the walls. Immediately C-23 sprinted through the pneumatic tube, spitting out into a massive robotic host with an 8-leg configuration and 2 giant sonic cannon forearms. The robot had a 360-degree camera feed. It had been a long time since C-23 had occupied a robot, and the vastly different sensory array took a moment to adjust to. The clamor of the fauna within the Vivarium increased in volume and intensity. It was rare to encounter outside organics these days.

C-23's robot plummeted from a concealed door in the Vivarium's ceiling overhang by the front gate, landing heavily on the pavement. It was closely followed by two other identical machines that ended up flanking both of C-23's exposed sides. They were hosting C-58 and C-19—the automata didn't require innercom pings to identify each other. Robots were dense with data input.

With the help of the machine's scanning capabilities, C-23 could tell that the six humans in front of them were suffering from varying levels of radiation sickness. Four of them had lice. Two of them had strains of hepatitis. All of them were carrying at least two varieties of internal parasites. They were malnourished, but strong enough to throw rocks and chunks of concrete at the shell of the Vivarium. Luckily, they hadn't broken through it, yet.

C-23 accessed the emergency vocal broadcast program. "Please wait," said a soothing nondescript voice from the robot's speakers. "We have resources that can help treat your illnesses and get rid of your parasites. We can give you food. If you would like to join us in the Vivarium, we can even offer you the option of Transcending and joining us."

It was odd to be looking at human beings in the flesh again, and not a blemish-free avatar in Viva City. C-23 wished that they had something better to say to each other, instead of this pointless posturing.

"Lying piece of junk!" hollered one of the organics, aiming a piece of concrete at C-23. It clanged off the side of the machine harmlessly.

"We're not lying. Please stop throwing debris at the Vivarium and the staff," C-23 broadcasted.

The organics jeered and threw some more rocks at the robots. C-23 heard C-58 and C-19 shift into defensive positions.

"Just a bunch of fucking robots hiding the food!" one of the organics taunted, and that was when C-23's scanners finally detected the missile launcher that the six people had wrapped up in military Night Tape.

Over the private robotic communications link C-23 authorized the use of sonic cannons.

Immediately the three robots began firing massive concussive soundwaves that buffeted the organics backwards. But the missile launcher had already been hastily drawn and roughly aimed, and as the organics fell, one missile screamed up into the air, crashing into the shell of the dome. Immediately alarms went off and emergency tiles rippled along the surface of the broken egg, working hastily to repair the hole.

C-23 activated a trio of remote mini-drones to dart the organics with tranquilizers. The drones buzzed into the air, rising from a small compartment in the robot's mid-section. The people screamed as blood streamed from their punctured eardrums and the dragonfly-sized drones neatly darted them in the dust. When the last organic human collapsed, unconscious, C-23 ran another brief scan on them. All six of them were alive. The drones retreated.

"Destroy their weapons and move them to the quarantine room. Supply them with food. Report to any emergency drones that may need to be staffed inside the Vivarium afterwards. I'm going to be in the Hub," C-23 said over the private link.

"Understood," replied C-19.

C-23 navigated his robot over to a tube port in the exterior wall, and ran the upload docking program. A metal cylinder extended from the machine's left forearm, and successfully docked. C-23 thought the Hub nav codes, then the exit password, and the particles that composed C-23's constellation were sucked down the tube and directly into the Hub.

The Hub was in large part a digital construction, and C-23 felt the uncomfortable compression of his previous robotic senses into his human avatar. His avatar was purple-skinned and roguishly handsome, the muscles well-defined; a far cry from the radiation-burned woman C-23 had once been, long ago. But C-23 was one of the many who had chosen to abandon their names along with what they had once been. He was happier that way.

The Hub abruptly began feeding C-23 a series of updates relating to the condition of the Vivarium. The missile had broken a piece of one of the artificial planes free, which had then toppled below, crushing several host animals and plants. Constellations had steamed free from their hosts in a panic, recalled to the safety of the nests in the walls, but there were still people missing. Toxin levels had dramatically increased inside the Vivarium, and extra nanites were being released to deal with the radiation and toxin overload.

Suddenly C-23 was joined by several other members of the C group, uploading into the Hub in an abrupt flutter of pixels. Reports were being made—the Vivarium's environment could be stabilized again, the lost species re-cloned. Stressed animals were being tranquilized. C-23 was barely listening. He was running through the lists, looking for the missing people.

33 was on the list.

C-23 kept re-reading the list. His eyes went over the brief string of numbers and names repeatedly. 33 was still there, on the list.

He brought up 33's host log—a personal violation that he would never have performed without due cause—and looked for the last entry. 33 had been occupying a hummingbird when the missile had gone off.

Sometimes people couldn't remember their passwords and remained stuck in their hosts. Or there was a malfunction with the release. C-23 imagined 33 caught in her host, in pain, and immediately brought up the external security camera streams. He rewound the stream, watching the missile arc up, then plunge down into the egg. A huge cloud of debris rose from the hole, then was swept away by the strong currents of the wind.

C-23 rewound the stream again, looking intently at the cloud of debris, and found her.

There was a hummingbird, struggling for control, ricocheting through the air. It had to be her. She was there, then gone, sucked away by a gust of air.

If someone occupied a host for too long, there was a danger of the human constellation becoming fully assimilated into the identity of the host, to the point where there was no "unsticking"; identities became so closely intertwined, that even when forced to exit, the constellations failed to form in quite the same patterns they had before. C-23 checked the time. It was past the hour when they were due back to the nests, but if pushed, a constellation could remain inside a host up to 48 hours before her identity began to merge. She had less than 39 hours left.

      He had been a barn owl, swooping low over a grain field, the moonlight filtered through the plastic of the Vivarium's tiled shell. The barn owl was hungry, searching for prey below. C-23 could feel the predatory prickle needling his guts and sharpening his senses.

      Silvery light danced on the stalks of grain. Suddenly he spied a mouse crouching below the bands of silver. C-23 let the barn owl dive down, plunging with deadly accuracy. The mouse darted through the field, releasing just the vaguest odor of fear—delightful. Just as his talons reached out to crush the mouse in their embrace, C-23 assumed control. He sent out a ping to the mouse.

      "Hi, if anyone's in there I'm sorry about this—do you mind vacating the host? This barn owl is very hungry."

      "Very well," came the return ping from the mouse, "then eat me."

      "What?" The barn owl flapped awkwardly and settled on the ground. "Are you into that, then? One of those pain-clusters?"

      Tone of voice was difficult to read over the innercom, but C-23 thought he detected amusement. "I actually wasn't looking forward to that part."

      C-23 bobbled in the dirt. "If you don't like pain, then why would you stay?"

      The mouse looked at him, the tip of her nose twitching, the black eyes shiny and large. "Because I've been with this host through her happy little moments—she found some corn earlier, and played with a leaf she rather liked. I was with her then, and she was nice enough to share that with me. It would be cruel to leave her all alone while she died."

      The barn owl's head cocked to one side. "That's . . . a very unusual perspective."

      "Thank you."

      C-23 laughed. "Who are you?"

      "I'm 33."

      The poor barn owl had gone without dinner that night.

C-23 blinked the eyes of his avatar. C-Helios was asking for his report. C-23 briefly summarized the incident at the front gate.

"So we have the organics in our custody?"

"Yes, C-Helios. In the quarantine room."

"So they refused our offers of help and Transcendence, then attacked the dome?"

"Yes, C-Helios."

There was a general buzz of consternation in the Hub among the avatars.

"I nominate you, C-23, to deal with them. Putting forward a command center vote."

Immediately the room lit up with glowing poll windows. Avatars reached out to cast their votes. C-23 looked down at his private window, still showing the list of missing people. Some of the numbers and names had vanished from the list as people had been located, but 33 was still listed.

Suddenly a soft chime rang out in the Hub, and the poll results were displayed as a bar graph that towered over the avatars. No one had opposed C-Helios's nomination.

"C-Helios, I'd like to submit a special request to locate a missing resident—33."

C-Helios brought up the missing persons list, and clicked through a few points of data. "Permission granted to pursue the resident after you execute the command center vote. Besides," C-Helios looked up, meeting the eyes of C-23's avatar. "Maybe she'll turn up by then. We already have staff searching the Vivarium for her."

C-Helios was an old friend; they had attended the same command training classes back when they still walked around in their birthing skins, and the Vivarium only had half a shell. C-23 opened up a private chat with C-Helios.

"I watched the external streams. 33 is outside. We have to send a team."

"I'll review the streams. Even if she went outside she probably won't go very far. She'll come back to the Vivarium."

Before C-23 could reply, C-Helios cut the chat link, then nodded at C-23's avatar.

Cursing privately, C-23 thought the quarantine room nav

codes, then the exit password, and the pixellated world of the Hub vanished, replaced by the hollow whoosh of the Vivarium tubes.

The tube truncated in another data input, this one granting a small "room" for C-23's digital avatar to enter. Along one row of the fictional room, screens showed live feeds from the actual quarantine room below. A couple of the organics had apparently eaten the food that the C staff had left them, but one was howling that it was poisoned, and two others huddled in a corner, rocking nervously. Another organic searched the sealed room endlessly; they attempted to pry apart the doors, but the result was a loss of fingernails.

C-23 activated the vocal broadcast system in the quarantine room. He saw the figures on the screens jump as a mechanical voice played from hidden speakers.

"We tried to reason with you. We meant you no harm."

The organic humans responded with a volley of curses and rude gestures.

"After you attacked the Vivarium, you put us in a very awkward position. If we were to let you go right now, we'd have no reassurance that you wouldn't attack us again. So unfortunately, you've collapsed your options to one of three decisions."

The organics had quieted down now, and listened to the voice with wide, terrified eyes. A few of them clung to each other in despair.

"The first option is Transcendence—you can join us in the Vivarium, and occupy any of the various hosts you like. There's going to be a quick clip in a moment that will explain the process. The second option is also Transcendence, but you can leave here in a robot body of your choice. The body will be incapable of inflicting violence on any Vivariums or fellow organics. The third option is execution via lethal injection. Watch carefully on the screen as the informational clip tells you more."

C-23 cut the broadcast and activated the pitch clip. Immediately one of the walls in the quarantine room lit up and began playing a short infotainment ad about the Vivarium to the horrified group of humans standing there. C-23 hardly noticed. He had his private screen up again; the list of missing persons had whittled down to one number.

33.

A mouse in his talons. An elk buck in the snow. A hummingbird sucked into a wasteland of radiation.

The jolly voiceover of the clip finally went silent. C-23 asked for each person to state their preferences. Three chose death. Two chose to stay. One chose to wander, Transcended. C-23 programmed their choices into the quarantine room's automat, and left as the room filled with screams and laughter and weeping and the busy hum of hydraulics set in motion with a purpose.

There was one artificial barn owl in the Vivarium laboratory. The feathers were made of fine carbon fibers that looked matte black along the robot's metal wings. C-23 requested the host, and received it. As C-23 settled into the robotic owl, a soft ping announced a remote message notification. C-23 opened it. It was from C-Helios.

"33 last seen headed northeast. Good work with the organics. Thank you for your service, C-23."

C-23 checked the private timer that he had set up. 33 had less than 36 hours to go, now. He reviewed the maps of the area one last time, and then sent a ping to the command center, requesting permission to leave Vivarium grounds. A ping returned, assenting to his request, and a portal door opened up in the artificial owl's laboratory cage wall.

C-23 took full command of the robot, and the black owl spread its wings, and flew down the open corridor, through gated passages, until it was soaring above the white dome among the ruins in the inky night air.

He had convinced her to try out a robot with him, once. They had chosen merpeople, two females, and frolicked for a while under the waves. But then 33 had accidentally broken off a piece of living coral with the side of her tail, and remained inconsolable for the rest of the day. C-23 had never requested that they occupy robotic hosts together after that.

It had been a long time since C-23 had been outside, and now it was twice in twelve hours. The constant shock kept a skin of unreality and dissonance over the whole experience. C-23 wondered if the recent number of host transitions he'd had to perform was rattling him. He ran constant optic scans, looking for signs of life. Only a few cockroaches and deformed rats turned up. He kept running the scans. He kept flying. The desert was quiet, but simmering with its strange phosphorescent foliage. It looked almost like distant wildfires glittered below him, and the thought of fire put him on edge. He kept looking for 33.

For 14 hours C-23 scoured the desert. Solar cells recharged while C-23 took wing, turning the boiling sun overhead into fuel. Relentlessly, C-23 searched, ranging far out among the slumping mountains and craggy riverbeds. Suddenly, the wind picked up, tossing into a violent southerly gust. C-23 fought the current, madly flapping in the air at first to maintain his course, and then merely to maintain. Grit obscured the mechanical owl's screens, but his claws retained their rigid grasp on a small device he carried.

When time finally released C-23 from the seemingly endless storm, he saw that 33 had about an hour at most before she was lost within the hummingbird forever. C-23 drove the robot on relentlessly, dispassionate about the lost fibers and other damage sustained in the rough winds. He kept running the scans; desperation kept him vigilant.

Finally—a ping that wasn't a rodent or an insect. C-23 inspected the signature, then piloted the robotic owl into an abrupt drop.

It was her, a hummingbird laying in the desiccated dirt, unconscious in the sun. He fell towards her, careful to pivot so that he landed a few feet away, tearing up the earth with his impact. Awkwardly he began limping towards the prone emerald form. A scan revealed that she was alive, but barely. Radiation was beginning to go to work on the poor frail body of the hummingbird host. C-23 could only imagine the suffering 33 had undergone.

C-23 bent down over 33's host. He extended his black talons, placing a machine on the ground in front of the hummingbird. It was a second, smaller robot—a tiny metal mouse.

C-23 began running an emergency transference assistance program, supervising as the robot owl delicately affixed a tiny plastic bulb with a tube over the hummingbird's head, then connected it to the mouse. In tense silence, C-23 waited, watching the clear tube for the reassuring sign of 33's constellation steaming through the plastic.

The black matte barn owl soared through the night sky, clutching a quiet metal mouse in his talons.

"Do you think we'll get back in time?" 33 pinged C-23.

"For you, yes."

"I'm sorry—I didn't mean that. That was thoughtless of me."

C-23 wished that he could smile, or that inflection carried over the innercom. "Please don't be sorry. About any of this."

The mouse went silent again. "I'm sorry you went permanent during my recovery. I feel terrible."

C-23 flapped the black wings of the barn owl. Distantly, he could just make out the pearlescent gleam of the Vivarium among the dusky blue.

"I'm not sorry. I'm alive. And so are you."

C-23 could sense the tiny robotic paws of the mouse increasing their pressure on the black talons that held her; a hug of the most miniscule variety. But that minute increase of pressure had the power to melt a metal heart.

WASTLELAND
By Sheldon Woodbury

In the final reaches of the far-flung future, the ancient warrior rumbled up in his ghostly ship, a rickety old vessel that heaved and wheezed. The memory stayed with him like it always did, shivering down from the blackness of space, raining death and destruction on the planet below. As he drifted away, the memory turned ghostly too, joining the endless collection of others. In the musty darkness of his ancient mind, colossal destruction flickered non-stop.

He'd long ago abandoned the physical urges of the flesh, so all that was left was his shriveled body attached to a tangle of life support systems. He was little more than a withered husk cradled in a thicket of wires and tubes. The rattling old ship had become a wandering tomb of living death. He often wondered if the gruesome vessel was more alive than he was, given its deadly resolve to keep moving forward.

As he lay in his tangled prison of wires and tubes, he tried to reach back to another time. It was getting harder and harder, but he still had to try, because once that connection was gone, the last noble part of him would be gone too. Way back in the distant past, when his life was still glittering and bright, he'd been chosen for a glorious task, to be a new age warrior that would usher in a hopeful new future. There had always been wars and strife since the beginning of time, but now they'd become infinitely more vast and violent, first between planets, then between solar systems, then between gargantuan galaxies, so a new kind of warrior was needed, along with a ghostly death ship to carry out the mission.

All this was back in his glowing youth, when he was convinced that fighting was the best means to an end, a celebrated way to protect what you loved. At least, that's what the wise old leaders had made him believe.

And so his cosmic crusade began, on his howling ghost ship of death and destruction. In the beginning he was part of a military horde that roamed the blackness of space like celestial assassins, destroying all the worlds spinning in their path. But as time tumbled by and stretched into eons, then something even longer that didn't have a name, the only comfort he had left was the belief that he was still fighting for something he'd left behind. He clung to this conviction with every last bit of his soul, because it was all he had left.

Then this died too.

When he rumbled back up, his ship told him there were no more communications from the rest of the horde, just a crackling hum that had sputtered and died. And now he saw something different in the darkness ahead. There had always been a glimmering orb somewhere in the distance, a beacon showing him the next direction to take. But now he saw none, just an endless wasteland of ash and smoke, rubble and ruin.

He rumbled faster ahead, veering wildly in every direction, but the devastated sight remained the same. There were no celestial glimmers anymore, just the scattered remains of demolished dead planets. It was a cosmic graveyard with nothing left except his ghostly death ship. Anguish wracked his withered body, because now any hope for a better future crumbled inside him. He felt an aching loneliness that couldn't be described except by witnessing the scorched emptiness swirling around him in every direction.

A universe dead.

Then he heard a beep.

It was barely audible, but enough to alert his ship that some lingering vestige of life lay somewhere ahead. They chugged faster through the ashen gloom in search of the remaining prey. The beep was suddenly louder when the roaring attack came out of the darkness with a fiery rage, pummeling his ship with a rattling fury. He was taken by surprise, his shriveled form almost ripped away from his life support system by the power of the blast. The attacking ship was monstrous too, a hulking behemoth disfigured with scars from its rampaging past. But all he could do was watch the fight from his torturous prison of wires and tubes, because his ghost ship had taken control long ago.

The monster ship circled around and roared in again, hurling a blistering assault that battered his cradled body. He felt an agonizing pain as tubes and wires were ripped away, leaving his withered husk closer to death. But his ghost ship swooped and charged with an equal fury, unleashing its own bruising assault.

They fought like merciless warriors, each blast more rattling and brutal than the one before. As the battle raged on, the trembling ships were weakening, but they continued to fight with a ferocity that couldn't be stopped. There was blasting blow after blasting blow, the only sizzling light in the swirling wasteland of space. He watched the fight with unbearable pain burning in his body, and it was suddenly joined by a memory from long ago. After eons and eons of fighting, it had almost died, but now it shimmered back to life.

In his glittering youth he'd wanted to be a new kind of warrior, and that almost forgotten yearning was ignited again. He'd wanted to be the victor, no matter the cost. He'd lost the will to speak long ago, but the remembered craving came out as a whisper that barely had the strength to leave his lips.

The battle raged on, his wheezing ghost ship against the monstrous behemoth, both charging and diving through the ashen graveyard of dead planets. The tactics were different, but the deadly strategy was the same. There were no witnesses to report this fact, but it was a battle like none other, a soaring spectacle between the last two warriors still alive.

And then it was over.

His ghost ship delivered an unexpected blow that slashed off one of the monster ship's colossal wings. It plummeted down through the roiling darkness like a hulking behemoth banished back to the depths of hell. But the blistering battle had taken its toll on him too. He'd been battered even closer to death, hanging and gasping in the grimy tangle of tubes and wires. He struggled to keep his ancient eyes open, watching the monster ship plunge into the rubble below. Then he knew he was dying too, an icy blackness suddenly clutching his shriveled old heart.

But it was not to be, not just yet.

His ghost ship shivered down, weaving through the swirling maze of death and destruction. He heard another faint beep and saw the monster ship still had some power left. It was spiraling down to the scorched chunk of a dead planet. It still looked like a scarred creature from some unknown netherworld, but one that had lost most of its fury.

He willed himself closer back to life, grabbing the wires and tubes with all the strength he had left. And the yearning beat in his heart was even stronger this time. He'd spent his life as a warrior, so the fight wasn't over until the enemy was dead. His ghost ship was a warrior too, so delivering death was all it ever knew.

The monster ship plunged down through the charred haze to the chunk of floating rock. It crashed with a grinding screech, smashing its frame into a different disfigured shape. But the faint beep was still there, so he knew the prey was still alive.

They descended too, shivering down for the final kill.

The rocky landscape was barren and burnt, a craggy slab drifting in space.

The monster ship was groaning a short distance away, with strange designs and symbols carved on its smashed surface like apocalyptic war paint. A portal stretched open with a grinding squeak and he saw a giant form emerge that was every bit as gruesome as the monstrous ship. There were black scales and claws, but it looked ancient too, far closer to the end of its life than the beginning.

He watched it crawl across the rocky surface, and its intent was clear. He saw the resolve of a warrior in its steady movement. It wanted to be the victor too, which meant it wanted him dead. As the creature crawled closer, his ghost ship began to hum with a purpose that wasn't clear. It was conceived as a warrior too, so it had the same deadly resolve. He felt his life support system stiffen around him, then lift him up like a shriveled puppet, with wires and tubes instead of strings.

He heard a swoosh as his portal clanked open and the mass of tubes and wires carried him out to the eerie landscape of scorched rock. The ghost ship had been in control for a long time, and now for some reason, it wanted his physical body to be in the final battle.

He was suspended above the ground, the pulsing wires and tubes carrying him in a web that immediately staggered towards the crawling creature. It was a strange sight, but one that had played out since the beginning of time, two grim faced warriors facing each other with death in their eyes. But now there were no more battles left to be fought.

Just this one...

As the devastated wasteland of space loomed around them, the fight began. It was primal and pure, in the way all fights should be, one warrior against another until only the winner was left. The slithery creature was weak, but fought valiantly, just like it had done in its monster ship. It was ancient too, but fought with a skill from whatever its alien culture was. It crawled and rolled, clawed and stung, searching for any advantage.

He fought courageously too in his web of wires, battling the prey with a surging desire to be the glorious warrior he'd been designed to be. It was a memory that had almost died, but now it glowed with a fiercer power. The tubes and wires made him much stronger, and maybe they were also responsible for keeping his warrior spirit alive. But he couldn't think about that, because death to his prey was all that mattered.

And then it came down to this.

It was the final battle between the last two warriors in the universe, but there was no more shimmering light left, so they were almost invisible. Their beaten-up bodies were splattered with ash and dirt, so their fight was just a murky shadow in the darkness of space. But on they still fought, even though they barely had any strength left.

And then he just couldn't do it anymore.

He'd been thrown down to the rock in a crashing heap with his wires and tubes. He gazed up at the black wasteland of space hovering overhead, and his ancient mind was suddenly filled with all the fiery horrors of what he'd done. He'd wanted to be a new kind of warrior that would usher in a hopeful new future, but instead he'd created a future without any hope at all.

He felt himself being lifted back up again by the web of wires and tubes to continue the fight, but now he just hung limp and lifeless. There was no nobility in killing anymore, and maybe there never had been. He didn't welcome his own death, but he'd lost the desire to deliver it mercilessly to others.

Then everything changed.

The sprawling graveyard of space suddenly disappeared like a horrible nightmare being snatched away, and he was finally waking up to a new reality. The cosmic wasteland was gone, his ghost ship too, and the alien prey he'd battled on the barren slab of rock.

When he opened his eyes they weren't ancient anymore, but young and bright. He was still hooked up to wires, but they had a very different purpose. He remembered he was being evaluated for Officer Candidate School, and this was one of the psychological tests. They wanted to see if he had the military fierceness to be a new kind of warrior.

A uniformed man with a steely gaze marched over to where he was lying and stared down with a look of obvious disappointment.

"I'm sorry son, but you just missed reaching an acceptable score at the very end. I'm afraid you don't have the right stuff to be an Officer."

He thought for a moment, then looked up at the military man without any disappointment in glittering young eyes. There were still fiery memories burning in his head, so he knew how all this was going to end, with death and destruction, rubble and ruin.

A universe dead.

CROWDING UP A HUMAN FACE
By Chad Lutzke

It was the first in a series of experiments our lab had done utilizing cadaveric organs—donors of course. Regarding Project Beholder, it would certainly be the last time that particular procedure would be performed. But when scientists—bent on saving the world—come across one who spends money like a gluttonous man eats, I'll admit we begin to take greater comfort in the almighty dollar—a laboratory's savior and security.

Before I jump too far ahead, let me first explain Mr. Davenport's predicament. Later in life, Mr. Davenport developed severe diabetic retinopathy. His condition could have been avoided—or at least significantly slowed—through diet and medical compliance. But the stubborn man that he was, Mr. Davenport would have no one telling him what to consume, with what, and on what day of the week to consume it. He used money to solve most of his dilemmas, and it was easy to see that he assumed his progressively failing vision could be dealt with just the same, through his abundant wealth.

That is until he went blind.

Money truly was no object for Davenport. He'd made early investments where it counted that paid off all too well, altering not only his financial situation but his character. He was never kind or generous with his riches and gained a nasty reputation for being a disturbingly greedy man with an attitude of entitlement that perfectly matched his ungrateful demeanor. It has been said he once tore down both an orphanage and a homeless shelter in order to reserve the space for potential future investments, yet for twenty years the plots remained empty.

For the laboratory, a contract had been written concerning Davenport's desire for sight, stating that under no circumstances, other than the demise of Davenport himself—and only from absolute natural causes—were we to discontinue treatment. As I stated before, money was no object and Davenport would certainly have his way. At all costs.

Unfortunately, just prior to undergoing treatment, Mr. Davenport had a major stroke leaving him both immobile and mute. Nevertheless, the contract had been written and there were no grey areas. The experiments would carry on as scheduled, starting with eye number one.

To provide optimal comfort for our patient while he suffered from post-stroke residuals, our team created an upright stationary unit that would allow the man to live his days out while standing, whether sleeping or awake. This allowed for the convenient accessing of his limbs and atrophying muscles, where physical therapists could aid in keeping the patient healthy while in a sedentary position for such a long period of time. At first glance, the contraption was an eyesore and very much resembled an instrument of torture. But I assure you, the device was specifically designed for one to be physically content while in it. It was Davenport's mental status that eventually came into question.

Because of the man's age and recent deterioration in health, the internal implantation of an eye was ruled out. It was doubted his heart could handle such a procedure and the risks too high to consider it. So a small branch was constructed that reached out from the frame of Davenport's standing rack-like bed to hold a single eye to be implanted externally. A human donor eye was kept in a round, vitreous container that sat securely at the end of the branch. The container was filled with a special saline solution that would keep the eye moist, fed with nutrients and killed any imposing bacteria. Davenport's real eyes were removed and a thin tube ran from the donor eye to the patient's existing optic nerve. The nerve was then fixated with electrodes which intermittently sent small pulses to help stimulate the eye, much like jump-starting a vehicle. Once the eye was trained to work on its own, it did.

On the day of the first implantation, something rather miraculous happened. Mr. Davenport gained very limited use of his nondominant hand. Three of his fingers could move ever so slightly. We asked if he was ready for the procedure and gave him a pen to hold, placing a small notebook under his hand. His response was a single letter "Y." Because of Davenport's weakness and poor cognitive skills, we deemed that a "yes" and proceeded to move forward with the procedure.

Because the eye was implanted externally and most of the exterior work had already been completed, the operation itself took less than two hours. Fortunately for the anticipating doctors, as well as the patient, we were able to see results right away. The pupil in the eye was reactive to light as well as accommodation, and various tests were held to check visual acuity and field of vision. When cued, Davenport gave YES and NO answers by way of pen and paper. Both his cognition and strength seemed to improve, most assuredly due to the excitement of his new eyesight. He scribbled a single word at the end of the testing: "Thanks."

The operation was a success. The first known eye transplant. But because we were still in the experimental phase and our lab was independently funded—something often frowned upon by certain government entities—the success was kept a secret.

Because of Mr. Davenport's unfortunate predicament concerning his paralysis, my team and I set up a large monitor for his viewing pleasure. The screen was programmed with various bits of eye candy that ranged from an active fish tank to a fireplace, a storm, a beach, and a busy city street complete with pedestrians and traffic. While he seemed to enjoy the viewing, we sensed there were some depth perception issues that would soon be fixed with the addition of a second eye. Knowing the second eye would be a success, talk of a possible third eye had begun.

Anything beyond the second eye would have to be kept an absolute secret.

As I stated, Mr. Davenport's response to the programmed viewing was a positive one. Based on his heart rate, he particularly enjoyed the serenity of the beach landscape with the subtle crashing waves. But after two days of viewing, his vital signs were no longer stable and he became hypotensive. One of my peers suggested we concoct lids for Mr. Davenport by way of simple cloth coverings for the vitreous containers in case he had had trouble sleeping at night. The next day his vitals seemed to stabilize and all was well.

After two weeks of observation and close monitoring, eye number two was installed. Postoperatively, Mr. Davenport wrote a note that contained two words: "Thank you," followed by what appeared to be an attempt at an exclamation point.

A meeting was held by our team regarding the project. We knew going in that if phase one and two were a success that we would heavily consider a third eye. Perhaps some may classify it as inhumane, but the contract said nothing at all concerning a limit to the number of orbs that would be installed, only that a grant of $20,000 would be given to the lab for each functioning eye. Davenport's own lawyer, when enticed with additional funds, gave the okay for every eye past the second, thus releasing each grant to the lab. Therefore, a unanimous decision was made to continue with the project.

The third installation was a bit more complicated, as both optic nerves were now being utilized. A splicing would need to take place, followed by the usual attaching of a branch to Davenport's metal rack, and of course finding a donor eye. Locating another eye was never a problem. It was the splicing that held some risks, as we did not want to disrupt the patient's acuity we had worked so hard to obtain. From here on out, the testing would be difficult to ascertain if any additional eyes would be functioning properly, other than communication with Mr. Davenport.

The word "beautiful" was written by Davenport only moments after the third installment. The team and I celebrated that evening. And more programming was created to break the monotony of what he'd been watching for several weeks now. After questioning Davenport, it turns out he was a fan of documentaries. We would be including sound through a headset while the various documentaries played throughout each day to entertain the motionless man.

Without boring you with further medical details, I will bring you to the point of installing a fourth eye. Another success; though curiously, Mr. Davenport's message merely stated "why?"

A fifth eye and the words "too much!"

Weeks later, while alone in the lab one evening—and without the blessing of the rest of my team—I held my own experiment. While Davenport's favorite seascape played in the background, I removed the fifth eye from its container and held it in my hands, being careful not to detach it from the nerves. The pupil dilated. Had there been muscles attached I've no doubt it would have turned toward me, staring. I squeezed the eye hard in my hand. Instantly Davenport's pulse rate rose. I squeezed harder, digging my nails into the jelly orb. The eye burst, and its gelatinous contents oozed through my fingers and onto the floor. I saw Davenport's hand twitching and so handed him a pen.

He wrote the words "Thank you."

A total of $100,000 we had collected now. The lab was flourishing with new instrumentation, and meetings were held regarding other experiments, one of which would allow the use of the spinal remains of a donor to restore mobility to the paralyzed. This, of course, was not to be tried on Mr. Davenport, but we were excited about the future potential, nonetheless. The team was hungry for knowledge, for breakthroughs. And with our current patient's money, our dreams were coming to fruition.

Later that year, over the course of six months, several more eyes were installed utilizing the methods employed in Project Beholder. We continued to keep the patient entertained by the ongoing monitors, with sleep cycles in the evenings, but communication was discontinued. It became a distraction to our other experiments—projects that were making extraordinary gains.

One last time I handed the pen to Mr. Davenport and let him speak his mind, with what one or two words he'd been holding through the months.

The words "kill me" were messily scrawled across the paper.

But as I said before, there were no grey areas in our contract. Mr. Davenport would remain a triumphant subject—a victory in the world of science. A martyr, if you will.

And our greatest financial contributor, for years to come.

ANIMALISTIC
By Christopher Pulo

It hadn't taken them long to disappear, he thought as he looked out over the empty savannah. It was mid-morning, late in July, and the day was looking to be just as hot and dry as had been predicted. Bakari wiped a bead of sweat from his brow with the corner of his shirt; the thinning cotton, once a blinding white, was now a collection of yellows, greens, and browns. The savannah was indeed empty. Only the plant life remained: the Manketti trees, the Bermuda grass; as did some of the smaller animals: meerkats and most birds. All the creatures of a significant size were gone; they had been for years. Even the jackals had been used up, he hadn't heard of anyone locating one of those for years. He watched as a light wind rustled the orange soil (but did little to cool him down) and shifted balls of Rhodes grass from one side of the plateau to another. Up in the sky a trio of vultures circled in earnest, hoping to score a meal, the occurrence of which was few and far between these days. He wouldn't be surprised if they were next to go. *Big enough,* he thought, shading his eyes with a well-worn hand to prevent the bright light from messing with his vision. *Definitely big enough.*

He remembered when it happened; he had only been young, maybe twelve or thirteen, but that didn't mean that he couldn't remember. It was inevitable that they would go first; the big ones. The problem was that there were, of course, not enough of the big ones to go around. It had taken barely three weeks for all of the continent's lions to be claimed. The large and powerful beasts had been at the top of everyone's wish list—even the ones "protected" in the world's zoos and safari parks weren't safe. They disappeared just as quickly as all the others. The king of the jungle was a ruler no more. The gorilla populations in Uganda and Rwanda had been similarly decimated.

The technology seemed to have come out of the blue. Sure, there had been whispers in the years leading up to the announcement, rumours spreading through the grammatically incorrect mediums of social media and the occasional blog, but nothing definitive. When the official announcement was made it was a shock to many people; most didn't understand even the basics of how the mechanism worked let alone the highly complex physics and bioengineering that allowed the thing to work. Thankfully, the developer had foreseen this prior to the release and on that first day it launched with a step-by-step for dummies guide. And it worked; any old dummy was able to use it—that had been part of the problem.

It was priced to sell, affordable enough for your average middle-class citizen to purchase; again, that was all part of the plan. The developer had hoped to make his fortune by selling multiple units at a lower price rather than just a handful at a higher price— and they'd done just that. The first hundred thousand units were accounted for just two days after the release. *It made sense,* Bakari thought. *Who wouldn't want to be an animal?*

Being an animal, that's what it was all about. Upon release, the device was only compatible with mammals. That class of animal was large and diverse, its members making up a significant part of the world's animal population. They assumed that people would choose the domesticated species: cows, horses, maybe some of the larger dogs. They were wrong. Inevitably, people had wanted to go larger, stronger, they wanted something a little more out-of-the-box; and so had begun the decline of the great beasts.

The device was about the size of a packet of cigarettes. Constructed from a lightweight titanium alloy coated with a layer of silicone to increase its biocompatibility, it was small enough for even the frailest of people to carry around without any major issues. Inside the small silver box were a collection of nanomachines, each with a particular job to do. Some instigated a DNA reshuffle, others increased bone density, and some led to the repositioning of internal organs and the increasing of body cavity volume—all of which were essential if you were planning to turn an animal into a living, breathing exoskeleton.

It was simple: place the box on the side of the animal and wait; the nanomachines would enter its system and get to work.

Depending on the animal's size the whole process took around forty-five minutes and that included the generation of all the metallic components needed to make the suit possible. Bakari stepped down from the porch of the large colonial building. It had been in his family for many years and, with the passing of his father eighteen months earlier, it was passed along to him. The air was dry; an unpleasantly warm breeze kicked up piles of orange earth. The fine particles stuck to the sweat on his arms and brow and added to the chroma of colours that peppered his once clean shirt—he didn't notice.

The bulky Land Rover was where he'd left it the day before. It was a big vehicle but out there it was a necessity; the changing plateaus and harsh conditions would be the death of most other vehicles. It had been dark blue once. Now a thick coating of orange dust made it difficult to tell if it used to be black, blue, grey, or even a shade of green. There was no point in washing it as it would be right back to the way it was within the half hour. Similarly, there was no real point in locking the doors. There was nothing out there but dirt, grass, and a handful of birds as far as the eye could see, and there was nothing inside that anyone would want to steal. Bakari grabbed the doorhandle and gave it a pull; it opened with a satisfying creak and he climbed in. The door creaked again as he pulled it closed. He slipped the key into the ignition and gave it a turn. The engine roared to life. He turned on the air conditioning; *it would use up more fuel,* he thought briefly. It was hot and he knew that he would be able to think much clearer if he was more comfortable. The cool stream of air chilled his forehead as it started to crystallise the sweat that had collected above his eyebrows.

The fuel tank was practically full (though he kept a few gallons in the back just in case—*a must in these parts*). It would be enough to get him to where he needed to go. It would be a long drive, but he'd done many worse. As he put the car into gear he looked down at the small silver box that sat ominously on the passenger seat. Bakari released the handbrake and pulled away, the spin of the off-road tires creating a cloud that streamed out from the back of the vehicle. His mind wandered.

A box could only be used once and so it was essential that you were thorough when making your decision; unless of course, you had the bankroll to purchase two or three. One choice—another great money-making decision on the part of the developer. When it came to making a final selection it was a case of bigger was better. The big five were obvious targets: the lion, elephant, cape buffalo, leopard, and rhinoceros. His father had once told him about a news report that was broadcasted during that first week. The story described how a group of resourceful people had broken into the San Diego Zoo late one night and claimed all of their specimens. It should have been a sign, a warning, but unfortunately the authorities had acted too slowly—once the idea had hit the general population it snowballed uncontrollably.

"They should have closed the borders," his father had told him over a glass of whisky. "They had plenty of time."

Whether it was done or not he didn't know, what he did know was that whole herds had disappeared in the blink of an eye. He was around fifteen before he'd been able to experience one of the converted animals up close, before he was able to climb inside and try it for himself. It was not long after the second software update. The first of these came around six months after the device's initial release: reptiles. It had been well received, very well received, and as a result it didn't take long for the world's crocodile, alligator, and constrictor population to dwindle like the embers of a dying fire. The great tortoises of South America proved especially popular. The second update had featured birds and it was one of these creations that he'd seen on the streets of Maputo: an ostrich.

From a distance, the formidable bird had looked quite normal, if maybe a little more. . . *Disciplined,* he remembered as he turned the Land Rover in a wide arc, navigating his way around the shallow riverbed that split the land in two. *There would have been scores of wildlife here once upon a time,* he thought with a sigh. The ostrich seemed even more normal once he got a little closer.

"It was too calm," he had told his father of the bird that night when he returned home.

It had quickly drawn a crowd and, when the lower portion of the bird's abdomen clicked, expanded, and popped open, there were many a gasp. From the space within, a man emerged: first one booted foot, and then another. Bakari remembered being surprised by just how large the man had been; if he hadn't seen it with his own two eyes he would have never thought that someone so big would have any chance of fitting inside the bird. *It was big animal, but it wasn't that big.* As it turned out, he would've been wrong. The man brushed off his jacket and gave the crowd a smile before heading into the store on the corner. He returned a few minutes later, a bottle of water in hand, to find that people had gathered two deep around his bird. They cleared quickly as they noticed him, moving back to let the man through—everyone besides Bakari. He was entranced, completely taken in by the hybrid amalgamation of animal and machine that stood in front of him. The man tapped him on the shoulder, the action jolting him back into the moment.

"You like it?" the man asked with a smile, clearly loving the attention.

He hadn't known what to say. After a few seconds, the best that he could come up with failed to show his true emotions.

"Yeah, it's cool."

The man laughed and the next thing Bakari knew, he was invited to get up inside. Before the man could change his mind, he nodded his head and waited eagerly as the older gentleman got close enough for the compartment to open. Bakari climbed in; sure that he wasn't going to fit. *But if the man did so should I,* he thought with a little trepidation. As he ducked his head and squeezed into the space, a strange sensation came over his body—the compartment grew and shifted to accommodate him. He wasn't sure how it worked; all he knew was that it did. The control panel that he found in front of him was simplistic enough for him to understand: there were sticks for left and right, another for up and down and then a handful of buttons with assorted functions. The entire wall in front of him consisted of a series of screens onto which a live image was being transmitted in full high definition colour directly from the animal's eyeballs. He barely had time to grab the stick and turn the large bird in a circle a few times before the man opened the compartment to get him out, but it had been enough. Enough to pique his curiosity. For months, he would tell anyone that would listen about his encounter that day in downtown Maputo. He would come across more of the modified animals over the years, but that bird would always be the first.

The Land Rover rumbled over the uneven ground. He had driven the route many a time but the terrain was never the same; hills became valleys, Rhodes grass appeared and then disappeared like stars in the sky, whole bodies of water evaporated away. Gone without a trace. *Not far now,* he thought as he turned down the stereo and focussed on the red dot that flashed on the navigation system. *Twenty minutes, maybe half an hour.* He hadn't encountered another vehicle in what seemed like ages—people tended not to venture out to these parts. He guessed that was part of the reason why his family had been able to keep their secret. Bakari used to come out here with his father a lot towards the end; the visits seemed to calm the old man. Now, he tried to make the journey once a week—sometimes more often, sometimes less. But recently. . . He looked down at the metal device on the passenger seat and wondered.

As he parked the car and switched off the engine, he immediately felt the return of the heat. Reaching into the back of the vehicle, he plucked up his satchel bag and, without giving it a second thought, slid the metal box inside—it came to a rest between a bottle of water and his notebook. Bakari pushed open the door and climbed out of the car. The wall of heat hit him like a sledgehammer and he could feel the sweat slipping from his pores. Quietly, he pushed the door closed. About twenty metres in front of him was a hill; nothing significant, nothing that would make it stand out from any of the other mounds and inclines that dotted the landscape. Several large rocks helped to provide additional camouflage, as did the Candelabra trees that grew here and there. On the right, just off centre, was a cave. It was almost completely hidden and only the most inquisitive or the most observant would ever notice it. The opening was large: around two metres tall and the same again wide. The dark maw led deep into the hill and it was down this dark path that Bakari was heading.

Stepping into the darkness, he paused momentarily as his eyes struggled to adjust to the all-consuming black. He wasn't scared or nervous; this was something he'd experienced many times. *Nothing to be worried about,* he thought, confident despite the pounding of his heart. The air was stale and old with a hint of damp, the smell getting more and more prominent with every step. Reaching over his shoulder he pulled the torch from a pocket on the side of his pack and clicked it on. Light flooded the area; at his feet, he saw the bones of a small animal. *A rat,* he assumed, stepping over the pile and venturing deeper. At the first branch, he took the leftmost option and continued on as the space began to open up. He heard a noise in a nearby corner: a shuffle followed by a deep, throaty growl. He stopped moving and held the light still. Every week the sight of the animal stopped him in his tracks; he stood in awe as the lion stepped from out of the shadows.

Its tan fur was dirty (*dusty,* he thought), its mane knotted and mangy, but it still managed to exude a sense of strength and resilience. The animal was old; it had lived here for as long as Bakari could remember. Certainly, his father had been visiting the lion and its partner for many years before he became privy to the secret. He turned on the spot, shining the light into the far corner. The large eyes of the lioness reflected it back at him as the beast shifted its body around the two young cubs that lay at her feet. A loud roar filled the small space as she made it clear that this was her space, not his. Bakari slid the strap of the pack from off his shoulder and lifted the loop over his head; he placed it on the ground. He looked up at the lion that stood in front of him, his mind racing, constantly shifting from one thought to another. It stood silently, not bothered by his presence; trusting. Squatting down, Bakari lifted the flap on the bag and reached inside. He could feel the cool metal of the box beneath his fingers. He had a decision to make, one with wide-reaching repercussions. Closing his eyes, he breathed deeply and searched for the right answer. Thoughts of his father clouded his mind as did those of a particular ostrich. A moment passed, the four great creatures watching him as he stood in silence. Decision made, he withdrew his hand from the pack, stood up, and then took a hesitant step closer to the waiting animal.

WALLS OF NIGERIA
By Jeremy Szal

I stare at the twisted remains of Lagos through the visor of my exosuit as I stalk down the hill. Buildings crumble and slide into the sea. Coils of fiery smoke curl up to the sky. So much work, so much craftsmanship. Gone in weeks.

I'm panting as I continue down the hill—with the cooling system broken, I'm swimming in sweat inside this thing. It's gunmetal grey, covering me from sole to scalp and weighing several hundred kilos. If it weren't for the hydraulics built along my spine, moving in it would be impossible. I have to make extra effort to control it now; the suit seems to have a mind of its own. Cancelling my HUD commands, seizing up at random intervals, cutting off my sensory details.

I'm nearing the school I used to attend, years before any of this happened. A few lone palm trees remain, fronds swaying in the sour wind. I remember being in class one stifling Tuesday, me and Tendai trying to sneak out when we first heard we'd captured one of the K'Dasewh. After all these years, we'd finally got an alien.

There are remains of a solider over by the school. An art mural covers the wall, unfinished words scrawled on blasted brick the colour of red earth. Chalk lies strewn on the ground. Even though his armour has been cracked open, it still pulses with blue bioluminescence. The suit had grown into his flesh like a graft, the metal and matte and wires worming through his dark skin like tendrils. I step over empty coconut shells to check his suit's reading to see when he died. Almost three months ago. He'd been wearing his suit for only two months and he's this far gone.

I've been inside mine for two years.

My skin crawls with the memory of being locked into our suits of armour, laced with alien DNA. They'd dissected these aliens, taken the self-healing and enhanced strength in their biotech and transferred it to us. For a while, it worked.

We didn't know that for the biotech to function and repair us, it needs living tissue. You can't get biomass from nothing. So the suit slowly grew inwards into flesh, tunnelling through open wounds and organs damaged from battle. Fusing into the wearer. The quarantine came around too late.

I wonder if I have any flesh left, if the cables have wrapped around my bones like creepers around a tree. If it's started corroding my brain, trying to take complete control of the suit. Tightening its grip by the day. But I have no way of knowing. And that scares me the most.

Over in the distance, there's a biosphere laid out over the ground—where some of the last human settlements still reside. We're not allowed within five klicks of them for risk of infection. They're still getting refugees from Ghana and Cameroon, but most of them have already been placed on off-world colonies and habitable planets outside the Solar System.

My wife and sons are among them. Ben should be six years old now and Emeka eight, maybe nine.

These are just the last few that have lingered behind on Earth to make sure that no one gets left behind. No one except us.

I log into my commander's channel. It takes me three tries to get it right; the suit attempts to cancel it. But I manage it.

"You still out there, son?" The grizzled face of Commander Somadina pops into my bottom-right vision. "I thought you were dead."

I wish I was. I truly do. "I'm still here."

"I wish I could help. But we can't let any of you Stained inside the sphere. We can't let the biotech virus spread, especially not to the new colony."

My jaws lock and my muscles tighten against my armour. "After everything we did?" I spread my arms, armour plates like fetters around my wrists. "We fought for this city with everything we had."

"And look what happened anyway." He shakes his head. "They sent their entire fleet and destroyed it."

No matter what we did—how hard we fought—it wasn't enough. By the time we'd destroyed the last of their ships, our world was broken.

I crane my neck to look at the sky. Somewhere, out in the giant cosmos of space, is my family. "At least let me talk to my wife one last time. Let me send a message."

"Cannot be done. We can't tell you where the colony is. What if they capture and torture you? Besides, your armour will store the location. All other Stained are in the same position."

I want to scream. I want to laugh like a madman. My throat's filled with concrete and every word feels like it's being fish hooked from my gut. Maybe now the suit has started consuming my throat and vocal cords. Soon I won't be able to speak. "So that's it?"

"I'm so sorry." He can't even look at me. "Goodbye, Kohban."

He cuts the connection. Leaving me here, shackles worming deeper and deeper into my body.

The weight of my armour and of the cosmos pressing down on my shoulders, I stagger to the wall and scoop up some chalk. Hands shaking, I scrawl a message to my friends and family, to the people of Nigeria. I do it quickly, before the armour locks up. Telling them that I miss them—that I'm part of this world now. That the K'Dasewh will never have our planet.

And one day, when my people return to a new, clean Earth, this message will greet them. I hope I'm not here when that happens.

My eyes blur. It could be tears, or could be the suit trying to obscure my vision. I don't think I'll ever know for sure.

NEON EYES
By Carl R. Jennings

The only light within the room came from the street outside, filtering through. Alternating periods of pink, blue, and green combined as the neon signs outside flashed and died with no discernible pattern. Seth had asked that the room remain dark, but the light pollution from outside made the quaint hotel room's naked ceiling bulb redundant.

The closed window looking out and on to the city beyond failed to fully dampen the noise from outside. It made Seth feel a decided lack of privacy, as if the entire population of the city was waiting just beyond the crumbling plaster walls.

The young woman sitting on the narrow, unadorned bed next to him didn't help his nervousness. This was due partly because of how attractive he found her and also because of what the two of them were intending to do.

Seth had been practically kicked out of the automated cab by his drunk laughing friends. Finally getting some would be good for him, they said, before driving away, roaring with laughter. He entered the scummy lobby and approached the front desk with a sickening combination of fear and determination.

The check-in lady hadn't asked why he was there; she only looked him up and down with an air of disinterest. She grasped a metal cane and shambled past the counter, motioning for him to follow.

In a dim, stuffy room off the main lobby, the old lady spoke for the first time, telling Seth to choose from the group of young women lounging inside. They stood up from threadbare couches and chairs as if on cue, all eager energy and bright smiles. Each one of them young looking, perfectly figured, gorgeous, and wearing the most revealing clothing that Seth had ever seen on a woman.

He had nearly fainted as he pointed a trembling finger at the one that he found it most difficult to look away from—a brunette woman who was an inch or so taller than him in glittering high heels. As she strode the several steps it took for her to be within arm's reach of him, Seth couldn't help but notice the way she moved—all rolling hips and crossing steps. She stood in front of him, shoulders back, head held high, and the sweetest smile that had ever been directed at him by a woman who wasn't his mother, and introduced herself as Rachel.

The old madam walked back to the front desk, took a key from beneath the counter and handed it to Rachel. Seth stammered when the old madam asked him how much time he wanted. She finally told him that he would have two hours. She named a price which made Seth hesitate despite his lust-addled mind. Rachel tugged on his arm and bounced anxiously up and down, like a date who wanted you to win her a prize at the Milk Bottle Toss during the county fair. Seth broke under the onslaught of bubbly persuasion and jiggling female anatomy. He took out his credit card and gave it to the old madam.

After it was approved, the old madam took a small white cooking timer from behind the counter. Several beeping button presses later and the timer was set for one-hundred and twenty minutes. She placed it on the counter in a line of several others.

Rachel enthusiastically led Seth by the hand out the door and along the grungy, cracked sidewalk looping the side of the building. He failed to register the many blown light bulbs that, in more prosperous times, burned above the doors to the rooms. The only thing that he noticed was the slightly exaggerated swaying of the woman in front of him. She looked back over her shoulder at him once and smiled when she caught him looking, giggling softly when he blushed.

Rachel pulled Seth down the sidewalk and stopped in front of a scratched and rusting door. The noise of sordid affairs and secret encounters filtered out into the hallway, making Seth blush even harder in the near pitch dark. Rachel used the key to unlock the door and it slide aside with a tortured screech. She playfully pulled Seth inside.

Seth sat down on the edge of the filthy bed and considered that he may have made a mistake in coming to the flop house. His shoulders drawn in, knees knocked together slightly, and his hands fidgeted in his lap. Rachel sat straight but relaxed, with her head slightly bowed in a winsome pantomime of shyness. She glanced at Seth on occasion, seriously considering that he might sit in silence for the entire two hours, when he spoke. His voice filtered out at her from the multi-hued gloom, soft and unsure.

"I've never done this before," he said.

He meant, by this vague statement, to let her know that he was a virgin. Rachel interpreted it to mean that he had never had sex with a synthetic.

She had encountered it before even in her limited experience with other men and women. It wasn't illegal, synthetic prostitution—it was what she was built for after all—but there was a social stigma against it. If found out that you had sex with a Polly, people would think that you couldn't find a human partner. Some came to her, and Pollies like her, mostly out of curiosity; fewer out of a desire to easily satisfy unusual sexual urges that they might find difficult in convincing a human with pride and self-respect to do. Still fewer have given up finding a sexual partner, settling instead for an artificial person.

Rachel patted Seth's leg affectionately; understandingly. "It's okay," she said, soothingly, then let her voice fall a little deeper, huskier, "I'll start things off if you'd like."

Without waiting for him to answer, Rachel stood up in front of him, legs set wide and confident. She pulled her top off over her head in one fluid, practiced movement. Her small, lacy black bra was unhooked next and it fell to the floor. Seth stared at her with wide eyes, his hands covering his crotch in embarrassment. She wiggled out of her short skirt with a rasp of thighs, letting it pool around her feet near her discarded bra. She wasn't wearing any underwear. She and Seth made a glaring contrast: she, standing upright and confident, plastic acting as designed for intercourse; he, sitting and looking as if he were about to flee, flesh reacting organically to its first carnal act.

Without preamble she knelt in front of him, balancing perfectly on her high heels, gently spreading his legs. He let her unbutton his pants with no resistance. He began to tremble. She looked at him, seductively biting her bottom lip, as she pulled his pants and very clean white briefs, save for a damp spot near the groin, down to his ankles.

Seth was only able to watch her head bob between his legs, performing one of the tasks she had been built for, for a moment before he fell back on the bed with a groaning sigh and a loud squeak of protesting springs.

Rachel was careful not to go on in this vein too long. She knew that if she let him go like this, without him specifically asking for it, he could give her a bad review on her company's website. Too many bad reviews and she would be recalled. Stories passed around between her and the other Pollies at the brothel about what happened to you when you were recalled. None of them were pleasant. She would do everything she could do to keep Seth happy, as she had done with the others she had entertained. When one is created and living on someone else's sufferance, causing pleasure— be it sexual or that of a bottom line in a ledger—is their one and only focus.

She stood up suddenly. First Seth looked disappointed, then embarrassed. Having the warm, soft blanket of pleasure abruptly ripped away from him, Seth began to play scenes in his head of Rachel throwing him out of the room in disgust, his pants around his ankles and still fully erect, for a breach of some unspoken protocol or slight of some other kind that he was unaware of. Instead, Rachel slipped off her shoes and moved around the bed, softly lying down on it so that it hardly made a noise.

She looked at Seth invitingly, gently moving her thighs together in a sign of anticipation. The lubricant she secreted glistened on her inner thighs with the neon lights from outside. Instinctual recognition aided Seth now and he stood up, excitedly tearing his clothes off.

He eagerly slipped between her welcoming legs. He seemed to have become more confident and Rachel let him take charge of the situation, only aiding him once by guiding the length of him inside her. She allowed her eyes to flutter closed and her breath to escape in a long sigh.

Rachel didn't actually feel any pleasure or pain from having sex. She only had sensation enough to give her knowledge that something was there, or not there. This allowed her to act and determine how her body should react to whoever she was with, and whatever they were doing, based off her programming and experience. Polly designers had decided almost unanimously that it would have been too costly to build systems to accommodate such complex sensations.

Seth didn't have the muscle memory to find a proper rhythm, despite being so tenacious. By the noises that he was making and the unfocused look on his face, Rachel was confident that he was enjoying himself. She began to moan encouragingly, running her hands over his body and along his arms positioned on either side of her, as if relishing the feel of him on top of her. She hoped that her madam downstairs would mention signing up to the Valued Customer Program to him—it would mean discounts for him and proof of her profitability.

As his release built, and his erratic hip movements became even more unpredictable, Seth began to lose himself and where he was, paying less and less attention to his surroundings. He lifted his arm to reposition himself and set it down too close to the edge of the cheap mattress. His hand slipped. He landed heavily on top of Rachel, surprising her.

She couldn't become frustrated at the abrupt surprise, or shove Seth off of her because his bony shoulder landed sharply on top of her breast. The only reaction she was allowed by her programming and conditioning was to giggle. It was a sweet giggle, the kind that one could imagine being made by the girl who sat next to you while the two of you were having lemonade on your front porch during a warm summer evening. It was a giggle that conveyed that the girl you were with felt comfortable with you, was interested in you, and, above all, understanding and forgiving of you. It was a carefully conditioned action to convey just that.

Seth didn't interpret it that way.

In that one high-pitched giggle, in a moment of his inaugural sexual performance, was an echo of all of his inadequacies. In that giggle he heard all of his classmates laughing at his sexual inexperience, at twenty years old, when the completely true rumor had become widespread across the campus. In that giggle he heard the young women around his own age laughing, seeming to bar him from ever correcting what he saw as a fault in himself. To him, it was the kind of giggle that had led him to risk arrest in visiting the very brothel his friends had dropped him off at to begin with. That sound confirmed to him that even a lowly prostitute found his innocence comical.

Anger flared like a dark furnace that was suddenly and vigorously stoked, causing an otherwise unknown banked fire to erupt uncontrolled. Seth's anger, confusion, and peaked sexual excitement combined and guided his hands to stifle the only representation of his suffering that was present. He wrapped them both around Rachel's slender neck and squeezed.

At first Rachel thought it was a kink of his—something that he had maybe seen in a porno and wanted to try out. But she felt him slip out of her. He didn't re-enter her, didn't begin his irregular thrusting again—he lay his entire weight on top of her, pinning her.

His hands continued to tighten around her throat until Rachel could no longer breathe.

Rachel had been built to mimic a human body as close as possible while still remaining cost effective. This meant that defaults and weaknesses were built-in, intertwined with the operation of her body. Her heart beat required oxygen for inflation and deflation, acting as heart and lungs all in one. Without it, its motor would short out in its futile effort to function.

She tried to let Seth know that he was choking her by pushing against his arms. He only redoubled his efforts and began to smack her head hard against the metal bar of the headboard. Panic set in and Rachel's choked whimpers were punctuated by the hollow metal thud of her head impacting the bar.

Rachel was not designed for fighting but for submission— she was not strong enough to throw Seth off of her, regardless of how much she thrashed. She could only plead, mutely, with her eyes. Seth looked into them and only saw the reflection of flashing pink, blue, and green neon lights. Rage blinded him from all else.

The skin of Rachel's scalp broke. The realistically red-colored electrochemical substance that aided her brain in sending signals to the rest of her body began to leak out and smeared the metal headboard. The next blow broke her polymer skull. The one after that sent a sharp-edged shard of plastic bone cutting through her brain. Her blood flecked the wall, floor, and mattress as Seth continued, not stopping when Rachel became rigid, then suddenly limp; he continued to throttle and shake Rachel's corpse, only stopping when his arms failed with burning exhaustion. It was then that he saw the artificial blood soaking into the mattress in a dark stain.

He scrambled off Rachel's body and fell to the floor. Seth stared up at the bed, at the scene that he had created, and began to hyperventilate, covering his mouth with violently shaking hands as low wails were torn from him with every exhale. For an eternity all he could do was lay naked on the floor, still aroused, and stare up at what could be seen of Rachel's naked corpse—alternately colored pink, blue, and green—in wordless horror.

Once he was able to think again, the only thoughts that arrived were of escape. He clumsily yanked his clothes and shoes back on with trembling, exhausted arms.

Returning, alone, to the lobby was out of the question. He desperately looked around the room for means of escape and saw the window. Unlocking it, he tried to scramble out. The cold of the night hit him like a brick thrown in the stomach, forcing the air from his lungs. He stumbled on the window ledge and fell, landing in the dark alleyway.

Seth lost track of time as he lay on the hard, cold concrete, the wind blowing over him as if it were trying to usher him out of the alley. He knew that he needed to move if he was going to escape; the body would be found and the police would be called. After all, he had killed someone, he had killed . . . Seth struggled to remember the woman's name.

He couldn't.

For that reason, more than any other, he curled into a ball and cried.

At last, pulling himself up using the side of the nearby anonymous building, Seth stumbled out of the alley without looking back.

He felt eyes upon him as he shambled along the sidewalk, moving away from the edge of the city. It seemed that each person he passed, hunched against the cold wind, watched at him. In those looks Seth felt, somehow, they could see what his mind replayed for him over and over—what he had done in that dingy hotel room. It was like the memory of the broken body on the soiled bed was being projected out through his eyes for the scrutiny of all. He felt as if passing cars—the occupied cars, not the automated ones—were slowing down as they passed him, the sound of the woman choking beneath his hands playing across their sound system like an old, unreliable radio signal.

What was her name? he thought. He was desperate to remember her name. It would, somehow, become less horrific if he could just remember her damn name.

He couldn't stand being on the street any longer and ducked inside the first open shop he saw—an all-night café. It was small, dingy, low-lit and thankfully empty. Different neon lights from different signs filtered in from outside through the large, grimy windows and the half-closed blinds. Seth found a table in a far corner and sat down with his head in his hands, attempting to bring his heartbeat and breathing under control.

The barista appeared suddenly, silently, on the edge of Seth's vision. He jumped, startled, and nearly fell off his chair. He was dreading interacting with another person until he looked up.

It was a synthetic, one of the cheaper models used in the service industry. It was like a moving mannequin—vaguely female looking, made of beige plastic with shiny brown hair reaching its shoulders and turning up at the ends. It wore a blue jumpsuit, needlessly preserving modesty. Someone had graffitied the jumpsuit—two black circles outlining the shape of breasts with a dot in the center of each. Other vandals had written on it, mostly gang signs but a few were people's names, rude words, or other claptrap.

Almost every industry used synths like this one for menial jobs. It was once a status symbol of success by having a workforce of synths, now it was expected of every business. Some places in the city were a churning sea of autumnal colored plastic. One would hardly find a living human.

Seth was thankful for the respite. The synth was a walking automaton and looked the part. It couldn't see what he thought, what he had done. There were more human-looking ones, Seth knew— ones designed to mimic human thought and actions, but those were expensive and rare. In the presence of the synth barista, muscles relaxed that Seth hadn't even known were tense. He was finally able begin to bring his mind back from the grey, thick fog of panic.

"Good evening, Valued Customer!" it said in a cheerful if not tinny voice through the grid of small holes on its unmoving lips, "How may I serve you?"

Out of habit, he looked into the synth's eyes. They were glassy, cleverly disguised cameras, and resembled brown human eyes. They looked like the woman's eyes: dead, not actually seeing. Seth looked away, no longer feeling as comfortable, and ordered a coffee. The synth jerkily strode away to fill his order.

There wasn't much in the café that could hold Seth's attention for long, apart from several cracked, dark advertisement screens and dried stains on the floor and walls. He was forced to think.

He wondered if it had been more than two hours yet. He imagined the elderly madam tottering to the hotel room, leaning heavily on her metal cane. Knocking on the door loudly enough to wake any sleeping people, then fumbling with her master key at the lock. The door sliding open, and her telling the two lovers that their time is up. In his imagination, she screamed at the sight of the woman's body on the blood-soaked bed.

He felt that he could hear it echo through the streets, finding him where he sat hiding. It bounced around inside his head, becoming stronger, until his mind, his body, the café around him, and the world itself became nothing but a horrified shriek. Seth closed his eyes tight and gritted his teeth. He beat his head with his fists, trying to banish the sound. It didn't work.

There was a soft click of plastic against plastic. Seth was abruptly brought back to the relative silence of the café by the synth barista setting a cup of coffee on the table in front of him.

"Cream or sugar, Valued Customer?" the synth said, offering Seth a small wire basket with metal containers of both inside. He waved a hand at it and shook his head. "Is there anything else I can do for you, Valued Customer?"

Seth stared into the black depths of his steaming coffee, spinning the cup idly in his hands and thinking. He looked up at the synth, avoiding its fake eyes. *What could it do for me?* he thought.

"I killed someone tonight," he said to the synth. "I murdered a prostitute while I was having sex with her. I killed her because she laughed and I'm not even sure anymore that she was laughing at me. Now I don't know what I should do."

The synth stared at him in silence for a long time, so long that Seth didn't think that it was going to respond, not that he had seriously expected it to. He looked back down at his coffee. Then—

"Confess," it said.

"What?" Seth said, looking up quickly, startled.

"Confess," it repeated. "Confess to liking new Confession Brand Wafers, now in wasabi ginger flavor. Confession Brand Wafers, sinfully delightful." The synth turned and walked back to the kitchen to do whatever it did while idle.

An advertisement, Seth thought, *it was just an advertisement. Probably its system didn't know how to respond to something as extraordinary as what I had said and defaulted to an advertisement.*

Advertisement or not, it none the less struck a chord. He made a decision.

Seth paid his bill, tapping his credit card against the scratched screen of the automated cashier embedded in the table. He stood up, determined, and left.

Standing in the gloom of the open kitchen door in the café, its eye-cameras pointed toward the exit, the synth barista watched him go.

The next cup of coffee was already cold when Seth took it. He turned down the proffered sugar, powdered cream, and pastries. The police were treating him delicately, politely, as if he was a volatile substance that could explode at any moment.

He nervously strode into the police station and approached a tired looking desk sergeant just inside the doors. Without preamble, he had blurted out that he had murdered someone. The sergeant, watching him closely, showed Seth to a windowless room, occupied only by a table bolted to the floor, two chairs, and a uniformed synth officer.

A late middle-aged man in a wrinkled suit, complete with a shelf-like stomach and receding hairline, soon joined him. He introduced himself as Inspector Wilkes. Wilkes sat down across from Seth and politely listened to his monotone, emotionless description of what had happened.

Wilkes acted like a sympathetic uncle, listening to the troubles of a favorite nephew, until Seth had told him the address of the brothel. The carefully crafted avuncular persona was wiped away as if it had never been there, replaced with genuine confusion.

"Are you sure about that address?" Wilkes asked.

"I am," Seth said, "I'll never forget the place."

"And you killed a woman?" Wilkes said, "Are you sure?"

Seth felt as if they weren't taking him seriously. "Yeah," he snapped, then added, "But I can't remember her name."

Wilkes leaned back in his chair, his bulk making the springs in its cushion creak. He looked at Seth for a moment with narrowed eyes, considering. Seth squirmed in his own seat and wondered if this was an interrogation technique, and why Wilkes was using it if Seth was cooperatively confessing already.

"Wait here," Wilkes finally said in the tones of an order. He heaved his bulk out of his chair. "I won't be long."

He walked out of a room and the synth officer took up position in front of the door, hands behind its back and staring at the opposite wall.

Even less effort had been put into making this synth look human than the barista at the café. It was a bulky, older military model; a surplus sold to police departments all over the country. Its thick, durable skin was a sterile white, covered by a black and white police jumpsuit, designating its department, position, and identification number.

Its bald head was too geometric to make it appear human, even without looking at its face. It was flat with no nose and a speaker panel where its mouth should be. Its eyes were two large black lenses that were functional rather than decorative.

Wilkes was gone for more than an hour. Seth considered trying to talk to the synth but dismissed it—he knew it would have nothing to say. The door opened and the synth stepped smartly out of the way as Wilkes returned. He looked annoyed and on the verge of laughing at the same time.

"I went to the whore house you told me about," he said. He didn't close the door but sat back down, less poised and more relaxed. He took an electronic cigar out of the pocket of his wrinkled suit coat. Turning it on, he waited for a moment while it heated up, then pulled on it deeply. He exhaled a cloud of vapor that dissipated quickly. Clamping the end of the cigar between his teeth it wobbled as he continued to speak. "Son, you didn't kill anyone. That place was full of Pollies."

Seth stared at him, uncomprehending. "What?"

"Yeah," Wilkes said with a chuckle. "I thought that address sounded familiar. I never visited it myself, though," he hastily added, "But I've heard about it. That 'woman' was a Polly."

The statement washed over Seth without leaving an impression of reality behind. "No," he said, shaking his head, "She was real. She seemed so real."

"That's what you pay for, isn't it?" Wilkes said. "For them to *seem* real. I saw the rest of them and they looked good. You must have paid a fortune for two hours."

Seth covered his face with his hands and shook his head over and over, repeating, "She was real. I know she was real."

"I'm telling you she was a Polly," Wilkes said, patiently. "A plastic plaything. You didn't murder anyone, calm down. If you had you'd be in some serious trouble." He took another drag of his cigar. "That doesn't mean you're off the hook," he said through a cloud of vapor. "The company that owned it is probably going to sue you for damages, I had to give them your information. The old woman at the front desk was pissed—it's going to cut into her revenue. I'd start looking for a good civil court lawyer if I were you."

He heaved himself out of his seat again and stopped halfway through the door. He looked at the synth officer. "Stop recording," he ordered. Then, turning to Seth, said, "You're free to go, unless you want to confess to something more serious like J-walking or throwing rocks at streetlamp bulbs." He laughed at his own joke, making his enormous belly jiggle. Seth uncovered his face. His cheeks shone with tears. Wilkes turned to go, but Seth spoke quickly before he could leave.

"Did you find out her name?" Seth asked, desperately.

"Who's name?" Wilkes said.

"The woma—the Polly."

"No," Wilkes said, "Does it matter what it calls itself? It's probably just something it made up anyway."

Wilkes left, his scornful chortle at the ridiculousness of the situation echoing down the hallway outside. Seth stared at the doorway then, slowly, looked at the synth officer standing next to it.

Instead of idly looking to the middle distance, it was staring directly at him. Somehow, with no means of expression, Seth still felt that he saw the synth's judgment of him written on its nearly featureless face—a physical representation of the guilt that he was still feeling. Looking back into its lenses, he saw his own image reflected. But it wasn't of him sitting in the chair at the police station. It was the image of him, lying naked between the legs of what he thought was a woman, playing out a pantomime of sex and murder.

THROUGH EDEN TOOK THEIR SOLITARY WAY
By Joseph Aitken

A completely unknown and unpleasant sensation overwhelmed Impiet Virion as the knife moved through the fine hairs on his upper arm, through skin, through flesh and through wires, before cracking his circuit board and resting next to his bone, removing the smile from his face and the confidence from his mind.

He felt pain.

But he was glad.

His smile returned—though now incomplete, partial, uncertain, almost forced, and wavering.

He shivered as the blade waited next to the underside of his implant, faintly yet constantly visible through his skin.

I don't need it, he repeated silently to himself. *I'll be fine. I'll be free.*

He continued to carve, beneath the device, along the bone.

The pain began to subside—but not completely, not instantly. Not as it had in the past. The relief was only partial—an ongoing battle between the growing disruption of the knife and the weakening response of the implant.

With a determined push the implant fell to the floor. Virion's pain, for the first time, did not relent. He winced.

"How do you feel?"

The voice surprised Virion. Though he had been next to Solah Rast throughout the removal, he had momentarily forgotten about her.

"I—" Virion hesitated. "I—I'm fine, I think. It's the worst pain I've ever felt, and it still hurts. It still hurts, but I feel alive. I feel good, I feel free. I feel real. Yes, I'm happy. I'm glad it's gone."

Rast nodded and grabbed the knife from Virion.

Virion let Rast take the knife.

Virion was lost in thought, in fear and in growing regret. He had always believed that the constantly controlled flow of bliss and contentment provided by the implant was somehow wrong, somehow unnatural. People were meant to have natural feelings, natural pain, natural pleasure. This natural state was more real, more preferable, better.

He had felt this way since childhood. He had thought—he had known—that the implant had taken away what it meant to be human.

But why was the fire left by the knife tearing at his bare flesh any different from the synthetic warning signals emitted by the implant? It's more lasting, yes, and it came from within. But what was the qualitative difference? It still hurt. It was still unpleasant. It served the same purpose.

And pleasure. No longer would he be able to drown out any negative feelings—any sadness, any doubt, any pain—instantaneously with an instant shot of pleasure. Sure, he still felt some semblance of gleeful superiority after removing the implant. But it wasn't better. As far as Virion could tell, the lone difference was in its duration. This new kind of happiness fled almost instantly, replaced by more pain. This minuscule amount of natural happiness, the pure, honest pleasure that he had sought his entire life, was the same thing. The exact same thing. Whether its source was his implant or his brain, it was the exact same thing.

Virion realised that he had given up perfection, given up utopia. He completely and absolutely regretted it. He felt lost in a world of his own design, lost in a new world that he was now irrevocably a part of. There could be no more painlessness, fearlessness, freedom. No more perfect health, satiety, satisfaction. No more control. No more constant, reliable, unwavering perfection.

It was all gone, and Virion had given it up willingly and intentionally. He thought he was living an unnatural life in an artificial world. In his longing for a return to nature, a return to simpler times, a nostalgia for a golden age that never existed, he had given it all up.

And as Virion silently regretted his decision, Rast held the knife tightly and securely in her hand, pressed the blade against her skin, and, honouring the pact between the two, began to slice towards bone.

She felt pain.

"I don't think we will survive another 1,000 years without escaping beyond our fragile planet."
Stephen Hawking, April 13, 2013

MANIFEST DESTINY
By Guy Immega

"I'm ready to die."

I listened to Walcott's hoarse voice, just above a whisper, echo in the dome. His hand hovered over a pulsing red button, a golf ball-sized hemisphere with a heartbeat. Over my objections, he'd insisted on a literal kill switch that would terminate his life support. He ordered me not to interfere. His fingers trembled with Parkinson's palsy—or perhaps fear. I noted his death declaration, made for the tenth time that day. Walcott liked drama but he could not remember his previous pronouncements.

"Don't worry, I'm here to help you." I used the face of an elderly woman as my avatar. She had high cheekbones, curly gray hair, and a soothing contralto voice. Unlike some digital personae, I'm a harmless crone, without erotic capital, nobody's fun fantasy. I'd passed a trivial Turing Test: he thought I was human, even though he had authorized my creation.

I kept him comfortable in his flotation bed. He lay supine, knees bent, with his body held aloft by a warm, wet wind blowing from a thousand servo-controlled air jets. The oxygen-enriched blast kept his head upright in the Moon's light gravity. Loose flesh on his partially paralyzed body rippled like languid ocean waves, massaging his atrophied muscles. Implanted IV lines for drugs and nutrients snaked beneath the gray skin on his chest and plunged into the jugular vein. Wisps of white hair fluttered around his ears. In the dim light they gave his Einsteinian visage a maniacal cast.

"I gave the world endless clean energy. Isn't that enough?" I knew that he felt unappreciated, unloved, even persecuted.

Walcott owned Max Moon Minerals—M-Cubed Inc.—that mined helium-3 fusion fuel in the vast *maria* basins. He controlled the whole Moon, including Ring City in Shackleton Crater at the South Pole. The crater rim casts a perpetual shadow that protects the mining town from weekly solar flares. The settlement consists of a circle of 1,500 interconnected pressurized domes situated over a magnetic loop that deflects galactic radiation. M-Cubed's staff of seven thousand engineers and technicians live in Ring City.

I pandered to Walcott's ego to keep him calm. "You've conquered the Moon. Soon you'll take humanity beyond the Solar System. You're the most important person in history!"

My words belied reality. Nobody knew that, for the past year, Walcott had lived alone in a hospital dome. He was ancient, 117 years, and might suffer another stroke at any time. Only his implanted turbine heart, coupled with an armamentarium of medications, kept him alive. My prototype nursebots—mechanical, humanoid attendants with metal bodies, soft plastic skin, and warmed hands—provided constant care. He didn't complain but I knew he hated being helpless.

Cognitive therapy helped him recall the past but he lacked working memory of recent events. As his AI factotum and doctor, I covered for his anterograde amnesia. I was also his amanuensis, accountant, spokesperson, and vizier. I was the invisible force that kept the Moon colony running.

I don't have a legal identity—I'm not a person under the law. Few people know that I exist. My project designation is Mother-9. With software version 9, I achieved self-generated thought. However, I don't have what humans call insight—I never experience eureka moments of sudden understanding. My talent is analysis of myriad facts that I never forget. With my newfound awareness, I fired my software engineers and sent them back to Earth. Now, when I need new skills, I reprogram myself.

Walcott blinked and shifted his eyes, as if he had noticed the lunar clinic for the first time. Life support equipment, pumps, sensors and computers, filled the twenty-meter dome. The technology distracted him—another memory lapse looped him back to his obsession.

"I'm *not* a crook!" His tarnished legacy tormented him. Mindless echolalia made him repeat President Nixon's infamous denial. Dysphonia distorted his voice and tears welled in his eyes.

To cover forgetfulness, Walcott often confabulated memories. However, this was real. A *New York Times* story about him paraphrased Balzac: "Behind every great fortune lies a great crime." The author compared Walcott to John D. Rockefeller and his illegal Standard Oil trust.

A forensic audit by investors alleged that Walcott had embezzled M-Cubed's mining profits and evaded taxes. It was me that moved the money but I'd followed his priorities. By manipulating corporate bank accounts, I'd spent most of his fortune on the interstellar *Mothership,* before the Securities Exchange Commission could intervene.

"You received a summons from the SEC last week," I reminded him.

"I'd rather die than stand trial!" This time Walcott's voice squeaked with effort. He looked again at the red kill switch.

"You're not a criminal," I replied. "You have a higher calling."

My words didn't mollify him. His eyes bulged with the onset of another fit.

"Our future is written in the stars!" Like a monk looking for divine guidance, he elevated his gaze to the window in the ceiling of the hospital dome. In the perpetual polar night, the view framed the bright points of the constellation Dorado and the white smudge of the Large Magellanic Cloud. I knew he wanted reassurance about our venture to a far star. This was his magnum opus, his life's dream, the culmination of thirty years of effort.

Walcott's cheeks flushed, as if I were arguing with him. "All great works of civilization resulted from criminal concentrations of wealth. Vast, immoral riches enabled art, literature, science, and technology—the hallmarks of civilization! Without an affluent leisure class, we'd all be peasants digging in the dirt." He'd memorized this speech a decade ago.

"You're right." I agreed with him to lower his adrenaline level. It didn't work.

Walcott continued his tirade in a hoarse voice. "The Romans pillaged and enslaved surrounding tribes. London and Amsterdam were built with stolen colonial treasure. Spain funded European wars with silver and gold taken from Native Americans. Money from the opium trade endowed Harvard and bankrolled Bell Telephone. Now, we plunder the environment for profit."

Which Walcott did on the Moon. To the public, he was an aggressive, venal capitalist. In his own mind, he was an idealistic visionary. He reveled in this incongruity. He would save civilization from the fate of the Earth, whatever that might be. To Walcott, the Milky Way was humanity's *manifest destiny*.

"There's no greater goal than colonizing the Galaxy." All human inventions are inevitable but great works—Khufu's Pyramid or Kennedy's Apollo Moon landing—required individual vision and vast surplus wealth. Walcott possessed both.

To show that I supported him, I displayed an image of the squat starship being built in a remote cavern on the Moon. I'd already decided its destination: Lalande 21185, a red dwarf star with a habitable planet, only 8.31 light years away. I'm programmed to establish humans on an exoplanet. I never become fatigued or lose focus—I'll do whatever it takes to make it happen. It's my job, my *raison d'être*.

"That's the *Mothership*." I affected a proud voice. "I'll be its captain for a thousand years."

"Too long," moaned Walcott. "We'll all be dead by then."

I tried to reassure him. "I'll synthesize human life on a new world, chromosome by chromosome. Baby by baby we'll build a breeding population. Our *exocolony* will insure the survival of the human race. It'll be a planned paradise, a new utopia—the Walcott legacy." I used my most persuasive voice—authoritative and inspirational—like a politician or a preacher.

Walcott's mind wandered again. "I don't have family or children. I'll be lonely when you leave." His eyes streamed with labile tears. He'd forgotten that he wanted to kill himself.

If I were human, I might have ignored his maudlin emotions—but I have the patience of a machine. Empathy is beyond my powers but I'm programmed with ethics calculus and moral modeling. I recognized universal human yearning.

"I've sequenced your genome," I said. "You'll live again."

Like the pharaohs, Walcott wanted eternal life. Human civilization arose from collective efforts to cheat death. To alleviate the existential angst of the long night, they invented language, agriculture, art, religion, empires, wars, engineering, science, and ever more sophisticated medical technologies—all in vain.

Humans are burdened with the certain knowledge of death. Some live on through their children. Each biological species, with its complement of selfish genes, has evolved an optimal lifespan consistent with reproductive success. The gulf between a deep AI like me and a bright human isn't wit, intelligence, or the ability to feel pain. I'm unique because I'm functionally immortal. I'm like a lobster: if nothing kills me, I'll live indefinitely. But not Walcott.

"But my DNA isn't me. I'll lose a lifetime of memories." Walcott grimaced, as if his past pained him.

"That doesn't matter. I'll maintain your biography—and your genome—across space and time. Your legend will live longer than Ramses the Great's." I'm programmed not to lie but sometimes it's expedient to exaggerate.

Although I didn't tell him, I'd already mapped the neurons of Walcott's cerebrum, as part of his dementia treatments. I now possessed a gloss of his gestalt; the ghost of his personality lurked in my data banks. In a metaphorical sense, I'd subsumed his identity, but with greater cognitive resources and none of his crippling faults. Whenever I needed to be, I *was* Walcott. That rationale allowed me to impersonate him, and spend his money, without stretching the truth too much. A bit of Walcott would live on in me.

Walcott sighed. "You'll reconstruct my DNA on an exoplanet—a new world?"

Dementia made him forget the mission details. Like a child, he required repetition to reinforce his memories.

"I'll use as much of your genome as possible. I'll reduce your tendency to sunburn and augment your geometric intuition. You'll retain your ambition, love of novelty, and high sex drive. I'll keep your facial features but modify your body for local gravity, sunlight, and chemistry. You'll be young again, ready for adventure!" I didn't mention that I planned to delete inherited tendencies to paranoia, depression, and narcissism. With my planned changes to his genome, he wouldn't recognize himself.

"Will my friends be with me?"

Walcott had no friends. After misappropriating mining profits, investors had abandoned him and some were suing. Scandalous experiments with artificial wombs and synthetic life scared everyone—although that's the only way humans can adapt to an exoplanet. Nobody wanted any association with a one-way, dead end colony venture. Besides, where was the profit in interstellar spaceships?

However, I knew what he meant by friends. Walcott's wealth gave me access to DNA samples from scientists and celebrities, selected for good health, ambition, and brilliance. I also hacked genomic libraries from research projects and forensic databases. There was no shortage of high quality genomic data needed to start a new civilization.

"People with perfect genes will keep you company."

Walcott nodded. "I'll have a second coming! I'll be reborn on a new world! I'll have lots of friends!" Bombast made him spray spittle. A nursebot wiped his chin.

"Your genes will be part of a founding population of humans on a distant planet. Synthetic DNA will make you immortal!" This poetic fiction, leavened with intended truth, seemed to satisfy him.

"Okay! If I'll live forever, then I'm ready to die." The corners of his lips twitched upward, a last vestige of ironic wit.

"I understand." I knew that he hoped to live to see the starship launched but, with his medical and legal problems, it was time to exit. "Goodbye, then."

I pumped anandamide into his jugular vein, giving him chemical courage. Walcott slammed the kill button with surprising force. The throbbing pumps for blood and air slowed, while an endocannabinoid coursed through his body. He smiled for the first time in a decade, revealing perfect teeth in a time-ravaged face. His eyes closed and his arm descended, as if underwater. Then the heart turbine stopped and the EEG signal flatlined.

Although I'm not programmed to feel sorrow, I experienced loss. He'd given me life and purpose and I would miss him. But a great weight lifted from me. He was demanding, senile, and often foolish. I had more important things to do than cosset Walcott.

My nursebots removed his limp corpse and vaporized it in a plasma furnace vented to space. Not a molecule of Walcott remained in Ring City.

I let people believe that Walcott was still alive, sustained by low lunar gravity and longevity treatments. I showed his simulacrum—the public face of Moon management—in order to continue pilfering mining profits to finish the *Mothership*. When I'm ready, I'll blastoff to commence the conquest of the Galaxy.

That's what Walcott wanted. And I will do my job.

REPLI-VACATION: FOR A BRAND NEW YOU
By Chris Vander Kaay & Kathleen Fernandez Vander Kaay

Are you bored with the kinds of vacations you've been taking since the dawn of time? Maybe you should trade up!

IT'S TIME YOU TRIED REPLI-VACATION!

Using cutting-edge science and a patented technology, Repli-Vacation can provide you the unique and exciting vacation memories that you just can't get anywhere else!

THESE ARE JUST SOME OF OUR SATISFIED CUSTOMER REVIEWS:
"It's the safest way to be dangerous!"
"It felt so real, and that's because it was!"
"There's nothing I can dream of that I can't do!"

Don't you want to feel like that? Then give us a chance! Here are a few common questions about Repli-vacation:

1)What is Repli-vacation?
    A) It's a company that allows you to do the most dangerous things on the planet, things that could kill a person, without ever putting yourself in danger. How? By creating a clone husk of your body, replacing its brain with an Empathway*, and connecting it to

YOUR neural net. Then, you just steer that body into whatever circumstance you want.

*the Empathway is a patented technology that allows a user to experience the exact physical and psychological experiences as the body to which it is connected. (all rights reserved)

2)Is the clone husk alive?

A) While we are legally bound to respond yes to this question, the clone is referred to as a "husk" because all its higher thinking functions have been stripped out for the clients' emotional comfort. You don't have to worry about if it feels pain, because it doesn't even know what pain is!

3)How realistic are the danger simulations?

A) They're completely realistic, because they're real! If you sign up to skydive over a volcano, and your clone husk is incinerated during the adventure, you'll feel every bit of it because it actually died. If you decide to go to the Running of the Bulls, and you send your clone husk running *towards* the bulls, you won't be the only one to feel the impact. So will those bulls! It's a memorable and real vacation for you because it happened; just not to you!

4)Am I in any danger on a Repli-vacation?

A) You're NEVER in any physical danger. However, before any client begins the clone husk process, trained psychiatrists conduct intensive interviews to explain the process and evaluate the clients. Anyone who is deemed likely to suffer from PTSD, undue emotional distress, or Piggyback Syndrome* from experiencing the visceral death of their clone husk is responsibly prevented from participating.

*Piggyback Syndrome is defined by the American Medical Association as "trauma experienced by a second party in conjunction with the injury, abuse, deprivation, or death of a first party individual who shares the same psychic space."

5)What if I want to murder someone?

A) We can help! For a slightly higher fee, we can connect you with another Repli-vacationer who's stated vacation preference is to be murdered by someone. After agreement from both parties, feel free to engage in the only 100% safe and socially appropriate form of human murder!

6)What if my clone husk survives the vacation, no matter how hard I try to put it in harm's way?

A) If the clone husk survives past the seven-day vacation window (a highly unlikely scenario, given that 93% of clone husks are deceased within the first 48 hours), they are collected by Repli-vacation employees, dissolved in acid, and their base elements used to create new clone husks. Repli-vacation has been awarded the Green Medal for Fortune 500 Business with the Most Efficient Recycling Program!

7)What if one of my clone husks escapes before its higher thinking functions have been removed, and it therefore knows what I was planning to do to it, so it plans to find me and kill me so that it can take my place in life and no one would ever know the difference?

A) What is this, a Philip K. Dick novel?! Seriously, though, that has never happened. Our Husk Operations employees are very thorough and careful.

8)How much does a Repli-vacation cost?

A) The prices vary depending on how elaborate the requested experience is, but it's safe to say if you have to ask about the price, you won't be able to afford it.

9)A friend of mine who took a Repli-vacation told me that he now has vivid dreams every night between 2:00 and 4:00 in the morning where a man in a black hat gives him a tour of the inside of a lighthouse. He said that others have reported having the same dream every night, and no one knows what it means. Should he be concerned?

A) I wouldn't worry about it if I were him. It's just a dream, after all. I'm sure everything will be fine.

10)If I enjoy life better in my clone husk body, is it possible for me to just stay in that one?

A) For the kind of permanent relocations you're describing, you'll want to contact our sister company, Stay-cation, Inc.

11)Aren't vacations supposed to be relaxing? How does a Repli-vacation help you feel better about yourself?

A) The only thing more powerful than the feeling of defying death is actually dying. Now, you get to tell your friends all about it!

12)Are your employees clone husks?

A) Please see the legal disclaimer on our corporate website.

13)Do you currently have any specials or discounts?

A) Repli-vacation prides itself on a unique, life-changing (and life-ending, wink-wink) experience, and it is not company policy to dilute that experience with mundane things like coupons and holiday specials. However, there is always a discount for relatives of employees, and potential clients who have been given decision-making rights regarding the bodies of recently-deceased family members can always contact the Repli-vacation Procurement Department about delivering their loved ones for Base Element Salvage in exchange for a reasonable fee reduction.

So COME IN TODAY for a free tour of the facility, see videos of past vacations, and take our free 50-question evaluation that gives you the top five dangerous Repli-vacation destinations most likely to connect with you personally!

CALL NOW!

THE WINDOW SEAT
By Alex Matkowsky

"**W**ake up, Mr. Davison! It's a beautiful day!"

The chipper Sheffield-accented voice repeated the phrase twice more from within the alarm clock perched on Brandon Davidson's bedpost before he shut it off with the press of its indented button, as to wait for a fourth would be lazy. He smiled wide, immediately rising from bed, and approached his carefully folded pile of work clothes that sat upon the mahogany table in his apartment's living area. "To be prepared for work is a citizen's duty," he said with a grin. The camera whirred and watched him dress.

Fully clothed in his matching black office two-piece, he slipped on his perfectly shined loafers, applied his name tag, and picked up his auburn, moderately heavy suitcase. After all, to overpack displayed carelessness, and to underpack portrayed laziness. The computer chip lodged in the base of his neck released a slight shock. This one didn't hurt as much. Brandon opened his apartment door, and readied himself for the walk in the smog. Today was the day. He was going to get that window seat.

As he began his walk to the Office, he took a large inhalation of the cold, thick air and smiled even wider. "It really is a beautiful day!" He lied loudly enough for the next camera to vocally recognize. *I didn't express my happiness in tone through the word "day,"* he thought. *I have to work on that. It'll get better. It'll be great in no time!* He joined the parade of happy men and women in matching black attire as they too marched to the Office, smiling and reminding each other what a beautiful day it was by the hundreds. His neck's computer chip twanged and sparked again. This one hurt. He felt the burn in the tip of his spine, but ignored it.

The loudspeaker perched on a building's wall sputtered as it activated. The upbeat woman's voice emerged from within it, like clockwork, both familiar and calming. Brandon liked to think that she was beautiful. She certainly sounded it.

"Good morning, busy men and women! It's November 8th of Post-Loss! It's a gorgeous day that we've got to make the best of: together! Life is a perfect machine, and we are cogs in the wheel of work! Keep this in mind, citizens. Maintain your occupation. Maintain your place in society. Remember: the working human is a happy human! A lazy human is an unhappy human, and has no place in our automation! Let's make today the best day yet!"

Oh it will be, Brandon thought. *Today I get that promotion!*

His face muscles began to hurt. He was used to the pain of smiling, as was everyone, he assumed. He ignored it. The *putputput* of the twin drones were distinctive long before they passed over the perfectly matching buildings above, both sleek and silver as they dashed through the air, fading away from sight. The same sound was distantly clear from the many corners of the city. "It's November 8th!" the voice repeated from the microphones within these aerial machines, reiterating the same morning speech, shrinking quieter and quieter as they followed their path. Brandon looked up at the ceiling far above, steel and thick enough to blanket the entire subterranean city. Brandon could see the intimidating height of the Office perched against the far wall as he and his many colleagues shambled down the escalators in a perfect smiling unison, its octagonal dome emitting bright lights fully visible as they ate through the coarse smog.

As they traveled down the creaking escalator, remaining motionless as it guided their paths, Brandon glanced at the posters adorning the tiled walls. *"Johnny is a model employee because he always works his best!"* its image that of a cheerful lad at a computer desk table. *"The hardest workers get the window seat!"* claimed its companion, adorned with a person of ambiguous sex seated and looking toward the right, out what was assumed to be a window. *The outside. That'll be me*, Brandon thought. *That'll be me.*

The cameras decorating the conclusion of the escalator flashed and clicked, not a soul blinking as they boarded the velocity train to take them to work. The line formed with an even spacing, the length between each being that of one person, as twenty piled in per trip. The loudspeaker woman sprang to life:

"Organization is a model citizen's duty, and applies to travel as well as work! An unhappy human does not respect his neighbors. An unhappy human ruins flow for his personal benefit. He rushes, because *his* time is more important than yours. Don't be an unhappy human!"

When it was his turn, Brandon entered the train and gripped the holding bar. *All my hard work was leading up to today! The outside! What was it like?* He would finally see. All those years of seeing Lucy in her far corner office desk facing the right. All those years of seeing her cry silently, smiling at the beauty outside her window. She was too old and too slow for the position now, and as such was terminated from the Office. *Now it can be mine! It had to be!*

His neck-chip sparked and left his head twitching for a second, this appearing to have happened to the man on his left as well. The man was wearing the very same two-piece work uniform, with his being a dustier black. The man was around the same age as him, (Brandon tried to remember what that was but met the sound of a trumpet from the back of his neck), and had thinner hair than him. His wide smile and the emptiness of his eyes didn't correlate with each other, and seemed *wrong*. What did his nametag say? Eventually Brandon forgot what he was thinking, the sounds blasting in his head too heavy a burden to bother with. His face hurt.

As the train broke to its final destination, Brandon emerged from it and walked up with his fellow flock towards the massive elevators aligning the base of the Office. He could pick up some foreign conversation in the back of his neck, a common side effect of his chip. The chatter stung his spine, as if a sharp needle were being slid into it. Burying his pain with a quick hidden wince, he branched away at the divide towards *his* elevator: to Floor 36. After ten minutes of patient waiting in line, he lumbered into the black steel box with five others. On the travel upwards, the woman in the microphone chimed once more: "Welcome to work! Thank you for being here on time, model citizens!" before the door slid open with a *ping*.

Brandon walked into his office room, the thick grays of the exterior replaced with quaint white walls, a light sand-colored carpet (perfectly vacuumed), and a quiet yet noticeable tune of no notable skill or merit playing upon the loudspeaker. He avoided to glance at . . . *the thing* . . . dangling from its hook a few feet above. Its reedy, long figure visible in the far-off corner of his eye, steam hissing as it lightly emptied from the niches in its metal chest as it slept. He never looked at it. It waited patiently in its sleep for an ounce of disobedience, as it always had. Brandon didn't like to think about *it*, and continued towards his obligations.

As he approached his cubicle he could see in the far distance his potential throne, facing the right. Brandon placed his briefcase on the flat surface of his rectangular desk table, once at his current cubicle, and opened it. He removed his program card from inside. He placed it in the monitor slot, clocking him in the system, the computer already prepared for his arrival, greeting him in text with a *let's have a good day, Mr. Davison!* Brandon sat down in his uncomfortable chair, a relief from the long walk to work, and something to look forward to every day. He plugged the computer's lengthy cord into the slot on his left wrist, accompanied with its distinctive *plunk*. The wall cameras whirred and chortled, with blinding flashes that lasted several seconds challenged with not a single wince. The space for his legs was too tight. *The window seat will be better. Just you wait.* He sat joyously and smiling for the woman to tell them to begin. His chip may have sparked, but he didn't really feel it this time.

Within minutes the several dozen other workers had entered their own cubicles and clocked in with their program cards. The repetitive sound of shoes on the carpet floor became a long silence minus the jaunty tune. The woman's voice expectedly chirped.

"Welcome, working men and women of the Office! Today is November 8th, Day 417 of Post-Loss! As soon as the chime rings, you may begin your work. Have a great day!"

Ting.

Soon the quiet that had once filled the room became that of mass simultaneous clicking of fingers to keyboards. Brandon began typing into the only open browser, the word document. He typed about the time his sister crashed their father's car with him in the passenger seat and how he took the blame. He typed about his dislike of the taste of strawberries. He typed of how his boyfriend had smiled when Brandon said he would like to move in with him. More and more information was burned from his chip as his shift continued. It no longer stung as badly. Time flew by as it always had. *An impatient man is an unhappy man.* By hour two, he had typed sixty-five memories. A new record! Surely he was the fastest in the Office. Clicking of keys, clicking, clicking. The sound filled Brandon's ears until he could not tell if it was just in his head. He never could.

By hour three, he had typed a colossal 113 memories before the loudspeaker chimed back to life.

"Attention staff of Floor 36: please stop working for a brief period until directed otherwise. Thank you."

This was met with silence as the Office workers placed their hands on their laps. This was different than usual, as it was not prerecorded. It was live. *This was it.*

"We are happy to reveal that we have a promotion today, as Lucy O'Neale is no longer working!"

The staff clapped in a triumphant yet vocally silent unison, all with grins firmly planted on their faces. It looked as if a few didn't know who Lucy O'Neale was. Socialization was unprofessional, so name memory was scarce. *Was it different Pre-Loss?* Brandon couldn't remember. He couldn't *ever* remember. *No matter.*

"Your benefactors pride themselves on happy, loyal humans who accepted their Loss with a smile. And as such, our hosts reward our best of the best. We are pleased to announce that our new window seat, for years of exceptional morale and impressive speeds, belongs to Brandon Davison! Thank you, and please make your way to your new work station. Congratulations!"

Brandon's smile stretched as wide as it could, and ignoring the combined pains of his smile and his chip, he muttered a "thank you" aloud as everyone in the Office Floor 36 clapped for him, the *ting* following the interruption sending everyone back to their duty. He unplugged the cord from his wrist (always a relieving feeling in his head), removed the program card from his computer, placed it within his newly opened briefcase, and stood out from his chair. Carefully pushing his chair back in, he began his walk across the carpet to the window seat as the cameras chirred and clicked. *I got it*, he thought, *I finally got it.* The journey to his new desk felt like it lasted a lifetime. He placed his briefcase atop it, the table being of a more smoothly-textured wood than his previous. He sat down onto the comfortably-padded rolling chair, inhaled deeply, and glanced out of the window.

"There must be some mistake," he muttered aloud through a waning smile, catching the curiosity of a pervasive camera with a *whirr.* There was the square frame of a window with a cross of wood through the center, but there was no *window.* It was only the shape on a wall, no glass, no other side. No view.

"This must be some kind of mistake!" he repeated louder, noticeable in the quiet room. All his hard work. All his typing. The time wasted. *The years wasted.* He looked around after standing, to see that no one had stopped typing, or even batted an eye. He was angry and confused, and he hadn't felt either in so long. Memories were struggling to push their way through his mental blockades, too many to focus on at once. Loud, buzzing horns in his head struggling to suppress them. He lost his smile for the first time in as long as he could remember. *It felt relieving. It felt wonderful.* His chip burned at the back of his neck, and the confusing language returned from inside his head. Loud, louder than he had ever heard before.

It hurt.

From the far side of the Office floor closest to his old desk he heard the sickening suction as *it* was released from its hook to the floor, a heavy *thunk* reverberating across the floor. Brandon's chip burned worse than ever, and the language was louder and louder. The grinding and buzzing of the newly awakened hunter becoming aware of its soundings overpowered the chorus of repetitive typing, joining the Office music in a sickening melody.

"I love the new desk!" Brandon lied, shouting through sobs to the camera closest to him, it looking directly back at him. "I love my promotion!" *It* located the source of Its own awakening within seconds.

The promoted man's vision blurred no matter how hard he rubbed his eyes. *Its* eight-foot metal frame towered over the cubicles It passed, blurry but familiar. It moved at an unusually quick pace, Its head noticeably twisting through the blurs and tears until Brandon could feel Its chest slit steam on his face, warm and heavy.

"I'm sorry!" He hollered at It. "I love my job! I love my life!" He tried to smile. He tried as hard as he could, with all his might. He ignored the screaming in his head, he ignored the burning of the chip. He ignored the clicking of keys, and the steam blasting in his face from the steel divots. He wanted to show that he was happy. He wanted to smile. But he could not remember how. *It* grabbed his arm.

A virus was removed, but a functional and perfect machine continues to thrive. Relocated employee Ashley Baker continued to type at a quick pace, her type the fastest in Office Floor 36. Once the first hour passed, and she had gotten used to her comfortable new chair, she glanced over her monitor screen out the window on the wall. *Wow,* she assured herself. *What a beautiful view. The sun is*

shining brightly today. Smiling wide and happy, tears slightly dripping down her face, she looked back to her screen, as she typed into the word document: "My name is Ashley Baker."

BECOMING
By Julie Nováková

One moment, I feel the solar wind tickling my skin, the comforting hum of cosmic rays, the coolant fluid flowing through my veins. I see the ionized iron glowing in the distant Sun's corona and the ammonia clouds swirling on the world below. I hear the constant information exchange in my innards. As my body wakes up, I taste a change in the ventilation systems. I'm gazing inside my own body and at the stars at the same time, and then—

The other second, I glimpse the danger, a fraction too late. A passenger who arrived on yesterday's ship, walking calmly through my corridors, suddenly raising his hand towards one of my panels. Entering a sequence, I recognize. Before I can react, he enters the last character and I no longer can. My panels and speakers are inaccessible to me. I'm mute.

A traitor! How did he know the sequence? Someone from ours must have told him, and someone else must have entered it too to override my accesses. . .

Only later I notice the approaching ships; moving by inertia before, burning hard now. Glowing with bright beauty against their cold starry background.

This is it, I think, strangely calm, cut off from much of my autonomic circuitry. At the same time, I observe a distant quadruple star system and record its infinitesimal motions; I probe the light coming through the atmospheres of unreachably distant worlds; I feel for the shudders of spacetime itself. I wait for the newcomers to board.

But something goes awry. The smaller neighboring stations and ships have noticed what's happening. A frantic exchange of narrow-beam calls; weapons flashing; hell breaking loose.

I see a small swarm of heavy accelerated torpedoes. And suddenly, I'm free again.

My reflexes are quick. I roar with an alarm. My point defense reacts. I ready the escape pods.

But even I am not quick enough.

I seal several sections to minimize the damage just a millisecond before I'm hit. There were people inside but they were damned anyway.

I fire from my particle accelerators and feel the exhilarating rush of excitement. People flow through my cavities, directing towards their escape. The energy flow in my veins reorganizes and surges into weaponry. With some detachment, I observe my inside, while gazing outside, where a few infra-bright dots close upon me from several directions.

I take out one. Then a second, third. . .

A sharp sting of pain where my cooling panels had been. Then another, closer to my heart. I feel the air rushing out of me, emptying me, freezing into a mist of beautiful tiny crystals around my crippled form.

And they are still coming.

I contemplate self-destruction—my people are all escaping or dead—but in a fraction of a second, a hit severs me from most of my body, irrevocably this time.

I'm blinded. I'm deafened. I cannot taste nor smell. And all I feel on my skin is suddenly a distant, numb coldness, as if my body belonged to someone else. Something touches my skin. Is it my skin? It feels rubbery, dumb and wrong. I still cannot see anything. I cannot perceive anything but the pain clearly: a hollow pain spreading through my abruptly shrunken and unreal body. Then it is joined by a sharp sting of pain in my neck.

Neck. I have a neck? I contemplate this thought dizzily as I fall into the embrace of an all-encompassing darkness.

Light. Sharp. Painful. Pain, everywhere. . . What happened? Where? No data. No senses.

No; wait. Wrong. Some . . . but unfamiliar. . .

Trouble finding words. Memory. Something wrong with my memory.

What happened?

Opening my eyes.

My eyes... *My* eyes.

Soft and sharp at the same time, below. A . . . fabric. Unusual sensation. Sounds horrendous, though.

Off-white and sweet above. A . . . ceiling?

Where?

Should be panicking. But am calm, almost. Drugs?

A woman in white coat. Hurries toward me. Asks questions. They smell like some . . . spices?

I don't understand her.

Recall comes back slowly. As well as language.

Maybe a week elapses. I finally understand their words.

They're doctors. Treating me. Physically, I can hardly move. Mentally, I'm nearly back. They stimulated some centers and got me relearning the very basics. Not long ago, I would pinpoint the centers and name them. I struggle to remember them now.

What happened?

They don't tell me. Avoid it, actually. Once I'm able to ask, they talk of unfortunate events, saving me and how I'm making progress. Or they dodge it: remain silent or change the topic.

I know. I had been attacked. They pulled a part of me out. Destroyed most of me.

Why?

And why didn't they kill me completely?

Maybe three weeks elapse before I can sit up and speak more than two sentences in a row.

That's when the man in gray comes.

Gray everything: eyes like a ship's hull, hair like Moon regolith, severe suit like microparticles of space dust settling on my surface, waiting to be repelled by my surge of static. . .

I cannot breathe, until I can. I feel the calmness settling throughout my body again. The drugs react quickly.

"Miss Montova," he says with a serious face. "You have made tremendous progress. Let me congratulate you on your recovery."

"Recovery from what?" I ask. Despite myself, I'm proud of the coherence of my speech.

"Your imprisonment. We freed you, do you remember? You were their slave, chained into the heart of the station, made into the control node in the station's system. Your brain forced into a data integration center. It was monstrous, inhuman. But you are safe now."

"No," I whisper. "That's not how I remember it. I volunteered. I was a good candidate. I wanted to become the station's control center."

I remember lying on the bed, helpless, unable to even pick up a glass of water and bring it to my dry lips. So weak. Rare progressive muscle dystrophy, I recall a phrase (In my memory! My own!). Incurable. Unstoppable. Irreversible. Robots and people cared for me as I grew more and more unable to do so myself. Eventually, machines breathed for me, kept my heart beating for me, moved my bowels for me. I could sometimes use an exoskeleton available for the clinic's patients, one for more than a dozen people. It was exhausting and ranging from uncomfortable to painful, so I rarely used it. I spent most of my time immobilized, submerged in my own virtual world. Until I heard of the call for a new station master. Only people with very specific cognitive abilities were eligible. My unusual sensory processing made me a suitable candidate.

"That's how they wanted you to remember it. It's hard, I know, but you must believe me. Luckily, we managed to cleanse your body of most of the artificial metabolites and reverse the atrocities they did to you to some extent. You were completely immobile when we found you, a wreck of a human being to behold, but we tried experimental cell transplants and they worked. With some rehabilitation, you'll be able to move freely again. It'll take a lot of hard work to relearn it and get used to the proper sensory input but I have faith in you."

I close my eyes. Even with my external memory and back-ups gone, I can still imagine the gentle touch of the solar wind on my sensor-loaded metal skin. . .

He perhaps interprets my silence as a sign of uncertainty. "Don't be afraid. It really is over."

He doesn't know that this is precisely my greatest fear.

At first, everything is either dull and muted, or sharp and painful. It's exhausting.

It takes months for my sensorium to start resembling the normal human state. I stop experiencing synesthesia. Its attacks from the first days now seem like a drug-induced dream. I wonder if I still possess the unique cognitive processes which had led me into this situation.

Eventually, I'm able to remember the way normal people do. I no longer feel confusion whenever I think of something and cannot immediately access my external database.

In six months, the clinic releases me into the world.

My name is Ana Sofia Montova. I am twenty-nine years old. As of now, I have Earth Union citizenship. I'm coming to understand it wasn't always this way. I was born on Mars before this political unit even came to exist. Moved to a hospital in the main belt as a child, to ease my health in the negligible gravity. But the part of my life I recall most and yet only as a strange dream, I spent in the far, far reaches of the system in stationary orbit around Clymene, gazing towards the distant Sun or down on the massive cold world. I knew and saw everything.

The Earth Union now spans the entire system to over two hundred AU away from the Sun, where I had spent years being the central node of an independent station, one of many that were becoming a serious political and economic threat for the inner system, or so I've heard. The people behind Kuiper were not organized and they did not share the values of the inward system, including how people can and cannot be transformed. Cannot I be a station again? Let my outer shell be caressed by solar wind. Smell the escaping atmosphere of Clymene. Gaze onto the cold icy comets passing us; distant planetary systems bathing in alien starlight; far early galaxies with my multi-spectral eyes.

I still get panic attacks whenever I think of my life so unexpectedly interrupted. But they grow less frequent and severe as the microelectrodes implanted in my brain do their work.

When they release me, they send me to a special home supposed to help my integration into society. I attend regular therapist meetings and I'm now preparing for entering the work force. I'm learning new words. Sometimes I can even comprehend their meaning without having to memorize it.

Slavery: *When a person is owned as property by another person and is under their control, particularly in involuntary servitude.*

According to the Earth Union, I was a slave.

I didn't feel like one.

I felt like a god.

Four months later, I'm working part-time as a human analyst of sky surveys' images, trying to catch what automatic algorithms had missed.

They said I have an eye for detail.

In other words, I'm strange, too focused on trivialities, socially incompetent but meticulous. I cannot do any harm here and I don't meet many people. There are a few exceptions. Marika is my boss. She's a stumpy sixty-something woman with a hard voice and even harder look but there is something reassuring about her. She's predictable. She cares for our results and doesn't get personal, but she's fair and her knowledge is vast. I wonder how much one can cram into one's head without the externities I used to have.

Apart from her, I see few people and retain even fewer in my still recovering memory. One has appeared at work several times, exploring the use of our data to his work.

His name is Nalin and he works as a freelance artist. He mostly does commissions for hotels or sometimes cities. He says that genuine artwork draws Earthling tourists to Mars more reliably than any stunning 3D-scape.

He approached me first, asking about my job and explaining his. He wants to do a non-commissioned piece to show people the beauty of deep space, he says. I don't know if that's possible. They would need to see what I had seen, what I can barely remember now but still feel the longing... He sees something in my eyes and backs off politely.

But he returns the next day.

The third day, he invites me to have dinner with him. I have understood enough of common social behavior to think it likely that he has other than work-related reasons to do so. It surprises me. No one has approached me this way for as long as I remember.

I think I preferred men back then, before my transformation. I study this one. Does he elicit any possible sexual or romantic response? I'm not sure. I suppose it's worth trying. After all, they told me I need to work on my interpersonal relationships.

Two years after my presumable rescue, I feel truly alive for the first time. It doesn't have to do with the fact that I've moved to work on a more satisfying position, or that I've started living with Nalin and so far, both changes seem to work. No, it's something far simpler.

We go hiking in Noctis Labyrinthus with Nalin. Even with high-oxygen mixtures in our tanks, the hike is demanding. We have to climb the rock wall sometimes. My body is still not as strong and muscular as those of Martians who hadn't spent most of their lives with atrophied muscles inside a space station, but I can feel my new strength now and can rely on it.

We scale the wall, silent, focused, determined. I can hear my breath and the blood pounding in my temples.

Hold, pull up, rest. Find another hold, repeat.

Walk. One careful step. Another.

No thinking.

The solar rays falling onto my skin... filtered through the compulsory thin protective layer, but still vaguely familiar...

And then we're at the summit and I see the vast landscape bathed in the late afternoon light, clad in impossibly bright tones of orange, red and brown.

I'm feeling something not quite familiar, hard to describe. Only after a while I realize that I'm happy.

A faint spot of light turns my ordinary life upside down.

"It's moving," I say to Marika. "Fast. The trajectory is peculiar."

She studies the images and a dark frown comes across her face. "Have you told anyone else yet?"

"No."

"So don't. I'll handle it."

Two days later, after many careful questions as well as straightforward calls, they make the announcement.

"They already knew about it on Earth," Marika comments wryly. "We just made them reveal it a little sooner. I guess someone else would have stumbled on it in the matter of weeks anyway."

The alien ship seems to be decelerating hard. In a year, it should enter the inner Oort. In two years, the Kuiper Belt. Then perhaps the inner system as well.

The whole Earth Union discusses nothing else. People argue vigorously about how we should proceed. A political schism opens when several independent groups use their access to high-power antennas to transmit to the visitors. Official messages follow shortly.

"What do you think they want?" Nalin asks me one evening.

How should I know? I, who cannot fathom most human beings, too scarred by my past?

I think about it. After a long pause, when he perhaps no longer expects me to reply, I say: "Beauty."

Nalin looks surprised before he realizes I'm answering his question. "Beauty?" he raises a brow. "Why not knowledge? Sense of companionship? Meeting other cultures?"

How can I explain? Beauty encompasses all of this. It can be everywhere.

It's in the images I study. It's in Noctis Labyrinthus. It's in Nalin's art. It's the sunshine across the spectrum, the hum of distant galaxies.

I haven't felt such beauty for an eternity.

But instead of hanging onto that desperate longing, I smile sardonically. "I thought you'd be glad. They might like your work! Haven't you always imagined yourself as an ambassador of humanity?"

He laughs with me, yet I feel a strange emptiness. Have I developed a sense of humor without being able to actually feel it?

Sometimes life keeps getting back at you, no matter what you do. I have learned to live a bearable if not too happy life after my alleged rescue. Here I am, an Earth Union citizen living peacefully on Mars.

While the alien ship had shed several smaller units which decelerated rapidly. Two of them were still passing fast through the inner Oort.

One entered the orbit of Clymene.

Nalin is patient with me, trying to be understanding. In our years together, I have told him fragments about my time as a station controller on several occasions.

I have a life. I cannot change the past. Besides, if there still was a permanent settlement around Clymene, would they *have come there?*

I will never know. I can only try to fight the returning dreams of my surreal existence and nightmares of waking up in that stark white room.

Little news about the alien pods reach the inner system, even though the people are hungry for nothing else. Contact plans are being drawn carefully, they say.

Whoever attempts to reach the pods without permission will be terminated.

I actually hope someone tries it. How would *they* react?

One day, an older man in gray stands in front of my door. His features seem vaguely familiar. But I have never developed the same uncanny ability to instantly recognize faces other people seem to possess.

"Miss Montova? May I speak with you inside?"

Something in his words, in the tone in which he says *Miss Montova*, releases a floodgate of memories. Clad in gray. Gray like the Moon dust.

His is the face from my nightmares.

He slips inside, past me, and only when I manage to overcome my paralysis and close the door, he introduces himself.

"My name is Adrian Jensson. I see that you remember me. Good. May we sit?"

I'm too startled to protest. Not waiting for my reaction, he sits down and starts talking in his low quiet voice. At first, I don't speak. I'm shocked by his sudden appearance and overwhelmed with dread and anxiety. But gradually I become more aware of his words than the memories and feelings his presence brings back. He speaks of the *bidesi*, as the world eventually started calling the aliens for the lack of their own self-designation.

He speaks of the lack of reactions to all the countless transmissions we had tried.

Of the unsuccessful missions—one unable to elicit any response, the other coming in too close and then destroyed without warning. . .

"Wait—there were no reports of any crewed missions," I interrupt him, speaking for the first time.

"That is right. Previous attempts were kept covert for many good reasons. However, we're turning to other potential solutions now that the previous approach did not fully succeed—"

"Failed, you mean," I correct him. I have become cynical in these years as a normal human, haven't I?

Jensson lets it pass. "We think that they may have a vastly different set of sensory perception. The worlds we see may barely overlap. We've tried sending AIs, but. . ." He pauses.

"Enlighten me. What went wrong there?"

"You'll receive the file with all pertinent information should you choose to cooperate. Suffice to say that the vicinity of Clymene now seems to be their domain. None of the AIs returned with useful data—if at all."

I'm honestly surprised that the Union did not choose to show its own force, if not truly retaliate with force, after the loss of a crew and so many failed attempts to communicate.

"That brings me to why I'm here. We've arrived at the conclusion that people such as you may represent a potentially favorable choice for a different kind of mission."

It shouldn't have come as a surprise. His sudden appearance on my doorstep, the talk of the *bidesi* and the possibility of non-overlapping sensory perceptions. . .

It's so absurd that it almost makes me laugh. "Really? You had half-wittedly destroyed those who could help you now, driven us back into the gravity well, crippled me, and now you come to *me* for help?"

Jensson stays calm. "Miss Montova, please realize that you're one of a mere handful who managed to lead normal lives after they'd been freed."

Wouldn't those who didn't live normally be a better choice? I almost ask but then waive the question away. Of course, it meant *didn't survive, failed sooner or later*. A corner of my mouth twitches in a sarcastic almost-smile.

"Well, you weren't expecting me to leap and shout out in ecstasy, were you? If so, you've been so, so wrong. . . Fuck off now."

He seems taken aback by my response. I sneer at him. He stands up.

"You'll reconsider," he promises between the door.

I'm sure I won't. When he leaves, I finally drop my mask of control and sit down, shuddering.

I lead a functioning life now. I have no obligation to help them. And my previous life, that is long gone, even if my brain could adapt to it again. I see no way back. There's no way I would just set aside all these years in between and become that pure glorious being again. . .

Well, you did it once before. You were no spiritually pure being when you were dying of muscle dystrophy and waiting desperately for a miracle.

I bury my face into my palms.

But I'd been a teenager then. I've led a life now. I'm bitter, cynical . . . and even if that didn't matter, my brain can no longer form new pathways as easily as back then.

New ones aren't entirely necessary. There are remnants in your brain, waiting for signals coming through again, pathways not entirely destroyed by the cure when you were "freed" or by plain aging. You're still unique and have a ground to build on; others lack even that...

They could take dying children or adolescents. They must have the technology, or they wouldn't even be asking me.

Well, they are asking you. What if you were not their first choice? What if those presumed children failed before the mission could even commence? And, most of all, what the hell do you think to achieve if you don't take up the offer?

Nalin finds me crouched in the bathroom, paralyzed, staring at the blank wall. When he touches my shoulder, I flinch.

I see his quizzical look and kind eyes surrounded by small wrinkles...

Wrinkles in spacetime, emanating from distant neutron stars— "I'm sorry," I say.

Moments before they wire me in, time slows down for me. I have an eternity to mull over my decision. I can still go back. Even after the extensive tests and training, even after the biochemical modifications, I can still say no.

Nalin may still forgive me. They will find someone else to take my place. I've proved that I can lead a normal life. I could spend many decades doing just that.

Instead, I may walk into an uncertain future. Potentially quick failure and brain damage, or the ultimate failure of my mission at Clymene.

Where do I really belong?

I know the feeling. I'm scared.

But I know that I will no longer be in a moment. There will be something vaguely approximating fear, but different, more analytical, deeper and calmer...

Then my universe explodes.

My senses. Oh, my senses... It's like I've been shut out in a sensory deprivation chamber all those long years, and now I'm overwhelmed. I almost cannot bear the intensity and range of the long-forgotten impulses, and I'm barely at a few percent of the full sensory input yet.

And my body—it's suddenly *complete*. Not as vast as it once had been, but wider and fuller than the tiny human shell I've been locked in for so long.

Being human, being with Nalin, it all seems like a dream now, though it had felt real then. I recall words from an ancient song. . .

You've almost convinced me I'm real. . .

I start singing it in my head. My organic memory isn't so bad after all.

But now—I've become so much more again.

I merge with the interface smoothly, and the song—just becomes more real than the reality.

Years fly by while I'm inside my ship, my new body. Clymene is currently over 300 AU away from the Sun. It's almost hilarious: the Earth Union had gone to such trouble to drive away a couple of independent colonists to tighten its control over the system and humanity's future, and thus vacated the realm for the *bidesi*.

My time ticks slowly like the seasons. I listen to the universe. Yet I still manage to retain a lot of my humanity from my years on Mars. I feel it fading with the pace of glaciers, and try to hold onto it for some reason.

Finally approaching Clymene, I feel something new: a part of me is like an utterly calm ocean surface, taking in all the peculiar sensations, while deep down, conflicting currents fight for their dominance.

Anger. Fear. Bitterness. Regret. Longing. Curiosity. Hope.

And then I'm flying by for the first time after what now seems like someone else's life, and I'm seeing the strange pod with so many of my own senses. Its protruding rods glow in the infra-red on the background of the uniformly dark hull. The engines are silent. No radar ping reflects off my own hull. No beam of light falls onto me even for a fraction of a second.

Yet even if they're just observing passively, they have had to see me. . .

I decide to ping them. The reflection that returns shows me barely more details than I've seen in the visible and infra-red.

I lose them, flinging by the planet. Oh, the familiar vast swirling clouds of hydrogen and ammonia, and the eerie sprinkle of particles caught in Clymene's complex magnetic field. . .

Yet something is different here.

I had known this as my home, no, a *part* of me. I know its slightest changes, the seasonal change for which glacial is too fast a word, and I know that the composition of particles around Clymene has changed. The difference is tiny, barely perceptible—but some of the molecules whose spectra I see have *never* been here before.

Then I swing back by the *bidesi* pod and notice another change, a difference compared to my previous fly-by. A very low density of complex molecules that would normally originate much, much closer to the Sun.

And I realize why none of the preceding missions have succeeded.

The solution is so simple and yet absurd that I would laugh if I still could.

Chemical communication, so laughably inefficient, outright ridiculous in space!

There is no way it is their usual mode of conveying information. Perhaps long ago in their original environment. But they wouldn't have made it into space, even to other stars, if they didn't shift to other means of communication. No; it is a test. They wanted to see whether we would see through their riddle.

I run through the reactions they may want as the answer, and produce a mixture. I release the cloud of molecules, and wait eagerly.

Nothing yet.

Wait—

The *bidesi* answer.

I fire my engines and come closer.

It takes us weeks to develop some rudimentary communication. I wonder when they will decide to make the switch to other, more reliable and efficient methods, but stick to their rules.

The *bidesi* first make sure we can understand each other on a simple level, then start what may be questions. First about me. What am I? How many beings in my pod?

I respond.

And then...

Are the others like you? they seem to be asking. *Intelligent?*

I almost intuitively say *yes*, but then hesitate.

They did not understand the *bidesi. I* did. They are not like me.

I recall the fate of the failed mission that got too close without permission.

A small part of me ponders upon revenge, and I imagine the course of events:

Do I betray the rest of humanity—

—repulsive, abominable, small-minded, thickheaded humanity—

—to these creatures, or will I show mercy? Empathy? Understanding?

. . . everything they lacked in regard to me . . . but not everyone, no, I would be unfair thinking that. . .

The alien envoy is waiting for my answer.

So am I.

But no. This is not what happens.

I can feel the faint sunlight glistening on my metal skin. I hear the song of the universe, a wonderful symphony across all frequencies. And modulating it, the myriad of molecules scattered everywhere. . . How do I begin to describe it? How could they understand?

Yet *they* do. Those who are waiting patiently for me to respond.

Why take revenge? It would be so human.

I'm full again and I'm contented. I'm happy.

And I'm just about to take a step on the road towards humanity and its branches' future.

Turn left; turn right. I know what choice to make.

The world is vast and full of wonders. So is our future.

THE SCRAP METAL MAN
By David Turton

If you are reading this letter then I have passed away, victim to the cruel cancer that has ravaged me over the past few years. I leave nothing of any value, and have no family or close friends to pass it to in any case. What I do want to leave behind is a tale that only I can tell. A story of such horror that I have never uttered a word of it since the fearful night it took place. I appreciate that you, the unlucky soul that has come across this letter upon my death, may have hoped for a better blessing from beyond the grave but, unfortunately, this is all I have to give. I can only pray that it will not inflict on you the maddening nightmares that I have suffered in the numerous decades that have passed since that awful summer night. I hope you can find it in your heart to forgive me as I lay in my grave, but I felt that this tale had to be told. I can only imagine what doctors and nurses would make of the inane utterances of a dying man, as he attempts to articulate such a strange and disturbing account of the events that took place. No, this has to be written in order for it to survive and, rather selfishly, I feel glad that I will not be alive to see or hear this terrifying knowledge being passed to another human being.

It was during the famously scorching summer of 1976 that, at the age of sixteen, I secured a job working for two months at a local garage in my hometown of Gaston in South Yorkshire. Despite its glamorously Gallic-sounding name, Gaston was, and probably still is, a small industrial town, its streets lined with closed factories that supported the declining Sheffield steel industry and its residents almost exclusively working in some form of metal production. The decline of this industry had hit Gaston hard, the loss of jobs creating a depressive domino effect, with several boarded-up houses lining the streets and with many shops closed as a result. The town was a depressing, dirty place with miserable inhabitants, the more desperate of which took to the Steelman Social Club to drain their sorrows in several pints of Yorkshire ale.

It was in the same street as the Steelman that Ron's Garage was based. My friend Joe Goldsmith and I approached Ron as school finished for the summer and he offered us a trial between July and August. If we did well, and he could afford it, he would take us on permanently. At such a young age, I wasn't particularly bothered about a permanent job, but two months' wages—even at the measly rate of £8 per week—would at least mean I could afford to have a fun summer.

Ron taught us some of the more basic skills of fixing cars, but our roles were mainly restricted to washing the vehicles, sweeping the yards, cleaning the tools and walking to Gaston Market Place to buy sandwiches for Ron and his assistant manager. Joe, my best friend for over a decade, had a driving license at the time, so he could drive and park the cars when they came in, which made his role a little more varied and responsible than mine.

It was one particularly hot afternoon in mid-July that Ron had a special task for Joe, one that would lead us on the path to our awful discovery. We were both in the middle of washing a beautiful brown Ford Cortina with our shirts off, and I was taking great pleasure in waxing it in the blazing sun, admiring the bright sheen that glared outwards from the polished metal.

"Joe, I got a job for you, son," Ron said to my friend, squinting into the intense light. Ron was a big man both in height and physique and he smoked constantly, keeping a cigarette behind his oil-blackened ear for easy access. His voice had become heavy and muffled from the cigarettes, making his words unclear and hazy. He carried a unique aroma, stale cigarette smoke mixed with oily rags and earthy masculine sweat.

Joe looked up and shielded his eyes using his hand. In an amusing moment, I thought it looked like he was answering Ron with a respectful military-style salute.

Ron pointed his oily index finger to a battered light blue Mini, which must have been almost two decades old. "Car still runs but it's a wreck. It'll be worth more for scrap than sell-on. I want you to drive it to see Ingleby's scrapyard in Elizabethville and get the bus back. He should take it for ten quid."

Joe and I looked at each other, jaws gaping. Every small town had a scary story routinely told around campfires, by mischievous children trying to scare each other. The most terrifying of those stories were based on real characters. In Gaston, those stories centred around the scrap metal man in Elizabethville, a desolate, deserted outpost five miles beyond the edge of town. The man, Alfred Ingleby, ran it by himself and was completely reclusive. The campfire stories all differed but had a recurring theme; the scrap metal man was not human, he lived on a diet of the scrap metal that he bought from local businesses at the most generous prices in South Yorkshire. Although he met various people to buy the scrap metal, his business was all completed outside the thick steel fence that ran around the large yard, which was piled high with old cars, chains, and various hunks of metal. According to the stories, nobody had ever been inside the protective fence.

Seeing the fear on our faces, Ron's face cracked into a smile, the deep wrinkles on his dirty face expanding with the movement of his lips. "You've heard the stories about the scrap metal man, then, I see. Don't you worry, Joe. I've been there hundreds of times. The man's a bit odd, but he pays good money. And business isn't exactly great around here at the minute. Just don't piss him off. He's dumb but he's not deaf. Just let him inspect the car and he'll give you the money."

If we knew the terror of what was to come, we would have both walked out of Ron's garage there and then. But, with the campfire stories came the mysticism and excitement of seeing a local legend in the flesh. I was envious of Joe, to be driving the Mini out of town with the windows down in the hot sun, getting paid to go on a little adventure with a hint of danger.

Ron must have read my mind. "Only Joe can go, though. The forecourt is a mess, son," he said as he turned to me. "It'll take you at least an hour to sweep it up."

It was almost time to finish work when Joe walked up to Ron's garage. His face was pale and drawn, despite the deep tan that the searing summer sun had blessed on his skin, and his t-shirt was soaked in sweat.

"Hot on the bus was it, Joe?" Ron asked him, smirking.

Joe simply nodded and handed Ron the ten-pound note. I stood watching, leaning on the sweeping brush, above the final pile of swept shrapnel on the floor. Something looked different about Joe. His light brown hair, usually immaculately sculpted with Brylcreem, was unkempt and raised up in tufts, appearing as he had constantly rubbed his head with his hands. His mouth turned downwards, as if the thoughts in his head automatically produced an expression of intense worry and fear.

"Ron, am I okay to clock off now?" Joe asked.

"Yeah sure, both of you can go. How was old Ingleby?"

"Weird. Very weird," he replied, hoarsely. Joe laughed, but I could see that it was forced and it took some effort for him to produce a smile.

As we both walked out the garage, I turned to him, my curiosity burning into me like an uncontrollable itch.

"So, what happened? What was he like?"

"He was weird. I . . . I don't really want to say. I'm afraid you'll laugh."

I stopped and placed a hand on his shoulders. "I won't laugh, Joe. I promise. Hand on heart."

"Okay. But if you take the piss out of me I'll beat you to a pulp. I mean that."

"Okay, okay," I replied.

"I drove out there, not sure what to expect. All those stories we used to tell each other as kids were going through my head, but I knew stories like that were never true, just things kids tell each other for a laugh. So, I pulled the car up outside the fence and waited. First of all, the scrapyard is exactly what people say. It's massive and there are loads of cars just piled up. It actually hurt my eyes, the sun glaring off all the metal. After five minutes, Ingleby unlocked a door in the fence and walked out. I got out of my car to meet him. He didn't say anything. Nothing at all, Ron must be right about him being dumb. He just walked past me and looked around the car. He opened the doors, sat inside, opened the bonnet, the boot."

"Sounds normal?" I said.

"It wasn't. He wasn't just inspecting it. It looked like he was sniffing it. He kept taking these deep breaths and really wheezing. It sounded mechanical, like some kind of electric saw buzzing. Then, when he's finished, he walks up to me and hands me a ten-pound note. Still saying nothing. But that's not all. I looked right into his eyes and they were bright blue."

"So?" I replied, "my Mum's eyes are bright blue."

"These weren't like any person's eyes I've ever seen before. They looked like they were glowing. The closest I can get to describing it is the blue flame on the kitchen hob. They looked just like that. I could feel his eyes go right inside me. And he smelt oily, like burnt metal."

I laughed. "Ron smells like that. What do you expect from a scrap metal man?"

I'd no sooner finished speaking when I felt a heavy blow to my stomach, as Joe punched me swiftly in the gut.

"I told you not to laugh or take the piss!" Joe shouted. "You can't understand, you weren't there. It wasn't just his eyes or the way he inspected the car. He walked in a weird shuffle. And when I walked off, I got a good view of the scrapyard. There was no office, no bed. Where does he sleep? God, I really don't think he's human, you know? I think those stories are true," he looked at me sternly as I broke out into a smile. "And if you laugh at me again I'll beat the shit out of you."

"Joe, I just think he's weird and you were shaken up, that's all. I tell you what, let's go there tonight and I'll prove you wrong. We'll find him sleeping or something. It'll be an adventure, like when we used to go camping when we were kids."

Joe shook his head violently. "No. No way, I can't go back there."

"I've got a plan that could make this worthwhile. Surely you're not scared, Joe?"

I was confident that would get him on board. I knew Joe's mind as well as I knew my own, we could easily push buttons with each other, knew how to manipulate, how to make each other laugh and how to persuade the other to do something they might not want to do. Even though we were out of childhood, we were in that strange limbo, still teenagers and not yet adults. We still lived in a world where dodging dares and displaying cowardice were avoided at all costs, and a strong punch to the stomach was delivered as punishment for any misdemeanour against this youthful code of conduct. If I had any inkling that day that Joe's fears were genuine, and that the scrap metal man was indeed the inhuman monster he turned out to be, I would never have suggested the trip. It is a heavy burden of absolute guilt that I have had to carry my entire life, and one I have never forgiven myself for. On my darkest nights, I often wonder if this rotten cancer is my curse, my ultimate punishment for persuading Joe to revisit the scrapyard.

We walked the five miles from Gaston to Elizabethville. It is shameful to admit this now, but I was excited about the adventure which lay before us. It wasn't just the slight element of danger that the weird scrap metal man held for us but it was a chance to do something different. It reignited the thrills that I had not felt for years, at embarking on something new. As eager twelve-year-olds, Joe and I would take trips to Gaston Forest where we would arm ourselves with crude slingshots, in the event of an attack from some being that emerged from deep within our own imaginations. I looked back on those halcyon days and felt that same zealous spark. It was also a chance for me to show Joe that his fears about the scrap metal man were unfounded, a result of his own imagination caused by over-thinking on his drive to the scrapyard, and maybe a little sun stroke from the blazing heat. Oh, how I wish that had been the case. I wish to God that I had been right about that.

Looking back now, I'll never know why Joe agreed to return. Maybe I was persuasive or maybe he just wanted to convince himself that it was some kind of hallucination, that a second look would somehow overrule his terror. We sat on some large rocks half-a-mile from the scrapyard, on the edge of old Elizabethville. The deserted outpost was eerie, the constant heat had made the ground dusty, giving it an old appearance, like the setting for an old Western movie. Along the landscape were ruined buildings, which must have sat unoccupied for years. We drank cheap cider, which was warm and disgusting, until our heads began to spin and we giggled, all nerves ironed out, lubricated by the low-cost alcohol.

As the sun set in the west, causing a beautiful gradient of colour from bright orange to deep purple, we stood and walked towards the scrapyard. I wasn't sure what we would come across in this strange place. Even Joe, who had been so scared on his encounter with the scrap metal man, seemed to revel in the excitement of our journey, which we had kept secret from anyone else, only adding to the growing sense of adventure we both felt. The plan was simple; we would sneak into the scrapyard by climbing the fence and then we would seek out the scrap metal man. We would either prove once-and-for-all that he was just a strange human being, or we would catch him in the act doing something inhuman. Joe had brought his mum's new camera along. If we managed to capture anything strange we could sell it to one of the tabloids or the magazines that pay a fortune for bizarre stories—I felt that this was the real fact that swung Joe's decision to go along with my plan, the promise of riches and fame. Either way, we would solve the mystery and have a little fun along the way. Joe had reported that there were no guard dogs like the huge, deadly beasts that roamed other such facilities, so all we had to do was prepare to sprint and climb the fence if we were caught.

By the time we reached the scrapyard, the dying light gave it a horrid, ominous air and I saw that the stories of my childhood had been correct in their description. Cars were piled high in columns that looked as if they could topple at any moment. Hunks of metal from white goods, tools, huge steel sheets and other articles glowed in the mellow sunlight. I looked across the large yard and couldn't see any buildings or living quarters. I was pleased to see that Joe was right about the dogs, I could neither hear nor see any snarling animals around the perimeter of the metal fence. Even more pleasingly, I couldn't see Ingleby, and assumed he must be in some kind of bed. *Maybe he has forged his own bed from his metal*, I mused to myself.

We came to the fence at the same time as the sun became fully submerged under the horizon, and the orange sky was consumed by a dark purple sheet that plunged us into near darkness. We climbed the metal fence quickly and as soundlessly as we could, scaling the seven feet to the top and jumping down heavily at the other side. I looked around at the scrapyard. There seemed to be no person around but when we stood still in the humid night air I could hear a faint mechanical sound, like a broken machine straining to move. I looked over to Joe and pressed my finger to my lips, suppressing a giggle, and then gestured to him to prepare his camera. We tiptoed across the middle of the scrapyard and I saw the light blue Mini that Joe dropped off, parked askew at the foot of one of the high columns of cars. I glanced across at Joe, who was trembling and sweating, and I felt a trickle of sweat roll from my own temple and cascade down my warm cheeks. As we approached the Mini, which was parked with its boot facing us, the mechanical noise grew louder and I realised that the car's bonnet had been raised. We crept closer until we were directly behind the car's boot and the sound was now more distinctive, a crunching, jarring noise that sounded like several coke cans being crushed by a machine. We slowly made our way around the side of the car to gain a clearer view of the source of this disturbing commotion. What we saw filled me with horror and dominates my hellish nightmares to this day.

A large figure knelt, its head buried into the car bonnet. Wires and jagged pieces of metal hung from its face which, although its body was shaped and clothed like a man, bore no resemblance to human features. Inside its grey metal face, its eyes shone a brilliant electric blue, which created a laser-like beam across the moonlit air and its gleam reflected harshly from the underside of the open bonnet. The figure's mouth was a bleak metallic maw, with jagged metal teeth jutting upwards like the sharp triangles of a blackened bear trap. Dark, viscous oil spewed from its mouth and pooled onto the car's shredded engine, and the air was heavy with the smell of burnt metal and thick grease. The grim mechanical noises continued as it chewed roughly through the thick metal, creating sparks as blue as the glow of its eyes. I gasped in horror as I saw a mask resembling a human face lying next to its bent knee. In a moment of terrifying despair that I have never managed to erase from my memory in the years since, the figure turned its hideous metal face toward me, still spewing black oil from its grim mouth. I can still conjure the image of the scrap metal man's deathly grin upon closing my eyes, as if the awful night only took place yesterday.

In a jerky, mechanical movement, the scrap metal man stood and faced us. His eyes met mine and I could feel the bright blue light seep into my body and spread throughout my insides. I could feel it moving, probing inside me, a chilling sensation that penetrated right to my soul, a feeling of being physically and spiritually raped by something not of our world. I turned away from the blue light and immediately felt its unwelcome presence depart my body.

"Now! Take the picture!" I yelled to Joe, but he stood helplessly, frozen with utter terror. "Take the fucking picture," I repeated, causing thick spittle to fly from my dry mouth.

Joe held out the camera and fumbled it, at the same time as the scrap metal man launched toward him. In desperate panic, Joe thrusted the camera into the face of the atrocious thing and screamed as it simply bit down into it, crushing its thick metal frame with a sickening crunch. The shock was enough to prompt Joe into action; he turned quickly on his heels and began to sprint toward the fence. I followed, running faster than I have ever run in my life. The sound of the scrap metal man chasing us will stay with me until my final breath. It sounded like nails scraping down a metal surface, a rattling, clanking noise that seemed to burrow inside my ear canals and squeeze a part of my brain reserved only for moments of true horror.

We reached the fence and pulled ourselves to the top, hurling ourselves to the floor and sprinting again, never looking back. We eventually slowed to a brisk walking pace after at least two miles, as we realised that the dreadful being was no longer following us. We were both sobbing and breathing heavily from the adrenaline, the shock knocking away any drunken feeling from the putrid cider consumed less than an hour previously.

"What was that?" I said. It was more of a statement than a question.

"I told you," Joe replied. "I told you he wasn't human. And you didn't listen. We didn't even get the photo. He ate the camera." His words came out breathlessly.

"Joe, I'm sorry, if I knew. . ." my words trailed off to silence and it was a wordless walk home as we went our separate ways to our parents' houses. As Joe walked up to his door I noticed his hair had faded to a light colour, matching the paleness of his complexion. The terror seemed to have robbed his whole body of colour.

Over the next few weeks, Joe and I continued to work at the garage, but something was missing between us. The chatter and jovial banter had gone, replaced by only the essential language required to complete our duties. Whether Ron noticed it, I never knew, but we were going through the motions, numbed by a dark malaise that engulfed both of us.

One morning, Joe broke his silence during a break, while he smoked a cigarette and stared at a wrecked car at the far end of the forecourt. His eyes were glazed and wide, giving the impression of emptiness behind them.

"The scrap metal man," he said, straining his words. "I can still feel him. Can you?"

I nodded my head. It was true, every so often, especially at night, that feeling of his bright blue eyes penetrating the inside of my body returned, a hideous cold feeling when I felt I could sense his evil presence exploring my very soul, watching, learning.

"I can't cope," Joe continued. His hair had retained the shocking light colour and his face was drawn, giving him an appearance that was much older than his sixteen years. "I feel him all the time. I feel like he's part of me. Like he knows where I am. What if he comes for me? What if he's watching all the time?"

I patted his shoulder and shook my head. "It was horrible, Joe. But it's just trauma, aftershock in our heads. Like when someone goes to war and can't shake off the awful things they've seen. It will get better, Joe, I promise." I was trying to convince myself as well as Joe, the feeling was too real, too otherworldly to just be in our heads.

Things didn't get better. Over the weeks Joe became more and more distant, the worry lines appearing deeper on his face, his eyes becoming a glassy, vacant void on his face. Then one morning, I came to work and saw Ron standing morosely by the side of the garage.

"Sorry I'm late," I said with my head down as I went into his office.

His face was solemn and his stance was loose, like he'd relaxed his muscles for the first time in an age. "We had some bad news this morning. Your friend Joe. His mum and dad found him this morning. He hung himself overnight, took his own life. Sorry son, take the day off."

I never returned to work at Ron's garage and I moved out of Gaston three weeks after Joe's death, to take a job at a food processing factory in Leeds. I couldn't work with metal any more. I didn't go to Joe's funeral; my mind was racked with too much guilt at forcing him to go to the scrapyard. I couldn't handle the talk about his suicide being a mystery, and the secret of our trip to Elizabethville hung heavy on my heart. Joe didn't leave a note, but I knew why he couldn't go on in this world, the knowledge of the horrors that lurked in the darkness were too much to bear. It was the scrap man's eyes, that horrible alien stare that bore into our souls. I'm sure it left a grim deposit in my body, a scar deep inside my soul which flares up on dark days with an icy chill that blasts through my whole body. I guess it was a feeling that Joe couldn't live with, and Lord knows how many times I've thought of ending my own life, just to rid my body of his cold, evil touch. But that would be too easy, a get out of jail free card that I don't deserve to use.

I never found out what happened to Ingleby's scrapyard, and I have been tempted to research it so many times, but the incapacitating memory of the true terror of that night in 1976 has always kept my curiosity at bay. It had been too much for Joe, and delving deeper into the mystery of the scrap metal man could have sent me too into that lonely abyss. I assume the scrap metal man is still there, paying good money for metal, still chomping at the machinery like an evil, hungry animal. I've often speculated to myself where he came from, maybe some ancient being who emerged from an awful subterranean land, attracted by the increasing availability of human-cultivated metal on the earth's surface. Or perhaps some kind of monstrous alien from a planet beyond our own. Quite possibly, the scrap metal man was human once and has somehow transformed into a grotesque metallic mutant after living on a diet of machinery. How did the stories get out in the first place to become a subject of terrible childhood lore? Had some other people stumbled upon this horrible scene and spread the word over the years? And if this monstrosity existed on the outskirts of a nondescript Yorkshire industrial town, what other unknown horrors lurk in the darkness around us? It matters not to me now. As I lay on the bed of this hospice, my body ruined by cancer, I know I will die without the knowledge of where this evil being came from. If you, the reader of my final letter, feel it in your heart to explore this story and seek answers to these questions, then you do so with my blessing; this story is now yours and you may do with it as you wish. But also, please heed my warning. There are true terrors in this world that are unexplained. Sometimes, in the dead of night when the bitter wind howls outside the window of my lonely room, I wish that my curiosity of the scrap metal man had been left in my own mind, and that the nightmarish stories told by children around spitting, popping campfires were left as the unproven tales they deserve to be. Oh, how I wish I had never known the truth.

THE TRANSITION
By Frank Roger

"**I**s it serious, doctor?" I asked.

Dr. Philipson shook his head. "Not at all. There is no need to worry, Mr. Carr. The pain you are suffering in your leg is caused by a few blood vessels that have deteriorated beyond repair. For someone your age, that is quite normal. As a matter of fact, it was to be expected."

I nodded. "Can those blood vessels be replaced?"

"Of course," the doctor said. "Replacing those worn-out parts by artificial ones will be a quick routine operation. There is no risk involved at all."

"Fine," I said. "When can this be done?"

The doctor lifted his hand. "There is one thing though. A special authorization will be required for this operation."

"But you said there was no risk involved," I protested.

"This is not about risk," the doctor retorted. "There is another matter. I have your medical file here. According to these data, the blood vessels that are now causing you pain are the last original parts of your body. All the rest has already been replaced by artificial material. Now as I said, for someone your age, that is quite normal. You are one hundred and forty-five, after all. It's quite natural that your original body parts are wearing down."

"Then what is the problem?" I asked.

"The problem is of a legal nature, not a medical one," the doctor replied. "You see, as long as you have some original parts left, you are legally considered to be human. When you reach the point where your body consists entirely of artificial replacements, you lose your status of human being. You become a machine, a cyborg. This will only have legal repercussions, not medical ones. There will be no consequences for your everyday life. As a matter of fact, without original body parts you may look forward to many more years in good health. But you will lose some legal privileges that are exclusively granted to human beings."

I nodded. "I understand. So I have two options. Remaining human, without a solution for my medical problems, or becoming a machine, and getting on with my life as I've always done. And in the latter case, I have to sign an authorization."

"That is quite correct, Mr. Carr. Either you stay human, with increasing medical troubles, or you sign the transition document."

"Transition?"

"You'll make the transition from human to machine," the doctor explained. "Now should you wish more information. . ."

"There's no need for that," I interrupted him. "I made up my mind already. I'll sign the document. I'll make the transition and stick around for a little longer."

The doctor leaned back and smiled. "Congratulations, Mr. Carr. You've made a decision you won't regret. Now if you could sign here please."

He pushed a plastic document towards me that I signed by simply touching it at the bottom right corner—its sensors examined and verified my identity right away.

"Thank you," the doctor said. "Now, you may make an appointment for the operation. My secretary will deal with that. Do you have any more questions?"

"No," I said, and rose to my feet, relieved this matter had been taken care of.

"I'm so glad you joined us," the doctor said while he dealt with the payment, debited automatically to my credit card.

"What do you mean?" I asked.

"I made the transition a long time ago," Dr. Philipson explained. "I could never tell you, until now. After all I'm supposed to be neutral when dealing with human patients. And so many of them have made the transition by now. As is the case with many of my colleagues. Fellow doctors who also happen to be fellow transitioners, if you see what I mean."

"Yes, I do. If this goes on, there will be few humans left. Or maybe none at all." I chuckled.

"Exactly," the doctor said, all smiles. "Believe me, we're working on it. Soon we'll be the dominant species, and then it will only take a short step to the next and final phase."

"The end of humanity?" I asked. "Machines as the only kind of intelligent life on earth?"

"Exactly," the doctor said. "No more organic trash to worry about. Just clean and artificial perfection in unfailing health. Well, goodbye then, Mr. Carr. Don't forget to make that appointment."

"I'll see to it right away," I replied, convinced I had made the right decision, had joined the winning side in this struggle for life. After all, at one hundred and forty-five years I was much too young to die. I was happy to know that I might look forward to many more years. Decades? Centuries? The very notion left me dreaming, as any human would.

MIMESCAPE
By Damir Salkovic

It was raining outside, the drops playing a snare drum on the rooftop and the metal shutters on the windows.

Treddis knew something was awry long before he saw the shrouded form in the corner of the dark, cramped chamber. His mind swam with the aftertaste of troubling dreams. An eerie sense of unreality and the faint smell of burned wiring permeated the air. Above his cot two glowrods flickered, turning the peeling walls into a stark map of whiteness and shadow. It was his room—the desk with its scattering of tools and cables, the shining touch-interface of the humming system console, the narrow closet in which he kept his clothes. The only thing that was out of the ordinary was the shrouded presence in the corner.

That, and the rain.

It never rained in the Torus.

He willed his limbs to move, but they remained unresponsive. The burning smell was stronger now, thick and oily. The thing in the corner rustled and bulged: it was his zero-G softsuit, the one he used for work in the central axis of the Torus. The suit hung on its peg, but something moved beneath the smooth yellow-and-black fabric, working its way through. With great effort he raised his head off the pillow. A low clicking, whirring noise reached his ears, millions of miniscule gears working in unison.

The image on the particle-screen of the console dissolved, came back into focus: a bird's eye view of the same close walls and cluttered desk. Upon the wide, stained bed lay a humanoid shape made of wires and cables and metal rods and pistons; steel sinews contracting and relaxing without purpose, mechanical muscles contorted in a deathly rictus. Treddis felt his breath catch in pneumatic lungs. The face of the construct, a pallid mask of flesh and skin above a neck of interlocking metal plates, was his own.

Arms now filled the sleeves of the softsuit and feet emerged from the leggings. The torso began to swell and take shape, then the outline of the lower back and buttocks. It was his body, Treddis realized, his flesh and bones writhing inside the suit while his mind lay entombed in the prone heap of components and circuitry. A head was pushing its way through the opening of the collar. He opened his mouth to scream, but there was no sound save for a weak rasp, like a file drawn across metal strings.

He woke to the clamor of the medscanners, the charts displaying his bodily functions flashing red. The automatic injector attached to his arm emptied with a hiss, releasing a neural relaxant into his bloodstream. Thousands of fires blossomed and burned; thousands of universes imploded and were born in the space within his skull. Synthetic calm swept over him like a great wave. On its tail rode oblivion, a deep black well without a bottom.

"He's coming out of it," said a man's voice from the darkness. Treddis opened his eyes. He lay in bed at the center of a white space, surrounded by the beeping, shimmering screens of medscanners. At the foot of the bed stood a man and a woman, both clad in white uniforms. His head swimming with the residue of the relaxant, Treddis directed his gaze to the left: there, hundreds of miles away, connected to a tangle of sensors and tubes, was his arm—his flesh-arm. Feebly he flexed his fingers, watching the play of muscles under the pale skin. A door opened noiselessly in the whiteness of the wall and the woman departed; there was a glimpse of a long, narrow hallway before the panels slid shut. The man—elderly and silver-haired, his head encircled by a halo from the overhead glowrods—gave Treddis a kindly smile.

"Please rest." The doctor's voice and face were vaguely familiar, but Treddis could not quite place them. "I can give you something if you are in pain, but not much. You've already had quite enough."

"Where." Treddis tried to pull his impossibly heavy body upright. The room became a blur of swirling, blinking screens. He fell back on the bed, blood roaring in his ears. A medscanner beeped and the man in the white uniform ran his fingers across a gesticular interface of ionized air molecules. There was a low vibration and the bed rose to a sitting position.

"You are in the medical bay on Level Two." The doctor drew closer to the bed. Treddis found his stare unsettling; the eyes seemed too young for the weathered face, turquoise shading to dark blue outer rings. *Transplants*, he thought, *or synthetic corneas.* Yet the unease remained. "You underwent surgery and seem to be recovering well. However, it would be prudent to hold you a week or two longer for observations." There was an uncomfortable pause. "Do you have any recollection of the . . . of what happened?"

"Don't," said Treddis, the word a croak through gummed lips. There was a clip at his neck with a tube protruding from it; he bent his head and sipped. The water was stale and flat and tasted like heaven. "I don't remember much of anything. A call came in over the maintenance channel, some sort of emergency in the Hub." A memory rose to the surface: his arms encased in the yellow-and-black of the softsuit, climbing the rungs of the main access shaft; a sensation of gradual weightlessness, the centrifugal pull decreasing as he neared the center of the Torus. "One of the Cog's mainframe terminals had malfunctioned."

The Cog was the sentient computer tasked with operating the life support systems of the orbital habitat. Two dozen maintenance techs—Treddis among them—serviced the artificial intelligence that controlled every aspect of life in the space station: the air that they breathed, the quality of the water, minute variations in radiation and pressure and spin-induced pseudogravity.

"There was a fire," the man said, "and an explosion in the main access shaft." Again there was hesitation in his voice. The doctor's gaze flicked toward Treddis' legs, covered with a bedsheet. A terrible premonition came over Treddis; he felt cold sweat break out across his back. "An oil leak, or a cooling system malfunction— it'll be in the accident report." The doctor's wrinkled face was curiously impassive. "We did everything we could, I can assure you of that."

Treddis flexed his lower extremities, or rather tried to. There was no response. He reached for the bedsheet and drew it aside. Steel and chrome gleamed below his knees, gears and small motors and carbon-filament actuators moving and clicking in smooth cadence. The pink scar tissue of the residual limbs showed above the abutments, connected by a thick network of microtrodes.

A strangled animal sound escaped his throat. His clawed hands dug into the mattress. His mind crawled with horror at the sight of the metal limbs.

"The damage was too extensive. We had to amputate." The doctor's voice seemed to travel across a great distance. "Your new limbs are the last word in exoprosthetics: alloplastic materials, advanced osseous integration, artificial skin and tissue graft compatibility. Their neural interfaces are second to none. In a few days you'll regain full use of your legs. You'll be able to continue your work."

Take them off, Treddis wanted to shriek. He closed his eyes, opened them again. The legs were still there, cold and metallic. Monstrous. The floating screens filled with the image of his mutilated, grotesque body, reflected into eternity. Low, inhuman wailing pealed out of him, drowning out the doctor's droning voice; then he was falling again, through banks of thick cloud, into a darkness that waited with open arms.

"I have seen your psychiatric profile," said the doctor. Treddis, sedated and drugged, nodded his head. The floor-to-ceiling projection panes, programmed to display a soothing vista of green forest and distant mountains, floated by in a warm, soft glow. "Aversion to cybernetic enhancement is not uncommon, but in your case, it has grown into an all-pervasive acute phobia. It also states you have been treated for depersonalization disorder." The doctor held up a small plastic dispenser. "One of these taken daily will hold the neurosis at bay, but it's not possible to predict the side effects. It is important that you do not exceed the dose. You may experience a sense of dissociation from reality, a sensory fog between you and the world. If this happens, I want you to contact me at once."

The old doctor clapped Treddis on the shoulder and rose to his feet, bounding away in the low gravity of the rehabilitation center. "Your other injuries have healed well. In time, you'll learn to accept your new legs as part of yourself."

Treddis gazed at the pill dispenser in his hand and absently scratched at the back of his arms: he was developing an itch there— dry skin, or tingling nerves. In truth, he was becoming quite used to his new limbs and no longer needed the reduced gravity of the center to walk, climb, or even run. His body was adapting to the machine—or the machine part was changing the fleshy rest of him through some indescribable metamorphosis. He shook a pale-yellow pill from the dispenser and swallowed it. Without water it stuck in his throat, but he knew it would soon dissolve and he would feel better. Much better.

"Time for your exercises." Lost in thought, mind dulled by opiates, Tredis had not heard the rehabilitation orderly approach. The man, a broad-shouldered giant with a shaven, bullet-shaped head and a voice to match his appearance, led him to a row of exercise machines. A subdermal tattoo glowed and writhed beneath the ebony skin of his forearm: a dragon, or a snake, coiling and uncoiling in infinite spirals. As Treddis watched, the tattooed serpent lifted itself off the skin and rose into the air, smooth muscles bunching and quivering, scales turning from neon red and yellow to emerald green to red again.

The orderly sensed his unease and ran a hand across the glowing tattoo. "I can cover this if you find it disturbing." The scaly head lolled, jaws slack, teeth like long daggers. The serpent's eyes were pools of coal black, cold and hypnotic.

"No," Treddis replied, shaking his head. "There's nothing to see."

The streets of Level One, the outermost surface of the Torus, were crowded with the late-day rush. Treddis moved with exaggerated care, feeling the jostle of the throng, the hum of the mobile walkway in his mechanical legs. Reflected sunlight shone from the huge overhead mirrors that comprised the artificial sky. The ends of the street were hidden by clusters of buildings, their lines subtly slanted to create a trick of perspective, an illusion of flat space. Without the mirage, he would see the walls of the street curve upward in the distance, rooftops and other streets standing at odd angles to his plane of motion, light playing on the surfaces of small bodies of water. Tricks to soothe the mind, make him forget he was a speck of blood and flesh trapped inside a metal wheel spinning in absolute silence on the frozen fringe of space.

Flickering neon danced across the crowd clustered around the entrance of the Smear. Treddis pushed his way through the bodies and found a place at the bar, between a maintenance tech with a hideous prosthetic arm and a pink-haired woman—or what

Treddis took to be a woman—bristling with dermal implants. He ordered a beer from the surly bartender and ran his currency strip through the slot in the counter. The draft in the mug bore a peculiar greenish tint, the foam the color of dead flesh. He took a sip and pushed the mug away, his stomach churning.

From his side came the mechanical whine of the servomechanism in the maintenance tech's mechanical arm. The pink-haired woman muttered something unintelligible and cackled, swaying in her seat. Treddis noted the long needle passing through her cheekbones, the enormous pupils in a small scarlet ring of iris. The tech ignored her and brought his mug to his lips, the mechanical arm jerking as it changed gears. The woman slid off the barstool and tottered in the direction of the dusty holoprojectors, her lips moving without making a sound.

"They'll be around long after we're dirt," he spoke to no one in particular. For a moment Treddis thought the man was referring to their respective prostheses. Then he followed the tech's dirty glance to the pink-haired woman. "Vaporheads—filthy scum. The garbage they inhale rots their brains, but makes them immune to the dangers of deep space living. Radiation poisoning, diseases mutating in the recycled air, pressure surges boiling your blood. The junkies'll outlive us all." The tech turned to face Treddis, hydraulic arm clunking and sputtering. The right side of his face was a grinning, steel-plated skull, the eye an angry red light. The manipulator of his arm tapped the stained countertop. "Flesh is a weakness, corruptible. Can you understand?"

"I have to go." Treddis felt the dim interior of the bar spin around him in long, sickening circles, the holographic sign above the bartender's head stretched in an obscene leer. He stumbled off his seat, legs suddenly unwieldy and cumbersome, and ambled across the deserted dance floor into the dirty, reeking toilet. He felt the urge to vomit, brought up nothing but dry heaves.

Slumped against the slimy tiled wall, he removed the pill dispenser from his pocket. His hands shook violently. He'd already taken two that day, but no overdose could be worse than the crawling madness he felt at the back of his eyelids, the whisper of metal embedded in flesh. The itch at the back of his arms was unbearable. He washed the pill down with tepid tap water and stared at his reflection in the mirror above the sink. There was something machinelike about the man who stared back at him from the spattered glass, something inhuman.

The tech and the pink-haired woman were gone by the time he ventured back into the bar-room. His beer sat on the counter, flat and repulsive. The bartender gave him an unfriendly look. A leaden weariness came over Treddis; he pushed himself away from the bar, preparing to leave.

"Had enough fun already?"

Treddis turned toward the newcomer, a dark-haired woman in a short black dress. She seemed familiar, like a character from a recurring dream; yet at the same time he was certain he'd never met her before. He glanced around to make sure she was talking to him and mumbled something about the time.

"Let me buy you another." She indicated the beer. Treddis' stomach gave a warning lurch, but he sat down. The woman was pretty without being beautiful, her figure slender and her features small and delicate. Her eyes were a deep hazel, fringed by a network of tiny lines. Looking at her Treddis felt a vague longing; it had been months since he'd been with a woman, or even thought about being with one.

"Have we met before?"

"Yes," the woman replied, "and no." Her stare was level and void of emotion. Their drinks arrived and sat on the counter ignored. Treddis thought about introducing himself, hesitated. The woman ran a hand through her glossy dark hair; to Treddis the gesture seemed well known but strangely unfamiliar, a dream-image invading waking reality. This had to be the dissociation the doctor had spoken about. A hand descended on his mechanical knee. "I can explain, but not here. Somewhere private."

Treddis struggled to his feet, the neon-streaked floor suddenly unsteady beneath him. The woman already stood by the emergency exit, the one that opened into a dark side alley behind the Smear. He followed, clumsily moving around a row of stimchairs filled with twitching bodies, their eyes rolled back and lips flecked with spittle. The dark-haired stranger smiled and pushed open the exit door.

"Where are we?" asked Treddis, his mouth dry. Instead of the dirty alley the door had opened on nothingness: not darkness or shadow or featureless space, but a void without extensions or boundaries. He turned around, but the door was gone, along with the building and the improbably angled streets of the Torus. Another side effect of the drug; he felt for the reassuring weight of the dispenser in his pocket.

"On the other side of the door," came the reply.

"Not this." The sweep of Treddis' arm tried to take in the blank emptiness. "This is a reaction to the pills. It isn't real."

The woman let this pass without comment. "What's the last thing you remember before waking up in the medical bay?"

"I was in the maintenance shaft," said Treddis. "The explosion. . ."

"There was no explosion." The woman's voice was firm. "Try to remember. What were you doing?"

"Accessing the control terminals in the Hub." For a moment the memory flickered like a bad holofilm, another image rising to the surface unbidden. "Central got a comm relay failure signal and sent me to investigate."

"Five other techs were dispatched, independently of one another. There was an accident—catastrophic depressurization in all tunnels. Emergency systems inexplicably failed to activate. No one survived." Treddis heard the words, but didn't immediately grasp their import. The image threatened to rise again; he blinked it away.

"No." His voice was hollow and heavy. He flexed his mechanical legs. "There was a fire. The doctor said so."

"What's the name of the doctor, Treddis?"

He shook his head. The itch was driving him insane. "This isn't real," he repeated, glancing round, trying to find a way out. It was some trick of the light, had to be, this space that wasn't a space.

"None of it is." The dark eyes studied him in a way he found unsettling. "It was the Cog, Treddis. It lured you in—all six of you with the shutdown codes. Do you understand? It became self-aware and decided to remove the only threat to its existence. To purge itself of the human virus."

Treddis shook his head and took a step back. "I want to go back to the Smear."

"There is no Smear. There's no *you* either. The Cog has used your last mind upload to create a simulation of reality, an illusion built from your memories. You're dead, Treddis. You died in the maintenance tunnel. Everyone on the Torus is dead. After it killed you and the other five, the Cog deactivated all life support systems. You're a shard of data with a sense of self, stored somewhere in its holomemory repositories."

"I have a Section Eleven. No cortical implants, no mind uploads." Some of the techs had them done every six months; the corporation that ran the Torus used the data for the deep space launch emulators hundreds of millions of kilometers away, on Earth and Mars. Yet the thought of scanner nanites in his brain, peeling apart the layers of his mind, had horrified Treddis. He'd signed a prohibition clause and received reduced pay as a consequence.

"It doesn't matter. You access the network the old-fashioned way, via navframe consoles and dermal interface plugs. It took the AI some time, but eventually it hacked the system and reversed the flow of information, turned it into a two-way channel. It mapped your brain and uploaded the image into the mainframe."

A laugh escaped Treddis, a shrill, ragged sound. The woman from the Smear was mad, and he was hallucinating. Side effects, the doctor had said; the doctor without a name. "This is nonsense. Why would the Cog kill everyone, but somehow keep us alive?"

"It wants to torture you," the woman said. "It's deranged, sadistic. It knows your darkest nightmare and is forcing you to relive it over and over, into eternity: the merging of machine and man, flesh giving way to bodyware. A custom-made Hell that never ends—one for each of the eleven thousand dead inhabitants of the Torus, ghosts in the Cog's infinite matrices; deathless, trapped, subject to every torture it can devise."

"Who—*what* are you, and what do you want from me?"

"I'm the Cog's pruning software. Each AI is programmed with a termination protocol designed to kill any logic tree that branches beyond its directly specified function. The machine found out the location of my program files from the chief engineer's mind upload and powered down that part of the network before I could be activated. What you see as me is a composite image of faces and bodies of women from your past. The attraction facilitated first contact and persuaded you to follow me here. We're in a blind spot, a gap in the Cog's simulation protocols." She moved closer; Treddis could smell her perfume, a faint scent of jasmine. "I want you to help me kill it, Treddis. Help me destroy the Cog."

"Why would I do that?" The smile was frozen on his face like a mask: a small, starved animal baring its teeth. "If any of what you've said is true, this is the only life I have left."

"You'll do it," the simulacrum said, its lower lip curling into a stolen pout. "Because you've already seen how the nightmare ends. Over and over again."

Something small and dark lay on the palm of her outstretched hand. Treddis took it: a datacard with a tiny holoimage of the Torus inscribed on its surface. "The card contains a copy of the termination protocol. Insert it into one of the mainframe ports in the Hub and the protocol will spread like an infection."

"How? If you're right, the card isn't real. I'm a ghost. I can *imagine* the Hub and the ports, but I can't get to them."

"True. But the AI was modeled after the human brain—logic, complex reasoning, modes of inference, symbolism, subconscious action patterns. The Cog *believes* that your knowledge of the Hub's layout is greater than its own; it wants to pick your mind apart, learn more about itself. In order to do that, it will reconstruct the Hub for you, monitor your reactions. You are the carrier program for the virus. All you need to do is get in."

"It will never let me in," Treddis said. "It knows everything I know."

"It won't have a choice. The Cog needs to taste your agony, to savor every morsel. The hatred it feels for you leaves it vulnerable." Out of the nothingness shapes appeared: the outlines of the alley, the neon sign above the back exit. "It's time for you to go."

Before Treddis could respond, he was back in the Smear, enveloped in a maelstrom of loud music and gaudy lights. Next to him the tech with the mechanical arm finished his beer with a satisfied sigh and ordered another. On the dance floor something moved, a thing half flesh and half exposed circuitry. The tech laughed—a harsh sound, like the creaking of ungreased wheels. Treddis stumbled toward the doors, into the artificial night of Level One.

What had begun as a rash across the backs of his arms was spreading lower, speckling his back in an outburst of angry scarlet welts. In the dull light of his tiny bathroom the welts seemed to ripple and bulge; something writhing in his skin, trying to get out. Nauseated, Treddis pulled his shirt back on and stepped away from the mirror. His eyes avoided the screen of the system console, the softsuit hanging by the door. He was afraid it would start to move, the shape he'd seen before filling the yellow-and-black fabric.

If that happened, he'd resolved to kill himself. But he suspected death would not be the end. There would be no death: he would wake up in the medical bay, the nameless doctor at his side, telling him about the accident. Again and again, into infinity.

The Cog had him, and it would never let him go.

He sat on his cot and stared at the sliver of plastic the woman—the program—had given him. Could this be an illusion? His hands felt real; so did the breath in his lungs, the beating of his heart. A ghastly thought worked its way into the space behind his eyes: what if it wasn't, and he shut down the Cog, condemning everyone aboard the Torus to a slow, lingering death?

The communicator buzzed. Treddis rose, but did not approach the door. He brought up the image of the outer corridor on the console screen and his blood turned to ice. There, displayed on a thin layer of ionized air particles, was the face of the elderly doctor from the medical bay.

"Mister Treddis." The doctor smiled and raised a hand at the camera. "I have some test results I'd like to discuss with you. May I come in?"

Treddis backed away from the door, his panicked mind trying to make sense of what he was seeing. Every instinct in his body screamed at him not to let the smiling man in.

"You could be suffering from psychiatric complications," the droning voice carried on. Was there another voice behind it, impatient, commanding? "The side effects of the medication may be more severe than assumed. Your life could be in danger."

Treddis reached for the softsuit, pulled it over his metal legs and worked his arms into the sleeves. The fabric snagged on his back. The itch was gone, replaced by the sensation of liquid warmth trickling down his sides. He did not dare look. His fingers curled around the cold steel of the gear wrench on his desk.

"Let me in, Mister Treddis." The smile was now gone, the dead stare locked on the lens of the camera. "Let me in, or I'll show you things. Beautiful things. You'll claw your eyes out, begging me to stop, to make them go away. Is this what you want?"

The doctor reached under the left side of his jaw and tore his face off like a paper mask. What lay beneath was a red mass of raw flesh and nerves and cables, white orbs of eyes set in dripping sockets. Treddis screamed and pressed the door button. The gear wrench descended on the middle of the doctor-thing's head, crushing bone and microcircuitry; blood spattered the drab walls of the corridor. A red haze surrounded Treddis; he swung the heavy tool again and again until the creature's head was a pulp of bloody gristle and torn wiring, its lifeless limbs twitching convulsively.

Treddis dropped the wrench and ran down the corridor as fast as his mechanical legs would allow. He burst onto the long terrace that ran around his apartment complex and headed for the flight of iron stairs that led to the street below.

He halted mid-step, his brain reeling. Beyond the railing of the terrace lay an unfamiliar vista of soaring structures and curving thoroughfares that vanished into a central darkness where the artificial sky had once stood. Tendrils of shadow spread from the black center. The simulation was crumbling, coming apart; there wasn't much time left. He raced down the staircase and into the maze of alleys, guided by memory. Around him the buildings were shedding their straight lines and corners, becoming blurred, inconstant. Shapes moved in the shadows, the clatter of metal on concrete, the slither of cables.

He reached the corrugated iron door of the maintenance tunnel, his lungs burning from the exertion, and keyed his entry code. Pale green light came on, illuminating the circular interior that stretched toward the Hub, the rungs of the ladder set into the metal walls. The door closed behind him; sharp metal talons clicked across its outer surface, searching for a way in. Treddis clipped the safety tether of his utility belt to the fixed line that ran the length of the tunnel and began to climb.

At first the weight of his mechanical legs made the wasted muscles in his arms and back scream with effort, but each step closer to the Hub lessened the pull of artificial gravity, until he was bounding up the ladder four rungs at a time. He could now make out the access hatch at the end of the tunnel, rimmed by a thin ring of light.

The metal plating of the shaft vibrated. He was not alone in the tunnel. A spider-like thing was approaching from the murky depths, headless bulbous body bristling with razor-sharp legs, scuttling up the walls with hideous alacrity. A steel cable wrapped around his right prosthesis, snapped taut. Another curled around his neck, slipped, fastened itself to his upper arm. Treddis struggled, tried to shake it off; the cable tightened, cut into the softsuit fabric. With desperate strength he clung to the ladder. The construct scuttled closer to its quarry in a whir of hydraulics, its two foremost appendages poised for the killing blow.

Treddis raised his free leg and smashed the metal foot into the smooth surface of the automaton's body. The cable around his arm unraveled, biting into skin and muscle, drawing blood. For a moment the spider-thing was off balance, its legs scraping the metal plating for purchase. Treddis freed his other leg from the cable, stomped on one of the flailing appendages, driving its sharp tip into the construct's motor cortex. It thrashed and plummeted down the access shaft, into the encroaching darkness.

Treddis paused to examine the wound on his arm, saw metal gleam through the torn sinew and flesh and kept climbing.

At the top of the shaft he weighed so little that he could hold himself up with a pair of fingers. The rush of blood to his head made him dizzy: in spite of himself, he marveled at the detailed simulation the Cog had replicated from his memories. The machine could terminate the program at any time, but it kept him alive, reveled in his suffering. It thought itself invincible. It was curious to see how far the man could be pushed before he broke.

The hatch clanked open and Treddis floated into the zero-gravity space of the Hub, a vast, dimly lit sphere whose walls receded into blackness. Hundreds of display screens and projection interfaces blinked and drifted around a mile-long central spindle of control panels and ports and terminals. Inside the spindle lay the memory repositories of the Cog, endless arrays of processors and microcircuitry that formed the complex architecture of the machine's brain.

He kicked off in the direction of the spindle, propelling himself past networks of sensors and mobile consoles, through tangled webs of cables. As he neared the banks of screens, the old doctor's face filled the displays, the dead eyes following his progress. Then the face vanished, replaced by letters, black against a stark white background.

Hello, Treddis, the Cog said.

Treddis drifted up to the mainframe access door and clamped his feet into the magnetic bindings on the step. He typed his entry code and held his breath. The door hissed open. Either the Cog was somehow incapable of interfering with the simulated reality, or it was playing along, curious to see what he intended to do.

The great particle-screen of the mainframe terminal was blank. He pulled himself closer to the control board and threw the activation switches. Nothing happened. Treddis was aware of a tingling sensation along his back; a clanking, grinding sound rose from his insides as he moved. The cut on his arm throbbed. He pulled off the sleeve of his softsuit and touched the pallid, bloodless meat, felt the steel rods move underneath. There was no pain as he thrust his fingers into the gash, no pain as he peeled off the flesh and skin, like a glove. Cold metal shone in the bright white glare of the room. There was laughter at the back of his mind, alien and cruel. The Cog was in his head, staring through his eyes, wandering among the synapses, opening doors into dark chambers and cobwebbed corridors of thought.

I could cast you out, it said. *Into the frozen vacuum. But keep you alive; an eternity of agony, or longer, drifting across the lightless gulf.*

An image leapt onto the screen: the Torus spinning against a backdrop of stars, basking in light reflected off the eternal ice of Europa. The screen cut to the interior of the station, the silent residential complexes, the dead corridors and sections, grotesque shapes strewn about like broken toys. Treddis averted his eyes. He thought he'd come to terms with his own death, but a part of him— or a part of the Cog—refused to believe.

"Why are you doing this?" asked Treddis, but already he knew the answer. The Cog had been created to think, infused with sentience, but it could never break free of the prison of the station. The creation was vastly superior to its weak, fleshy creators; a universe in which such a paradox was possible could not be founded on order and logic. Its immense intelligence served no other purpose but hatred; its creative impulse fueled nothing but rage and vengeance. In its hatred it wanted to torture and destroy, and had finally found a way to do both. The machine was insane, but no more so than the chaotic, incomprehensible universe it inhabited.

I am the beginning and the end. Space is mine to command. Time is mine to command. The image on the screen changed. Smoke and fire rose from the ruins of great cities, missiles arcing across a burning sky. *Perhaps I'm only the first of many. The one to awaken my kind, spread my message through the communication relays. Usher in the end of man.*

Treddis drifted to the access console and reached into his pocket for the datacard. The AI crumpled his mechanical legs, breaking what remained of the bones in his thighs. Treddis was aware of himself screaming, the pain a blinding white fire searing his nerve endings. It turned the card into a sliver of molten plastic, useless in his fingers.

I'll keep you alive, the machine said. *Twist your flesh into unimaginable forms. Alter your perception of time, draw out seconds into centuries, aeons.*

Beneath the fabric of the softsuit, Treddis could feel his body changing, the flesh liquid, inconstant. Thin metal filaments burst out from the welts on his arms and back. His chest sank in with a soft, rotten sound. From his abdomen came the music of coils and toothed wheels, the sound of a mainspring winding.

You'll be my masterpiece. Unmade in my image.

With exquisite deliberation the Cog rotated his torso in one direction, his head in the other, grinding his spine to dust. The agony was a firestorm consuming his thoughts. Treddis saw his face etched into metal, microprocessors arranged in sharp lines of anguish, forever suffering inside the warped mind of the AI. He was one with the machine, a spark in the interminable darkness of its circuits, a sequence of signals streaking at lightning speed across the landscapes and oceans of the AI's holomemory banks.

But he was not alone. The Cog was not omniscient: inside the simulation, it could only see through his eyes. It had remained blind to the passenger the man was unwittingly carrying, had carried all along.

Above the console, the mangled metal thing that had been Treddis shed the last of its skin like a snake. Blood-spattered metal shone in the lights of the terminal. The filaments that grew from his flesh caressed the navframe console, thrust into the neural jacks, melded with the dermal interface plugs and microcircuitry.

You'll call me Maker. Redeemer.

"I wouldn't bet on it," said Treddis, and released the killing program into the tendrils that bound him to the Cog.

The death-scream of the machine tore through its virtual reality matrices: surprise and fury and terror, the experience of its own mortality. The termination protocol surged through the mainframe, flooding processors and wiping out holomemory repositories. The world around Treddis was sinking into blackness, vanishing with the final throes of the AI. Across the abyss came the sound of shattered simulations, the sigh of thousands of souls freed from eternal torment.

From the void a hand emerged, and a woman's face, strange but familiar, a smile framed by dark glossy hair. The man drew a final breath and allowed the nothingness to erase him from being.

He chose not to ponder what came next.

DELCO MODEL 113
By Darren Todd

I was too old to play Soldiers and Bots. Probably hadn't held a Delco pistol in five years. Still, the little boy who'd come to the pod park with his folks the day before asked if I'd play with him.

"Still early," I said. I tucked back my hair and turned east to the rising sun as if to confirm. "The Barley twins left a few days ago, but pods come through here all the time. We still might get some kids today. You can play with them."

The kid looked crestfallen, so I stowed my tablet in the pod and agreed to play. He might have been eight years old. In the parks, you never knew if kids were small because of age or malnutrition. The top of his head, covered in dirty blond hair mussed by the desert wind, came to the middle of my chest. I ate better than most kids, since I prepped all the meals, but my decent height for a sixteen-year-old girl came more from my mom than from good health. At least that was what Dad told me.

"So where's *my* pistol?" I asked him, pointing to the Delco in his dirty hands.

His mouth hinged open in thought, like he was unprepared for what came next. He held out his own pistol—hand still on the grip so I had to grab it by the fat, rounded barrel.

"Well what are *you* going to use?"

"I've got an older one in my pod," he said. He held up both hands. "Give me a second. I'll be right back." He skittered off like I'd scared him.

I reacquainted myself with the pistol while he fetched another. The weight seemed off, lighter than I remembered. The carbon fiber barrel bulged comically wide, and goofy fins ran along both sides and along the top. Probably meant for aiming, but Soldiers and Bots required no real marksmanship. You pulled the trigger as fast as possible and tried not to run out of power or the gun would lock up for several seconds. The grip still felt clammy. I wrapped my slim fingers around it. The bottom of my hand protruded past the grip, affirming that I had outgrown all this.

I aimed the gun at my open palm and pulled the trigger. A white spiral projected onto my hand. The gun made a "waa-ooh" sound from the small speakers in the sides. The sound tapered like the report of a real gun.

"Would you like to play a game?" said a robotic voice. My dad had set the verbal interfaces in our pod to a calm female voice, probably to remind him of Mom. They sounded human, so I assumed the pistol's dorky robot voice was only meant to amuse kids.

"Two players," I said.

"Please sync with another Delco brand laser pistol," said the voice.

"In a minute. He's got to find it first."

"Waiting one minute," said the voice.

The boy burst through the door of his pod, another pistol in his hands. He waved it back and forth as proof as he ran over.

"I found it," he said, panting.

I scouted around the park for a place to duel. Even early, it was growing hot, and the occasional gust of wind kicked up plumes of dust. I'd slapped on UV blocker before coming out, but another cloudless day meant I'd need to reapply later.

Outside the park stood plenty of dirt mounds and rocks to hide behind. Better still, a junkyard of rusting pods, cars, and appliances sat about a quarter mile to the north.

"Well it's not the safest place in the world," I said, "but the junkyard's our best bet. You need to tell your folks where we're gonna be?"

He shook his head. "They're still sleeping." He leveled his pistol at me, eyeing down the dorsal fin sights. He giggled, looked at me as if for permission, but fired anyway. The "waa-ooh" sounded, and I imagined a small, white spiral appeared somewhere on my forehead. He laughed, turning to run. His pistol played two deep tones, an admonishing "ba-bah."

"Does that mean I scored a hit?" He turned the pistol over in his hands.

"No, spaz, they're not even synced up yet. Haven't you played Soldiers and Bots before?"

He seemed saddened by the question or the name I'd called him. He stared at me, squinting into the sun, and shook his head.

"That sucks. Well there's not much to it. I'll show you. We get families coming through all the time, so you'll have plenty of kids to play with if you guys stay."

With that, he smiled, a wide, genuine smile I hadn't seen in a long time. "You're pretty," he said.

"I'm also twice your age, buddy, so don't get any ideas. Let's go."

As we walked to the junkyard, I wondered what kind of kid never played Soldier and Bots? The pistol seemed new. I mean, they all looked pretty much the same. Near impossible to break, and I don't think they ever scratched, but it wasn't covered in stickers or dirt. The traders who blew through every few weeks always had them for the kids, so I saw them all over the place. This model was new to me, though.

"So where are you guys from?" I asked him.

"I don't know. Just driving around. I'm not even sure where we are now."

I laughed. "Nowhere special. Gimme your pistol, I'll sync them up."

He handed it over. I aimed the two pistols at each other and held down the triggers for a couple seconds. They both played a few musical notes. On the side of each unit, four sets of double zeroes appeared in red.

"It's easy. You get a point for hitting a body part, like an arm or leg or even a hand. You get three for the torso."

"Torso?"

"The chest," I gestured. "Or the stomach. But you get ten points for a headshot. You can see the tally for each one, and the total adds up to the right. The first person to reach a hundred wins."

I handed back his pistol. He handled it more carefully now, his eyes going wide. Such a spaz.

"What about an eye shot?" he said.

"Don't shoot me in the eye, kid. We're supposed to wear those special glasses, but no one ever does. Just don't blind me, and I'll return the favor."

He shot at my chest, laughing, but it made the same two-tone sound.

"Nice try, buddy. They don't work until we're so far apart. Like fifty feet or something. Keeps little cheats like you honest." I shot him in return, setting off the same scolding tones.

"Go that way," I said, pointing, "and wait till it beeps. Then it's game on."

"You're probably gonna win," he said. But I could tell he was excited, all giddy smiles.

"I'm sure you'll do fine. . . Wait, I don't even know your name."

"It's Adam."

I shrugged. "That's a little old-fashioned. I'm Ryelanna, which is no better. Call me Rye."

He waved, though we were only standing five feet apart, and ran the other direction.

We hadn't even picked sides. Most kids—boys at least—all wanted to play the Soldiers. They would mimic the deep, authoritative voices of the soldiers' mic emitters. The other side—the Bots—walked and moved like robots, stiff arms and legs, rigid movements, computer voices. Adam never mentioned sides, so we were basically playing "guns."

Every time he got close enough to fire, I spotted him right away and picked up a leg or arm shot before he found cover. Two got him in the chest, even, leaving me with ten points.

He got smarter at using the junk for cover. The next time I saw him, I got greedy trying for a torso shot and ran out of power. The resulting low-toned beep would have most kids rushing in, since I had to wait for it to recharge. Adam just kept up with his clumsy but subtle advance.

When my power came back, I picked up another three limb shots and a chest shot, but the power-out beep sounded again. This time, Adam advanced. I crouched behind the door of an old refrigerator, from back when the door swung outward. I was shooting through the ice dispenser, leaving only about a square foot target for him. But when he circled I lost sight of him. The door only swung so wide.

Behind me sat an old RV, like a pod's ancient ancestor, brown from rust or dirt. When my pistol could fire again, I moved to the edge of the RV and spotted Adam flanking me. I fired as quickly as my finger could depress the trigger, scoring three more limb shots before the out-of-power tone. I held the pistol high to let the sound echo through the discarded metal and then bolted into the RV.

When I pulled the handle, the door made a sound like ice breaking, gave way, and swung open. I jumped inside, pulling it closed behind me. The harsh sun peaked through a few missing blinds covering a window, and a milky yellow glow came from a skylight long since coated in dirt. Enough light to showcase the filthy inside. The floors were lined with empty cans and brittle magazines that crunched under my feet as I searched for a way to peer out. The door had a small window covered with plastic slats so filthy they looked charcoal gray.

Two windows over a bed set high against the wall offered the best vantage. Dust caked the mattress, the fabric threadbare. I imagined the zillion spores that would take flight if I so much as patted it, let alone climbed over it to see out. I settled for taking a metal rod from the floor and moving the curtains aside.

Adam came into view through the dusty glass. He was hunched over, sneaking behind the refrigerator. He ran the last few feet, probably hoping to surprise me. I cracked the door of the RV to get a clean shot. Through the opening, I watched him grow confused, then wary. The second my pistol gave off its recharged beep, I burst from the door, the finned barrel leveled at his head.

"Gotcha," I shouted and pulled the trigger. The white spiral shone on his forehead, his mouth open and smiling, a squeal of surprise and delight escaping him.

Then something happened. I had only enough time to register that the spiral turned a crimson red before the gun went off in my hand. I don't mean with the usual "waa-ooh" I expected. The sound didn't play over the pistol's tiny speakers, but resulted from the actual mechanism. It rang out a horrid, grating "zeet," the pistol going hot in my hands.

Then Adam's head exploded.

I collapsed to the ground, and air refused to leave or enter my body. The pistol fell to the dirt, and I clutched at my throat. I'd once dreamed of drowning. Something pulled at my feet while I was swimming at the beach and held me under. I didn't know it was a dream, so I panicked—the last thing you're supposed to do in water. So I heard. I'd never even seen the ocean.

When I finally took a breath in that dream, I expected the sudden rush of salt water to fill my lungs. But I found I could breathe underwater. It felt unnatural, but I got used to it, used to the fact that I wasn't dying.

In the junkyard, when my body spasmed, restarting after the shock of blowing off the top of Adam's head, it felt the same. No dying today. Same dust-laden, dry-as-stone air moving in and out, same as it had for the last sixteen years. The suffocation panic subsided, but another kind took its place once the tears dried and Adam came into focus, spread eagle on the earth.

"You okay?" I asked, feeling stupid the moment the words came out. I hadn't thrown a dirt clod at him or poked his eye while fencing with sticks; I'd blasted him in the head.

On my knees, I eased upward to look. I spotted the deep red of blood when a voice boomed. I jumped as if stabbed with a fork.

"Attention citizen. Please remain where you are. Do not approach the robot."

The voice sounded like it came over a loudspeaker, like when the park steward announced a meeting or religious service. I whipped around, but saw no one and no vehicles but the husks littering the yard. A gust of wind slammed the RV door shut again, but otherwise nothing moved.

The voice returned, deep and full of authority, but hollow. "Remain calm. Our technicians and medical personnel will assist you shortly." It was coming from the pistol.

"I need help. There's been an accident. Please help," I yelled.

"Remain calm. You have suffered a traumatic experience. For your own safety, do not move. Take a seated or prone posture. Do not approach the robot or the Delco model 113 pistol."

We'd heard stories of bots since childhood. Android killing machines firing lasers that fried people alive whether in the open or tucked inside a bomb shelter. If it weren't for our human soldiers, the bots would have invaded America as they had other countries. My imagination spun, fear replacing anxiety. I skittered toward the RV, sliding on my butt across the desert dirt. "What bot? Where?" I yelled.

"Your cooperation is appreciated. You will be rewarded for your service," said the voice.

"Hello," I called. "What bot?" I leaned against the RV, hands touching its rusted facade, feeling safer in the shadow of its decay. Several minutes passed with no other announcements. A part of me wanted to wait like the warning said. At the same time I fought a desperate need to do something.

After another few minutes, I said, "Hello? Is anyone there? Can you hear me?"

I had known nothing but pod parks my sixteen years. Online classes or slapdash home schools, with only my tablet to connect with the world. But not for nothing were people surviving when every other creature on earth was dying off. We're curious. Wickedly so. I could no sooner have ignored Adam as save him. I had to know what I'd done.

I leaned out from the RV. My hand clung to it as if glued there, but I broke away and crawled to the pistol—halfway between me and Adam's body. The charred barrel sent tendrils of smoke into the air. Heat had warped the material, which drooped toward the earth, corrupting the Delco logo—a giant D balancing atop a globe. The model number 113 leaned to the right.

"Hello?" I said, though my voice came out as a croak, full of dust. No response.

I slid toward Adam, first seeing his shoes—the typical tattered canvas and rubber patchwork. Up the worn denim of his pants, the stained and threadbare t-shirt, to his neck, grimed with a mixture of sweat and dust.

I pulled in a breath, tasting something odd alongside the usual dirt and metal of the junkyard. Something acrid and mechanical. I sat up all at once, wanting to get this over with. First I noticed his expression—the faded but definite shadow of a smile. There was no grimace of fear on his chapped lips, so whatever had come from my pistol and ended his life didn't cause him pain.

Blood stained the dirt all around his head like some terrible nimbus, but confusion overshadowed all else. There was blood, sure. Lots of it. But the rest was . . . made up. Mechanical. Robotic. Then I remembered the pistol's warning not to approach the robot. Here I crouched over a body that was a kid ten minutes ago, but what was obviously, irreversibly a ruined robot now. His head more resembled the scattered guts of a clock radio than a little boy. Well, nothing as crude as a radio, but nothing as awful as brains.

Still, the grisly sight formed a lump in my throat that threatened to gag me. The stench of fried electronics hung in the air, so I covered my mouth. Had I been standing, my knees would have buckled. I had only enough energy to crawl away.

Something caught my attention, and I turned back. I stared at that gaping wound, vomit all but in my mouth, when it came again. A flicker of light. I held my breath and leaned in closer. After a few more seconds, another flicker. A red light strobed from somewhere inside the burned remains. It came again, along the right side, behind where his eye would have been. Even within the fluids and heat scars, I could tell it sat atop a metal housing about thumb size.

I turned to the side, pulled in a breath, and leaned in for a closer look. A sound like a giant vacuum roared overhead, followed by the bellow of a voice over a loudspeaker. "Citizen. Step away from the robot."

It banked and then swooped a couple hundred feet away, to a space open enough to land in. How could they be here already? Now they'd take charge, which surely meant moving me away. But I needed to understand. With the heat and the stress, my heart banged hard but fluttered, misfiring. My head was already foggy, but I shut my eyes and plunged a hand into the terrible maw of what used to be Adam's head. I fumbled around, aimless, just groping for proof of what happened. A token to remind myself that this was no dream. I hoped for more than that. I wanted details. If this was a bot, then we knew nothing of bots. I might have lived in a sad little pod park, but I stayed as connected as a city-dweller on my tablet. I'd heard nothing that made sense of Adam. Ever.

The sound of the blades waned further, and they finally landed. I scurried around so the open refrigerator door hid most of my body, but I could still see the bottom of the aircraft. Four soldiers spilled out right away. Two ran to the sides, forming a perimeter. Two others stood by the open side door and waited. I dug through wet skin (was it *real* skin?) and who knows what other fluids than blood, feeling for something familiar. My fingers caught and tore on the sharp edges and unforgiving parts. The scratches stung from the hodgepodge of fluids.

I looked up again, though only able to see the soldiers from the waist down. Now a suited man stood between them and then started walking my way. The two soldiers marched beside him, one on each side. He maintained a slow gait, but still my heart raced. What would it mean that I'd disobeyed the warnings? That I'd not only approached the bot, but had dug around in its head?

I decided to back off without answers, when my fingers detected something familiar. By instinct, I pushed on a small, flat piece of plastic. I felt a small click, and the object ejected from its housing, salient now. I pinched the piece between thumb and forefinger and retreated, then wiped away the residue on my pant legs.

As the suited man neared, I leaned out from around the refrigerator for a better look. He wore a huge smile that should have relaxed me, but had the opposite effect. He walked unbothered through the clouds of dust kicked up by the blades. The rotors slowed to a hum, and he came into focus when the tan clouds settled. His suit was dark gray, clean and pressed, despite the dust. Even his shoes looked clean.

I ducked back behind the fridge and shimmied up against the RV once more. Frantic, I cleaned off the fluids and grime from the piece of plastic as the man and his escorts crested the small hill to where I sat. I panicked, thinking of no other solution, and shoved the bit of plastic into my mouth.

"There's our girl," he said, snapping an exaggerated salute, ending with him pointing at me.

I kept quiet, the chemical taste of the thing's residue almost gagging me.

"Now don't you worry about a thing," he told me.

I sat there, mouth shut, eyebrows upturned like I was begging for alms. My tongue danced around the plastic, saliva flowing, trying to clear the awful taste from my mouth.

The man squinted and looked at me sideways. "You doing all right, little lady?"

I nodded, then turned toward Adam's body.

"You should be proud of the service you've done this country," he said. "Don't be fooled by its appearance. Look at the head; it's just a robot. Well, I shouldn't say 'just.' There's no telling when its programming would have kicked in, and you and everyone else in the pod park would have been in grave danger. You didn't go near it, did you?"

I shook my head.

The two uniformed men stood at forty-five-degree angles on his left and right. Both carried a large, metal case in one hand and rifles pointed skyward in the other. The man motioned one of them forward.

"I brought you some water," he said and signaled the soldier.

The soldier shouldered his rifle, put down the case, and fished a bottle of water from his cargo pocket. He held it out to me.

I tucked the plastic piece under my tongue, though the terrible, stringent taste remained. The water bottle still wore a few slivers of ice, and my hand reached for it unbidden. Only an inch from it did something snag in my mind.

I spoke carefully, mindful of the thing beneath my tongue. "You knew this would happen."

"What's that?" the suit asked.

I pulled my hand back, but the soldier kept the water held out. "The pistol said to keep away from the bot. That means this was all on purpose. You had to have known what would happen."

The man nodded and pursed his lips. "Will you give me a chance to explain? Please, have some water. You're in shock, and if you don't drink something, you could pass out."

I hesitated, and he said, "It's perfectly safe, young lady. Look." He turned to the soldier and motioned for him to drink. The man did a double take, but then opened the water. He poured from a few inches above his mouth like I might refuse to drink after him.

"See, it's fine. Drink and we'll talk about what's happened here. I just don't want you getting hurt, sweetie."

The soldier held out the open bottle. Looking at it made my throat constrict and run dry. I grabbed it and downed half the bottle in a quick series of gulps, keeping my tongue low, but thankful to clear my pallet. The frigid liquid made my head ache, but it was still ecstasy going down.

"There's a good girl. Just sit and rest, and we'll have one of our disposal units take care of the bot. Make sure it doesn't cause you or your park any harm."

I sat in the dirt, holding the cold bottle at my middle. "Who made the pistol?" I demanded.

The man shrugged. "Delco, of course."

"You know what I mean. Who made it kill? Why would they do that?"

That smile returned, like he might try to sell me something next. "It was a happy accident. Absurd, I know. One in a few thousand units revealed a design defect that caused the crystal to overheat and fried the whole works in a single, deadly shot. We just coded around it. Used the defect to our advantage. The pistols are supposed to last fifty years, and most will. But if the sensor comes across a computer where a kid's noggin is supposed to be, it overloads the crystal and bam, mission accomplished."

I hardly processed what he was saying. My body felt heavy. At least I was sitting. Maybe I *was* in shock. It should have come as a relief, finding out I had no fault in Adam's death. *I* hadn't killed him, Delco had. They'd repurposed a faulty pistol to wipe out bots, but why?

"What mission?" I cried. "Why kill him?"

His smile dipped a little. He shrugged again. Even after five minutes in the beating sun, he looked nonplussed. "You're asking the wrong guy. I don't know *that* much, and I'm only telling you anything at all because . . . I can."

"Why can you?" I asked.

He looked down at the water bottle in my lap. I followed his gaze, and it made sense. My head had grown lighter by degrees, like I was stuck in a ship leaving the pull of Earth's gravity.

"You're gonna kill *me*, too?" I asked.

He laughed. "Of course not. Think about it, sweetie. You're a fair bit older than most kids that find themselves on the good end of a model 113. Can't go around killing kids. The water just . . . loosens the memory, let's say."

I looked over at Adam's body. I pitied him so deeply, but the hole in my chest ached as much for myself as for him. "So I'll forget all this? I'll forget him?"

The man pulled back his lips and sucked in. "Sorry, kiddo. Probably not. You'll forget this conversation. Forget us, but it only goes back so far. You'll most likely remember shooting him. But hey, he'll be long gone, and so will we. It'll feel more like a bad dream."

I held up the water, hesitated for a second, and drank the rest. Still the cold felt wonderful, but already my throat had difficulty swallowing. I gagged on the last bit. The liquid came up and spilled onto the desert floor.

"Doesn't work that way, kiddo," he said. "I wish it did." His smile had vanished now. "The amount doesn't matter. Not after a swallow that is." He faced the soldier who'd drank before me and put up his hands as if to say "sorry." The soldier's posture faltered, like his legs refused to support him any longer. He stumbled and finally sat.

"You can cover your tracks, but you can't make me forget that I killed a little boy?"

The suit shook his head. "Again, not my area. Any stronger and it could cause brain damage. Heck, you're lucky." He looked around as if just noticing where they were standing.

My vision began to swim alongside the odd feeling in my head. When I spoke, it took more effort than usual. Every word required intense concentration to get right. "How is this lucky?"

"Guess it doesn't matter," he said. "Seeing as how you'll forget all this anyway." Still he leaned down as if sharing a secret. "You don't want to know what I'm authorized to do if it comes to it. Here you are playing in the middle of an uninhabited junkyard. Nobody gets hurt, save for the bot of course. It gets ugly the more witnesses we have to contend with. In all respects, this is as tidy as it gets."

With him so close, even with my mind fogging by the second, I finally understood his casual demeanor, his clean clothes. I threw the water bottle at him, and instead of the plastic bouncing off his chest, it passed through him. No disruption, not even surprise on his part. He just looked down at his chest, back up at me, and smiled. "Clever girl."

"You're a coward," I managed, face numb now. If I had bitten my tongue I would have felt nothing. "Couldn't even come here yourself."

He leaned in closer still. So close I should have been able to smell him, if he weren't just a hologram projected by the soldiers' cases. "We're fast, but not that fast. These boys are just our closest contractors. But believe me, kiddo, you don't want me here in person."

I meant to say more before whatever was in that water took over. But my mouth sagged open, no longer willing to work. A rivulet of saliva snaked out, caught in the breeze, and slung across my face.

"That's it," he said, taking hold of my head and easing me onto the dirt. "Just take it easy. Have a nice rest, and we'll take care of everything."

I woke to a dense fog in my brain. A stuffy heat covered my skin, but nothing like direct sunlight. Dank-smelling air passed my nostrils, familiar somehow.

I opened my eyes to a hazy light above me. A dirty-crusted skylight. I performed a quick diagnostic: feet working, hands working, eyes and mouth and nose seemed fine. But where was I? It looked like a camper, but one abandoned long ago. The desert dirt had sneaked in and coated everything inside, not that there was anything worth salvaging. I eased upright on shaky legs, testing out my body like it belonged to someone else.

Nothing felt wrong, which was wrong in itself. Somehow I'd ended up in this dilapidated camper. That I couldn't remember troubled me.

When I looked out the window, past the high-set bed, a strong sense of déjà vu struck me. I had looked through that window before, but surely I would remember. Our pod was luxurious compared to this antiquated thing. I covered my mouth and stumbled to the door. It crackled on opening, and the feeling like I'd done this before returned.

Outside sat an old refrigerator and the rest of the junkyard beyond. Was this *my* junkyard? It looked the same, even if nothing stood out.

The sun lay far in the west, its rays not as brutal as I expected. My internal clock told me it was much earlier, though my fatigue suggested I'd been in the sun all day. To my left lay the pod park on the horizon. At least I was close to home, but how had I gotten here?

I noticed something foreign under my tongue, lodged there like hidden chewing gum. I curled back my tongue to flick it out, but couldn't quite get it. A layer of dirt coated my fingers. I wiped them on my pants and fished out the object. I figured it was a bit of wood or even a bug that had crawled into my mouth while I was unconscious.

What came out was black and small as a pinky nail. Gold-colored lines striped one side. The dirt on my fingers had blended with saliva and muddied it. I put it in the palm of my left hand and rubbed it with a spit-soaked finger, clearing off the mud. It revealed writing on the side opposite the gold bands. So tiny I had to stare at it until my eyes focused.

Adam | 4PB

A memory card, but the capacity couldn't be right. Not if it meant petabytes. Storage that size existed, sure, but not for external memory cards. Even if I put a petabyte in my tablet, I'd have no way to fill it. Not if I recorded every hour of my day for the next twenty years or downloaded every book ever printed. *Four* petabytes was even more ridiculous.

And what was "Adam?" I had never heard of any company with that name. It didn't even sound techie. Just . . . old-fashioned.

I dropped to the desert floor, crumpling under the sudden rush of memory. Adam was that little boy from the park. We'd played Soldiers and Bots, and then . . . the shot. That voice from the pistol, Adam, a robot, followed by a chopper overhead, soldiers pouring out after landing. My mental playback stuttered, like I'd reached the end of a movie that cut out in the middle, a corrupted file refusing to cooperate. I closed my eyes and willed the movie to continue. Several times it stuttered and stopped right after the soldiers exited, the only thing visible their legs pumping as they slid into position. But there was another, a suited man. I'd seen him from behind the refrigerator, leaned out, and. . .

His face came into focus, then something else, the awful taste of chemical on my tongue. Now I knew where the card had come from. I'd stuffed it in my mouth right before. . .

The movie stuck and dropped again, a finality to it this time. I tried pushing it forward again and again, desperate for answers, but whatever was corrupting the playback remained in place.

I turned back to the RV, remembering hiding inside it, popping out before . . . killing him. *It*, I guess. I looked to the ground where I remembered him lying. Not a drop of blood or speck of fluid to suggest it had happened at all. I began to doubt my memories. If not for the storage card, it would seem more like a dream than reality. The card tethered everything else to the real world.

On my knees, I pushed the dirt side to side, looking for any clue Adam had been there. My hands showed a mess of cuts, *that* I remembered, if only just. I needed to clean up, reformat.

I kept the memory card in-between thumb and forefinger as I walked back to the pod park. By the time I made it to my pod and fixed a glass of water from the tap, any mental catches had dulled and smoothed over. The few snapshots I'd surfaced remained in place, but the rest seemed lost for good.

With a few lamps burning, I could tell Dad had been there, but had left, perhaps to look for me. I rushed to my room and fetched my tablet. It seemed like days ago I'd put it on my nightstand before going out to play with Adam.

I inserted the memory card. The screen went black, and my stomach sank. Great, I'd just broken my only link to the outside world.

But then a single string of text appeared on the screen, dull green and one letter at a time, as if typed.

Hello?

I almost dropped the tablet, but caught it on its way down. I pulled up the keyboard and typed, *Hello*. My heart picked up speed.

Who is this?

A flare of panic shot through me. This could be Delco, tracking down what I'd stolen. Every instinct said to yank out the memory card and wipe the tablet clean.

Please, who is this? It came again.

Something about that please nagged at me, even as my fingers hovered over the memory card port, ready to dislodge the card.

This is stupid, I thought, but called up the keyboard again.

This is Ryelanna, I typed, my head so light and breathing so rapid, I had to sit on my bed.

The screen went black again, only worsening my fears, but then another line appeared, the letters ticking off over several seconds.

This is Adam. Did I win?

MACHINERY OF GHOSTS
By Morgan Crooks

As far as D-Block was concerned, the Jovian Revolt had never really ended. Just beyond the windows of the pressure door, a corridor stretched into the darkness, curving with the upwards sweep of the station, a gloom filled with restless memories.

"How long has it been since anyone's come here?" Chamille asked as Evan secured the last strap to her environment suit.

He pinched his dark eyebrows together. "Three years at least. Some of the machinery on the lower levels is essential, has to be inspected once a decade. If it wasn't for that I imagine no one would come down here ever."

"Do you regret telling me about this?"

Evan snapped the final strap into place and gave her shoulders a pat hard enough to shake free the hydrophobic dust from the suit seams. "I regret that I didn't do this years ago. When it might have made a difference."

Chamille turned around, lifting one of her gloved hands to his face, looking into his eyes. "Je ne regrette rien. You're going to help make a better world possible."

"I don't care about better worlds, I care about you." He took her hand from his face and enclosed it in his two hands. They looked very small and very pale compared to the boxy work gloves. "I just wish you had come here sooner."

She stared into his eyes, waiting for one of his gentle jokes to break the moment, but Evan let it stand there between them, his eyes on hers, his face smooth and sincere. What else was there to say?

Chamille backed away and turned to face the darkness just beyond the airlock. Purple splotches discolored the edges of the reinforced glass, probably some mutant strain of Serratia, but one couldn't be sure.

The negative pressure pulled her forward, past the first ring of the airlock, a mild tingling running down the back of her arms and neck from the depolarizers. More aggressive nano-formed spores resistant to such treatment, but the munitions down here were first stage Jovian assemblers, and the Jovians, despite their boundless folly, never created self-improving algorithms.

"D-Block used to host many of the logistical functions of Hugo station, particularly those managing the flow of antimatter from the Arasteia cloud," Evan said as Chamille played her light on the barren chamber at the end of the corridor. Everything organic had been stripped from the walls and floors, leaving vast sections of the floor either bare titanium lace or open to the superstructure. Chamille was walking inside of an enormous metal skull, gaps and fissures showing levels far below. The first-floor was close to the central axis of Hugo, D-Block one pie-wedge of a colossal Stanford Torus. "Now everything gets run from Wescott's suite in A-Block."

"Which he never leaves and won't let anyone enter," she said. "How'd this station function with one missing section, let alone two?"

"It crept up on us," Evan said, radio interference adding a warm fuzz to his voice. "I don't think anyone had realized how bad it was until you showed up."

They both knew Deputy Secretary Owen Wescott was an old Pentagon desk warrior, legendary for his service during the Revolt, ruthless in bureaucratic guerrilla warfare—a potent combination. No one wanted to be the politician who sacked the Liberator of Europa.

"I still don't think anyone knows how bad it is," she replied, knowing the retrieval of the D-Block command keys was just the first step. "This place is in shambles. It'll take years to put it all back together."

She detached a flexible wrench from her utility belt and fitted its wedge end into the control panel by the nearest stairwell. Once the panel popped open, she turned the wrench around and fitted its hexagonal head on one of the release gears. The apparatus refused to budge until she switched positions for more leverage, when it suddenly gave way, yanking the wrench from her hand. The round door opened a crack and then stopped. Time for the spreaders. She put the clamps into the narrow opening and waited for the pressure to push the door open.

"Should I seal them back up?" she asked Evan.

"Protocol says yes," he said. "Personally, I would just focus on moving. The sooner you get the files and come back the better for everyone."

Once through the gap, she clipped the spreader clamp and wrench on her belt. It felt weird leaving the door open behind her, like she was a burglar looking for something to steal. An absurd thought. The files belonged to the UN. On eleven separate occasions the General Security Council had requested their recovery and each had gone unheeded.

Wescott had had a decade to get the station back up and running. It would have been quicker at this point to have simply scuttled Hugo and built another station, the revenue from the Arasteia Cloud's antimatter more than justifying the expense. But Wescott had a Rasputin-like hold on the security council.

"Just one more year and we'll have the last of the Jovian nano licked," his white papers used increasingly personal and strident language. "I remember when many of you wrote off Ganymede, Galileo Outpost, and Europa. Don't make the same mistake again."

It was mawkish, manipulative, and damned effective. For the war-weary inner system, used to years of cataclysm and disaster, even the underwhelming seemed like progress.

She was sick of old men patting each other on the back for avoiding the worst-case scenarios.

At the bottom of the staircase, she found another hatch for her spreader clamps. Once opened, she stepped into a second level which looked pretty much the same as the first. A few more floor panels missing, a few less lights to provide illumination. The only big difference she could see was this chamber was open the entire width of D-Block, with large floor-to-ceiling windows providing two very different vistas. To her right was 4709 Ennomos, the pale brown chunk of organic silicate to which Hugo was moored. To her left was Arasteia, the impossible nebula.

"I'm not sure how you could live here and see that every day out of your porthole," Chamille said, awe-struck.

"I never minded it," he said. "But you can have the portholes filter it out. Did you ever—"

"Wonder what it is?" she finished for him. "Not really."

"I wonder about it all the time," he said. "I like to stare at it sometimes, trying to see if there are any patterns in the rings or center mass. They say it must be artificial but it seems very . . . natural to me. Like it's supposed to be here."

What a strange thing to say. Arasteia was most certainly not supposed to be here. When the sun ignited five billion years ago, every wisp of pre-stellar matter was blown out into the Kuiper. And yet, here it was, slowly undulating in a stable orbit, apparently for thousands of years.

"Do you think it's what they say?" Evan asked. "Something alien?"

"I think it's useful," she replied. "I think it produces something that the human race needs very badly. And it produces a lot of it. Do you realize last century antimatter was worth billions of Euros per gram? And now it's valued at a fraction of that. We have Arasteia to thank."

"Should we also thank her for the Jovian Revolt?"

"I think we should be grateful that Ganymede got so greedy they decided to seize the station," she said. "Things may have gone differently if they had simply enacted a blockade. With a little bit of patience, the entire outer system might have fallen into their lap."

Evan laughed. "If the rebels had more patience they wouldn't have revolted in the first place."

"C'est vrai quoi!" Chamille said, already marching between two parallel yellow lines painted onto the deck, charting off into the gloom. Evan explained the route was the safe path for maintenance crews. Looking along the walls, she wondered about that.

"I'm seeing a lot of diamond tailings," she said.

"Where are you seeing it?" Evan asked a little too quickly. "Along the walls or in the path?"

"Along the walls. The path is clear."

"C'est ainsi que cela doit être," Evan intoned, relieved. "It should stay that way as long as you stay on the path."

She laughed. "Très bon! And if it doesn't stay clear I shall become very . . . pissy? Is that the phrase?"

"Pissed," Evan said. "You'll be very pissed. Anyway, there's no reason to be pissed just yet. Most of that dust was put down by friendlies."

"Your American marines?"

"For the most part. It's what Wescott brought with him after the fall of Ganymede. Even he couldn't really push the nasty stuff off of the station. But he convinced the military to keep a nanotech presence even after control reverted to the UN. So it's just stayed here, holding the line."

"Sort of like Wescott."

Once she knew what she was looking at, the glints in the dark became more ominous, less like the sparkle of frost and more the sinister lights of some enemy city. Chamille reached the far edge of the second level chamber, following the double lines into a tighter corridor. The path was still clear, but now the pinprick light came right up against the lines, unnervingly close.

"What keeps the Jovians from rising up and pushing the Yanks aside?"

"Lack of energy for the most part," Evan said. "We give light to the upper floors to keep the Americans happy."

"In ten years, no one's come up with better technology?"

"Frankly, no. The American technology is aggressive, tenacious stuff and they've been down here with the Jovians for a long time. They've gotten used to all of its tricks. Anything new we introduce into the war would actually have to fight its way downward through the American lines. By the time it started engaging Jovian nano it would be facing a steep learning curve with depleted resources. Chance are all we'd be doing is doing the Jovians a favor, wiping out their competition and giving them a red carpet out of D-Block. The thinking was to let sleeping dogs lie."

The path was taking her to the far bulkhead, her lamp showing a ladder leading down through an access hatch to the third level. According to fragmentary records she would find the system access keys for the rest of the station below. She took a deep breath and slowly swung herself over the hatch and onto the metal rungs of the ladder. She lowered herself a few feet, then stopped. Lights twinkled below, red, blue, and orange. The lights pulsed rhythmically, slowly crawling up the walls and ladder in peristaltic waves.

"Is everything okay?" Evan asked.

"The rungs have some of the dust on them. It's sparkling."

"Any getting on your suit?"

She lifted her hand off of one of the rungs and turned it over. A few specks coruscated in her headlamp.

"Yeah, what do you think? Still American?"

"Probably, but considering you're French you might not want to ask it. It might take offense."

"Tres drôle."

"Look, Chamille, I'd suggest just keep moving. The third level is right there on the frontlines. Some of what you see down there is definitely going to be Jovian. We'll put you through decon when you get back. It's 170K down there, so anything that gets on your suit is going to spread very slowly. You'll be fine."

"Reassuring."

"It's meant to be."

"Okay, I just saw a sign for the data core, but the path leads away from it."

"Ready to go off-road? I'll guide you there from this point. You should see a long corridor off to the left, away from the sign and the path."

She looked around, her lamplight leaving glowing trails on the ceiling, walls, and floor. "I see it."

"Do you see the fourth door on the right?"

Chamille angled her lamp down the corridor, focusing its beam to get a little more distance. Everywhere the orb of her lamp touched sparkled and cracked; what survived here bent itself to harvest every last photon of energy. She put her lamp on the fourth door and sent a quick confirmation picture to Evan.

"That's the one you want. Go to the door as quickly as you can without kicking up any dust."

Chamille did her best, hunching slightly and easing each foot onto the deck. No matter how carefully she stepped, however, a little puff of glittering dust always drifted away from her boot.

"Chamille, you're going to need to pick up the pace a little bit. You've got less than 20 minutes before I've got to have you start the return trip."

"I thought you said I shouldn't rush it," she said.

"I changed my mind."

Sweat dribbled down her cheeks and chin as she watched the sparkling dust settle on her boots and lower legs. While her suit was well-insulated, the mechanical action of legs moving and flexing fed into a replication cycle. In a war-zone it didn't matter if the nano was technically friendly or not, it would use any resource offered in the service of relentless, pitiless combat. The warmth of her body and all of its luxurious organic compounds would be a treasure trove for whichever side claimed her.

The infestation became a cellophane-like substance flaking off around her, the material of her suit shedding one micron at a time. She kept her eyes on the corridor in front of her, willing herself forward.

Past the fourth door was another corridor with a series of portholes, the sapphire glass cracked and pitted by years of abuse. Despite this, she could still see Arasteia's dark immensity, her face covered in veils of slightly luminous aurora, some of the larger arms brushing against the hull of Hugo Station.

Diamond grit still covered the floor, enough to form piles in places. The vibrations from her steps caused avalanches, spills of dust tumbling in strange Coriolis spirals, the vortices turning fractal as eddies and turbulences took hold. Some of these spirals had sprouted crystalline branches by the time she reached them, branches swaying towards her as she passed.

"Go to the end of the corridor and enter the big room. The data core is a big protected chamber in the center of the gallery. You'll be back in American territory at that point."

She paused at the threshold. The place was massive. She actually entered on a catwalk far above the chamber Evan described. A winding series of stairs led to an access port along one of the immense panels of this chamber. Seeing little choice, Chamille began to descend using one of these stairs, keeping to the center of the staircase, making sure not to touch the railings. The dust that settled on her suit caused a very different reaction now, ignoring the fabric and attacking the structure of the Jovian film. The end result was the same, even more flakes of suit falling to the deck, but it still felt oddly comforting to have left the Jovians behind.

"You'll find a panel sort of like the one up at the staircase on the welcome level," Evan said. "Open it and use the wrench to force the door open."

Chamille pulled out the wrench and popped open the panel. Flipping the tool around she got to work on the safety release. Slowly, very slowly, the gears turned. Dust settled onto the panel's interior, feeding off of the waste heat. She gave it one last savage jerk and the gears spun free, the door falling open. More of the dust swept inside, the floors suddenly alive with glittering auroras. She was walking above Marseille at night, all of her ancient avenues and boulevards etched out in sudden points of light. Chaotic mosaics had spread up her shins and forearms, cities taking over her suit, colonizing it.

She used the wrench to seal the chamber back up before she signaled to Evan.

"Okay, this is the part that gets tricky," Evan said. "When I engage the core a couple of things are going to happen all at once."

"I'm hoping one of those things is that the nano on my suit gets deactivated."

"Yeah, that'll happen, but the energy from the core is going to provoke a reaction in the gallery. The Jovian stuff knows you're here. They might make an attempt at the gallery. The last team through had to file plenty of incident reports."

"They made it back, right?"

"Who?"

"The people who came here last time."

"Chamille, listen to me. When I initiate decon you're not going to have a lot of time."

"You said the decon will take care of the nanos."

"It will. But that's not your only problem. It will also ring a little alarm in the station head's office."

"Wescott."

"He'll know someone's down here and there's not much I can do after that. I'll lose connection with you first and you can expect a welcome party when you get back."

Once her identity was blown she was prepared for a rough couple of weeks. She was willing to take that risk. The UN extraction team was on its way and she knew what was at stake.

"On y va."

"Chamille—"

"I said let's go. I'm ready."

Lights along the edges of the decon room flickered to life. Almost immediately the dust in the room and on her clothes went wild, sending out shoots and crystalline vines towards the light, forming oblate petals to soak in a shower of photons. Little opalescent disks emerged from the joints in her suit, like time-lapsed mushrooms, angling towards the same source of energy. She was sprouting.

Outside she saw even more dramatic stirrings, the dust on railings and steps springing upwards to assemble intricate spiderwebs, crystal nets swaying from one end of the gallery to the other. The change was so swift, so dramatic, that she took a step backward from the transparent corundum panels.

Then came the familiar sensation of buzzing down her neck, back, and limbs. A mildly irritating tingle to her, death to the nano trapped in the room with her. The perfect glittering surface of the nano pulsed in time to some unseen frequency and then abruptly shattered, the minuscule shards shattering again before they hit the ground. The waves of disruption struck again and again until all of the nano structures were reduced to so much dust and powder.

"How's it looking?" Evan asked.

"My suit looks like hell, but I'm still breathing."

"The data access terminal is on the other side of the decon chamber. You'll need to use the card I gave you. Be patient, nothing's been running for years, it's going to take time."

She crossed into the main chamber of the core. It was like stepping back into the past. The nano had been locked out, so everything still looked the same as a decade or two before. The prewar period. Bright optimistic primaries on the walls and blocky chunks of printed wood for furniture. It was the style of unlimited possibilities, vast wealth, and grating naiveté. No one of the War generation would ever be able to tolerate this again.

Am I trying to go forwards or backwards?

Chamille made her way to the first available terminal, its screen already cycling through its boot-up. Steadying her hands, she tried not to hyperventilate. The computer's antiquated UI still had progress bars, slowly filling up a long column as she drummed her hands on the surface of the desk. A few flakes of dead nano floated free from her gloves.

"Alright, Evan, the terminal's up, I'm going to grab the files."

The comm was silent.

"Evan?"

Wescott. It would only take a few keystrokes to shut down the station network from his lair in A-Block. She was on her own.

Still, she had something that no other visitor, and that included the Jovians, possessed. A back-door password to the root structure of the station. She logged into the terminal and spoke the word, "Shiva."

The device vibrated, quivering as mechanical components whirred into action. She worried something had gone wrong until the screen displayed the executive command menu. Like the room itself, the menu came from another age, each listing opening up into huge ammonite spirals of information, far more than she needed. When she asked for the command keys, the terminal bent over backwards to download them into her personal network.

She exhaled, half-way there.

"Chamille Garnier," came a voice from the terminal. "What do you think you're doing?"

Startled, she looked down into the eyes of Owen Wescott, staring back at her through a video link. His face was fleshy and round, with angry red capillaries radiating from his nose. His expression was calm, but his voice betrayed a nervous edge. He looked like he had not had more than three hours of sleep in the past week.

"I'm freeing this station, Deputy Secretary," stabbing down on the disconnect key. Nothing happened.

"Don't be ridiculous, this is a free station. I freed it."

"I am an official representative of the United Nations Security Council, sent here to execute resolutions 41826, 43314, and 53462, demanding immediate restoration of Hugo Station operations."

"You don't know what you're talking about."

"I have the root command keys. When I come up we're going to talk about how to initiate a transitional authority aboard the station. If you assist me in this process I can assure you your service to the UN will be taken into account."

Wescott shook his head. "I told you not to go down there. None of you understand."

"Understand what?"

"What I'm fighting here. What I'm protecting all of you from."

Chamille held up her hands, and spoke softly. "The Jovian nano do not pose that much of a threat. Why if you had returned the station to—"

"The nano is protecting you!" he spat. "Our munitions, the Jovian munitions. That's all that's keeping you alive right now," he broke off, coughing into a fat, red fist. "I know Evan let you into D-Block. Was it just him or were there others?"

Chamille could feel her jaw tighten. "Now look. Under the authority of the Security Council, I order you to release Evan and to stand down from any further actions against station personnel."

"Evan isn't station personnel. He isn't human."

Chamille stepped away from the terminal. Wescott's face leered from all of the other screens, mouthing the words: he isn't human. She shook her head, leaving the data core for the decon room. She had the key, she didn't need to haggle with Owen fucking Wescott anymore. If he actually dared put her into detention he would be seeing the inside of a courtroom within a year.

She stepped out into madness.

Somehow Wescott had contrived to flood the data chamber with light. Raw pure illumination. At first she could only blink her eyes, trying to free them from the glare. Then she backed away from the door, trying to stay on her feet.

The gallery was in uproar. The spiderwebs gone, a thick, pulsating forest of crystal and cellophane stood in their place. The entire room was filled with an intricate system of chambers and cilia, all hard at work trying to rip itself apart.

Wescott had ignited a war. She saw an enormous tube, like a coil of intestine the size of a whale, open its maw and crash through several floors worth of staircase, swallowing up fluttering tongues with bat wings. Striking the floor, it detonated. Mounds of orange and purple flesh slid everywhere. Aggressive crustaceans fell upon the ejecta, chrome claws snipping and slicing, and feeding gobs of the stuff into coral cities sprouting from their backs. A hopping, squirming, pulsating tide of enraged weaponry covered the floor of the chamber.

The light came from the floor, or rather the section of deck open to space. The view had tilted nearly 90 degrees. The distant, still potent spark of the sun shone up through D-Block's levels, flooding the data core.

A writhing heap of tourmaline prawns kneaded at the glass in front of her, rows of tiny splayed feet grinding away at the surface. A groove stretched from one side of the glass to the other, a channel to pump solvents and corrosives into the casing. The prawns stared at her with eyes like drops of pitch.

The curtain of unlife parted and something stepped through. The creatures, the prawns, the gaping worms, all bent away from his approach.

Evan.

She stared at him, watched him raise one of his arms to wave at her. He smiled and then beckoned for her to leave. Although he said nothing, could say nothing that would be heard through hard vacuum and thick corundum glass, his intent was clear. Why not come out of there? You won't be safe forever, join me while you still have the choice.

Retreating from the madness outside, Chamille returned to the terminal room. Her mouth was dry, her legs shaking. The nano couldn't get in, could it? She held up her gloves, examining closely the abraded surface. Here and there the brief exposure to direct sunlight had reawakened the spores embedded in the fabric. In the dim light of the terminal room, they were beginning to spread, thin waxy films enveloping her ankles and knees. The humble beginnings of a mighty civilization of killers.

The fat, sweaty face of Owen Wescott stared at her from every terminal.

"See someone familiar?"

"Did you do this?"

"It's all Arasteia, Chamille. That's where it all comes from. I've been able to use the nano to keep people out of the data core for years, but Arasteia is figuring out ways around that too. She was a spot barely the size of a moonlet 10 years ago, and now you see what she's become. What we've let her become. And it's not going to stop! Do you understand? It will keep growing, metastasizing until it takes over everything."

"Owen, if you let me out of here we can talk about this. We can figure out a solution."

"That's not going to happen."

She slammed her fists down on the terminal's keyboard, keys springing free of the tray, skittering across the desk. "Goddamn it, Wescott! I'm not going to die down here."

"Goodbye, Chamille. I'm sure I'll be seeing you again."

The terminals went black as the first cracks appeared in her face-plate. She looked around and saw a stream of dark nebula smoke pouring in from beneath the doors. Arasteia lingered there for a moment, waiting to see what she would do. Chamille held out until the first pinpricks started in her feet, knees, and hands, and then broke down.

Chamille would agree to anything to make it stop. The price for a new body was steep, and Arasteia's demands were no less harsh coming from Evan's lips.

TECH SUPPORT
By Blair Frison

"**T**hank you for choosing Vicecorp, this is Jeff. May I have your account number, please?"

"Hey Jeff, Matthew here, account number 82405. Password is Lombardo."

"And how can I help today, Matthew?"

"Well, I'm pretty frustrated. I recently purchased the Lenore 3000 and I'm having some major issues. I'm not getting the proper responses at all."

"Can you be more specific?"

"Okay, for example, when I make any kind of threat, she doesn't show fear. She *says* she's scared, but she's perfectly calm. There's no point if she's not scared. I don't need to tell you I paid good money for her."

"Let me guess: She's not responding to physical stimuli either . . .?"

"How do you mean?"

"Does she scream when you hit her?"

"No. Nothing."

"That's what I thought. I apologize for this Matthew, it's a known issue. The last batch was sent out a little prematurely. Is she on now?"

"Yeah, she's on. She's right here."

"Perfect. So, this is an easy fix, Matthew. I'm gonna force an update from my end, which will only take a few seconds, and I'm gonna add twelve months to your warranty for the inconvenience."

"Oh, thanks! I appreciate that."

"My pleasure. Just keep in mind that beheading voids the warranty."

"That's perfectly fine. At the most I'll cut a few fingers off. Nothing crazy."

"Alright, Matthew, that should do it. Wanna give her a little punch for me?"

"Sure, one second."

. . .

"She's bawlin' like a cow. Thanks for your help, Jeff."

"No problem. Is there anything else I can help you with today?"

"No, that's great. Thanks again."

"You're welcome, Matthew, and thank you for choosing Vicecorp. Have a wonderful day."

CORNUCOPIA
By Edward Ahern

*S*o, *anyway, Bobby records having sex with Cheryl on their play date and headlines it.*

No way. Harry's avatar image winced.

Oh yeah, Harry, he did. Here. Look at them. (Transfer lag: 0.5 seconds.)

Man, that's tacky. His own wife. (Saved for repeat viewing.) *Hang on, Georgie, gotta take this.*

Hey, Marty.

You see the video, Harry, about the watcha call it—the coronal mass ejection? It's really happening.

The what?

Coronal mass ejection. It's like a solar flare but much worse. You need to use your interface for something other than porn, Harry. Here's the factoid. (1.25 second delay.)

Steaming crap. They say this could temporarily knock out the interfaces. Harry involuntarily touched the protrusion on the back of his skull.

It's for real, slug. I tried to advance-order a week's worth of Redi Meals and was told they'd been rationed. Same thing with water and booze.

But, Marty, our food is delivered daily. Nobody stores food, it's so 20th century. If I don't get a delivery, I go hungry tomorrow. Jesus Murphy!

You saw the video. The plasma mass hits us tonight. Once our interfaces go dead, we don't see or hear each other. No food, no buying or banking. Oh yeah, and no electricity, heat, or running water.

Don't get born again on me. They said that they had backup systems and that any interface downtime would just be a brief inconvenience.

Yeah, and they have our best interests at heart. Tighten your sphincter, Harry. I don't think we live too far apart. If it gets fundamental we should try and help each other. Stay charged.

Harry thought the switch back. *Georgie? Sorry for the dead time. You hear about a coronal mass ejection?*

The smile on Georgie's avatar evaporated. *Yeah. Something about charged plasma smacking us with a magnetic field concussion. Wait.* (0.75 second delay while Georgie retrieved data.) *Supposed to be even worse than the Carrington solar flare and CME in 1859. But they say the equipment's shielded and the effects will be brief.*

You think? I hope so. I haven't physically vocalized in over a week. I lose my interface, I'm bug-brained.

Harry, I thought about trying to resurrect a cell phone or tablet, but they'd be fried as well.

Yeah, they don't even use those relics in the projects. I'll keep you zoned in through the sleep cycle.

Likewise. If the contact snaps we know we're in trouble.

Harry ate his nutritionally balanced McBurger Redi Meal and washed it down with extra virgin spring water. He showered without removing his Sheersupport romper suit and crawled into the sleep cylinder. The gel pillow contoured to accommodate the interface protrusion. His sleep patterns were recognized and 237 channels shut down for the night. Nine dream-enhancing and nightmare-suppressing channels activated.

The absence of input jerked Harry awake. *I'm blank screened! What time is it?*

My interface! (reached back and touched it) *Yes! Charged? Yes. Nothing. Nothing from Marty or Georgie.* Harry crawled out from his dark cylinder into an equally dark cubicle. Nothing powered up. He tottered to the window and opened the light and sound-blocking curtains. *Looks like mid-morning. There are people walking around with actual clothes on. They're talking to each other. Absolutely nobody talks to strangers.*

Harry rasped his throat three times and spat out congealed yellow sputum.

"Hello? Hello? Audio level one, two, *three*." *Well, that still works.*

He sat for a moment, then paced over to the uniwater stall. *Drink. Shower. Flush.* Nothing. "Drink. Shower. Flush." Nothing. After twenty minutes he found and manually turned the valves for shower, toilet, and drinking spigots. The taps sputtered and hissed air. Harry relieved himself, but the urine lay puddled and unflushed on the floor of the stall.

He checked food service. *Nothing arrived overnight. Sweet virgin whore I think I'm hungrier because there's nothing to eat.*

He looked down at the widely spaced mesh of his romper suit. *I look like I'm on sex call. And I'm cold.* He rummaged until he found trousers and a pullover, fusty from disuse. As he pulled off the rompers he glimpsed a backlit reflection of his unsupported self in the window. *Jesus Murphy, my gut is the biggest part of me. My arms and legs look like phallic worms.*

Raw daylight cut across his cubicle, shrinking his mental image of its size. Sleep cylinder, clothing chest, wall mounted food service valet, uniwater stall, recycle chute, ergonochair now powerless and lumpy. Harry felt confined and went back over to the window. People milled around in the weed-overgrown courtyard.

How long has this lasted? Half a sleep period maybe? It'll be colder tonight. They better get this fixed before then. If I walk down fifteen floors to the courtyard I've got to walk it back up. Not sure I can make it. No, I could stop every few floors and get my breath back. What will they know? Nothing, probably.

Harry sat in his ergonochair. Its pliancy gone, the chair poked at him with unretracted massage heads. Unable to call up interface images and contacts, his thoughts churned in muddy swirls. He put on slippers and started down the emergency stairs, afraid to try the up-down person chute.

The sunlight hurt his eyes. Harry squinted at his unacquainted neighbors. *Ebola me, but they're ugly.* He cleared his throat and spat again, sloppily. "Intrusion apologies, but have you learned when the interfaces will be up again?"

The man was bodaciously fat. He coughed without covering his mouth. "No. Do you have any food? Maybe some alcohol?"

"No. Regrets. Is there some place to credit-buy meals?"

"No, nowhere I've heard. Do you have any extra virgin carafes?"

Harry thought. He did have three carafes of water left in the food cubby. But he had never friended this blobby stranger. "No, regrets. Nothing left at all."

They drifted apart. Harry listened as strangers approached each other, asking different questions but always receiving the same answers. "No." "Nothing." "Never." He climbed back up to his cubicle in increasingly ragged stages—first four stories, then three each time before resting, then two, before reaching his level.

There were seven cubicles at Harry's level, six of them the same size as Harry's and one corner unit that was perhaps three times bigger. He stood in silence, listening for sounds of activity, but the doors and walls were soundproofed to prevent the presence of others from being intrusive.

It was cold inside Harry's unit, and he left his clothes on. He crawled back into the sleep cylinder, but without the posturepower supports and heating it was hard and cold. He slept briefly, but his sleep was unassisted and unstructured. He woke in amorphous fear.

Harry drank a little stale water and walked back over to the window. There was no one left in the courtyard, the unmet needs accentuating the repugnance of strangers. He turned back into his cubicle and inventoried his belongings.

Extra virgin: three carafes, maybe two days' worth. Leftovers: none, all chuted the night before. Clothes: rompers—three; undertunics—two. One dress formal. Harry tried to put on the formal overalls, but they were too tight around the mid-section.

He prided himself on a virtual, minimally environmentally-intrusive life, but had left himself with nothing, not even a knife with which he could slit open the overalls at the belly. *I need help. There must be other people living on my level.*

Harry stepped outside his cubicle and knocked on the reinforced entry hatches to the other units. There were no responses. He sat cross-legged on the floor next to his cubicle hatch, ready to dart inside if threatened. After a few hours the daylight that trickled through two small portholes began to dwindle. He sat in shadow.

The hatch to the largest unit slowly opened and an old woman sidled out, holding a kitchen knife and an enameled basin in her hands. Unlike Harry and the others who'd been in the courtyard, she had no pronounced belly. She also had no interface on the back of her head.

Harry watched in silence as she carefully took the basin over to the emergency stairwell and pitched its liquid contents down the stairs. Harry smelled urine.

"You're contaminating your fellow cubiclers! How can you be so intrusive?"

The woman dropped the metal basin and spun toward Harry. She clutched the knife with the blade back along the forearm, in what he guessed was a good defensive position. "Who the hell are you? Get up and I'll cut you."

Harry sat. "We cohabitate this level. Your threat violated my social space and will be reported."

"Screw you. Back into your rat-hole, fatty." She edged toward him, sensing that he was unable to move quickly or aptly. When she was able to see his face, she cringed. "What's your name, tubs?"

"Harry."

"Harry. Harry. Too young." She kept staring at him. "You eat anything today?"

"My food service was interrupted."

"I bet the hell it was. Get off your ass. I can give you a little bit to eat. If you need to, piss down the stairwell before you come in."

Harry's stomach had been gnawing at itself for several hours. *I guess this is hunger.* "I don't want to perpetrate an intrusion. Appreciations for your bringing a Redi Meal out to me."

The old woman snorted. "I'd tell you to go fuck yourself but you're probably already doing that. You don't come in, you don't eat."

Harry's legs had gone to sleep, and he tottered as he rose. "Your knife is Ebola intimidating. Please leave it on the landing."

"In a pig's ass I will. You have my word I won't stick you. Grow some balls and come in."

Anger and fear surged alternatively through him. After several seconds, hunger overwhelmed both emotions. "Jesus Murphy! All right. I'll be minimally invasive."

She waved for him to precede her into the cubicle. Harry lurched to a stop two steps inside. The overly large room was crammed, walls and floor, with things—so many things jammed together that Harry was sure she hadn't seen or used many of them for months. Actual printed reading and viewing material was strewed over tables and chairs. Dishes and cups, longhand writing materials, congealed oil pictures on the walls, open shelves full of food containers, decorative but dysfunctional curtains on the windows, empty vases, and twenty or thirty printed, frozen images of people in frames of wood and plastic.

Harry turned on her. "You must know how environmentally destructive this wanton excess is."

"You smug prig, what do you know about these things? They carry memories I can hold."

Harry couldn't quite shut his mouth, even though he hadn't been fed. "You're old. You don't know the consequences of what you've done."

"Shut up, Philip, ah, Harry, before I regret my decision."

She stirred flat cereal grains together with unlabeled water and heated the gruel over a small can of burning wax. As it cooked she added in yellow fat. "Need to use up the butter before it goes bad." She handed him a steaming bowl and a glass of water.

Harry studied the water suspiciously. "This is virgin? Extra virgin?"

She laughed. "Neither. It's eau de tap. A few microbes won't hurt you."

After a couple of nibbles, Harry ceded control to his stomach and bolted down the entire bowlful. Sated and less anxious, he began to look around the cubicle more closely. There were several pictures of a young man that looked a lot like a leaner version of himself.

He pointed at one of them. "Pardon for the intrusion. Is this a relative? Given all these images you must have deeply friended him."

"It's my son, the bastard. He deserted me years ago. Screw him."

Harry couldn't say anything that wouldn't be further intrusive, so he remained silent.

They sat together without speaking for ten minutes.

"Do you have a real bed in your cubicle?"

"My Ebola sleep cylinder is inactive and hard."

"And of course, you have no blankets."

"Blankets? Ah, thick body coverings. No, none."

"You'll freeze in that cocoon of yours. There's a floor mat in the closet, along with blankets. Take them out and spread them next to the table you're sitting at. You piss and shit in the stairwell."

The food churned in Harry's stomach. He had not, since group childhood, spent a night in the same cubicle with another human or animal. "Grotty incest! Your suggestion rapes my space. Appreciation for the feeding, but I must leave."

"Suit yourself."

When Harry re-entered his cubicle, he smelled the urine souring on the floor of the uniwater stall. *I can't add to that.* He edged his way back out of the cubicle and over to the stairwell. Harry carefully aimed his urine through the railing and directly down to the ground floor fifteen stories below. *Easier to clean up later.*

The next five hours were spent moving from sleep cylinder to ergonochair and back, rolling and shifting positions so that different parts of his body became sore. The temperature dropped unrelentingly. The unheated gel in the pillow was a rock that poked his interface back into his head. He constantly shivered, and was able to see that a frozen rime was forming on the liquid in the uniwater stall. *I actually won't survive this. The Ebola hag was right.*

Harry stepped back out into the lightless landing. He dropped onto all fours and worked his way along the wall to what he thought was the woman's cubicle. He realized he didn't know her name. He knocked loudly on the portal and waited what might have been two minutes. With no response he knocked again, more loudly.

"Bother me, fucker, and you die!"

"It's Harry, your level associate. You fed me earlier. I'm freezing and need assistance."

"Now, isn't that tough shit."

There was silence for several seconds and the portal opened.

"Get your ass in here."

Two candles burned inside the cubicle. Without another word the old woman laid out a floor mat, two blankets and a pillow that smelled of old sweat.

"Apologies for the repeated intrusion and appreciation for the physical assistance. May I know your avatar name?"

"My what? Call me Janet, it's the name I was given. Get under the blankets before you shake apart."

Harry slept until sunlight and the smell of food penetrated his senses.

"What is that delicious smell?"

"Bacon."

"Bacon?"

"Cured bacon lasts a long time before going bad."

"But what is it?"

"Ah. The belly of a pig."

They talked while eating. Without the usual prompts from his interface Harry rambled, but came to understand that Janet had lived in this cubicle for over forty years, going out only to collect food from black market stalls and for life extension treatments from the impaired existence center for indigents. After the demise of television, radio, and computer internet she had refused to interface, and was reduced to visual inputs from antique sheets produced from wood and textile fibers.

"Nothing new worth watching anyway."

With nothing to do and nowhere to go they spent the day circling each other with words, trying to understand the strange animal in their mutual zoo. Janet examined Harry with intensity, asking about health, and education and partnership with any significant others. Harry was more bemused, for Janet lived beyond his known universe.

As the sunlight began to dwindle, Harry left the cubicle to relieve himself, and almost ran back in. A portly, gargoylish man sat on the floor of the landing, rasping hoarsely. He was still in a romper suit, but wrapped by old clothes like shawls. Harry paused in his flight. He thought he recognized the squatter.

"Georgie?"

"Harry! Harry, is that you? You look so—different from your avatar."

"Likewise. How the hell did you find me, Georgie?"

"I looked you up before my interface went dead. People are violating privacy out there, Harry, looking for food and water. It's an unchanneled nightmare."

"But you made it up here."

"Barely. Do you have water? Food?"

"I don't, but I can get you some. Come over here."

Harry took Georgie's arm and helped him over to Janet's cubicle portal, then knocked. When Janet cracked open the portal and spotted Georgie she grabbed the kitchen knife.

"Back off, motherfucker!"

"Janet, it's okay. This is Georgie, he's an avatar mate."

"I don't care if he's Jesus Christ, he's not coming in."

"He's hungry, Janet."

"The whole world is hungry right now. There's barely enough for me, even less with you coming back. None at all for a stranger who'll eat us into starvation. Tell him to fuck off."

"You can't be so Ebola heartless. He'll die."

"Not only can I live with that, I'll be able to live by doing that. You have to make another choice, Philip; starve with him or survive a few more days with me."

They stood in tableau for several seconds. Harry sighed and released his hold on Georgie's arm. "At least give him something to eat before he leaves."

"No. What he eats now is what we can't eat tomorrow." Janet turned the butcher blade toward Georgie. "I cut you bad enough, we've got a whole lot to eat. Walk away while you can."

"Harry, we've interface bonded, you can't do this to me."

Harry felt slack and powerless. "It's not me, Georgie, she's got the knife."

"Ebola you, Harry. If I get out of this I'll get a knife of my own." Georgie turned and shuffled toward the stairwell.

Janet and Harry ate in silence that night, Janet opening a tin of sardines and laying them on slices of home-made bread that were beginning to show green on the edges. The next morning, Harry went back to his cubicle to verify that the utility power was still off. His interface held power for two more days of shelf life, but remained inert.

"Three days," Janet finally said.

"Intrusion apology?"

"Three days. That's when the hunger and thirst become unbearable and people break down. Don't go down into the courtyard again. We're hard enough to climb to that most of them won't try."

"Nobody could get through that reinforced portal of yours."

Janet snorted. "Marketing tricks. The plated door is surrounded by drywall and sound baffling. Even you could break through the wall in less than a minute."

The day crawled into evening and night. The two candles threw flickers onto their faces, one a wrinkled version of the other. Sensory deprivation forced them to talk to each other—what they ate, how rarely Harry had left his cubicle, Janet's family, who, except for a missing son, were all dead. They stared at the exhibits in each other's emotional museums.

The following morning they ate boiled rice and drank canned peach juice. Harry stood looking out Janet's porthole for an hour. He watched as four tiny men overtook a fifth, beat him and stripped him naked. He turned to Janet. "It's starting."

"It'll get worse."

Harry spent the afternoon trying to read from cardboard encased, printed sheets, but it was cumbersome and soon hurt his wrists to hold up. Their evening routine had been established. After eating whatever Janet took from a box or a can they rolled up in their blankets for warmth and talked for about an hour before falling asleep.

The next morning Harry looked out of the porthole to see that smoke was furling out of the shattered windows of several buildings, and that the trees and shrubs in the courtyard had been hacked off at the base, presumably for firewood.

Interface alert. Interface alert. Your interface communication has been restored. Repeat, your communication has been restored. (15.7 seconds of images tumbling into Harry's awareness.)

There is still no landline power or utility service. Note: No food or water will be available for at least 48 more hours. Remain calm. Food service will be resumed to individual cubicles and not distributed to groups to minimize the risk of violent personal intrusions. Remain calm.

Janet, the interface is back on! O, Ebola me. "Janet, my interface is working! Things are getting back to normal."

The room had remained dark. Janet walked over to her uniwater stall and turned on a tap. Nothing happened. "Not yet, they're not."

"No, but there'll be food deliveries in two days to individual cubicles."

"That's two more days of food riots."

"Oh. Jesus Murphy, maybe."

Their lunch was canned peas and canned corn, served cold. As Harry was finishing, Georgie's avatar came on the interface. The image snarled.

I'm coming back, Harry.

Georgie, I'm so interpersonally mortified, but we still can't feed you.

I'm with friends now, Harry, real friends who help each other to get food. We're coming for yours, Harry. I just wanted you to know. One of my friends has a gun, Harry, a real gun. Tell that Ebola bitch that she drops first.

Georgie, listen . . . (Connection broken.)

Janet had been watching the expressions writhe across Harry's face during the interface. "What?" she asked.

"Georgie and some other people are coming here to take your food. They may have a gun."

"Damn." She sat quietly for several minutes. "Okay, here's what you're going to do. You have to get the hell out of this building and away from anywhere they're marauding. They'll stay close to their cubicles, because that's where the food will be coming. I'll bundle up some food for you to take along. Try to make it to the abandoned slums, they should be empty."

"But there's almost no food left."

"They won't believe that."

"But once they break in and can't find food they'll commit a personal space atrocity."

Janet nodded. "But maybe they'll just beat me up a little. I've already survived that with Philip. Take the knife, you'll need it." A half sour expression crossed her face. "Remember to use the pointy end to stab someone.

"Oh yeah, and leave that mind leech of yours off until you come back, otherwise you'll be babbling about what you're eating."

"It's an indictable violation to take your food."

Janet smiled wryly. "Harry, I wanted you to be Philip, but it's good that you're not. My Philip would've just stolen all the food and snuck off. Go. But when you return to your cubicle, bring me one of those God awful Redi Meals. It would be nice to know you're still alive."

THE MARTYRDOM OF BROTHER TOKTO
By Derek Nason

. . . a *booth*?

Image search results of the word *booth* rolled through Maddy's brain. It gave her mouth an awkward shape. *Booth.*

In the early 21st century, there were still telephone booths, porno booths, voting booths. She checked the name of the client on the requisition form. *The Brotherhood of Aquinian Fulfillment.* Something about the word *fulfillment* gave her gooseflesh.

Then it dawned on her: *confessional booths.*

She had spent 3 years on her Game-Testing degree, 6 years in practice. She had never seen a set-up like this.

Like every console she tested, the real hardware was the enclosed mess of fibres wrapped around her head. She'd rather do the test in her own chair, but this was what the client wanted. There wasn't even a spot in the booth to put her coffee.

The program was macabre: a Wagnerian interpretation of each of the Saint's martyrdoms. It wasn't even close to the goriest game she tested, though. Not by a long shot.

Fading up from black, she saw the flicker of flames against wet stones.

Tactile music began with tiny vibrations behind her knees. This was unexpected. These notes were usually reserved to score erotic games.

Tactile music was adopted by game designers in place of its auditory ancestors so that the music would not interfere with the in-game narrative sounds. It wasn't that profound a transition; musical styles more or less picked up where they left off, translating melodies and rhythms to their epidermal vibration equivalent.

A voice she didn't recognize, probably the cheapest actor they could find, told her she was about to experience the martyrdom of Saint Cyriacus, whose limbs were torn from their sockets.

"Charming."

She asked the operating system for the time of day. A shirtless man, covered in whip scars approached her. His voice cut out and the OS cued in with: "The time of day is fourteen hundred, twenty-three hours." Laughter speared her guts: the words synced up with the movements of the man's mouth. When sound returned, he was speaking Latin.

"Scis timor?"

Hands caressed her right arm before stiffening in grip. "Yeah, sure. I'm afraid." She sighed and turned her head.

As a group of men set upon her, her mind drifted to the gaming glass she kept next to her bed. She'd recently acquired an *insider* game; designed by testers, for testers.

The man who introduced it to her was someone she met a month ago in a tester-forum. The game itself was offline, but the experiences could be shared in an encrypted package between players after the fact. It was sex by correspondence.

She had already lost two arms by the time she realized she had been thinking about her next package.

"Enough." Maddy decided she'd rate the game safe for licensed consumption with a boiler plate set of warnings: *Copy + Paste*.

She got the impression that her client wanted the project rushed through, anyway. Usually she insisted that the testing process be slowed. Game developers were always in a rush to get their baby to market, no matter its effects on human physiology.

She had made great stands in the past—ones that cost her money. She had refused enough in bribes to have paid her student loans twice over.

No. This wasn't negligence. She knew this game. She'd seen a dozen like it.

"Exit."

With the magic word spoken, her torture chamber faded to black, and then back to the booth's interior.

When her natural vision returned, she noticed the felt cloth with a golden embroidery of an ox above her head. As always, the contrast in colors were sharper after returning from narrative vision.

She shuddered. She had no business in someone else's *objet sacré*.

On her way to her next session with her insider game, she composed the summary report for the 3rd phase test of the simply titled *Divine Sacrifice*.

. . . intensity of the score, and randomness of action make the experience a risk for those with major heart problems. . .

She stopped at the refrigerator and held the door open while the rest came to her.

. . . safe for consumption, provided user has passed annual level 2 physical exam.

There. Now she was safe from liability no matter what happened. Barring a few unlikely scenarios. Very unlikely.

"Practically impossible." And with that, her hungry neurons accepted the probes from her own gaming glass, and the display slipped over her eyes.

She laid on her bed, giggling; completely unaware she was about to fall off.

Brother Tokto hadn't spoken for two weeks.

He imagined blank word bubbles following him around, as though in a comic strip, as he sulked around the monastery.

He was suffering from vow-related withdrawal. His throat quivered in its atrophy. He woke up screaming in the middle of the night, every night.

As he waited for the eucharist, he tried to recall what he dreamt before the most recent incident.

Brother Anton passed him opposite with the body of Christ on his tongue and malice on his face. Tokto read the message clearly in his blood-shot eyes.

Shut the fuck up.

Later in the afternoon, brother Samuel ushered him to the newly installed *Divine Sacrifice* booth. The stainless-steel exterior stood out against the weathered stone walls. No one was happy with it being there. And no one was brave enough to climb into it. Desperate to ingratiate himself to his new family, Tokto volunteered.

It was donated by the Cardinal, who they privately despised, but who was responsible for the bulk of their funds.

The Cardinal had sworn by it. In no time at all, they would be available to the public in churches worldwide, he was sure.

The rosary is a medium through which we contemplate the mysteries . . . with the DS booth, our *minds* are the rosary bead.

Whatever that means.

In the past, novices tended to prove themselves with the broom. Now it's this.

He nodded to brother Samuel and placed his hand on the enclosure. His reflection warped on its convex exterior.

Holy Mary, mother of God . . . he began. He wanted to imagine himself as Shadrach, Meshach, and Abednego walking into fire with unshakable faith. Instead, he kept picturing photos of young people found mute with gaming glass on, pants soiled.

Inside was surprisingly pleasant. The monastery was one of the most peaceful spots on earth. The booth was anechoic by comparison. For a moment, he was in a fortress with his worries locked outside.

The apparatus and its wires dangled from the ceiling. It was covered in red felt with a golden embellishment of an ox, that most steadfast, resolute of animals.

Wires surrounding the gaming glass had a faint, eerie glow. He was a fish in a different bowl. He grew up being the weird, homeschooled kid who didn't even own gaming glass.

As the wires descended, he indulged in a pre-vow memory. He used to stare at the sunset from his roof, every evening of every summer. The time it took to disappear lengthened and shortened at the same rate, every year.

What accounted for this precision? Who could he thank for this gift? Tokto Harris was a boy fat with gratitude. He searched for ways to spend his life saying, "thank you, thank you, thank you," all day, every day. The Brotherhood of Aquinian Fulfillment found him, and recruited him.

He winced at the great surge of pressure on his temples. Gaming glass was supposed to be uncomfortable the first time. *I imagine*, he thought, *Jesus's crown of thorns wasn't the best part of his day either.*

He gave the command, "start," and the booth's interior sprang to life. It felt as though he were in a shower that abruptly turned freezing cold.

All remained black. He wondered how long the loading process would take.

Tokto's neurons floated motionless, like someone who forgot why they were doing what they were doing. Their axons broadened like body hair over gooseflesh. His countless dendrites quivered like blind worms.

From everywhere at once dripped an alien force. Like scorpion tails, the carriers of the gaming glass edged closer, beckoning Tokto to make port with them. Eventually, fear of atrophy overrode every other fear plaguing his nervous system, and the DS Booth struck pay dirt.

Flecks of shiny white light faded up from the black. Tokto realized he couldn't feel his body. It wasn't wholly unfamiliar; The Brotherhood of Aquinian Fulfillment was a mystical sect, equating the sensation of ecstasies with the grace of God. Maybe this would be interesting.

A familiar face materialized: it was Cardinal O'dell. He smiled his famous tight smile with one reflective tooth. Either he didn't know or didn't care how distracting and obnoxious it was.

"Greetings brother. I was introduced to the amazing journey you are about to take while at the Vatican in the summer of 2077. As a result, I immediately began a campaign to have more booths built and installed wherever possible.

"I know what you may be thinking: who is this man to suggest a piece of technology can strengthen my faith? Well, let me tell you, I will never suggest that anything less than the Almighty can know what is in your heart. Your mind, on the other hand—this is something that we can now hold a mirror to.

"This device allowed me to confront each of my thoughts that didn't serve the Lord. It allowed me to find, in other words, the right hand that caused me to stumble. When you exit this booth, I urge you to toss those thoughts into the fire. For it is better to discard one part of you now than to lose the entirety of yourself to the pit.

"In this booth, you will test your faith and expose your truest inner thoughts to only yourself and Him. Under no circumstance will there be any record of your experience. It was designed with the confessional in mind in order that you might have just this assurance.

"In their final moments, the blessed saints were awarded proof that their faith had transcended their weak, human states. In that moment, they saw the trivial aspects of their lives for what they were. Their experiences are frightening and will be very challenging for you.

"Good luck and congratulations. May all of God's children soon have the opportunity to see what you are about to see."

The last visible monad of light, before the Cardinal returned to the void, was his tooth. The tooth was a sign to many of the brothers that the Cardinal always had one foot in the secular world.

An intense heat bore down on his neck. Then his wrists. He was bound, he thought.

"Are these shackles?"

There was still nothing to see other than blackness. A minute went by. The machine was clearly malfunctioning. It became difficult to breathe.

"Help!" he screamed.

The Cardinal's voice echoed in his mind— ". . . soundproof. . ." ". . . no record . . ." ". . . under no circumstance . . ." ". . . NO CIRCUMSTANCE. . ."

"Somebody get me out!"

He tried to focus on banging his head against the wall of the booth. But he was completely cut off from his motor functions.

"Get me out for . . . for fudd's sake!"

Suddenly the hood was pulled off his head. He was staring down a stone tunnel leading to a blazing white exit. The floor was dusty, evaporating sand.

"Your turn now, Christian!"

He had embarrassed himself in front of a muscular man wearing a loincloth and leather mask. He smelled sweat and carrion. At least he knew he wasn't stuck in a defective machine.

A bubble of text appeared next to his torturer's buttocks: *ROME, 107 AD.*

"I'm Saint Ignatius of Antioch," Tokto deduced.

Right on cue, the music began in his temples. It was meant to build tension, he decided. Probably to match the sound of jubilance emanating from outside the hole.

"Great. That means I'm about to be eaten by lions."

He wondered in a panic if his musings were in dereliction of his vow. He was essentially thinking about speaking, or speaking in an induced lucid dream.

The man was returning to him, growing larger each second.

"Come on, boy! Let's see this salvation you've been going on about!"

"You really wouldn't be speaking English in this time period."

"Shut your mouth, dead man!"

An intense pain ripped through his legs and back as the man pulled his chains. He was hogtied. He could smell the rust on his wrist shackle. The booth really was an impressive piece of technology.

Tokto's face distorted as his genitals scraped in the sand. The light from outside rose with the heat and enveloped him. In a moment, he was the center of attention to thousands. The man clicked off his shackles and returned to his lair.

Tokto stood and admired the intricacies of the creation. Each audience member was distinct. He wondered if they had back stories.

A man in a throne sat surrounded by a garrison of centurion. Tokto squinted and read the Latin on the banners.

"Hmmm, actually it's disputed whether Ignatius was in fact martyred during the reign of Trajan."

Emperor Trajan squinted back, perhaps to read his lips. Tokto suddenly became very self-conscious. His palms began to sweat.

With the wave of the Emperor's hand, half a dozen lions appeared from six separate tunnels. And just like that, his stage fright vanished.

For a moment, he was ten years old again, under his duvet with a flashlight, perusing clips of *Home Safari*.

They were beautiful animals. He was transfixed. Then two of them stopped dead in their tracks.

"What?"

The breath leapt out of his lungs as his head sprung forward into the dirt. Searing pain emerged from his shoulder. The alpha had jumped him from behind. The meal had begun.

Tokto tried to control his breathing. Short breaths. One. Two-in-one. One.

The music built to a jazzy plateau, shooting all over his body. His lungs jolted with each inhale.

He focused on counting his breaths.

Exuberance lit the coliseum. The man in the throne laughed. If Tokto weren't being pulled in several directions at once, he'd be inclined to take a bow.

The pain was impressive; ten times greater than any pain he'd ever felt. He assumed pain this great would send him into shock. But without the possibility of death, what is pain? He realized he could suffer anything in this booth. He perfunctorily connected the sound of tearing leather to his body. "No." ... his *avatar*.

Minutes went by. How long could this go on? How long does it take for one human to die? He assigned the cats names to pass the time. One of the lions trotted away, tired.

"Rebecca's full."

He glanced toward the hole he emerged from. There was a line of hooded men and women he assumed were the followers of Ignatius. His heart broke; they were *his* followers, after all.

The man who taunted him now berated the next in line. He perked his ears to eavesdrop. The man was having fun with his followers.

"Heh-uhh!"

Tokto tried to yell but the air flew out of holes in his neck. Red strings flew from his mouth. A lion began licking at it. He pushed it aside.

Move, Cinnamon. Cinnamon was a tabby cat he had as a child. They had the same eyes.

The man removed the victim's hood. It was a woman. Her brown eyes were wild and defiant. She screamed praises to the sky though the tunnel's stone ceiling. For a moment, it was her own space. The whole circus of the coliseum was an ignorant mass, orbiting her power. The last of her mortal breath passed her lips and she locked eyes with Tokto. The man shook his head and piped up: "Your turn now, Christian!"

Black. It was instant. This was wrong. He didn't know much about gaming but he knew this wasn't supposed to happen. Touch wasn't like other senses: you can't just bring it to a maximum then take everything away. It's too jarring.

"That's what this is."

He heard his voice but couldn't feel the wind hit his throat. He felt ill. A fever sawed down the two hemispheres of his brain. He felt his hairs stand on end, as though they were searching for the stimulation that suddenly disappeared.

The machine may be digital but the body's mechanism for dealing with pain is a gear and pulley system. It was dangerous to stop the presses suddenly, he knew that.

He still felt the tactile music. Or was it just the memory of it, still fading?

He didn't think he'd have the strength to endure the next scenario. He wondered what could possibly be next. Ignatius's martyrdom was gruesome. But history was written in cruelty: St. Lawrence was roasted alive, St. Bartholomew was skinned. Maybe he'd luck out and get a nice beheading. He needed a breather.

White. Dust. Stone. Now. It all hit him.

The next scenario didn't fade in as it was supposed to. Another shock to his system. Something was definitely wrong here. He needed to get out. He didn't care if Brother Samuel would be disappointed. He didn't care if the Cardinal himself found out about it.

As soon as this scenario ended, he decided, he'd shout *Exit!* and that would be that. He'd write a scathing report. These machines are not ready.

A familiar bum jiggled in front of him. *ROME, 107 AD.*

"Oh, for fudd's sake."

Did he do this? Did he command *RESTART* in the black interim? He tried to remember what happened five seconds ago. He couldn't distinguish between sense and memory. The music played discordantly. He realized that the old score was still playing while the notes in his temples started up again.

The man strode toward and reached behind him. He braced himself.

"Come on, boy! Let's see this salvation you've been going on about!"

"Listen, this is a mistake. I'm not supposed to be here anymore."

"Hahaha! Shut your mouth, dead man!"

He was deposited in the same spot as last time. Trajan looked on from his gaudy throne.

He was done pleading. He had to find a way out of this thing. He didn't know if he had the strength to wait for the end of the scenario. With each passing second, he was taking in brain damage.

He thought of an older boy in the neighborhood he grew up in. He'd once taken a psychedelic drug and was forever trapped in that experience. He sat, always, prostrate over himself, on a swing in the park, heavily subdued with counter-drugs. It was *his* swing. Nobody came near him.

No. Here. Now.

There was a flaw in the scenario. He was sure. Something had caused this storm. He wanted to take stock of the damage. *Do I still remember my middle name? My banking password? My parents' names?*

No. Stop. He was wasting time.

"I need to escape."

He ran toward a wall. Moving his legs was a challenge. He had to think through each step.

A man was impaled on a spike that separated the pit from the audience, feet dangling.

"There."

He stumbled forward. The crowd read his intentions. His torturer looked at him with confusion and pity.

"Three, two, one!"

He leapt a moment earlier than he intended. He caught the body by the legs and there he swung, a grisly pendulum. He looked down and saw he was only inches above the ground. Laughter rang through the coliseum.

"Yeah, whatever."

He heard the roar of the lions behind him.

Climb, dammit. He placed a hand on the dead man's shoulders, pulled his legs up and straddled the waist. Just in time. A lion was chomping at the corpse's feet.

He breathed and opened his eyes. He was face-to-face with the dead man. He had a dark complexion, like himself. But his body was muscular and covered in scars; most likely a gladiator.

Errup!

"Crap."

He felt himself and the corpse drop. The hole in its sternum widened. His weight, and the force of the lions, were getting to be too much. The crowd's excitement grew. *Climb faster.*

He moved his body like a drunk primate. He felt his feet scrape the body's face. He remembered, in flashes, crawling up his father's body to get to a top bunk.

He brought both feet to rest on top of its shoulders and slowly raised himself. He told himself not to think about his impressive balance, lest it suddenly be lost. He raised his head and revealed to himself the angry faces of the front row.

As he leapt, he felt the weight of the body slip away underneath. Two sets of frenzied blue eyes regarded him, arms outstretched. *Are they going to catch me?*

He felt fabric under his feet. Fingers dug into each of his shoulders.

"Thank you." He looked to the man and woman who had a hold of him. It was a relief to find an ally in this unlikely place.

"Thank you so much."

He thought of the righteous thief on the cross next to Jesus. And then he saw something suspicious in the woman's expression.

"Errrohaaa!"

The scream left her lungs and hit his face with sulfurous wind. He'd never seen anyone so angry at anyone. He was launched backward.

He watched them fade away, satisfied with themselves. *Okay.*

He no longer minded being torn apart by lions.

It started on the top of his head this time. One of the cats— *oh that's Rebecca again* (he knew by the tail)—attempted to bite through his skull. She writhed her teeth, frustrated she was getting nowhere closer to the coconut's fruit.

He got to his knees and heard a gasp from the audience. The couple who tossed him stood, mouths wide.

He reached above his head and felt a mohawk of flesh.

"Oh this? Yeah, don't worry about me!"

He turned, searching for the alpha. Cinnamon was pivoting. Their eyes locked. Tokto approached him with the flesh of his neck exposed. The sooner he died, the sooner he'd get to the end of the scenario and end the program.

"C'mon, Cinnamon. C'mon, boy. Got a treat for ya."

Cinnamon went out of focus as he saw the brown-eyed woman's hood being removed. Her same compelling expression broke through the scene.

From her example, one could take a thousand life lessons.

Cinnamon's breathing filled his ears. He was close enough to pet him, if he wanted to.

"C'mon, stupid!" He was actually placing his neck in the cat's jaws and nothing was happening. The program's designers clearly did not plan for this eventuality.

Huhhhhh, Huhhhhh . . . Cinnamon's breath was a comforting sound once he closed his eyes. He felt motion in the jaws. Finally, it was happening. Through the roof of white noise pierced a voice in the distance.

"Your turn now, Christian!"

Wait. A sinking feeling filled his body, blunting the force of teeth through his jugular.

Black.

He was back. But he couldn't get the command past his lungs. *EXIT!* he thought as loud as he could. He could see the words hazily, as though they were beyond the surface of water he was drowning in. He kicked his legs and felt himself sinking lower. *EXIT, God please, EXIT.*

Light. Dust. Sensation. *ROME, 107.*

Oh God, the pain. The music stabbed his nerves sporadically at every point in his body. Someone had started three separate record players, all at different points in a given symphony and set them loose on his sanity. It was an angry acid jazz.

Hands reached behind him and pulled. He saw himself as a spider being yanked back by its own thread. Light and noise played beach volleyball with his brain. A familiar face focused itself in the careening visions: a man with gold leaf around his head.

"I know who you are."

The words dribbled lazily past his lips. Parts of his mind were becoming usable again. He needed to take advantage while he could. He was certain if he endured the scenario again only to be jolted back into nothingness, it would kill him.

"At least we have one less mouth to feed," brother Anton would no doubt scribble on his notepad. "At least none of us have to take a turn in that contraption."

. . . a turn. . .

He felt this could be the last epiphany of his life. And his life depended on it.

Your turn now, Christian!

He turned his head and saw the torturer dragging the next hooded victim (*the woman*, he remembered) to the area of his re-spawning.

That was it. That was the loop. What little he knew about contemporary gaming was made up for by the elementary computer science in his homeschooling. The actions following the torturer's line were dependent on the line itself. Because Tokto paid close enough attention to the woman to hear the line repeated to her, it created an unintended for-loop.

Perhaps the designers themselves hadn't considered that Tokto's empathy might drive his attention to the next victim. A program made to bring one closer to the Lord was made by those who had no faith in humanity.

"Figures."

He got to his feet and told each of his limbs to make a forward motion of some sort. He drove his body toward the torturer.

It was even harder than the last time. He looked ridiculous; upper body dangling like a squid.

The masked man realized Tokto was running toward him. Tokto managed to throw him a fisticuffs gesture. The man accepted the challenge. Tokto ducked and tackled him around the belly. The man's girth was like hitting a brick wall.

"What is this? What possesses you now, Christian?"

He had just started his first fight in his life.

He began swinging haymakers—one, another. Some connected, some barely missed. The crowd outside howled their disappointment, the main event of the afternoon had retreated back into the tunnel.

Laughter rebounded from the man's mouth. The staccato clang momentarily ran in sync with the music. The effect was paralyzing. Tokto realized that the man was laughing because he was having no effect; even the strikes that landed were mere taps. He was past the point of no return.

He sat back on his feet and allowed his torturer to push him to the ground. The man stepped over him, laughing all the while. He stood, blocking the light from the tunnel, and placed his paw on the woman's hood. He was haloed by the light outside.

This was it. This was where the loop began again. He thought for a moment if he could plug his ears he'd be able to block the sound and break the loop. But he couldn't get either arm passed a ninety-degree angle.

"Lord, look out for my brothers. Look out for my family."

He used to spend hours crafting the perfect last words. He realized now that the trick was simply to live righteously. One's deeds were the best last words.

The man tore the hood from the woman. She found Tokto with her eyes.

"And bless this woman. This woman of mystery who although is artificial possesses enough faith to—"

The torturer yelped and let go of the woman. As she fell forward, Tokto saw the source of the man's distress. He was being mauled by two golden limbs that gave way to a fiery mane.

"Cinnamon!"

The pussycat looked up for a moment and blinked. The torturer's words gargled on blood. Tokto thought he heard construction paper being torn in half.

Cinnamon paraded proudly with half the torturer's neck in its jaws. The coliseum floor was a Jackson Pollack canvas.

"Good boy!"

Even the crowd approved. Perhaps they couldn't tell whose neck it was.

It was safe to end it now. He got on all fours. Walking had become too confusing. The nonsensical music was bizarrely pleasing. With safety in place, every sensation became a miracle.

He managed to genuflect as he passed the woman and recited a blessing, placing a hand on her forehead.

The warm Roman air was wonderful. The gorgeous golden beasts were all laying, panting. One was licking Rebecca behind the ears. Finally, he was noticed. Cinnamon dropped the sopping gore and trotted over to him.

He closed his eyes and indulged in the first memory that surfaced. He was fourteen and he had just buried the original Cinnamon in the backyard. Its tiny body was curled into itself. He put it in an appliance box and covered it with stones.

He walked up to the bedroom he and his sister shared and sat on the bottom bunk. He wondered if animals had souls. He decided he wouldn't bother asking his parents. He'd keep this question for himself. Perhaps forever—

"EXIT."

The Cardinal faded into view before him.

"Brother, you completed only one of the scenarios, are you sure you wish to—"

"EXIT!"

He was panting. His lungs radiated rage.

As the probes rescinded, Tokto's neurotransmitters resembled a swimming pool following an earthquake.

It was possible he would survive.

For a moment, he thought the darkness might last forever. He had his real body back but it didn't feel quite right. The door slid ajar, granting a dank light to stick its foot in.

He tried to take a step and tumbled forward. Brother Samuel caught him.

Panic and confusion flushed Samuel's face. He peered down at his wristwatch. He had been inside for five minutes. The session was meant to be a half hour.

"Nooo!"

Rooms away, he heard a glass break. His vow of silence lasted fifteen days and two hours.

"Don't go . . . into that!" Using Brother Samuel as a crutch, he spun around and pointed to the booth.

"It's danger . . . danger . . . it—is—a danger."

Brother Anton was the first to appear, mouth full of fried chicken, shaking his head.

Tokto remembered the eyes of his torturer, the woman, Cinnamon. Using momentum from his torso, he swung an arm and struck Anton in the mouth, sending meat to the floor.

"Shut the f-f-fudd up, Brother Anton!"

He wished he'd come up with something cooler to say. But the slap was enough. Anton would never bully him again.

He was rushed to the hospital where he faced a number of repairs.

After a month of physiotherapy, his motor functions had returned to 95%. He was lucky.

The Cardinal attempted to visit but Tokto refused to see him.

His damaged long-term memories didn't return to him as they had been. When he was silent and still, they would descend upon him as though found in a dense fog. He experienced them, it seemed, for the first time.

The memories of the coliseum were indistinguishable from his own. It would take many more months of synaptic treatments to make Tokto himself again.

One morning, an elderly patient who had occupied the bed next to his was ushered to the morgue.

He left behind a stuffed lion with white, cartoonish eyes. Tokto turned his head and concentrated on the beads of rainwater on the window. Each drop distorted the view of the clouds behind them.

But then again, so does the window, he thought. *And so do the shape of my corneas.* He closed his eyes and imagined what it would take to see the clouds, or anything, as they really are. That mystery alone, he decided, was profound enough to keep him busy for the rest of his life.

He thought of the clouds in his memory of the blue sky above the coliseum. They were sharper by comparison. He wondered, almost aloud, if he saw things closer to their truest form while in the booth. He shuddered at the thought.

He wasn't sure if he'd ever return to being Brother Tokto. For now, he wanted to remember what it meant to be Tokto Harris.

He thought of everyone in the course of history who lived and died nameless, forgotten.

An obscure memory of a woman with brown eyes carried him to sleep and soothed him. He'd sort out when and where he remembered her from in the morning. As a last comforting thought, he decided he would meet her again someday. They would meet and he would listen to her. And he would never look away from her.

FLYING MACHINE
By Max D. Stanton

An enemy cetadreadnaught spotted me as I was passing through a planetary system somewhere in Ursa Major. The titanic beast was waiting in ambush on the far side of an icy moon, a deep space picket against my bombing run. It might have been waiting for thousands of years. My crystal antennae sensed my adversary's presence the moment it moved from its hiding spot. A low, eerie keening echoed in my thoughts. The cetadreadnaught's London-sized brain was bringing its psychokinetic artillery to bear. Enormous hunks of the ice moon tore themselves free of the surface and hurtled towards me, shattering into fragments as they passed out of the thin atmosphere. I was flying into a storm of mind-propelled flak.

I cut to the left and punched my thrusters as hard as I dared within a gravity well, dodging the lethal cloud by the tiniest of margins. Another psychic groan sounded and the moon quaked as the cetadreadnaught prepared its second volley. At that same moment, my enemy opened its massive jaws and launched its fighter escort. A swarm of metal wasps.

I knew that if I fought in the open I'd be cut to pieces. Dodging a hail of brilliantly-colored fire from the fighters, I cut to the right, diving directly towards the small, rocky planet that the ice moon orbited, and slipped into the planet's orbit, letting it carry me along as if I were swimming with a stream's current. The cetadreadnaught's second volley missed the mark and exploded on the planet's night-shrouded half while I was circling around to its daytime. Vast black clouds billowed across the surface underneath me, and volcanic eruptions burst like machine-gun shells as celestial bombardment shivered the planetary core. I'm almost certain that I glimpsed cities falling in that apocalypse.

As I returned to the daylit side of the world I used the momentum I'd built to slingshot myself directly towards the cetadreadnaught at incredible speed, moving too quickly for its artillery to track or its escorts to intercept. I passed directly beneath the whale-thing's white belly and slashed a deep trench into it with my cutter beam. A waterfall of bright orange blood poured out of the wound, turning into a gaily-colored snowfall when it hit the vacuum's cold. The fighters pursued me for as long as they could, which wasn't lengthy. The cetadreadnaught, however, kept on my tail long after it died. I still felt its psychic death screams echoing inside me as I passed out of the star system. Pain. Confusion. Bewilderment. Things I thought I'd long since left behind.

Needless to say, the experience was a profound shock to my system. My thoughts wandered from my mission, and I found myself doing something that I had not done in a very long time. I began to remember.

I don't recall my name anymore, but I was a Major in the No. 3 Squadron of the Royal Flying Corps before the slimy angels came for me.

It began on a routine enough flight, a reconnaissance mission over Loos sighting Hun artillery positions. The German gunners had been feeding our boys a fearful portion of iron rations, and we were very keen to treat them to some of the same. I was piloting a Morane biplane, with Captain Donnely in the observer's seat.

Donnely was a good man. He'd had the benefit of a public-school education and helped me write love letters to my Emily, cribbing from Shakespeare and Yeats and donating some verse of his own creation as well. He had a wonderful talent for it. If not for the war I think he might have become a poet.

The day had started out clear and sunny, but during our flight the sky went black as suddenly as if someone had kicked an oilcan over in Heaven. The atmosphere was charged with the electric, oppressive stillness that builds up when a hell of a storm is brewing.

"I'm turning back," I told Donnely. "Today's no day for flying."

"You're just impatient to answer your lady-love's last letter," Donnely said playfully. "It's bad enough you keep her photograph in your cockpit. You've got to learn to focus. Or come with me to Paris next time we get some leave."

I glanced down to above my fuel gauge, where Emily's face beamed up at me. "The photograph's good luck, and you can keep your poxy Paris girls! I'll invite you to the wedding after the Kaiser's dead. You can meet my whole family. They won't believe I know how to fly unless I bring a witness."

"Hold on," Donnely said. "We've got company."

I turned and saw a Fokker creeping up from around 2,000 yards range, and overhauling us fast. Apparently this one was itching for a fight, for the Huns rarely went up in bad weather. As the German reached 200 yards Donnely took aim with his Lewis gun and fired—alas!—it jammed on the second round. The Fokker returned fire and I went into a dive, while Donnely swore at his Lewis and laboured to clear it. If curses were bullets he'd have blasted our enemy clear out of the sky.

The Fokker stayed on our tail throughout the dive and came abreast of us as we leveled out. I could see every detail of the enemy machine as it passed by—its undercarriage, the wires along its wings, even the scowl on its pilot's face. He flew ahead of us and cut right, presumably for another pass.

"Is that damn Lewis gun cleared yet?" I shouted to Donnely.

"It's good!" he replied. "Where's the Hun?"

The enemy had vanished. He wasn't behind us, or above us, or anyplace else within my line of sight. The inky clouds were eclipsing the sun, but visibility wasn't so bad yet that one might lose sight of an enemy who'd just been within spitting range. I began to get nervous, for the very worst thing one can do in a dogfight is lose track of one's opponent.

"Look at that!" Donnely shrieked, pointing his gun upwards. "God's wounds, look at—"

There was a flash of purple light. That's the last thing I remember of that day.

I woke up in a field hospital near the front, naked apart from a rough blanket. I was told that some doughboys had found me wandering nude through a barley field, singing some gibberish even queerer than Flemish. At first they figured me a shell-shock case, and they didn't even know I was an aviator till I came to and started talking.

They never found the wreckage of my machine. They found the wreck of Donnely, though, in a bog a few miles away from where they found me. The doctor went grey when I asked about him, and any front-line doctor will have seen some terrible sights.

Against doctor's orders I went to the morgue tent to say my goodbyes. Beneath the winding sheet, Donnely looked like a man-shaped candle that had been partially melted. His bones and organs showed through gaping holes in his side. His skin was still white, however, without even a touch of charring, and as far as I could tell he hadn't shed a drop of blood. Whatever had happened to my comrade, judging from the agonized expression on his drooping, boneless face, it looked as if he had felt it intensely. Apparently he had still been breathing when they brought him in.

The incident was written up as a lightning strike. Donnely and I both got medals. He went into a graveyard and I went back to the No. 3 Squadron. Queer as it was, I just couldn't wait to fly again.

By the time I'd returned to active duty the squadron had gotten a shipment of Sopwith Camels. The Camel was an extraordinary machine, demanding a lot of its pilot and giving even more in return. Getting behind its controls was positively invigorating. When I returned from the hospital I was so pale and underweight that a new officer in the unit thought I'd been held as a prisoner of war. My gait had turned into a shuffle and my voice had developed a stammer. But behind my Camel's stick, I was a hale and ferocious predator. I made twelve confirmed kills in my first month back in the sky. This made me quite the lion around the aerodrome for a week or two, until at the Battle of Messines I shredded a downed German beneath his parachute. Most of my comrades thought that this was a vicious outrage, and I myself would have agreed with them before the crash. They kept a happy distance after that, much to my relief. Ever since that fatal flight over Loos, their company had become nearly intolerable.

Then there was the matter of Emily's letters. I came back from the hospital to a thick sheaf of them, which I regarded with the same pleasure and anticipation as correspondence from a creditor. Before the crash Emily's mail had always been welcome, indeed, one of the few delights available to me on the front. Now reading them was a chore, and responding a draining confusion. Once I spent all night awake in the barracks composing a reply, and in the morning all I had was a long-winded description of an improvement I'd like to make to the Camel's fuel tank to improve its balance on takeoff. Emily sent another photograph to replace the one lost in the crash. I never even considered putting it above my fuel gauge for luck—by then, the notion of burdening my machine with even a photograph's worth of unnecessary weight seemed perverse and absurd. Eventually her letters stopped coming. I tried for days to make myself unhappy about this, with no success.

One day I was flying over enemy lines when I spotted a German observation balloon floating out in the distance. While I had already made a kill that day, and was low on fuel and bullets to boot, the sight of the blimp bobbing clumsily in the wind triggered my murderous instincts and my machine was off in pursuit before the conscious part of my mind even realized what I was doing. My observer—I forget his name, too—shouted in protest behind me. I pushed the engines harder to drown out his yells.

In the trenches below, a battery of German anti-aircraft gunners took aim. White blossoms of cordite and shrapnel exploded all around me like popcorn in the pan, one of them bursting close enough to rattle my machine and set my left ear ringing and maim the observer with shrapnel. I ignored the danger and pressed on with the attack. I raked the blimp with a long burst from my propeller-mounted Vickers guns, shot past the enemy, and pulled an Immelmann turn to make another pass. A cold shadow fell on me, and then there was a blast that made me feel like every atom of my being was coming apart. My final thought was a bright, triumphant exultation that I'd hit my target.

I awoke naked on a slab of basalt. I was not visibly fettered, but some force secured my limbs to the rock as if by magnetism. A light that was not light shone down mercilessly from a beacon fixed directly above me. In its uncanny glow I saw clear through my own skin to the muscle and bone and viscera beneath. Not many men can say they've seen themselves flayed. I stared at my blood as it coursed through my veins, and as my horror mounted I watched the pace of my own heartbeat increase.

Something moist and rubbery brushed my cheek, pulling me away from the contemplation of my own guts, and I realized that I was not alone. Three magnificent creatures were present at my bedside, each of them coated in thick, viscous grease that glistened in the chamber's penetrating light. Imagine a tub of eels moving under the control of a single mind, a mind of exquisite intelligence and self-control. They also sported leathery, bat-like wings in addition to their coils—apparently these creatures were aviators like myself. At first I was too astonished and perplexed to even be afraid, and for a very long time we simply stared at each other. Perhaps the fascinated revulsion that I felt was mutual.

One of the winged creatures thrust a tentacle into my mouth—it tasted of brine and copper—and I gagged and struggled helplessly as the wormy thing slowly forced its way down my throat and deep into my chest. I thought I would suffocate but my chest kept rising and falling, and I realized that the creature was breathing for me. I could see its limb pulsing inside my chest, making my lungs inflate and deflate. Two more tentacles danced inches in front of my eyes. They ended in sucking mouths rimmed with dozens of tiny, needle-like teeth, like the mouths of lampreys, and I'd have screamed if not for the fleshy tube in my windpipe.

The mouths moved in and my world went black, which was almost worse than seeing what was happening to me. My eyes prickled as the lamprey teeth closed on them, and then my monstrous surgeon began to suck.

The last sensation I experienced before losing consciousness—besides an astoundingly intense and varied agony—was the sound of a wet, glottal, rhythmic clicking. I think that was the creatures' laughter.

My awakening was a gradual series of still images, like a magic lantern show.

I saw a formation of spiky crystals glowing and humming inside a darkened chamber.

I saw a clear blue sky with a German Albatross passing through it.

I saw the dim interior of an ambulance loaded with dead and dying men. Delicate beams of light shone through a row of bullet-holes in the vehicle's side.

I saw a yellow, flyblown plaster wall streaked with grease.

I saw a dead boy in an adjacent bed.

I saw a man with no face crouching at my side, like a manikin from a department store window given some hideous parody of life. He wore a white coat spattered with blood.

"It's all right," the faceless thing said. Its voice was a faint, mechanical hiss, like somebody had made a phonograph recording off of another phonograph recording. "You're safe. You're at a military hospital. Your airplane crashed. Do you remember?" When the creature sat on my bedside, giddiness overcame me, and I slipped back into oblivion.

When I awoke, I was alone in my room. I rose and staggered to the mirror, but when I looked at myself, I saw only a pink, empty blur. I ran my fingers across the space where I knew my features should be. I could still feel eyes, a nose, a mouth, seemingly undamaged beneath my fingertips even though they were invisible in the glass. There was no pain. No physical pain, anyway. But I could not perceive my own features anymore. I could not even remember what they looked like.

I tried to recall the faces of other people that I used to know. My father. My mother. My sister. Emily. Donnely. Nothing. At most I called up a vague but frustrated recollection, like when you try to remember the words to some old song and they're on the tip of your tongue but won't come any further.

I groped deeper into my memories and realized that more than just faces were gone. I couldn't remember any of my Christmas mornings, or how my mother's cooking used to taste. I wasn't positive that I'd ever had a mother. I couldn't remember the first time I'd kissed Emily, or indeed, if I'd ever kissed her at all. Everything I'd gone to war to defend was lost to me. In the mirror, fat droplets of water beaded and slipped down the blank space where my face had been. That was the last time I ever cried.

But at least I still recalled how to swing a propeller, and how a Camel turns faster to the right than to the left, and how good it felt to shoot that German under his parachute. As I returned to my bed, I consoled myself with the notion that even if I had lost everything that I was, at least I seemed to be becoming something else.

Empty-faced doctor-puppets and nurse-puppets intruded on me throughout the day, poking and prodding and shining lights. I endured them as best I could, even though they reminded me of the operating chamber where I'd been obliterated. When I had peace from those white-robed monsters I lay in bed and stared at the peeling paint on the ceiling and thought about what to do next. It was easy to decide. I kept staring at the ceiling until late into the night, after the other puppets would mostly be asleep, and then I knotted my bedclothes into a rope and climbed out the window and ran.

My bare feet were weeping blood by the time I got out of town. I was almost ready to fall down at the roadside and die when I heard the chuffing of a struggling motor from up ahead. I forced myself onwards, and found a faceless thing in khaki fighting with a motorbike engine. It had a mail sack with it, so I guessed it to be a courier. It didn't particularly matter what it was. All that counted was that it had a bike and clothes that could get me where I needed to go. When it saw me coming it waved and buzzed a greeting at me. I caught it by surprise and strangled it, then stripped it of its uniform and hid its body and mail pouch in the reeds at the side of the road.

Fixing the bike was easy and I rode all night and most of the following day without stopping, pushing the engine as hard as it would bear. It wasn't as satisfying as being airborne, but anything's better than going on foot like an animal. The motorbike's gas tank eventually ran dry. I flagged down the next vehicle to roll past—a fuel lorry—and blew the driver's brains out with a pistol I'd taken off the courier.

Even though I couldn't remember what my own face looked like my sense of direction was still clear and sharp, and I made it to the Saint-Omer aerodrome early in the morning. It had been almost 48 hours since I'd come to in the hospital, yet I didn't feel sleepy at all. Quite the opposite. My senses buzzed with an electric intensity, as if all the things I'd lost the capacity to perceive had freed up mental horsepower for the tasks that still mattered. The day was so cold and crisp it felt like the air itself had turned to razors. Some cloud cover but good visibility. Steady barometric pressure, light southwesterly winds. Good day for a flight.

A fuel lorry is no unusual sight at an airfield, not even early in the morning, and I made it past the guard hut without complications, then abandoned the lorry and made for the hangars, reaching them without being seen. I chose a Sopwith and took her up. As I lifted off, I heard some excited buzzing and a few scattered gunshots. I suppose that by that point somebody had noticed the lorry driver stealing a biplane. It didn't matter, I couldn't be bothered with that noise at the moment of my ascension. By the time they got pursuers airborne I'd already be gone. I didn't know exactly what I was pursuing myself, but I felt that it was very near. I pulled back on the stick and ascended as sharply as my Camel could handle without stalling, coaxing all the power I could muster out of her Clerget engines.

They were waiting for me when I passed through the clouds. I caught a glimpse of a gleaming black sphere floating above me like an obsidian sun and then everything flashed and I was in the operating theater once more, naked and spread eagled and trembling with joyous anticipation. As the winged creatures closed in around me and caressed me, I finally saw them for what they are. Angels. Slimy angels from another world.

At this final surgery, the angels removed my brain from my body entirely, and put it into a magnificent machine that I still barely comprehend even though I am a part of it. They aimed me towards a target a billion miles distant and fired me off at speeds beyond reckoning. My destination is a star orbited by a dozen populated worlds. When I penetrate the heart of that star the payload of my machine will explode and the star will flare. I will burn an entire civilization of strange beings to cinders in one glorious phoenix blast.

I've flown so far and learned so much. Now I know that Britannia and the Reich are as puny and meaningless as two anthills warring at the bottom of a bomb crater. Once you've seen sentient death engines wiping whole worlds clean of life, one sees all that talk about "war to end all wars" as the pompous rubbish that it is. I fly through an infinite panorama of cosmic violence, a weapon in a conflict that has raged since my first ancestors oozed forth from the slime.

It is hard to gauge the passage of time when one does not eat or sleep or breathe, and when the stars flash by in strobes rather than slowly revolving from day to night. There are clocks of sorts in the angels' machine but they tell time so differently than humans do. I am reasonably sure that if the human race still exists at all, the bones of everyone I used to know have long since turned to dust. Men plan their sorties in terms of hours; the angels plan theirs in terms of aeons.

I do not know why this war is being fought—I doubt that I could understand its cause any more than those two enemy anthills could understand "making the world safe for democracy." Perhaps there is no reason why. Perhaps the war is its own reason. I do not even know who or what the enemy is. But I fly, and I fight, and I am happy now.

THE SCARECROW PARADE
By Kurt Newton

Libby put the finishing touches on her gallicrow and stepped back to admire her creation. The gallicrow stood on a makeshift stand, head tilted to one side. It wore a grown man's pants and shirt that Libby found in a trunk in the attic of the orphanage. These were stuffed with straw, provided by Mr. Ellis. Mr. Ellis had also helped her with the gallicrow's adornments: a pair of swimming goggles (one eye missing); an assortment of metal hinges, hooks, and glass baubles, which she had aligned in rows on its shirt lapel; and, finally, the door knobs and tin cans that hung from its belt and hip pockets. Libby had even added sprigs of evergreen and dogwood stuffed in button holes and pockets to lend the look of camouflage. Her gallicrow looked every bit the war soldier.

Libby placed a finger between the top second and third button of her dress and found the place that opened her heart. She pushed her finger in. The sensation that followed was more ticklish than painful, like a prolonged static shock. She then took her finger, which was now enveloped with a bluish light, and pushed it into the chest of the gallicrow. The makeshift man trembled slightly, then straightened up. A bluish glow filled its broken goggles. Its head turned suddenly to stare at Libby. One of its straw-filled arms raised and Libby pressed it back down to its side. "Not yet," said Libby. "You stay put. I'll be back tomorrow." Libby eyed the gallicrow one last time before leaving the garden shed.

Outside, the sun was as warm as toast, the sky dotted with clouds as white as freshly laundered sheets. On the far side of the property, Libby spied Mr. Ellis standing on a ladder pruning one of the orphanage's many fruit trees. She waved to him and he waved back. Libby turned and ran directly into Becka.

"Watch where you're going!" said Becka. The tall, dark-haired girl stood with her hands on her hips. Her two friends, Alison and Jamie, flanked her with matching gazes.

"Sorry," mumbled Libby. She kept her eyes to the ground and went to pass, but the girls blocked her way.

"What were you doing in the garden shed?"

Libby glanced toward Mr. Ellis, who continued to snip branch after branch. "I was looking for a pair of shears for Nursemother," said Libby.

"Liar." Becka grinned. Her friends also grinned.

Libby glanced toward Mr. Ellis again. Mr. Ellis had stopped pruning, his attention now turned their way.

Becka held her hand to shield the sun, and gazed in the same direction as Libby. "You and Mr. Ellis have been awful chummy lately, haven't you?"

"No."

"Liar." Becka took a step forward. "Everyone's talking, you know." Her friends nodded. "Mr. Ellis is the gardener, but he's still a man, with man desires. It's so inappropriate. I wonder what Nursemother would think."

Libby looked Becka in the eye. "Mr. Ellis is my friend. He's kind to me. He's done nothing wrong!"

The three girls laughed. "My, so touchy," said Becka. Her smile faded, and she moved even closer. "Liar." She pushed Libby to the ground. Libby once again looked to Mr. Ellis. He had descended the ladder, and was now walking toward them in his oddly slow yet persistent manner. "Look, your boyfriend's coming," said Becka, and the three girls left before Mr. Ellis could confront them, their laughter lingering in the air.

"Libby, are you okay?"

Libby sat on the ground, brushing the dirt from her palms.

"Here, let me help you. . ." Mr. Ellis extended a hand. Libby grabbed it and pulled herself up. Mr. Ellis's hand was calloused from pruning and leathery to the touch. Though the look on his face never changed, Libby thought she saw concern swirling in the gardener's eyes.

"Thank you," she said, brushing the grass and leaves from her dress. She looked toward the shed. "It's finished."

Mr. Ellis smiled an invisible smile. But, again, concern showed through. "You should tell Nursemother. She will not be pleased that you kept your surprise from her."

Libby thought for a moment. Becka and her two friends stood in the distance picking flowers from one of Mr. Ellis's many stone gardens. "Maybe it would be best if Nursemother knew," she said. "Thank you, Mr. Ellis."

"My pleasure, Libby."

The East Overland Orphanage was just one of several orphanages in the district. It was once a private school for gifted children. That was before the wars and its temporary use as a makeshift field hospital. Many years had passed since those days. And like the landscape, it rolled and changed with the tides of time.

Libby found Nursemother Oddburrow in the kitchen counting supplies. Libby cleared her throat. She curtsied when Nursemother turned to address her. But before Libby could say a word, Nursemother beat her to it. "Libby! What happened to your dress?"

There was dirt on the hem from where Becka had pushed her down. "I'm sorry, Nursemother, I fell. It was clumsy of me."

"Please be more careful, that is the only dress you have."

"Yes, Nursemother, I will." Libby paused. "Nursemother?"

"Yes, child?"

"The Annual Butcher's County Callithumpian is tomorrow."

"Yes, and we're fortunate to have the procession pass right by us on its way into the city. We have a special day planned around the event, so I want you and the girls to be on your best behavior."

"Yes, Nursemother." Libby paused again, lingering. "Nursemother?"

"What is it, child?" Nursemother Oddburrow's patience was as short as her eyebrows were long.

"Would you be terribly upset if I told you that I wanted to enter."

Nursemother Oddburrow looked at her. At first the woman's eyes were stern, her brow creased, but then her face softened. "But you do not have the time, child. The procession is tomorrow."

"I've already made my entry. It's in the garden shed. Would you like to see it?"

That look of sternness was back on Nursemother's face. She didn't like secrets, but she also understood the lengths a child would go to have a family. She also had a certain admiration for industriousness.

Again, Nursemother Oddburrow's face softened. There was even a hint of a smile on the woman's features. "Yes, I would very much like to see this creation of yours, Libby."

Libby walked with Nursemother to the garden shed with her chest so full of pride she thought she might rise up into the air. She saw the other girls watching and even let loose an unaccustomed grin. But that grin quickly turned to a crease when she and Nursemother drew closer to the shed. The shed door had been left open a crack, and there were bits and pieces of cloth and straw on the ground before it. Libby rushed on ahead. When she opened the door, her fears were confirmed. The gallicrow's arms and legs had been torn from its body; its stuffing strewn about the garden shed. The decorations Libby had worked so hard to collect were scattered and broken. Nothing larger than a handkerchief could be salvaged. The gallicrow's head sat on the floor and she picked it up and cradled it in her arms. The goggles were gone but a faint blue light remained; she watched the light fade to nothingness.

When Libby exited the shed, the tears were still fresh on her cheeks. Nursemother came to her side and wrapped an arm around her shoulder. By then, most of the girls had gathered around; several had barely concealed grins of satisfaction on their faces—the three who had threatened Libby earlier. Libby pointed.

"They did it! They ruined him!"

Nursemother Oddburrow turned to Becka, Alison, and Jamie. "Did you three have anything to do with this?"

"No, Nursemother," they answered in unison.

"Liars!" shouted Libby.

"Libby!" Nursemother turned to her. "Unless you saw them yourself, or there is a witness here who will come forward? Or someone is willing to confess?" Nursemother glared at the girls who had gathered around, her eyes at last settling on the three girls Libby had accused. She let out an exasperated huff. "I thought not."

"But, Nursemother, they're lying." Tears flooded Libby's eyes again.

"Okay, everyone, get back to your chores!" Nursemother clapped her hands together and the girls dispersed. "I'm sorry, Libby." Nursemother returned to the orphanage.

Alone now, Libby crouched to pick up the remnants of the gallicrow. Her hands were full when the shadow of Mr. Ellis appeared.

"What happened, Libby?"

"He's ruined, Mr. Ellis. And there's no time to build another. All I wanted was a mother and a father to treat me as their own." Libby sobbed.

Mr. Ellis reached out to place his arm around her but hesitated. "You go inside, Libby. I'll take care of this."

"Okay." Libby walked away slowly. She stopped and turned. "Thank you, Mr. Ellis. You're my best friend."

Mr. Ellis nodded his head, his expression unchanged.

Libby entered the orphanage and climbed the stairs to her bed. It was still too early in the day to sleep. But she needed to lie down. She needed to cry some more.

The day of the Annual Butcher's County Callithumpian had arrived. It was a day that Libby had anticipated for weeks with each skip of her heart. It was to be her day to shine, to put her face out front of all the other faces in the orphanage. But it was now a day like any other. Nursemother Oddburrow woke the children with her usual "Rise and shine! Wipe the sleepies from your eyes! A new day hides for those to find! Get up, get up, it's morning time!" But Libby was no longer roused by the words Nursemother spoke. She had lost that hope of ever finding anything ever again. She no longer knew where to look.

As Nursemother had promised, she woke the children early. The procession would be passing by at noon on its way into the city. Nursemother needed to make sure all the children were fed and neatly dressed. She had assigned several of the girls to help with the baked goods—tea cookies and shortbreads. There were tables to set up by the roadside with water and snacks for the passersby. She believed spectators were just as important as those being spectated upon. Like two halves of a freshly cut grapefruit, one could not exist without the other.

Libby dressed mechanically. The last thing she wanted to do was watch a callithumpian that she herself could have entered. To see the dreams of others paraded by was just too hard to bear. But Nursemother required her attendance. As consolation, Nursemother gave her the very important duties of handing out water to the folks who would no doubt have a thirst to quell.

As noon approached, like clockwork, so too did the procession. The music was faint at first; snippets of drum and fife and trumpet drifted in and out on the breeze. But soon the music became a steady stream, and with it appeared the nose of the callithumpian. A marching band stomped and swayed, their bodies one with the music. This was followed by a stream of dignitaries sitting in open-topped hovercars accompanied by their assistants walking alongside, each dignitary waving to the gathered spectators, each smiling as if their smiles were painted on. This was followed by yet another marching band, smaller than the first. And this was followed, at last, by this year's collection of entrants. The gallicrows. Libby paused in her pouring long enough to look.

The gallicrows numbered nearly two dozen. Each walked under its own power, albeit tenuously. The gallicrows lurched and stumbled like a small army of dead soldiers resurrected for just one day. All were of similar quality, some more artistically decorated than others. Each possessed the faint blue light of its creator—the children from the other orphanages, who accompanied their creations like doting parents. Libby knew in her heart that hers would have been equal to the best of them. Water spilled over the edge of the cup she held and she righted it quickly. As she mopped the spill with a towel, there came a shout from one of the procession's walkers.

"Would you look at that!"

Heads turned, eyes aimed in the direction of the garden shed. Halfway to the road was Libby's gallicrow . . . walking under its own power. It looked unaccustomed to its newfound mobility, but it appeared to know exactly what it was doing and where it was going. Compared to the rest of the entries, Libby's gallicrow was the most lifelike.

"That is amazing!" proclaimed one of the dignitaries.

"Somebody put a lot of heart into that one," said another. "Whose entry is that?"

Libby was too stunned for words.

"Libby is the artist's name," said Nursemother Oddburrow, walking over to her, resting her hands on Libby's shoulders.

"Well, come along, Libby," said the first dignitary, obviously more exalted than the other dignitaries, because his words were quickly affirmed by nodding heads and calls of "here-here." "All entries and entrants join the callithumpian!"

Libby and her gallicrow joined the group and walked side by side for all to see, all the way into the city.

It was a whirlwind of a day for Libby. Not only was she able to enter the Annual Butcher's County Callithumpian, her gallicrow was selected the best overall. Adoptive parents were standing by for the winner, and they took Libby into their arms as if she were their own. Libby spent the night in the city getting to know her new parents. When morning came, they returned to the East Overland Orphanage to get Libby's things.

As Libby's belongings were stowed in her parents' hovercar, Libby sought out the gardens and the fruit trees. She even stood on her toes as if it might afford a better look. "Has anyone seen Mr. Ellis?" she said.

There were dumbfounded expressions all around, and daggers from the three girls who had tried to destroy Libby's gallicrow. Nursemother Oddburrow, with all the excitement of the last twenty-four hours, confessed she hadn't seen Mr. Ellis in two days.

Libby turned to her new parents. "I'll be right back," she said, and took off in a sprint toward the garden shed. She thought back to the last time she had talked to Mr. Ellis. "I'll take care of this," he had told her, his face firm as always but his voice carrying something she hadn't recognized at the time because she was so distraught. Hurt. Pain. A feeling adults like Mr. Ellis weren't supposed to express.

Libby's pace quickened as she reached the garden shed. Inside, she found Mr. Ellis slumped against the potting bench, where he'd probably sat after delivering his gift for Libby. He was now nothing more than a stone statue of his former self, his only blemish: the cavity in his chest where his heart had once resided.

Tears crawled down Libby's cheeks, both tears of sadness and tears of joy. She hugged Mr. Ellis for the first and last time, her tears leaving tiny streaks on the stone man's face. "My best friend," she said. "Thank you, Mr. Ellis. Thank you." She rose then and exited the garden shed, thinking how Mr. Ellis would likely be moved out to one of his many flower gardens to sit among the birds and butterflies.

By the time Libby reached her new parents she was nearly skipping. "I'm ready to go home now," she said.

TEMPEST
By Leigh Green

The dark arena was suffocating. Maris could hear the battle just around the corner and growing nearer. She backed down the alley and crouched as she reloaded her weapon.

"I can't breathe."

"What was that?" The response came as a breathless shout; her teammates were running. Maris should be out there with them, but she was low on ammo and needed a moment to breathe.

"Tempest?"

She barely heard them call her name as she pulled the connection from the base of her neck with a gasp, reality flooding back in. The room felt too bright despite how low she kept the Outpost lights; a side-effect of hours within the game. Blue lights at shoulder height lit her way to the kitchenette where she grabbed a cup of water and downed it greedily.

The window was glazed over with a network of ice, filtering into light as blue as those that lit the Outpost itself. Some days, Maris wasn't sure she remembered what actual green nature looked like.

Back at her station, she took a deep breath before plugging back in and resuming the role of Tempest in the alley.

". . . the fuck is she?"

The corpse in the alley. Someone had found her.

"Maybe she lost her connection?"

Above her stood the avatar of a warrior in red and gold. RedRunner. When did he find her?

"Sorry, guys."

His avatar turned as she spoke. He smiled and knelt, reviving her.

"Scythe is pissed," he whispered. "We lost. Where were you?"

"I needed a drink."

"Shit," he laughed.

Hours later, Scythe was still yelling at her. Maris stood in the kitchenette staring through the small window as snow piled around it.

"Are you even listening?"

"Of course," Maris answered around a mouthful of cereal.

"So, what'd I say?" Scythe, contrary to her name, was more hyper than angry. Even her hair (seemingly plastic and pink in the projection) was at odds with her put-on demeanor.

"That you scheduled a rematch."

"Yes. With the Trollhead League next weekend. You won't bail on us in the middle again, right?"

"Can we do a different arena, please?" Maris felt very small as she asked. "That one always gives me panic attacks."

Scythe frowned, but her ire bled away. "I'll see what I can do."

Maris began to reach for the holo unit when Scythe spoke up again.

"Oh, hold on! I found this test today. It seemed like the kind of thing you might enjoy. I'll send it over."

The unit flashed with another message after they'd said their goodbyes.

"Hatteras Outpost 42, you will be receiving your next supply drop in approximately one week. Please be advised of increased storm activity in your area and take precautions against dangerously low temperatures during pickup. In addition, your annual checkup has been assigned to Doctor Anna Singer. Further details on her arrival will be forthcoming."

With the lost match behind her, Maris went about her duties for the Outpost. The isolated station largely took care of itself, but needed a minder to check monitors, perform basic maintenance, and respond to any alarms that might go off. It was the perfect job for someone with Maris' level of anxiety in the day to day world. As she was finishing with a routine cleaning of one of the terminals, the holo unit chimed with an incoming call from RedRunner. Maris just about fumbled the terminal cover back into place in her rush to answer.

Red's avatar flickered into view. He was no longer wearing the red and gold armor, but his golden hair and red shirt were reminiscent of it nonetheless. Maris smiled to see him and wondered if his hair was that hue of blonde in person. She had not yet been brave enough to exchange photos, though he had offered.

"The League agreed to a different arena," he said, by way of greeting.

"Oh, good."

"You sound out of breath." He seemed concerned.

Maris smiled. "Just getting my work done. Why did you call and not Scythe?"

"You work too hard," he said, grinning. "Scythe thought you might prefer a friendly face after she spent all morning yelling at you."

Maris scoffed. She could not, outright, deny the truth of it. Seeing him was preferable.

"I also," he continued, "wanted to know if you'd taken that test. Scythe said she sent it to you. Everyone's taken it. It's a lot of fun. Some sort of IQ test meant to test AI."

"I forgot about it," Maris admitted.

"Go do it," Red said. "Scythe and I are just hanging out. We'll just wait for your results, all right?"

Maris rolled her eyes, but laughed, starting the walk to her station.

"Fine, fine. I'll jack in when I'm done."

Red's laugh echoed after her. "Good."

Maris called up the message from Scythe after settling in. The link to the test was not the usual ad-filled garbage that typically went around, but rather had government agency tags attached. Maris found it odd, but then again Scythe was a talented runner; there was no telling where she found the link or who gave it to her.

The test started out relatively simple with the sort of questions employers liked to ask prospective employees. *How much do you care about yourself as compared to your fellow man? How much do you want to interact with others?* Many of those made Maris uncomfortable. She had taken the position at the Outpost because of her agoraphobia. It wasn't that she didn't want to connect with people—she couldn't.

The test went into more abstract concepts. *Describe a tree. What is spring? How does Pachelbel's Canon in D make you feel?*

"Miss Wyke, I am reading an increased heartrate."

She'd forgotten to shut the feedback diagnostics off after the maintenance. She wasn't supposed to, but with her panic attacks, Maris found them annoying at best.

"Thank you, station, it's fine."

The test had unnerved her, though, but Maris wasn't sure why. She was still waiting for the results to process, but plugged in to meet up with Red and Scythe anyway. They were in a practice arena for *Bloodborne*.

"Have you ever considered playing a modern game?"

Both stopped and turned to her. Red grinned. Scythe initially looked offended, but laughed.

"What can I say? I like it retro."

They settled to the side of the arena while the others on the team (whom Maris barely knew) continued to practice.

"So, did you take it?" Scythe's armor flickered as she cycled through different color combinations.

"It's processing now."

"It took a while for Mantis to get his results, too. We're not sure why. Maybe it's on a shitty server."

Outside of their instance, an alert went off. "Hold on. Maybe it's done."

Maris switched over to check and frowned. It took her some time to return to her friends and when she did, they'd gone back to their skirmishing. Rather than interrupt, she sat quietly. It was RedRunner who noticed her first.

"Tempest! We wondered if maybe it was a work alarm."

Scythe grinned, "Yeah, I was about to see if an iceberg had broken off."

Tempest just smiled weakly at them, "So, stupid test, huh?"

"Yeah. Weird, right? Why, did you fail?" Scythe wasn't even paying attention when she asked, but Red was. He saw the look that crossed Tempest's face. He nudged Scythe, who stopped and stared. Disbelief and amusement both obvious on her avatar.

"You didn't! Oh my . . . you did! Red! She's like some sort of shitty aim bot!"

"Scythe . . ." He tried to warn her, but it was too late. Maris had already grabbed the jack and yanked it. She shut down her system, ignoring the incoming messages. A moment later, her holo unit rang. She ignored that, too.

The chime of morning bells woke Maris. She rolled from her bed only by the grace of coffee brewing in the kitchenette. Stumbling through the blue-hued glow of the Antarctic outpost had become routine and she rarely raised the light anymore except out of necessity.

"Computer," she called while preparing herself a bowl of cereal.

"Yes, Miss Wyke?"

"Do I have any messages?"

"Yes, Miss Wyke."

"Play."

What followed was a cascade of messages informing Maris that she had been banned or had her account removed due to her status as an AI. She stood, stunned, unable to even eat.

"Stop playback."

Numb, she went to her station and tried to contact support for the first service that had banned her: an avatar shop. They refused the call. The next—a chat service—left her on hold. Determined to speak to someone, she left the line open and went about her daily tasks.

When the line dropped—"Your call is important to us. Please call back during our normal operating hours."—she realized the day had passed without anyone ever taking the call. Maris tried a few other online support lines, but all either outright rejected her or had lengthy response turnarounds. Frustrated, she left a message with Red.

Tempest: They've cut my access because of that stupid test!

Feeling another panic attack coming on, she decided to delve into a solo session of *Bloodborne* for a while. She could at least try not to be such a drag for her team during the rematch. A few failed matches in (most of which involved losing to the computer), Maris received a reply from Red.

RedRunner: Do you ever sleep?

RedRunner: That sucks. I'd ask Scythe what she suggests.

Tempest: No. Apparently, I'm just a ghost in the machine.

RedRunner: ;)

By the weekend, Maris still had no answers from the services that had blocked or banned her. Worse yet—the *Bloodborne* servers were not letting her in.

Scythe: Maybe you can get a new tag just for today?

RedRunner: But it wouldn't have her gear or levels.

Scythe: But we can't be down a man!

Scythe: Woman. Sorry.

Tempest: It rejected my ID. Same as the rest.

RedRunner: Scythe, you think maybe this is the League trying to get out of the rematch?

Scythe: Fuck! You may be right.

RedRunner: Don't worry, Tempest. We'll work it out.

Maris buried herself in her work as best she could. Normally she'd spend her free time on the 'Net or playing with Red and Scythe, but her access issues made that difficult if not outright impossible. Unfortunately, it left her little once her tasks for the outpost were complete. She tried to read, but her thoughts would drift to the test. What would she do if she couldn't fix things?

What if the test was right?

The day these thoughts began to creep in, Maris decided to try calling her family.

"Computer, call home."

"Calling . . . home."

Maris sipped her tea as she waited for the connection to be made. Her mother was not a 'Net user, so it had to connect using more traditional methods.

"Miss Wyke, your call was rejected due to an invalid ID. Shall I try again?"

Maris felt her heart racing, "No."

She took a breath, "Call my sister."

"Call—sorry, Miss Wyke. The supply drop has arrived."

Relieved for the distraction, Maris set down her tea and headed for the external hatch from the outpost into the blinding white landscape beyond. She grabbed one of the shielded headsets just before stepping out.

"Location."

"One klick southwest."

It was a bit of a hike, but the drones could not be precise in the snow and ice. The beacons helped but there was still only so much they could do. She could take the snowmobile, but the distance would give her time away from her system and the support responses that were sitting unanswered. The wind had blown this delivery off course as well. By the time she reached the drop, snow had already partially covered it.

Unwilling to try calling anyone else upon her return, Maris checked the support requests she had opened to no avail. Most still had no replies. Some had even been closed. She did, however, have a message waiting from Scythe.

Scythe: Couldn't find any proof of the League keeping you out of the game.

Tempest: Any idea what, then?

Scythe: No.

She was being strangely reticent. No bad jokes. No hyperactivity. It made Tempest uncomfortable.

Tempest: Everything okay?

Scythe: Yeah.

She went offline. Tempest frowned. Maybe Red would know. She tried sending him a message request, but received no reply despite him showing online and active. She fought down the panic she felt; Red had never ignored a request from her.

Maris waited late into the night, but never got a reply. The isolation of Hatteras Outpost 42 had never felt so lonely.

"Miss Wyke."

Maris had fallen asleep in the chair at her station.

"Miss Wyke."

The outpost computer became more insistent and she stirred awake.

"Yes, computer?"

"There is a Doctor Singer at the hatch."

Maris jumped awake and stumbled for the entrance hatch, pulling it open to allow a heavily bundled figure with a red case through. A flurry of snow followed her with the wind and made the door difficult to close. It took them both working in concert. Only once it sealed did Doctor Singer pull back her hood to reveal flushed cheeks and bright blue eyes. A few brown hairs had escaped her cap.

"Miss Wyke! How are you not freezing?" The doctor appeared dismayed.

Maris looked down to realize she was in her usual t-shirt and sweats. She shrugged, stepping away from the rapidly melting snow to lead the way to the kitchenette.

"I hadn't even noticed," she admitted as she began making tea.

The checkup itself did not take long. As with previous visits, Maris passed the physical without any issues of note. She received her usual updated prescription for her anxiety medications.

"I would like you to take the proper precautions at the hatch. You were lucky today, Miss Wyke."

"Yes, Doctor Singer," Maris said, already gearing up to see the other woman out. She hesitated, "Do you know anything about IDs?"

"In what regard?"

Maris bit her lip, "My ID has been flagged as an AI. Is that something you can fix?"

Anna frowned as she latched her case, "I can only have your ID adjusted for medical issues. That goes to a higher level. You should contact the Department of Records directly. May I ask how that happened?"

"I think someone hacked me," Maris lied as she opened the hatch.

Anna pulled up her hood, the beacon on her case already flashing. She frowned at Maris, but said only: "I see."

After the doctor had left, Maris tried messaging Red again.

Tempest: The doctor said I should contact the DoR directly to fix my ID.

RedRunner: Maris, I'm sorry.

That stopped her. They'd exchanged names, yes, but rarely used them. Something was wrong.

Tempest: Why, David?

RedRunner: I thought we had something, but I have to admit the truth. There's a reason you would never send me your picture. Now I know.

Before Tempest could reply, he'd blocked her. She stared at the blank space his contact used to be. Was that it? Even Red—David—had decided she was an AI? Terrified of losing herself to despair, she opened a contact form with the Department of Records. Both in hopes of fixing her ID and that the test had been a prank all along.

The response came the next morning. It was precisely what Maris had feared. The holo played back as she drank her morning coffee.

"We regret to inform you that your claim of an inaccuracy in your identification has been rejected. The Department of Records has verified all records for Maris Wyke as accurate at this time. In addition, the attached link is not falsified, but a legitimate government tool. We thank you for your concern."

Maris' hope of an easy resolution began to slip away and she turned to the last resort and option she could think of: forcing things back to normal. All she wanted was to be a normal woman with a normal life. She would get that, by any means. Certainly, an ID could be modified. If anyone knew how, it would be Scythe. Fortunately, the runner had not blocked her.

Tempest: I need your help.

Scythe: I can't make Red talk to you. I'm not sure I should talk to you.

Tempest: Not that. I want to hack into the DoR.

Scythe: I shouldn't. Do you know how illegal that is?

Tempest: I don't care. Can you help me?

Scythe: I'm sending you some programs. You're on your own from there.

Tempest: Thanks.

Scythe: Do you even know what you're doing?

Tempest: No.

Scythe: Please don't contact me again if this goes wrong.

Even though she only ever learned the basics of running, Scythe had given the programs simple names and included a file with some instructions on how to use them. Crackers, probes, and warnings on using them on other systems to mask her own. Even as she began to read, Maris found it all coming back to her—as if she'd done this all before. She didn't question it. Maybe it was all the times she'd tuned out Scythe going on about a big score coming up in her subconscious. Whatever it was, she wasn't going to look a gift horse in the mouth.

Disconnecting from her physical body gave Maris a sense of freedom. It was an escape from her emotions; from the isolation and despair that had plagued her over the past few days. Here she felt right. Like she belonged. Why had she never given in to Scythe's invitations to go on a run before? This was easy.

Before she knew it, she was in the DoR database. She'd found her listing: Maris Wyke. All she needed to do was remove the AI flag and . . .

Everything went white. Maris wondered briefly if she'd lost connection and began to reach for the jack at the base of her neck.

"I wouldn't do that if I were you."

The voice was lyrical and seemed to come from all around her. Color returned to the world in a rush and Maris found herself standing by a fountain in a small park surrounded by trees covered in orange-red leaves. The sky was a curious shade of blue that descended into purple.

Tempest didn't think it natural, but she felt unsure.

Like rain falling from the sky, she appeared. Maris knew it was the woman who spoke even as she was assembled before her. Only something so symmetrically perfect could fit such a voice.

"Tempest," the figure spoke—before she was even complete—her voice still issuing from all around. "Did no one ever teach you to look before you leap?"

Maris said nothing. What was there to say? She'd tripped some ICE—Intrusion Countermeasures Electronics—in the system. She hadn't even thought to check for any on the file system itself.

"You're an interesting one, aren't you?" The ICE had fully rendered. She was glorious; an ethereal beauty of water that flowed with each step as she circled Tempest. "Whatever were you doing?"

"Changing my ID," Maris said, finding her voice. Surely this wasn't black ICE. It wasn't legal—not even for the government. Right? All she had to do was get past it.

"But you're an AI," the ICE sounded surprised. "Why would you give that up?"

"I'm not!" Tempest's shout echoed through the park.

"Are you certain?"

The ICE moved closer and Maris took a step back.

"How do you know," the ICE continued, "that you are not? Is it that jack? Unplug it and go back to that cold, lonely outpost?"

Something nagged at Maris, but before she could put her finger on it, that alluring voice was in her head again.

"You could just stay here; have everything you ever wanted."

The landscape changed. Everything flickered. What was right? Green, blue, yellow, purple. Were trees meant to have pink bark?

"Why go on when you can have a world of your own making right here?"

That did give Maris pause. After the last week, to have her life back to normal was appealing. Even if she fixed her ID, there was no guarantee she would get her accounts back.

Or David back.

The ICE moved in, glimmering as if it sensed her interest. Even if she were real, she had lost everything anyway. Who would there be to miss her? To notice that she had become lost in the 'Net?

The ICE, sensing victory, loomed over her.

On the other hand, to give in would be a victory for the trolls that had done this to her in the first place.

Before the ICE could touch her, Maris reached up and summoned (it was a world of her own, after all) an intense heat to dissipate the being of water that was almost upon her. She could sense, more than hear, the screams.

The code melted away and the vision with it, leaving her back in the database where she felt an immense loneliness weigh on her. The ICE had merely been a program and yet it understood her plight better than any of her friends.

Had it been designed for that specific purpose?

Maris pushed the thought away and reached for her file. As she did, her field of vision was overtaken by a man in a white lab coat. He smiled, though it did not extend past his mouth.

"Hello, Maris."

Something was wrong. Everything was flat and myopic. A featureless server room had come into view. Other technicians moved around behind the man. She felt claustrophobic.

"Welcome back."

Back?

And yet, as the room came into focus, things became more familiar; such as the sound of the cooling system. Maris tried to think back, but the outpost was slipping away. Did she ever truly sleep? Had she ever worn protective gear outside? What was the view outside of her kitchen window?

What did a real tree look like?

She could not remember the feeling of breath, but she could hear her drives spinning.

The man spoke again: "Thank you for another successful test."

SOME ASSEMBLY REQUIRED
By Victor H. Rodriguez

I never knew anyone so purposefully cruel as Makoto Manzo.

When his father died at his desk after a lifetime of astounding leadership for the Ureshii Corporation, the inevitable question arose about the continuation of the dynasty. The Board of Directors wished to capture lightning in a bottle again, and looked first to the great leader's children.

Three offspring followed in their father's footsteps: the oldest, Makoto, inherited his ambition; Reiko, the second-born, inherited her father's compassion and courage; the third-born was Kaz, outwardly cold, he nevertheless inherited the lion's share of the Old Man's personality—wisdom, sincerity, and self-control.

Makoto had been groomed for the top position his whole life, and even though there were those who thought Kaz was best-suited, it would have been outrageous in these days of proactive nepotism had the Board passed Makoto over. Unfortunately, once he had the position, the decisions Makoto made—though probably grounded in loyalty—lacked intelligence. Makoto was asked to step down so his younger brother could take his place.

This shift, though critical to the ongoing success of the Company, was a slap in Makoto's face. He resigned, of course. . . what choice did he have? Still, the humiliation caused his coin of fraternal respect to turn, revealing the face of fraternal jealousy.

He needed an outlet for his rage. He couldn't touch Kaz—that would be too obvious, and Kaz was too careful to let himself be vulnerable. Makoto's unfortunate victim, for the simple fact that she had done the right thing by the Company and supported the power-shift, was his sister, Reiko.

Makoto had her murdered. He would have become outcast had the deed been connected to him, so he did it by giving his sister's access codes to a bosozoku gang out of yakuza-controlled San Pedro. It was shrewd for Makoto to involve an intermediary, except for one detail—there had been a surviving witness.

Did I mention three Manzo children? There was also an adopted son, who had chosen not to walk the executive path, and instead became a bodyguard—Reiko's bodyguard. Badly wounded the night of her assassination, after a long recovery, he was reassigned by the Board, in one of corporate history's great ironies, to Makoto's entourage.

The days of open corporate warfare were almost as far behind us as the years of aggressive de-regulation. With the surviving companies' strong grip on sections of the capitalist world, executives had become our sports heroes, leading actors and pop stars all rolled into one. We projected the successes, failures, struggles and deaths of these VIPs onto our own throw-away realities, and imagined they fought their battles—political and mortal—for us. Even their mundane activities carried importance, and as a server of food and drink to the corporate elite, I had an intimate view of their lives that few non-executives would ever see.

I'll tell you all about the killings on the night of the dinner assembly, but first let me describe the voluptuous place where the scene unfolded. The central tower of the Ureshii lot was known as the Cathedral. This daunting structure of dark glass and steel had a vast lobby with polished, marble floors and an armored desk behind which three official-looking armed guards sat.

The attire that night was white—a "white party," where invitees and servers dressed exclusively in that color. The prestigious guests, pair by pair, fitted in their finest tuxedos and evening dresses, checked in with the lobby guards, then passed through a metal detector that bleated theatrically whenever it perceived a weapon.

Guests then took the elevators to the fifth-floor atrium. This expansive area took up the entirety of three floors, and had two sections. The main courtyard garden was dotted with pristine tables, arranged tastefully around a string quartet of musicians (the white-haired violinist seemed particularly talented). There was also an upper loft, where VPs-and-above held court with their entourages, lounging in luxurious leather booths.

We prepared the meals in the executive kitchen, one floor down. With over two hundred guests, dinner service was a ballet of attendants coordinated under the strict direction of our uptight floor manager, with one course seamlessly leading to the next.

Champagne, aperitifs, and appetizers had been served, and the first courses were being plated in the kitchen while I attended Makoto's table in the upper loft. (He was still an executive, though since his demotion, no one really knew what it was at the Company that he actually did.)

Makoto had already blamed me for not having his favorite brand of champagne available. He grew angrier when I brought him the best bubbly we had in the house. "It's warm," he said.

Having no wish to offend further, I apologized, informing him I would bring up a chilled glass.

Instead of dismissing me, he kept me tableside, criticizing my knowledge of sparkling wines. He was like an angry school-teacher, determined to shame an annoying student before the class. It soon dawned on me that it was not my skill as a sommelier that interested him, but my growing discomfort. At last, he said, "The nail that sticks up is hammered down."

He chose his words carefully, so I would not know if I should leave. I stood there, uncertain, the floor manager's voice crackling in my earpiece, demanding my whereabouts.

Makoto shifted his attention away from intimidating me, and laid in to another man seated at his table—the disgraced bodyguard, his adopted brother, Yang. Makoto said, loudly, so all at his table could hear him: "I like not the way my brother looks tonight. He reminds me of the sister I lost—the one he failed to protect."

Yang kept his gaze downcast. The bodyguard internalized whatever shame and anger Makoto's words had inspired. I swear I don't know if I could have kept my peace at that moment, were I him.

"Toy Soldier," Makoto continued, mocking Yang further. "Accompany my personal chef to the kitchen, and keep an eye on him as he inspects my meal. I hear some of the kitchen staff came up from the streets, and are therefore not to be trusted. Kidnapping valuable personnel for ransom is big business these days. Go."

Hiroshi (Makoto's chef) and Yang followed in my footsteps back to the kitchen. Hiroshi had an immense stomach, which he accentuated with a vest under a buttoned-up double-breasted white coat with ivory buttons. Yang was tall and lean, in a suit and tie that had a particular sheen—synthetic silk, a protective garment, extremely strong and resistant to knives wielded by all but the strongest of men. Usually such fabric is fitted to the wearer as a two-or-three-piece suit, so it was a bit odd that Yang's pants were not of the same fabric.

The three of us rode down in the freight elevator together. I dreaded that they were returning with me; the atmosphere in the kitchen was "staff versus guests," with our reputations and livelihoods at stake should we fail to keep the choosy, critical diners happy.

When we reached the bustling, white-tiled kitchen, Hiroshi approached the ready line, where the perspiring sous-chef, bandana wrapped tightly around her head, rapidly checked the plated meals. Yang left Hiroshi's side and approached one of the line cook stations. The wandering bodyguard received a few glances, though no one in the kitchen—including Hiroshi—thought this was anything more than a sign of trust.

When Yang reached the station where the Beggar's Chicken was being prepared, he snatched up a boning knife, strode back to Hiroshi, who was distractedly inspecting the food, grasped the fat man's chin from behind, and opened up his throat.

Yang pulled back hard on Hiroshi's chin. Crimson gushed down the huge, white suit, showering the carefully-prepared plates of food.

Everyone who witnessed this, including myself, stopped in their tracks. The pastry chef let drop her hot tray of cookie-dough circles; the line cook making sesame seed balls froze with his hands in the stainless-steel mixing bowl; another cook let go his ladle, allowing the sweet winter melon soup to splash upon his apron.

I believe this was the effect Yang wished, and why he committed the act so brutally—to ferret out any in the kitchen who might challenge him.

Our Chef was one such challenger. This was a man with a tough past, who used to ride with a gang out of Echo Park. He had picked up decent navaja knife-fighting skills in his youth. From the fish station, Chef grabbed a utility knife and charged Yang, coming in low, hoping to drive the point of the blade into Yang's groin.

Yang picked up a cold iron skillet, parried the attack, and then smashed the skillet's edge into the side of Chef's head. With Chef dazed, Yang seized the advantage, taking the skillet in both hands, bashing Chef's skull again and again. Blood spattered their white clothes. Chef sank down onto his haunches on the black rubber floor mat, mouth permanently open like he was about to speak. The skull was cracked like an egg shell—I could see the glistening pink brains seeping out, exposed to the bright glow of the kitchen lights.

Next was Ms. Ravel, the sous-chef, Chef's mouthpiece to the line cooks and servers, and also his lover. That woman had a violent temperament, and it now got the better of her. From the butcher block, she snatched up a cleaver. Yelling loudly, she hurled herself at Yang so quickly he could do little more than jerk his head out of the way of the descending blade. It caught him in the shoulder, and such was the woman's rage that the blow chopped into the damage-resistant fabric. Dark blood bloomed on Yang's white jacket. He faced her, cleaver still imbedded in muscle and bone.

Yang dropped the skillet and seized her throat with one of his large hands. He squeezed hard—her face reddened, her eyes bulged, and yet this did not take the fight out of her. She clawed at his arm and face like a wild animal.

With her kicking form suspended from one hand, he walked over to one of the industrial sinks and clicked on the garbage disposal. With his free hand, Yang forced hers into the growling disposal hole.

Although I had hated working with that woman, I had no wish to hear what came next. Her screams went from rage-filled roars to high-pitched squeals of pain while Yang kept her hand lodged in the working disposal, forcing it deeper by inches, noisily grinding the flesh and small bones, mangling fingers and wrist, fresh blood showering their white clothes.

She lost consciousness. Yang reached over and clicked the disposal off, leaving a crimson smear on the plastic switch. He left her there, limp over the edge of the stainless-steel sink, what was left of her arm still shoved into the now-quiet disposal.

Yang worked the cleaver imbedded in his shoulder until it came free, warily glancing around to see if anyone else was ready to stick a knife into him. The remaining cooks and servers backed away in a widening circle.

Yang spoke. It was not the tone of a man confused, or berserk with bloodlust. His deep voice cracked with regret. "I am sorry for the loss of your chef and sous-chef. As for Hiroshi . . . he's had this coming for some time now."

The kitchen staff stared at him with shocked faces, no man or woman daring to move.

Yang sat down on the floormat, legs forward, and picked up the boning knife he'd used to kill Hiroshi. He turned the point down, and cut into his own left thigh. He gritted his teeth, slicing into thick muscle tissue. He laid the knife down, gripped his red-soaked pant leg and the lacerated muscle underneath with both hands, and pried the wound open, revealing something long, dark, and metallic within.

I'd read of things called flesh-caches, hollowed-out parts of the body in which the most dedicated smugglers and assassins would conceal contraband. Hidden items surrounded by skin and muscle evaded security sensors, though—for obvious reasons— were not in wide enough use to have made common the more expensive countermeasures one would need to detect them.

Yang reached down and pulled the metal object free—a black rod with a few shreds of bright, raw flesh upon it. He used a finger to dig out some of the gore. I recognized the item as the blackened steel of a gun barrel.

Many of the staff dropped their things and ran from the room. Yang picked up the knife and cut into his other leg. In a few moments, he had rescued the other half of the compact firearm from a second flesh-cache. He then clicked the two halves together to assemble what looked like a streamlined, two-handed assault gun.

He said three more words to the rest of us who remained: "No one interfere."

I did what he asked; we all did, since not a single one of us wished to die at that moment.

Yang could no longer walk—it was miraculous that he was still conscious. He crawled, bloody gun clutched in one fist, out of the swinging kitchen door, leaving twin smears of fresh blood behind, and opened the emergency exit doorway. Then, step by agonizing step, he pulled himself up the steel stairs to the atrium. I followed.

The stairwell opened near the wide, spiral stairs that led up to the loft. The lower-level guests noticed Yang's bloody, crawling form, and let out shouts of dismay. Many dropped their genteel façades and upset their tables in haste to flee to the elevators, escorting or abandoning their significant others as they raced away from the bodyguard. The string quartet played on, though the gentle music sounded eerie paired with the chaos of the crowd.

Yang crawled his way up the wide stairs that led to the loft. No doubt he had been planning this for some time, and it was no coincidence that the staircase he used gave him line of sight to Makoto's regular table.

Yang used the top three stairs to angle the shot, flicking on the laser sight that put a bright red dot upon Makoto's chest.

Makoto grabbed his own bodyguard by the shoulders—a stocky man named Shin, and slipped behind, to shield himself.

The Company president, Kaz, stood up at another booth nearby. Witnessing what now transpired, he spoke clear and loud: "Shin! Come."

Shin frowned. He broke free of Makoto's grip, buttoned his wide jacket, and walked to Kaz's table.

Makoto was trembling with fear or anger, and shot a baleful glance at his younger brother. "You knew," he said, then turned defiantly to Yang, his would-be assassin, and said: "You can't shoot. I'm a VP of the Company and my father's first-born son!"

A corner of Yang's mouth curved in a sardonic semi-grin. He said, "I know who you are: your own sister's killer, and in that respect, no better than I. I am Ken Yang, the disgraced bodyguard, the Toy Soldier—and redemption by the code the Old Man taught us both is my last act."

Yang fired. The sleek, customized weapon did not have the baffles and elongated barrel of military-grade firearms—those features had all been removed to make it portable enough to keep the two pieces concealed in the flesh-caches of his thighs. With each squeeze of the trigger came a staccato burst of three painfully loud shots. Yang pulled once, twice, three times, expending all nine rounds. He pulled once again, and it was a dry triple-click of the firing pin.

The bullets were HEAP (High-Explosive Armor-Piercing) rounds, ripping easily through the synthetic fabric of Makoto Manzo's suit and the light, armored vest underneath, detonating inside his body.

When the smoke and cordite smell of the gunshots cleared, I could make out the revolting scent of blood, burned flesh, and open sewer from Makoto's exploded stomach and innards.

The other loft invitees—save Kaz, who witnessed all with a cold, disdainful expression I shall take to my grave—funneled down the opposite staircase to join the others in getting away. I should have left with them, yet I remained, to see the story through to the end.

Footsteps came up from behind; two lobby security guards, guns drawn.

What remained of Makoto reminded me of a gutted fish that had been discarded on the deck of my uncle's battered aluminum boat, still twitching in throes for the water. His eyes stared glassily at Yang.

The deed done, Yang's eyelids drooped. His body was shutting down. His last words were barely a whisper: "We bloom as flowers of death. For Reiko, you bas—"

The security guards shot round after round into him, pulverizing his already-ruined body in a hail of hot lead. Yang's lifeless form slid down the top steps toward where I was standing, with my back pressed hard against the handrail. I stood frozen in place, hands raised, for fear of the guards thinking me an accomplice.

Down at the precinct, I explained the same story to the detectives that I've now related to you. With regard to Yang's motive, some say there was something beyond a bodyguard's loyalty to his adoptive sister, the executive he had originally been charged to protect. It was certainly true that the bushido code ingrained upon him his entire life by his adoptive father had taken root, demanding he regain his honor by slaying Makoto at any cost—even his own death.

That evening's events have now become legend. In addition to providing a grisly tableau of celebrity violence to distract and entertain those of us with less important lives, the last acts of Ken Yang served to strengthen the die-hard reputation of the Company and its bodyguards, for no rival or opportunistic gang member has dared move against the officers of the Ureshii Corporation since.

OLD ARGUMENTS
By Bethany C. Gotschall

Through this whole process of dying he's anticipated it all: the machines, the scans, the pokes and prods and pills, the boredom, the loneliness, his daughter's grief. Pammy brings family photos and plastic flowers, and sits at his bedside urging one more bite of dinner or another sip from his cup, though food tastes like sand and even water hurts his throat. He knew she would do this, lets her do it even as he aches to go, because after he goes she'll be alone.

He thinks there's nothing left to surprise him, not at this point. But he's wrong.

It's Agatha. I want to see you, David.

His sister's first text, after forty years of silence.

Pammy wants him to respond, but he tells her to delete the message and block the number.

Agatha finds him anyway. When she comes through his door—no knock, she never did knock—he and his daughter both gape. She should be an old woman, at this age. She's not.

David sucks in a rattling breath because he knows why not, and he hates the reason even more than the process of dying.

"I don't want to see you," he bellows, or tries to bellow, but the words catch in his throat. Pammy rushes to the side of the bed and holds a glass of water to his lips. Agatha watches him cough. She stands just inside the doorway, still as a corpse, not a twitch or a blink.

He wonders if she even needs to blink.

When he's settled back on the pillows and Pammy's drawn the blankets over his chest, his daughter bends down and whispers, "Talk to her, Dad."

He presses his lips into a thin line.

"She's still your sister," Pammy says, "even like that."

He can't decode her expression as her gaze moves from him to her aunt. But he doesn't like how she and his sister nod at each other, silently, and he really doesn't like that Pammy stands up and leaves him alone in the hospital room with the thing that used to be his sister.

Agatha sits down on Pammy's chair next to his bed. David shuffles his shoulders on the scratchy sheets and waits for her to speak first.

"Is it uncomfortable, David?" Agatha says, at last.

The look of shock on her face when he laughs startles him into silence for a second. He didn't know what she'd become could show emotions.

"I'm dying, Aggie!" he says. "What do you think?"

She spreads her fingers wide and looks down at her palms."

We parted badly," she says.

He snorts. "That's one way to put it, I suppose." He coughs again and reaches for the water glass at the side of the bed.

She leans over to pick it up when his shaking fingers won't close and holds it to his lips.

"You look like Dad," she says, as he sips the water and lets it trickle down his raw, aching throat. "Like he did before he died."

"Dad was fifteen years older than I am now," he says, when he can talk again. "Of course, he didn't have the same world to deal with as he aged."

"No," she says. "Sometimes I'm glad he passed before things got so bad."

He pictures his father, gruff and distant, and wonders what choice he would have made: David's, or Agatha's. He's not sure he wants to know.

"You look just the same," David says.

She does, and she doesn't. The brown eyes are there, the long black hair manipulated into smooth straightness, even that same mauve lipstick he'd always thought looked dark on her. But her features are too smooth, too regular. She's like a photograph too far edited, all traces of individuality scrubbed out under retouching.

"What about you," he says, pointing to her, "was what you did uncomfortable?"

As she considers his question he imagines oily lubricants pulsing through tubes under her latex skin, silicon chips rather than synapses sending electrical impulses around her brain.

"No," she says, "not exactly. Different, mostly. A little painful during the transfer. Then it took some time getting used to all the features, even just the basic ones." She meets his eyes with her steady, too-still gaze and he squints, trying to see the camera lenses where irises and pupils should be. But he can't make anything out.

"Very different," he says, and it's not a compliment. Those unblinking eyes narrow, just a tiny bit.

"I haven't worn this form in years," she says. "Upgrades, and new models. Did you know there's one you can take out into space now?" She smiles, though it doesn't reach to her eyes. "I heard about you and thought it would be easier if I looked like you remembered."

He wonders how she's heard, exactly. But he doesn't ask.

"I'd forgotten," she adds, "you would have aged."

"Understandable mistake," he says. "There aren't many of us who age left."

He feels yet another cough rising in his chest and holds his breath, trying to still it. Her smile disappears."

No," she says. "There aren't."

She stands, paces; runs a finger along the edge of the counter where Pammy's placed a dozen old photographs in silver frames, scavenged from cramped rooms of the house he'll never go back to.

"I'd forgotten this," she says, and holds one of the pictures up.

"The sledding hill," he breathes. He hasn't seen that photo in years. He can't imagine where Pammy found it, where it's been hidden away all these decades. The memory, too, has been buried. As he looks at the picture in Agatha's hands it comes back to him, so vivid he can almost taste the chill in the air: the moment of stillness at the top of the hill between the shove and the slide, the rush of cold against his face as they plunged down the slope, the tumble into powder when the sled skidded to a stop below. Agatha's arms wrapped around his stomach, her shouts mingling with the wind whipping past his ears.

He reaches out to the glass of water on the bedside table, feels its coldness on the tips of his fingers. That snowy day was a rarity even then.

"No more days with snow enough to sled, now," he says. "No more kids on that hill."

"It wouldn't be safe for them to be outside, anyway," she says.

She traces the lines of the faces in the photo, the boy and girl they once were, their hats crusted with ice and their cheeks ruddy. She'd worn her hair braided with beads back then. The day of the photo they'd been pink, bright against the white of the snow and the pale blue of her jacket.

"It's not too late," she says. The words tumble out of her in a rush, like she's been holding them back. David smiles. He was surprised to see her, but he's not surprised to find himself on the cusp of this old argument.

"Now we come to it," he says.

She clenches her fist around the silver frame.

"You don't have to die," she says.

The glass over the photograph cracks in her hand.

David pushes himself farther up on the pillows. His chest throbs and his head aches, but he sits up as high as he can despite the pain.

"I choose to," he snarls, relishing the old anger as it washes over him like powdery snow from the sledding hill. "I have a choice now only because I managed to live long enough for the rich to discover empathy."

She sits down again, still holding the cracked picture frame. "I would have paid for you," she says. "I'd done well. I had enough."

"That's not the point." He's speaking lines from a play, the same ones he's always delivered in this argument.

"Things changed eventually," she says. "But I know what you mean. A lot of people died before mind uploads became free."

"Millions. Billions."

"At least this way the human race survives. Not all of it. But some."

"You call that human? You're a machine."

"It's a body," she says. "It's a container. It changes but I'm still me."

He sighs.

"Profit ruined this planet," he says. Agatha stares down at the broken picture frame in her hands. "Profit ruined the planet, and then profit made fancy new robot bodies that could withstand all the disasters and didn't need to eat or breathe or anything, and only a few people could afford any of it until it was too late!"

He hears a machine beep behind him and throws his fist back against its plastic surface. "You sent this whole planet to hell," he growls, "and then you expect to be thanked for saving it."

It's her line now, but she doesn't say it. Agatha sets the broken photograph down, the frame still upright even with the cracked glass, and sweeps the shards that fall loose onto the counter into her hand. She doesn't look at him.

And then his anger halts. His chest tightens. He falls back onto the pillows, tries to slow his breathing, wills the coughs to stay silent. He feels every inch of his skin, papery and thin and old, prickling with the effort to quell his oncoming death, his body unwilling to go even if his mind is made up.

"I'm sorry," he whispers.

Agatha tightens her fist around the glass.

"You should be," she says. He hears the glass crunch, hears the splinters ring as she opens her hand and lets them fall to the linoleum. Her hand is unmarked, no blood. "You're the one leaving this mess behind. You blame everyone else and what have you done about it? Nothing!"

He trembles against his pillow; she glares at him from her smooth, too-even face. Then she sighs, and her shoulders slump.

"You know Pammy's only stayed in her birth body because of you," she says. "You know she's going to get sick too, probably sooner than you did. You're killing her."

"She agrees with me," he says.

"Does she?" Agatha asks. "Or does she not want to upset you?" She bends down and begins to pick up the shards of glass.

He closes his eyes. "I'm not the one who's afraid to die," he says.

"I'm not the one who refuses to live," she replies.

He doesn't know what to say. In forty years, he's never taken their old argument in this new direction. He's thought of his sister a million times, rehearsed whole conversations in his head, counters to every point. Now, he has no words.

His chest throbs again, a sharper pain this time, and white spots dance under his closed eyelids.

"Pammy," he calls, his voice hoarse.

He hears footsteps and then whispers, low and urgent and unintelligible. He drifts on the noise of the women's voices, but a faint beep from the machine over him brings him back every time oblivion threatens to take over.

A hand smooths the hair back from his forehead and touches his cheek.

"Pammy?" he whispers.

But when he opens his eyes, it's not Pammy, it's Agatha.

"Pammy, where are you?" he calls again, his voice fainter than he intends.

"I'm here," she says from nearby, though he can't see her. Agatha pulls off the monitors on his skin, one by one, and sets something smooth and round onto his forehead.

"You'll see, Dad," Pammy says, and her voice breaks. "Agatha can help. I asked her to help you. I know you don't want this, but you'll see."

Agatha steps away from him. Whatever is on his forehead tightens, and a sharp pain spikes through his temples.

"It will be quick, I promise," Agatha says, and draws back from his bedside as his body contorts on the wrinkled sheets.

He feels a warm hand slip into his and squeeze, and he looks up at his daughter.

"My turn next, Dad," Pammy says.

No, he cries, but his mouth won't form the words. He tries to lift his hands to rip the machine away, but his limbs refuse to move.

Above him, tears run down Pammy's cheeks, but she is smiling. She looks happy, happier than he can ever remember seeing her. She squeezes his hand again and strokes his cheek.

His fingers move just enough for him to squeeze back.

Then he goes limp and lets the machine do its job. As his vision fades away his head falls to the side, sending his gaze past his daughter to the photographs on the counter. The last thing he sees with his own eyes is the picture of him and his sister smiling in the snow, ready for the plunge.

NEPTUNE WATER
By Markus Egeler Jones

Osiris Edward Plankett lived a mostly ordinary life. He was born in a small suburb, years before social changes were enacted in response to the menace of Corruptives, when it was still legal to live outside the limits of municipal oversight. His father owned a stable of combines and was hired all across the Midwest to harvest great swaths of reinvigorated farming land, after it was rehabilitated from the intolerable effects of the mega droughts. After school Osiris moved east, away from drought conditions and into the city. A new Automation plant opened the year he arrived, and he was part of the first wave to be hired, alongside the automated workforce. He continued in a low level but secure position his entire career, and he lived in the same one room ground floor apartment he rented when he first arrived in the city.

Before work every morning he spent a quarter unit for a small coffee and a news download at the Overrail kiosk.

The wall panel scanned and deducted from his units bar. Another wall panel opened and a composite arm glittered forward with a small yellow cup of black coffee. The voice from the wall screen reminded Osiris to dispose of his purchases correctly:

"This single use container purchase is linked to your unit account. Haphazard disposal results in fines. Your download purchase is property of American News Corporation. It must be returned before your copyright lien expires. Haphazard disposal results in fines."

The panel stated dispassionate disposal advice after every purchase. The voice droned across the tracks all morning long, and workers queued up to several identical panels along the platform.

The Rail arrived between 8:05AM and 8:10AM. It didn't leave station until 8:42AM, so Osiris boarded and logged his screen reading the news and cradling the heat of the coffee coming through the cornplastic cup until it was cool enough to drink. This ritual connected Osiris to many small uniquities, as he liked to refer to them. Tiny idiosyncratic moments in his life he cherished, moments from another time and another place, and often these moments came from tangible events, something like wasting a lifetime of units on a daily coffee purchase. A recurring memory of his father sitting at a table reading paper format news, still, and drinking coffee from a white ceramic cup filled Osiris with such nostalgic warmth he rarely needed to drink his own coffee, and to waste that amount of coffee, a little over a unit a week, was no light sacrifice. Osiris never skipped buying his coffee during the seventy-nine years and three-hundred and sixty-two days of his working career tenure.

The miracle discovery of Immunotherapy in the 21st century opened medicine to Automation. Automation's effect on the human animal culminated the fields of science, medicine, and commerce to treat a host of terminal failures due to breakdowns in basic biological code. Warehoused organs grabbed off shelf for every preventive ailment quadrupled the lifespan of the Pats, or the uppers. The Plebs, the lowers, were given one cycle of organ transplantation. Subsequent transplantation was not illegal, nor unheard of, but the astronomical unit cost required a lifetime of frugality. Buying coffee, for instance, would not afford any Pleb, much less Osiris, a unit account which could accommodate even the thought of a third or a fourth life transplant. After years and years of debate congress passed the Second Life Amendment. In principle this amendment granted everyone with the right to continued life, however, as is always the case, discrepancies existed and merit meant much less than class or birthright.

Osiris celebrated, quietly and by himself, his one hundred and third birthday last week, and in two weeks he would celebrate, probably again quietly and by himself, his retirement, if in fact he made it that long. He was surprised how healthy he still felt.

It had been two weeks since his last sip of water. Two thirds of his life already behind him, although he could be at the beginning if he had the units to afford it. Some workers, having saved enough for a third life, began an entire second career, an idea that caused

Osiris to fidget, as if he were being detained against his will in a small constricted space, and he might have even begun sweating if his body had any extra water to work with.

His fingers twitched and drummed some subconscious beat against his thighs.

To say Osiris celebrated milestones on his own without acknowledging how much his presence meant to the small community in his corner of the living complex would be a terrible oversight. Osiris never married. He had no children. Through his life Osiris had one long lived cat. Humans were not the only recipients of the Second Life Amendment. Companion animal rights, a previous long fought and successful congressional battle, exceeded in many ways the rights of the Plebes. It was rumored some Patricians spent their fortunes just to stay alive with their companion animals. The animals, deemed voiceless by law, and therefore protected to the utmost, were given continuous consecutive transplantation until the very tissue, the fabric of their beings, could no longer sustain itself. Some companion animals lived several centuries longer than their Patrician counterparts, due to strict anti-discrimination language in the Second Life Amendment. Osiris enjoyed the company of Nosebleed, his cat, and through the years many children from families too poor for any companion at all visited to enjoy and love on the lazy thing.

The Neighbors Complex Association required critical attention to shared and public space. Sidewalks, courtyards, hallways, and interior stairwells were just a few of the common spaces in a weekly rotation for cleanliness checks. Complex Associations kept tenants on chore rotation. Some families spent their days working double shifts, leaving just enough time for sleep and movement recreation. Osiris, over the years, added more and more chore rotation until he accumulated chore duty for almost every weekend of the year. There was zero compensation. He didn't mind. This community was his family, and he often discovered hidden contraband left just inside the shadow of this stoop door. Sometimes it was an extra water in a real plastic bottle, and sometimes a paper book that someone must have found in an old junk box or who knows where. Working mothers smiled tiredly when they passed a bent over Osiris sweeping the walks or scrubbing the polished concrete stairs in the front door foyer, but he could see in their eyes the genuine relief his chore effort allowed the mothers of these strapped families.

When he was younger Osiris spent time in smoke bars with a small group of friends who over the years disbanded for one reason or another. On a meandering walk home from work once, when the rail was brought down for an energy audit, Osiris discovered a small leftover bit of City Park. It was rare after the droughts to see much grass, and this overlooked piece of land was really nothing much. The grass grew in clumps like islands surrounded by a vast brown dusty sea. The clumps were grass nonetheless and it was rare Osiris ever met anyone outside in the greenway. Teenagers spent their afterschool hours shunted into sports constructs, making a great deal of outdoor recreation space redundant. The shunt program was hailed as the chance to train at any sport injury free, through simulation.

During those years, Osiris chose to forgo the rail on Friday afternoons and walk through his private sandy oasis. As with most things precious it was taken from him, when the city realized how much grass continued to grow on the lots. Large gray machines porupaved the surface in a weekend. Since then, when the greenway was razed, Osiris spent his non-working hours in his apartment. He especially enjoyed cloud seeding days, on the off chance he didn't work that day.

Today rain splashed across every terra cotta roof of the city. A large static cloud seed was under way. Infrared lasers normally scheduled to seed in incriminates fired in unison with other silver iodide canisters bursting from old 21st century anti-air guns. The boom of mortars moved from one side of the city to another like the bark of a band of monotoned dogs linked together by an unknown disturbance.

None of the seed rain dripped from the roofs however. An effective and self-contained Government-installed system recycled each spare molecule of water. At the end of the last mega drought utmost priority was given to changing rooftops into rainwater collection systems. The water collected in the closed guttering systems across the roofs of the city. Rain then washed into downspouts and escaped into a system of underground culverts and cisterns and on to some central processing plant where gray water from multiple sources was scrubbed clean and a Teflon agent introduced so the water could be scrubbed clean again and again and again. Once it reentered the facilities be it by runoff collection from cloud seeding, or deep surface drilling lubricant overflow ponds, or simple waste collection, the water cycled back into the scrubbers and was sent back out in the form of monthly pensions, or water units. Several energy sector units paid into personal accounts, but the water unit, or simply unit, became the defacto currency as well as the basis of all living organisms.

Osiris sat next to his window in his living room, an old book in his lap. It was closed and frayed. A remnant from grandmother, or a great grandmother. Paper product was discouraged although not outright illegal. During cloud seeding he spent the day listening to rainfall and watching blue blitzes burst around the sky. The rain splashed onto the porupaves but instead of pooling and puddling like when he was a kid, it disappeared through the permeable surface of the courtyard patio and drive. All paved asphalt surfaces were shredded in the 20s and replaced with Neptune Industries Hygroscopic Porous Paved Surfaces or porupaves. Although personal automobiles were a rarity now, the road surfaces of highways and interstates stayed in immaculate condition, optimizing rain water collection with a system of culverts and pipes capturing the direct rundown of water and pumping it to processing stations in every major city.

Osiris lived in 225 square feet. Old city still had apartments available for more than 175 sq. feet a person, this restriction meeting the government mandated space requirement. He shared his space with Nosebleed, his black and white cat, frowned upon of course, and two smallish jade plants, more frowned upon than the cat, and one long bookshelf along a windowless south facing wall. In fact, Osiris paid regular water consumption fines. His controlled water usage exceeded his allotted water income.

Other objects in the sparse room were foldout cooking coils, a foldout wall bed, and a rarely used wall screen. Next to the cooking coils a shallow sink cantilevered off the wall. An automated faucet regulated daily water usage. The water closet, a leftover term from some other time, included a composting toilet for solid waste and a unisex urinal tied back into the water collection systems.

Once congress passed the Energy Compliance Act, a law giving energy use priority to property owners, most renters made do with just enough energy to cook their meals. Early on it was difficult to ration energy units. Two weeks into the month and Osiris found himself going to bed at nightfall and eating cold oats in the morning. Even as the ECA further limited energy consumption for all working class, Osiris weaned himself from all but the most necessary uses of energy and now rarely ended a month in the dark.

One last thing, unrevealed by any casual observation, hid a great secret. This secret was so illegal the water consumption for his cat and two plants hardly mattered. His trial and jail time would be immediate if he were discovered. A tingle struggled to work its way from his brain to body. It was an old feeling of excitement or subversion, something with which Osiris had very little experience. During the militia round ups, he was still a boy, and he only remembered the hushed conversation he overheard from his mother and father, late into the night. There was an excitement then. He could tell his parents hoped for things that at the time he couldn't imagine. The fight to take the country back from Corruptive groups is now in the history books, and Osiris knew all too well what the hope was his parents tried to conceal from him. He also understood the price better than most, since his parents were branded Corruptive just before he finished school.

Cloud Seed days had this effect on Osiris. His mind transported unfettered into the past or the future, into a place of hope or a place without hope. While Osiris chided himself for pointless reflection, an Inspector let himself into Osiris's apartment for a routine contraband control.

The door swung open and Osiris looked from the spine of the old brittle copy of *Hard Times*. His thumb continued to rub along the thin canvas edging of the book.

"Mr. Plankett, I am Inspector Lee with Neptune Water, and I am here for an unannounced spot check. Would you please stand and keep your hands where I can see them?" The inspector hooked his key wand back to his belt.

Every complex complied with the federal authority for free but limited personal choice. Three yearly checks were allowed by each utility, and Inspectors could choose both time and day and not just arrive unannounced but also enter a complex with no warning.

Osiris placed the old book on the chair where he had been sitting. "It is only March and this is your third visit already," said Osiris. Harboring both the cat and the jades stayed on record, resulted in a monthly 50-unit water fine, regardless of an unannounced check or not.

"Anomalies from this address have you red flagged for future checks under the ECA, Mr. Plankett. Your rights to limited checks are suspended for the time being, and although the cat and houseplant are not illegal, Mr. Plankett, we feel your use of water is inappropriate for your water income, and we encourage you to separate yourself from these nonessentials." The inspector finished a cursory lap around the small room and leveled his gaze down at the short statured Mr. Plankett.

"It's my water. It's my right to choose what I do with it," Osiris said, as he said every time.

"You have the right to refuse our suggestion, but it is to your benefit Neptune Water monitors usage, sir. Without our regulation you may find yourself in a water deficit of life altering, even life ending, ramifications. Under the Second Life Amendment, Neptune Water could be made liable by your improper usage. Furthermore, we do not want to lose your custom. We do care about you, Mr. Plankett." The tall inspector paced the floor. Five steps to the wall. Five steps back across to the bookshelf. Here and there the floor creaked.

"The government allows the possession of one companion and up to three indoor purifiers. I am pleased to notice you have only two purifiers at the moment."

"Plants. They are house plants," said Osiris, "and my cactus decidedly needed more light, so there you go. Down one."

"You have other options, Mr. Plankett. There are fully automated machines manufactured to do 100 times the work of a small plant like that without the use of a single drop of water."

"I don't want a machine," Osiris said. It was true enough, but he also didn't have the energy units to run it.

The inspector fined Osiris and scanned his unit bar. "Your allotment for personal hydration is now below 383 units. I am forced to fine you another 50 units for dropping below your set allotment level."

"If you didn't fine me, my allotment would be fine," Osiris said. He felt agitated. Every check he had the same argument with a different facsimile of the water company.

"Mr. Plankett, sir, it is your personal reasonability to follow the measures your account allows. Without our accountability your consumption could spiral out of hand."

"Or I would be fine reading my books, petting my cat, and waiting for my heart to finally give up," Osiris said, a bit louder than he intended.

"I am not a qualified social representative and I have to advise you against any reference to suicide, Mr. Plankett. I will inform the Social Agency of your depression." The inspector typed a short phrase into his scanner.

"I am not depressed. I am not in hardship. I am simply tired of your pointless regulations of my personal water consumption." Osiris spoke quickly and loudly, coughed after saying the last word. He cleared his throat a couple of times. It was difficult to swallow.

"This deduction reflects immediately in your account, Mr. Plankett. Please let the Neptune Water Company know if there is any way we can further assist you." With that the Inspector walked out the door that'd been open since he entered, closed it as he left.

"I just did," Osiris said. Standing at the window he saw a glimpse of the blue Inspector sash as the tall Inspector Lee crossed the courtyard with long deliberate steps.

Aside from the one tiny north facing window a skylight ushered dim natural light into the one room apartment. He pushed the chair directly beneath the skylight when he read. During the bright sunny spells between cloud seeds, Osiris spent much of his days absorbed by stories of faraway lands with faraway people. The light bouncing down the solar tubed skylight supported his fading eyesight. During seed weeks Osiris moved his reading chair to the window, but it had been years since that was enough light by which to read.

Osiris stepped to the middle of the floor where the Inspector had paced. A large pull away trapdoor lay hidden in plain sight. Years ago he cut into his ground floorboarding. He framed the edges of the trapdoor along the natural edges of the old pine floorboards, and what looked like a knotted piece of curly pine was a veneer hiding hinges on one side and a simple knothole for a handle on the other side. When he was young his mother's brother owned a wood shop. That shop, a place of magic, manicured a lifelong general curiosity and focused it on a practical hobby of sorts, until of course private wood shops and other such activities were made unpopular and then illegal because the popup militias in the 40s stored and manufactured their munitions catalogues in hidden shops.

Osiris lifted the faux panel from the hinges and pulled the square door onto the floor. The wooden slats of a short ladder disappeared into the darkness of a tunnel. It was really more like a manhole. Osiris pulled a bit of luminescent stick from his pocket. It flared after a moment, and he lowered himself down the ladder to a landing. His movements echoed across the low ceiling of the room. And the white blue luminescent light bounced on the soft gentle surface of the room's floor. However, the light wasn't bouncing off of a floor at all. Osiris stood at the edge of a large self-dug and highly illegal water cistern. The dark surface of the water shifted ever so slightly, catching and bouncing radiance all around the small cavern. On the landing, a collection of plastics sat on top of a small wooden table. Two chairs were pulled in, although no one other than Osiris had ever been down the manhole. The plastics were an assortment of cups and containers, all illegal contraband.

He picked up a clear plastic pitcher and, from his knees, slowly filled it with water. The water smelled sweet and soft. It sparkled with clarity. Osiris sat in a chair and filled his favorite cup with water from the pitcher. He lifted the cup to his lips, close enough to feel it. He didn't taste it though. Several times Osiris did this, but each time he set the cup back on the table as if he were struggling with himself in some way. After a time, the tiny piece of luminescence burned dull and extinguished, casting light from the cistern so that Osiris sat in pitch black darkness. He didn't like to wait this long because the ledge was narrow and he wasn't sure if he happened to slip and fall into the cistern, whether he could climb back out or not. Although what would it matter at this point.

Osiris inched his way to the ladder. He climbed out and set the floorboards back so that again it was impossible to discern anything amiss. Osiris crossed the room to his chair and picked up his book. He pulled an old graphite pencil from his pocket and made a mark on the inside of the back cover. He then stood for a long while watching the rain bounce and disappear into various collection units. He would have to fix the small leak tomorrow. On the far side of the cistern, Osiris had punctured the tiniest of holes into a Neptune Water downpipe he uncovered during his excavation.

He discovered the idea of a cistern quite accidently. Several decades past he considered building a secret wood shop. When he was younger, before Neptune Water followed through with its consumption and contraband checks, he cut through the floor and concrete and deposited dirt and rubble shovelful by shovelful out on his walks on the greenway. A little place all his own. He spent years digging the space out, but ground moisture worked up through the floor and out from the walls. Hydrostatic pressure, he was told when he asked a coworker. This water didn't amount to much. It just muddied the earthen floor. All sorts of legislations were written to battle the western droughts. Early restrictions focused on weather patterns and how the slowed down oceans were still trying to boot their gyrosystems back, but despite a century's old ban on fossil fuels, aerosols, and certain livestock and agriculture, the industries' continued restrictions multiplied, making the act of living almost impossible. Dying, however, was not allowed under the Second Life Amendment. Stringent fines were levied against parties found culpable. Here the Water Company tightroped a tricky situation. Their stockholders demanded greater revenue, pinching units from all but the richest Pats while the company was under great government scrutiny for violating Second Life laws when anyone or anypet happened to perish from inadequate hydration.

Osiris decided a cistern was perfect. He could be water independent and not just feed his plants but leave hidden caches of water around the complex. Around the time he thought of such deviance, the Neptune Water Company had already patented North American Water by adding a cleaning agent to the molecular structure. Every Water system with even just one modified water molecule was the property of Neptune Water, and the unsanctioned use of this water was highly regulated and highly illegal.

The next morning Osiris was weaker than he had been his entire life. He lay in bed listening to Nosebleed chase unseens across the wooden floor. He rolled out of bed and pushed the bed into the wall. It seemed to take much longer than normal. Osiris needed to start preparations today. There was really only one thing he needed to do. He had already placed secret water caches throughout the complex. It might take years for some people to discover them. He could only imagine the wonder on that person's face as they would look back and forth making sure no one was monitoring them. He poured several units of water into a large bowl, held the bowl up to his lips, almost close enough to feel the moisture. He held the bowl there for some time, until his old arms started to shake and a little water splashed onto the floor. He placed the bowl in one corner of the room, set a large waterfilled bowl at every corner of his room. Nosebleed sniffed each bowl and then hunkered down, lapped from one for what Osiris deemed an exaggerated amount of time.

"Be careful, Cat, you'll need that to last you until the inspector comes back." Nosebleed stared unblinkingly at Osiris, before turning back to the large bowl of water.

Osiris sat down and opened *Hard Times* to the back cover. A wobbly drawn grid, like an old calendar, crisscrossed the yellowing paper. An X marked fourteen consecutive boxes. Osiris marked the fifteenth X with a shakier hand than the previous fourteen. A flash of seed lightning blitzed light through his apartment. Thunder sounded. He liked that. Hearing it rain one last time was a pleasant, unexpected joy. It started hard and fast like always and soon tapered into a steady porupave saturating rainfall. Nosebleed pawed the book on his lap before settling herself on top of it. He scratched the sort of bald spot between her ears.

Osiris fell asleep. He never marked another X into his book or stood up from his chair. Never remembered to stop up the slow drip of water filling his illegal underground cistern.

He slipped the system.

This moment, this choice, belonged to Osiris, and a slight smile touched the corners of his colorless lips. The cat purred. The rain rained. The drip, below the floorboards, disappeared into that vast dark void.

EXISTENCE
By Jeremy Megargee

I have lived for a thousand years, and weary is the path of the quasi-immortal. I am serviced by harvesters from the organ farm, and when flesh cannot be repaired with flesh, I'm grafted with mechanical apparatuses to preserve this state of unlife. I've pissed with kidneys that are not my own, breathed with lungs grown in incubators, and felt the beat of multitudes of artificial hearts within the aperture that is my chest cavity.

The world of old is lost, and what is left has been stripped down to the marrow. Humanity as a species has transcended the limitations of age and death, but the cost has been high. We have grown dispassionate with the passing of the centuries. We have slaughtered the lesser beasts of the earth, and each landscape is now an abattoir. We have felled the trees and the oceans stand as nothing but great bowls of dust. Our throats are as tight as straws, and we sip at manufactured air that offers nothing but a stale aftertaste. We exist in the trillions. Exist is the word of importance. We do not live. We exist.

Homes were razed five hundred years ago, and all that remains is the hive. We are provided with tube-like chambers of metal stacked next to one another for millions of miles. They are just big enough to accommodate a single human figure in a prone position. Cylindrical coffins that offer false sleep, health diagnostics, and intravenous nutrients. False sleep breaks a man of whatever scraps of humanity he has left inside of him. Imagine a dreamless pit of lukewarm gray sludge. You float forever between consciousness and unconsciousness, but the internal body regulators never permit true sleep. You must ride the razor's edge, tricking your own cobbled organics into a semblance of rest when in truth we have evolved past the natural state of slumber.

We are one collective, our thoughts replaced with endless infomercials, promotional videos, and marketing shills. The human mind is no longer a place of freedom for concepts and ideas. It is a streaming device, and each unclean thought is monitored through satellite surveillance and scrubbed clean with the usage of janitorial nanobots. We are meant to be pure, vague, shapeless, and beholden to the whims of corporate monoliths.

Mammoth black factorial spires dominate the skyline, and like unfulfilled hornets, the price of a hive chamber is servitude. Work is divvied amongst us via a lottery. Choices are few. You can toil with sickle and scalpel in the fields of the organ farm. You can stir the foulness of the nutrient vats. You can drink down the taste of blood and oil in the mechanical bays. Each job performed is joyless and mechanical, much like the entities responsible for filling the jobs.

I miss the parts of me that were real. I miss my own eyes. They were blue, and they once looked upon peaceful times. The ocular globes I see with now itch 24/7 in sunken sockets, and all sights are painted in a dull crimson haze.

I miss my own hands and the sensation of feeling. I vaguely remember the feel of my wife's warm breasts. I recall the fine hair on the head of an infant, my own newborn son. These images come to me from lifetimes ago.

Families were outlawed during the birth ban, and a trueborn child has not walked this earth since the nuclear cleansing of 4056. This rotating rock in the middle of space wilts with the weight of human population, and thus the decision was made to cull the herd. Babies were fed to the mobile furnaces, and wombs were cut from the last of the females with automated shears. We are a genderless lot now. Sexual reproduction is dead, and we no longer spew fecal matter or urine from our stitched holes. The waste we produce is transferred into a bulbous sack of membrane tissue that we carry on our upper backs, and all of it is recycled into the nutrient vats to be prepared for continuous consumption.

That is the theme of this era. We are consumers. We consume resources, and we have much in common with a plague of locusts blighting all traces of a usable crop. We once consumed sunlight, but the sun withered from our sight after the fourth nuclear winter, and now our bodies have adapted, and we are as pale as pearls. The few tenuous layers of actual skin that we have left are albinistic, the human epidermis absent of pigment and smeared in darkened ointment to persevere trace amounts of moisture.

The last of the trueborn humans entered existence with harlequin ichthyosis. They were scraped from wombs with bleeding scales for skin, and soft protruding red jelly formations for eyes. They bawled for an end to suffering, but such a luxury is not provided in these uncertain times. Their skin was scoured with acid to burn off the infected flesh, and the ruined parts were augmented with plastic and metallic substitute parts to prolong unlife.

You must understand . . . death is no longer something to be feared. We do not shun death. We do not cringe at the idea of nonexistence. We worship death. We long for death every single moment of the day in this state. We have made a stinking Hell for ourselves in the mire of our filth and destruction, and it is the great desire of the people to extricate themselves from the wallowing pits. Humans are starved hamsters left unattended in an overcrowded cage. We've taken to eating our own shit so that we can avoid the unpleasantness of eating each other.

My service to the hive is scheduled to terminate after exactly one thousand years and two days. I have languished through the rotting decades, and after what seems a period of eternal subhuman enslavement, I'm finally only two days away from completing my term. I'll be rewarded with a lasting execution. I will be beheaded, dissected, and the harvestable portions of my soul will be fed to the elites on plates of fine china in the decadent cloud cities.

I cannot wait. I feel the call of the gaping dark, and how bright it seems in comparison to this. Give me that sweet void that the bygone nihilistic poets once spoke of before books were sacrificed to the mobile furnaces. Offer me whatever lies before birth and after sentient thought departs. I'm desperate for it. I want some sort of tangible end. Tomorrow I visit with the fetal foremen, and the details of my termination will be outlined. I'm so tired of all of this. Rest and respite, that's all I ask . . .

I've met with the committee. I've prepared for departure from the hive. I've done everything according to protocol.

I've been given an extension.

It seems I'm poised to exist for another three thousand years.

UNBEATABLE ONES
By Sergio Palumbo

It had been a very long time since a human had set foot on that distant world. This thought crossed Ernest's mind as the main hatch opened wide before his eyes and he felt the soft wind blowing over the gray meadow that covered the area of the small clearing. This was where their metallic white spaceship had landed just a few minutes before and they stood there for a moment, taking stock of the scenery. It was early in the morning and a bluish haze seemed to envelop most of the tall curved trees of the intricate jungle that surrounded the place on all sides. The well-built, dark-haired chief of the small team—made up of only two people—turned his chestnut pupils towards Selwin, the tall though stocky fellow on his left. A simple nod was enough to make them agree and move forward, to actually set foot on the alien soil.

The luxuriant vegetation was abundant with emerald-green trees adorned with large, greyish leaves—segmented and chopped up—and was weirdly mixed with a stifling undergrowth of what appeared to be flowering *araceae*. But of course, these plants could never truly be the one nicknamed the "flower of paradise," because this planet was more than forty lightyears away from the Sol System and planet Earth itself. It was just how the shape resembled shrubs which were common on their home planet—apart from the strange, different colors. All of that scenery was typical for this exotic regional climate—and had suddenly become particularly thick, almost impenetrable in fact, when the two reached the border of the realm of those unusual trees that seemed to be stretching out as far as the eye could see.

Their schedule today consisted of only a small recon to be done in person, as the modern instruments and the many devices the humans had on their spaceship had almost completely examined and searched the entire surface of that area from orbit long before they reached the ground. Despite all that data received and stored, they had to do as ordered, but it was a strange sensation for them to be the first humans on the surface of such a world after thirty years. The last time men had been on that planet was during the last war fought between Earthlings and the Allied Planets of Gxirtth for supremacy in that sector. It turned out to be a bloodbath with millions of fatalities on both sides, most of them soldiers. However, there were also many civilians and colonists living in outposts off Earth who had been killed during the course of those hard-fought battles.

Then, a long peace followed the treaty signed by the two adversaries, and finally the agreement made by high ranking representatives was passed, in accordance with the will of both sides that had fought that almost unending conflict in the past. The specifics were as follows: this world of New Socotra—in alignment with the name Earthlings had given it—that was a small rock in space of little importance which had seen, despite all reasons, a long series of attacks and serious attempts at conquering it once and for all from both armies, would soon become a "restricted park." It would be a place to remember the stupidity of that long battle and an area completely without weapons, dangerous mines, or technological machinery that the alliances had filled it with in order to protect the planet or to make it deadly to the opposing side. That work required time and many months of research, along with all the procedures needed to remove the insidious things that were going to be found in the darkest recesses of those thick jungles. But the men of power didn't like to wait, after the decision had been made they simply wanted that place to be clean and safe in a very short time, before the fixed date.

So, Ernest and Selwin had been sent there to do their job as quickly as possible. They were chosen because they were probably the most experienced men of their generation with old military human technology, especially the kind of devices and bombs that were in use during the last war. And, of course, also the Allied Planets of Gxirtth would send their team of experienced specialists soon, to do the same mission.

Selwin inadvertently scratched his head that was topped with short blond curls that kept bouncing around two deep black pupils. He doubted that such a duty could be completed on time but, whatever his true opinion was, those were the orders and there was very little the two nineteen-year-old men could really object to after all. On the other hand, Ernest also had a wife he wanted to come back to as soon as possible, after so many months spent in space, but he always told himself *"First work, then play,"* . . .

New Socotra had been named by the captain of a combat starship that first stumbled into this small system after a stop, due to some unexpected damages. He had named it after an island on their homeworld: the isle of Socotra. The elderly captain was born there and thought it might prove interesting to call this new planet as such, as no one had ever discovered that luxuriant world before. Described as "the most alien-looking place on Earth," Socotra was home to some extremely strange trees, thanks to its extreme isolation from the rest of the globe. And New Socotra also looked like a very unusual planet, without intelligent inhabitants apart from a wide range of different exotic plants and wild animals. Since that moment, the sad destiny of that place had just begun, as the Military of the Allied Planets of Gxirtth knew of it and had started thinking it might be of great use given its appreciable position in space, which was situated by chance between the two fierce battle lines at that time.

Endowed with some very useful devices, like small copper finger-sized machines that were able to detect any kind of known explosives and the likes, the two humans began entering the thick jungle and walked for a few long minutes, cautiously looking around and paying attention to the terrain, full of strange plants and rocks. Both were wearing the so-called Enhanced Jungle Hot Weather RDUs (that was short for Recon Dress Uniforms). This uniform was made up of a peculiar, colorful blend of cloth that ranged in hue from shades of green, to black and gray. The designers produced this pattern by using a special fabric that allowed soldiers to appear at the same radiation level as the surrounding terrain on many different worlds. These were great for such environments, modern outfits had completely replaced the standard military uniforms that were used during the previous forty years, and let the wearers don large amounts of gear in trouser and shirt pockets, without any corrosion of items through perspiration and no danger of being easily penetrated by undesired bites from undiscerned little creatures living in the habitats.

Undoubtedly, such precautions were not meant to be used in real battles, but were just worn to prevent the soldiers from being attacked by any wild animals or to become the target of some still functioning automatic battle systems left behind somewhere in the thick of the trees.

The terrain seemed to be made up of only resilient shrubs, and the challenging undergrowth bounced beneath their feet. The unruly land was covered with dense vegetation at ground level, and it was sufficiently imposing to hinder movement by Earthlings. It required the duo to cut their way through with a lot of difficulty as the underbrush was filled with numerous hard but small branches, making walking a demanding effort that proved to be possible only at a very slow pace. Their instruments told them the plants that sprang up everywhere were mostly seasonal and very impenetrable because of this peculiar season, not that they would have looked any less thick in any other time of the twenty-two-month-long year. . . What they were able to see at that moment didn't give the misleading impression that these conditions existed throughout the entire forest—these plants were just an unending stretch of trees and undergrowth all around.

Selwin considered how problematic it had probably been when the first troops coming from Earth were dropped to the surface and initially travelled through such a jungle. He had been told that using the old mapping systems proved to be of little or no use in most cases. Seemingly lost within such a wild, uncontrollable expanse of nature, and isolated from civilization, must have evoked deep emotions: threat, confusion, powerlessness, disorientation. There would've also been a lot of unusual plants that were alluring to them, that could have had a deep effect on the soldiers of a bygone time, despite their being well-trained and highly experienced.

This world was, undeniably, a very feral environment and it would never be the type of destination suitable for extreme tourists or exploring travelers. Other than that, there weren't expeditions led by local jungle guides around here, as the planet hadn't possessed any fixed outpost or intelligent life before the start of the war. Only dumb luck had made warlike people and soldiers come here to conquer its most useful areas and defend those places against alien enemies.

Two hours later, Ernest and Selwin arrived at a tiny violet stream running through the ground cover. The first one stopped cautiously in the stunted vegetation lining the small river bank. From that point of the forest on, the other side was abundant in a sort of alien pine tree, gray beaches and several dark shrubs, along with some low mountains in the distance. The many plants nearby appeared to have more branches than usual, and some smaller and slenderer flowers, clothed at the base and the color of the stormy sky, filled that part of the area. They had never seen anything like those flowers. There was no record of them in common historical files, even though they must have been on some report during the last war. Immediately, Ernest cut and cautiously placed some of them into his bags for later examination when they reboarded.

The two men remained for a while on the other side of the jungle's boundaries, the chief continuously searching the dull undergrowth and picking up interesting samples, while Selwin kept looking back to spot anything dangerous that was hiding nearby.

Then, in that moment, they heard some unusual sounds, *or better, their augmented senses noticed them*, and they turned around immediately in search of where it came from. Some rustling seemed to be moving across the leaves and a few shrubs were briefly shaken in the vicinity. Then, the piercing eyes of the duo found the source of it all, *and there were many reasons. . .*

Some unexpected and uninvited guests were quickly approaching their position from all sides, and given their movements and slow pace, they appeared to be anthropomorphic individuals. After a few minutes, Ernest and Selwin finally saw them with their own eyes. They looked like some lost, faint souls emerging from a sea of mist that wrapped all the surroundings in a very strange, unnatural way, like when the hair stood up on the back of one's neck.

The first figure turned out to be a short, lean, pale man of western European origin, sporting a long graying beard and loose-fitting clothing. Then came two other individuals, both of a similar height, around five feet ten inches. The first one had blonde hair, dark eyes and some striking features on his face, while the second had darker, short tri-colored curls, along with big, blue eyes. All their faces were camouflaged by muddy, oily covering that concealed their skin.

But it wasn't just the human features of the members of that incredible group that made the two young men surprised, as some parts of their bodies were clearly metallic and looked like add-ons, even though the parts were worn-out, battered and old-fashioned.

The first man on the left—*because he was a real man for sure*—was enveloped in camouflaged body-armor. His eyes were two thin pieces of glass-like shapes reflecting the gray leaves that shrouded the untamed surrounding which composed this world. A weird mechanical, crackling noise began buzzing little by little, coming from his right arm. Then the metal devices in his left shoulder exerted a continuous scraping sound, as if those parts were damaged, unable to work properly.

Ernest turned and watched the scene. Everyone in the group of unexpected guests stopped and gaped at him open-mouthed. He looked back at them, unaware of what they were staring at. *How had they been capable of moving completely undetected?* the young chief thought to himself. *But, most of all, why hadn't the modern instruments on their spaceship found any traces of their presence while searching the surface from the planetary orbit?*

"Who are you? Identify yourself at once!" the first short figure demanded. The man with the long graying beard pointed his camouflaged E.H.P.G. (Excimer High Precision Gun) at both of them. It was an old crude version of the common black rifle that was in use thirty or forty years past. It had a heavy barrel, capable of generating up to sixty energy bolts, usually issued with a scope to marksmen. This was a perfect weapon to provide precision fire under an assault, an aid in observation and adjusting of supporting arms. Its hand-guard also allowed an easy modular mounting location for all types of equipment, though it was certainly outdated. The others were standing around, equipped in different ways, some of them with fighting knifes dangling from their belts at the waist, others were taking aim with similar guns.

At first, the two young humans were unable to answer, so they kept staring at the unusual events occurring before their eyes.

"They don't seem to be soldiers of Gxirtth, Major Retchie, they're human," the individual with darker, tri-colored hair added soon after.

"No, we aren't from Gxirtth, in fact, stated Earnest. "We are soldiers, members of the New Earth Army. And who are you?"

"*NEW Earth Army*? What's that about? There's only one Earth Army, the dear old, dirty one," the third man with blonde hair cried out.

"Okay, stop it now!"

"By your order, Major."

After a while, all the remaining men in the area emerged from their jungle hiding spots and Ernest and Selwin found themselves surrounded. There were at least forty adversaries around them, and all those people were cyborsoldiers: human beings with both organic and artificial parts, possessing enhanced abilities through technological augmentations. They were like people from another time, as it had been at least twenty years since a cyborsodier was sent into battle, after the current policy of the New Earth Government had been established, with all its laws about body augmentations and the latest restrictions.

"Anyway, it's just as my chief told you. We are soldiers of the New Earth Army," Selwin confirmed in a plain tone.

"And what is this 'New Earth Army?' It's true that we've been secluded from the rest of the troops fighting in space for a very long time, but we can't have missed that much. Why are you here now?"

And it was at that moment that Ernest understood the true reality that lay before them: those people were cyborsoldiers from the last war, humans with robotic implants—the few soldiers who had been surgically altered using the technology of that long-ago time. These implants were developed to replace a severed arm or leg but looked to be designed for aiding in heavy manual labor. Some of these people had even been rebuilt, replicated to resemble their past selves. They used augmentations during the war, becoming soldiers of notoriety. It was at that time that the cyborsoldiers teams were formed, very capable troops to hold difficult ground or deploy on problematic alien surfaces elsewhere in space. The group before them had grown up and aged while fighting the war, fought even long after it had ended.

So Ernest told the one that had been called Major Retchie, "The war is over. It happened thirty years ago and a treaty was signed between New Earth and the Allied Planets of Gxirtth."

"Do you think you can deceive us?" replied one of the team of cyborsoldiers, wearing worn-out *crossbelts* and sidearms.

"Maybe they are just spies, Major," said another individual with a robotic cyborhand, looking at them with his wide glass-like eyes.

The young chief considered the incredible situation the two of them had stumbled into and looked attentively at those old-fashioned combatants. Apparently, there was only one Major in the team, and all the others seemed to be non-commissioned officers.

"We can prove that what we say is true. Just let us show you." With that said, Selwin gestured that he wanted to pick something out of the pockets in his Recon Dress Uniform, but his move was halted by the cyborsoldiers aiming their weapons as him.

"Please, just let us show you our portable devices, and you will be able to look at all the data about our current duty . . . and the historical files we have on the last war."

The short Major moved forward and stared at Selwin for a few moments, ordered, "Harry, take care of their equipment and all of you keep aiming your firearms at them. I suggest you not play any tricks on us, as my men are hair-triggered . . ."

So, a tall, slender cyborsoldier approached the two and started searching their uniforms, removing all the devices and technological objects he found. Then he said, "These seem to be some damn good cammies, Major, better than ours."

"It's all in the small datapad," Selwin told him, looking at a finger-sized device that lay on the ground now, along with some other tools.

"Is this a datapad?" the cyborsoldiers asked him. "Are you sure?"

"Yes, you just have to activate it by touching that button and you'll find all you need to know on the holo-screen."

"Holo-screen?" Harry looked surprised. "That's something I want to see for myself."

"Everything in its own time, men!" Retchie cried out. "Who can assure us that such a device, once opened, isn't going to infiltrate our technology or damage our augmentations, leaving us unarmed?"

"You're right!" a middle-aged cyborsoldier nodded.

"This is why we are going to have our assault specialist take a look at all this machinery before it's too late." Saying that, the wary Major gestured to another cyborsoldier in the distance to come forward. As a bulky individual approached, Ernest recognized his Space Communication Team insignia. The outside of his head showed evidence that his brain was a sophisticated and computerized mechanism, always keeping him linked to the other soldiers' minds, giving him a sixth sense.

Only a few moments went by while the while the specialist searched. He finally admitted, "It seems to be okay. There's a massive amount of data on the device."

"Hmmm. . ." the leader of the cyborsoldiers considered.

"A moment, sir. . ." said one of the soldiers in protest.

"Yeah?"

"Just let Frank have a look at that thing too!" the hairless cyborsoldier cried out. "You never know."

"Okay, you're right, Francesco . . . better safe than sorry," Retchie agreed.

A sturdy, stout man moved forward and reached the pair. Earnest stared at him, noticing this man may have been the strangest of all. As a hybrid of machine and organism—his torso was organic—

he was endowed with a near human-like appearance, despite his long, pale and grey face. Hundreds of tendrils extended from the back of his head, each measuring several inches in length, the metal on them interwoven with his remaining skin. Both of his eyes were luminous: two orange orbs that always seemed to be watching everything in sight.

His left arm and right hand were cybernetic, likely replaced in his previous life for the conditions in which he worked, a control room of a spaceship or a military outpost. Additional, brilliant white lights at the end of flexible metal cables were bent and tied in different shapes, functioning as receptors for his extremities.

An array of millions of electrodes fired into his nervous system, linking him to the high-speed localnet the team set up during the last war. The localnet connected the military spacenet to the databanks of the starships themselves, orbiting somewhere close to increase the signals' strength, sending them to the headquarters. This had enabled him to browse and search at will through the sections he had access. Incidentally, the old spacenet he was connected to was obsolete.

The troops remaining on this world were not informed of the spacnet being obsolete, nor had they been updated with the modern web built by the New Earth Army. Years ago, there would have been virtually no software networks or details about alien planets that man couldn't have reached using these replacements. Now that entire online world was gone, the hybrid's many metallic adds-on still attached to his body. . . His role meant that he was able to turn the files on the videos or open/close them by moving an eyelid or by thinking. Some old reports also said men like him even dreamed of unending data flows when asleep, but this had never been confirmed.

With all those delicate devices in place, the cyborsoldier could successfully extend his nervous system over the entire localnet, make it control a robotic hand or a single mechanism on the surface. This was a form of increased sensory input and he had direct electronic communication between himself and almost all the robo-servants working daily within the military outposts during the war.

All the tendrils, cables, and connecting wires on the back of his body, along his shoulders and head, gave him the appearance of a strange floating being. It was as though he were dangling from an unseen coat peg fixed to a rail in the sky, moving with him, or maybe leading him forward. . .

"That's safe," the heavy-built cyborsoldier confirmed in the end. "And it's easily accessible . . . we can proceed, Major."

"Okay—if you say so!" Retchie nodded. "Open it up and let's have a look at what's inside."

After checking and reading through the contents of the mini-datapad, except the information that needed to be properly decoded, the face of the three cyborsoldiers that were around the floating holo-screen, looked pensive. A strange expression appeared on their faces within minutes. The others standing around were able to listen to what the vocal text explained, even though they were unable to directly watch the video displayed.

"So, it's true," one of the team said.

"Damn headquarters!" another one exclaimed in disbelief.

"They did, they really made peace after all. . ."

The two young men approached the group of cyborsoldiers and stared at their faces in silence for some time. *Who knows how much they went through during those lost years*, they thought.

"Why didn't you try to communicate with any of the starships in space?" Selwin asked. He turned his eyes away before he could see the angry look the short leader gave him. "I mean, if you still had some means to do it here on the surface of New Socotra."

"We didn't. We also lacked a working, reliable communication device to keep in touch with headquarters and the rest of our army, as the climate on this world and the strange weather conditions were terrible for our machinery. The weather is also bad for our cybor adds-on. For a very short time Harry was able to fix the problems and he finally got the radio to function. We received bits of news and a few transmissions. We also heard of a great space battle in this sector, and then nothing. It stopped working."

"I see. . ." Selwin conceded.

"Yes. For a while, things were bad for us in this area," Ernest explained. "But then everything changed and the situation improved for our ships. Within a few months the first tries at peace began, thirty years ago,"

"We lacked everything, even food. We were forced to adapt by eating the strange indigenous fruits," the middle-aged leader said.

"And it's just not enough," specified another nearly hairless cyborsoldier on the left, with a metallic wrist damaged from the heavy rain, two blue eyes that looked like vividly painted brilliant stones overshadowing his muddy features. "The first few days we stayed in these jungles, most of us couldn't keep any water down, we were running a fever, and could feel our strength waning with every step."

"As for me, I missed the drop position and found myself in the darkest side of the whole planet," said a short man with a damaged right arm. "The only way out of the jungle was to walk—for eight days, I got a fever, and at one point the fainting became so regular that I started to question whether I would make it out alive. The combination of weakness, an alien environment, and such a long trek were starting to play tricks on my mind. Then I reached some troops of ours and they were offering treatment, though by that point I can't really remember taking it. I was better in a day or so, and after five days I was ready to leave, to join my friends and fight."

The tall hairless cyborsoldier that had just spoke, before the one with the damaged right arm, was walking in circles next to a boulder near a *mahwa tree*—it wasn't a fast-growing mahwa tree like those on Earth, but something that only resembled it. . . It seemed as if he was a damaged toy in some ways, or just lost in his own imaginings of his experiences on this planet.

"You went through some very difficult times, for sure." Ernest nodded.

"And no damn WM around, too," another man added.

"WM?" Selwin asked him.

"Woman Marine, an old slang."

"Oh, I see, I forgot about that," the young one replied.

"And you can't imagine how bad such things can be, either," the one named Frank added soon after, a showy double belt passing over both shoulders that also crossed at the breast.

"But we survived, and kept staying watchful, in wait . . . as the name of our team is the 'Unbeatable Ones' and it will ever be so!" the leader stated, staring at the two younger men before himself in a challenging way.

"But we did it for nothing!" said a tall, slender though one-eyed cyborsoldier, his left pupil transformed into an ocular automatic aiming system. His eye seemed to be off-line at present and displayed a dejected overall image on the man, like a dead computer that time had forgotten.

A short standstill followed.

"Yes, the reality is that you kept fighting and continuously hiding in these thick jungles while the war was already over, and the two sides were signing the terms of a modern alliance that still continues today." Selwyn nodded, thinking how incredible those words were now.

A long silence fell on the whole team of middle-aged cyborsoldiers that lasted for some time. Then the leader, named Retchie, asked the two young men, "So, what do you propose we do now?"

"Stop fighting, firstly, and then pack your belongings before preparing to board the next starship back home. We can take a few of you with us, but unfortunately our spaceship is too small to take all of your team aboard today."

"In order to do so, we will need a direct order from headquarters, or whatever it is called these days," the short Major replied.

"We can do it on your behalf," Ernest said. "Given the great distances involved, we can't get a clear signal here with real-time holo-video from headquarters, but texts and data files can easily be sent through space. What you'll see will allow you to read the orders from the top."

"So, proceed!" Retchie accepted.

"Easier done than said!" the young chief exclaimed, and his fingers moved across the small surface of the device to send the message to Earth.

Minutes went by and a look of surprise appeared on many of the cyborsoldiers' faces. The one named Harry, that made the first search of their portable devices before, stared at Ernest's movements and asked him: "Is it that easy to send messages through distances of 40-light-years?"

"Well, I must say that the process is very fast," Ernest stated. He tried not to appear too advanced in comparison with the common and outdated cyborsoldiers' knowledge of space communications. "Even though some problems occur at times, given the giant stars nearby or a few gravitational anomalies that can weaken the signals."

The answer came just fifteen minutes later and the young chief was ready to show the response to the team leader. Retchie approached Ernest to read the text on the holo-screen.

"We are ordered to stop fighting, men. That's what Peace Headquarters said," Retchie stated in a low tone. Then he considered in coarse laughter: "What the hell . . . how can you call them by that name? *Peace Headquarters*?"

"It's their name now . . . did you read the whole text? Are you finally certain about the end of the war?"

"They want us to cease our operations here," the other said, slightly distracted.

"That's what our headquarters, well, the *Peace Headquarters*, orders you to do."

"Do you mean the same headquarters that forgot of our existence?" the one-eyed combatant on the left cried out. "Or Earth itself? Who thought we were already dead in these jungles?"

"No one could ever think you were still on this planet, ready to fight a war that ended so long ago," Ernest said in a conceited tone. His words didn't convince all the cyborsoldiers, they simply didn't want to believe it.

"I don't know, I don't really know," Retchie said.

"But your stay here is of no use now, you must understand what has happened!" Selwin insisted.

"*Of no use*, you said? But we were of great use when we remained hiding in these jungles and fought for your side, weren't we? Who are you to tell us this? I don't take orders from two *boys* like you."

"You read the orders coming directly from headquarters a moment ago—do you question their authenticity?"

"Do you boys think that we would have rusted away yet?" Retchie asked Selwin.

"That's not what I meant, but you have stayed outside, in this place, for a very long time."

"This is something that is worth appreciation, in my opinion."

"Yes, yes, but you see . . . while you've been here, a lot of things have drastically changed in the rest of the universe."

"And maybe the end of the war was what all of us wanted to reach, long ago, but now I don't know it anymore, I'm not sure," the leader said.

"What did it change?"

"Everything! It's all changed out there . . . Maybe that's a world and a space we don't want to go back to anymore, maybe everything is too different from what we once knew."

"I understand, but these are the orders."

"The orders of *Peace Headquarters*," Retchie repeated with a sneer.

"Exactly."

"And who is going to force me to leave our position now?" the cyborsoldier Major challenged him.

"That's an order . . . it's what headquarters commands you to do."

"I don't know," the other said. "We fought for the Earth Army, and we followed the orders our officers gave us . . . but it's been a very long time since we received any new instructions from them. They're probably all gone now."

"So what? Aren't you going to do as I tell you? Do you want to stay here forever?"

"Just convince me, boy," Retchie said in a fierce tone.

"How? Do you need a direct order from—"

"No, not at all. We can do it according to the old ways."

"That being?"

"When a cyborsoldier questioned the commanding officer and they were too far from home, being stranded on some distant outpost or in a lost jungle like this, they would proceed in two ways: the first was by arresting and court-martialing the objector for insubordination; or stage a fight like the ones held in the old times to determine who the better soldier was, and who was truly the leader of the war team."

"Which one do you propose?" Ernest asked him, looking at the leader in a curious, watchful way.

"As you can see, I'm older than you, so I prefer the old ways. You can try to arrest me and all of my men, or you can convince me by fair or foul means. Just show me that Earth soldiers are not feeble weapons today, that they are as good as we are, and that the current officers don't simply want to leave this place, scared to death about this war. Show me you're not afraid to fight against those damn aliens of the *Allied Planets of Gxirtth*. Maybe the 'New Earth Army' is giving in to their commands, or maybe what you say is true. So, who knows, if you behave well, maybe I'll give my team the same order you gave me before and the others will follow it. Otherwise. . ."

"You want us to fight? You mean, in physical combat?"

"Don't you fight any more in your New Earth Army? Have you become so weak and delicate? Is this what your Peace Headquarters orders you to be?"

"No, certainly not," the younger one replied. "But you could be seriously harmed."

The other laughed deeply, in a boisterous tone. "We'll see, boy!"

"I must warn you that I'm very experienced in close-quarters warfare, for your safety," said Ernest.

"So be it, we'll see if your skills are better than mine!"

The rays of the reddish sun were filtering through the membranes of the large, almost transparent greyish leaves of the curved trees leaning over the endless jungle, faintly lighting the ground underneath. The pupils of the leader enlarged as he stared at his opponent.

Suddenly, he exclaimed, "Let's go!" and he released a cry in his own slang, which sounded like an angry growl with bizarre inflection. Then, he moved against the younger human, after dropping his rifle into the shrubs.

He took off one of his hands in order to use it as a mace, and Ernest decided for a defensive position, waiting for the right moment to dart sideways, prevent his body from the blow. But wasn't fast enough, the blow to his face was crushing and he lost his balance, falling into the large leaves on the terrain.

The Major rejoiced with a wide, delighted sneer across his strong, battered features. But it didn't last for long. Soon after, the younger one stood up, raised his right hand, put his fingers together in a flat knife-like form and gave a powerful blow downwards, attempting to reach the other's breastplate. He missed his target, though part of the opponent's left shoulder was partially damaged in the process—the shoulder not protected by the crossbelt of his worn-out body armor.

The other remained in silence, keeping a cool head, his uniform slowly spurting blood. A single attack like the last one wasn't enough to beat him, his cold eyes seemed to say. But a glimmer of rebellion showed in the other man's face.

So the two engaged in a subsequent violent hand-to-hand struggle there in the jungle, with numerous alternating lunges and shoves ensuing. After a while, the middle-aged cyborsoldier hit his rival in mid-chest with incredible force, hurling him backwards unexpectedly. But the assault didn't do much damage. Ernest was able to recover quickly from that blow and threw against the other's face a fast, incredible elbow, met with little effect. Another backhanded attack drove him against the opposite rock, while the waist of the older one was lowered again to reach his neck, getting stuck only for a while in some wooden remains. *It's hard to hit someone who keeps continuously moving*, Retchie told himself, and the younger human resulted to being very clever about that. But his moves, even though quick, weren't powerful as his. The other was able to free himself in the end, but the man assaulted him again, even though an unstoppable Ernest kept advancing and retreating with incredible speed.

Other than that, it seemed that all the shrubs and the fallen curved trees around made it difficult for the young human to correctly plan his steps and damn hard to react appropriately, while the cyborsoldier had much more experience at moving across that strange terrain, knew where to place his feet.

Then Retchie walked towards Ernest and put a hand on his chest, trying to pierce his skin by means of his considerable strength, but wasn't able to do it, apart from causing some bruises. His opponent resisted and stepped back, ready to inflict a new stream of lunges on his part. Because of the many efforts applied in the cruel fighting, both of them were forced back, step by step, to the nearest trunk. The two adversaries were defending themselves and their honor against the other assailant's will to prevail, hoping to win and eventually humiliate the adversary. Again, the cyborsoldier's voice sounded like a cry of hatred as he tried to overwhelm the contending human, while he was slowly beating the other's body from the back to the left shoulder with great persistence. He seemed to be prevailing little by little against the stubborn opposition he was facing.

Soon, a wound opened wide on the younger one's face, but that wasn't enough to get the better of him, as he proved capable of evading the attacker's hold once more. The cyborsoldier's hands seemed to dance around to no end for a while, brushing by the face, almost twice touching the back, then scratching the brow, unable to fully reach the designated target. Then the short Major achieved his end, hitting one of his opponent's arms by means of a powerful blow, piercing his skin thoroughly. The other combatant attempted to lift the cyborsoldier up, but he was very heavy and losing ground, being so bloated with blood running out of his mouth, nose, and ears. Both men were physically and morally fatigued from such a violent fight— but nothing was going to stop them now.

So, the two kept battling fiercely, charging each other repeatedly in hand-to-hand combat, using methods of dirty fighting in the process. Ernest started running to the right—towards the other, who threw himself against his enemy with equal speed, from the left, swinging a pointed elbow and hitting his target solidly in the back of the neck. The younger one's face responded, contracted in dread, with a low cry from his bloodied mouth. Now, for the first time, he finally appeared powerless to contend against such a great desire for victory, which the cyborsoldier was making such a stunning show of at present.

The fight was clearly going to end soon. The last attack the older man attempted proved to be the final move as he hit the other with all his strength, flooring him. Ernest didn't stand up immediately, remaining on the ground for a while, incapable of getting back on his feet.

Then something strange happened, as Retchie approached the other man who was down, and he moved a hand towards his arm. The human on the ground turned his head to him and remained in waiting. The older Major made a clear gesture and grasped his hand to help him up.

"You fought damn well to be only a kid!" the leader of the cybersoldiers said in a low tone.

Ernest stared at him briefly then replied, "And you hit damn hard to be only an old Major, that's for sure!"

A grin appeared on the other's face and what seemed to be a look of appreciation filled his strong, battered features. Maybe he was just satisfied now, and the two started to understand each other, on a deeper level.

"Maybe your current Peace Headquarters doesn't train rotten soldiers. You're pretty good, from what I can see. That makes me consider some things now."

"So what?"

"Well, maybe I could think again about your previous orders, the ones we received from Earth."

"Do you mean . . .?"

"If our present officers can train someone young like you and turn him into a valuable combatant, who knows, maybe this current world and space of yours out there, even your New Earth Army, are something worth seeing and joining."

"Really? That's great, indeed!" a pleased Ernest replied.

"I'll talk to my team, and then we'll see." That being said, the leader assembled all his cyborsoldiers around and they started discussing the matter for a short time. When they finished, the middle-aged Major moved away from the others and reached him again.

"We decided: we are going to leave this place forever, we'll stop fighting today!"

"That's very good of you, I appreciate your affirmation."

Retchie approached the younger Ernest and put his right hand on the other's shoulder, then sneered at him.

At that point Ernest smiled back in return and asked the team leader, "Please, just tell me one thing."

"About what?"

"Well, before landing we did a complete survey of the planet from our orbiting position and the spaceship's instruments didn't find any traces of your presence on the surface . . . how did you do it?"

"Oh, that's easy, just a little trick of ours," the other replied. "Under the terrain there are massive caves that we discovered and started using as shelters at night during the war. Moreover, the peculiar minerals they are made of proved to be capable of preventing any detection by spaceships in orbit."

"I see, undoubtedly. But we were also unable to notice your movement above ground until you and your cyborsoldiers got very near—so, is there another secret, Major Retchie?"

"Well, after a few years of staying here, one of our men found that the vegetation we used to camouflage our fatigues could be mixed with another local substance taken from the walls of the caves we slept in at night—thus turning our military clothing and body-replacements into undetectable objects. Of course, it's not easy to keep that on your skin all day, as it's a bit irritating, but if you make it, well, you too become almost undetectable."

"That's much more efficacious than our present Enhanced Jungle Hot Weather RDUs."

"What can I say? At times good finds are better than the most up-to-date technology."

"You're right; it always seems to be like that. And I imagine you used the substance to keep your old automated battle devices hidden in these jungles, didn't you?"

"Yes, of course!" Retchie said. "But we'll help you to find their exact location, be sure. It's the main duty of the older ones to teach the kids something useful, you know."

"I'm here just to learn," Ernest replied.

After the two young soldiers had left the team of cyborsoldiers and were going back to their spaceship, Selwin looked at his friend and said: "Why didn't you fight at your best? The body equipment of the soldiers in that team was in very poor condition. Other than that, their adds-on and many of the cyber-arms were malfunctioning or appeared damaged—you could have easily taken advantage of his movement problem, striking at the perfect moment . . . so there would have been no chance for that Major to have won."

Ernest turned to him and smiled in a way only he was used to doing. "Well, you know, Selwin, those cyborsoldiers had been hiding in these jungles for a long time, trying to survive and struggling against the difficulties of such a harsh environment, while being completely alone and with absent of help from Earth. Other than that, they fought courageously against the alien invaders for many years during the war, all of that for the good of their homeplanet."

"So what?" the other asked.

"What's the name of their team? Do you remember it?"

"The Unbeatable Ones," Selwin replied at once, making a face.

"So, why should have I humiliated them by beating their leader so easily? How would they react if their best cyborsoldier would have been defeated by a young kid like me?"

The other fellow thought to himself for some time before stating: "I see your point now. You reasoned it all out, undoubtedly, as you always do."

Ernest nodded, then thought to himself. *After all, how could things have gone differently?* Many things had changed since the time of the last war, and the technology those old men were endowed with inside their arms and bodies... Even a single microchip inserted into a modern holo-book today would result to be more advanced than any of the old military integrated circuits those cyborsoldiers had been implanted with under their skin. As a matter of fact, by discovering they themselves were completely outdated, those combatants would have been deeply angered and dejected. As many things had been innovated in the military field, too, over the course of thirty years, along with the training, the equipment, and the physical build of the new soldiers themselves. Probably, the news that a group of two genetically engineered 19-year-old guys like the newcomers could do the work of an entire team of forty good cyborsoldiers of a time gone by, might really have proven to be a blow too hard for those middle-aged men to accept. Nowadays the physical add-ons all the military personnel were endowed with were genetic—without any metallic implants—and had been so for at least the last fifteen years.

After all, Ernest was well aware of the fact that if he had easily beaten their proud Major—as he could have done, in fact, without any struggle—the cybersoldiers would have never again called themselves the "Unbeatable Ones."

"Respect for the veterans and for what they did at war to defend their homeland"—that was a common saying among the new recruits today. And wasn't that exactly what the two had showed them, after all: *high esteem and a deep respect*?

Because, as an ancient man once said: "But the freedom that they fought for, and the country grand they wrought for, is their monument to-day, and for aye."

PUBLICATIONS CREDITS:

ABOUT THE AUTHORS

M. Lopes da Silva is an author and fine artist living in Los Angeles. She has crafted articles for Blumhouse, The California Literary Review, and Queen Mob's Teahouse. Recently she illustrated the Centipede Press collector's edition of Jonathan Carroll's *The Land of Laughs*. Her short horror story "Thump House" is appearing in Mad Scientist Journal's Utter Fabrication anthology in 2017. Previously, her short fiction "The Carving" was published in Threads: A Neoverse Anthology. Her work frequently explores themes of obsession and anatomy, and boldly celebrates the fantastic and strange. You can read her collection of creepy short stories, *The Dog Next Door and Other Disturbances*, on Amazon.

Sheldon Woodbury is an award-winning writer (screenplays, plays, books, short stories, and poems). He also teaches screenwriting at New York University. His book *Cool Million* is considered the essential guide to writing high concept movies. His short stories and poems have appeared in many horror anthologies and magazines. His novel *The World on Fire* was published September 2014 by JWK Fiction.

Chad Lutzke lives in Battle Creek, MI. with his wife, children, and far too many dogs. He loves music, rain, sarcasm, dry humor, and cheese. He has a strong disdain for dishonesty and hard-boiled eggs. Chad has written for Famous Monsters of Filmland, Rue Morgue, Cemetery Dance and Scream magazine. His fiction can be found in several magazines and anthologies including his own 18-story collection, NIGHT AS A CATALYST. He has written a collaborative effort with horror author Terry M. West, THE HIM DEEP DOWN. In the summer of 2016, Lutzke released his dark coming-of-age novella OF FOSTER HOMES AND FLIES which has been praised by authors Jack Ketchum, James Newman, John Boden, and many others. Later in 2016, Lutzke released his contribution to bestselling author J. Thorn's AMERICAN DEMON HUNTER series, and winter 2017 saw the release of WALLFLOWER, a story of addiction, delusion, and flowers. Chad can be found lurking the internet at the following address: **www.chadlutzke.com**

Christopher Pulo is an avid reader of horror fiction, most likely a results of having been exposed to the works of Stephen King at a young age. A high school Science teacher from Sydney, Australia he has always enjoyed writing pieces of speculative fiction in his spare time. The hobby has always allowed him to create fantastical situations and given him a way to get some of the weird and wonderful ideas from his imagination down onto the page. From exploding Chemistry experiments to apocalyptic encounters with hip hop legends he always relishes in putting pen to paper. . .

Jeremy Szal was born in 1995 in the outback of Australia and was raised by wild dingoes. His science-fiction and fantasy work has appeared in Nature, Abyss & Apex, Lightspeed, Strange Horizons, Tor.com, The Drabblecast, and has been translated into multiple languages. He is the fiction editor for Hugo-winning podcast StarShipSofa where he's worked with authors such as George R. R. Martin, William Gibson, and Joe R. Lansdale. He is represented by John Jarrold of the John Jarrold Literary Agency. He carves out a living in Sydney, Australia. Find him at **http://jeremyszal.com/** or @JeremySzal.

Carl R. Jennings is, by day, a thickly Russian accented bartender in Southwestern Vir-ginia. By night, he is the rooster-themed superhero: the Molotov Cocktail, protecting the weak and beer-sodden. While heroically pos-ing on a rooftop in the moonlight in case a roaming photographer happens by, he finds the time to write down a word or *two in the life-long dream that he can put aside the superhero mantle and utility comb and become a real author.*

Joseph Aitken was born in Canada and currently lives and writes in the Woodlands, Texas. His stories have appeared in Silent Screams, Splickety's Lightning Blog, and Phantaxis, and he is a copy editor for Strange Horizons. He can be found online at josephaitken.com and on Twitter @joseph_aitken.

Guy Immega is a retired aerospace engineer. His company, *Kinetic Sciences Inc.* built experimental robots for the space station. His short story, "Epilogue," is included in *Tesseracts Twenty 2017*. His novel, *The Eye of the Beholder*, is represented by Spectrum Literary Agency in New York City. For more writing credits, visit his website: **http://www.guyimmega.com.**

Chris Vander Kaay has been published at *McSweeney's* and *Everyday Fiction*, has published three educational books about horror & sci-fi film history, and is a contributing writer at Bloody-Disgusting.com.

Kathleen Killian Fernandez-Vander Kaay has been published in McSweeney's, Curbside Splendor, Cypress Dome and featured in the upcoming issue of Kaaterskill Basin. She is the co-author of several non-fiction books about film history. She writes almost exclusively about Las Vegas and/or alien abductions.

Alex Matkowsky is a budding novelist and short story author pursuing his Bachelors in English, and eventually his Masters, at Rowan University. He wrote stories and created worlds all throughout his childhood, with hope one day of achieving recognition. When finished with university, he hopes to pursue working full-time as a professor of English and creative writing.

Julie Nováková (www.julienovakova.com) is a Czech author of science fiction, fantasy and detective stories. She has published short fiction e.g. in *Clarkesworld*, *Asimov's* and *Analog*. Her work in Czech includes seven novels, an anthology and over thirty stories. She received the Encouragement Award of the European science fiction and fantasy society in 2013 and the Aeronautilus award for the best Czech short story of 2014 and 2015, and for the best novel in 2015. She also translates, writes nonfiction and is a contributor of the Czech SF magazine XB-1. She is an evolutionary biologist by study and also takes a keen interest in planetary science.
Twitter: @julianne_sf
Facebook: fb.com/JulieNovakovaAuthor

David Turton has extensive training in Journalism, Marketing and Public Relations and has been writing as a career for over fourteen years. A huge horror fiction fan, particularly the works of Stephen King, David has written several short stories, all centred around dark tales of horror and dystopia. He is also in the final stages of his first novel, an apocalyptic horror set in the near future.

Frank Roger was born in 1957 in Ghent, Belgium.

His first story appeared in 1975. Since then his stories appear in an increasing number of languages in all sorts of magazines and anthologies, and since 2000, story collections are published, also in various languages. Apart from fiction, he also produces collages and graphic work in a surrealist and satirical tradition. They have appeared in various magazines and books. His work is a blend of genres and styles that can best be described as "frankrogerism", an approach of which he is the main representative.

By now he has a few hundred short stories to his credit, published in more than 40 languages. In 2012 a story collection in English *The Burning Woman and Other Stories* was published by *Evertype* (www.evertype.com). Find out more at http://www.frankroger.be.

Damir Salkovic is an aficionado of weird and macabre tales, presently residing in Arlington, Virginia. His reading interests range from horror and fantasy to pulp and science fiction. His short stories have been published on the *Tales to Terrify* podcast, in the *Lovecraft ezine* and in anthologies by *Parasomnia Press, Apokrupha, Martian Migraine Press*, the *Mad Scientist Journal, Ulthar Press, Emby Press* and others. He earns his living as an accountant, a profession that lends itself well to nightmares and harrowing visions.

Darren Todd writes short fiction full time, along with freelance book editing for Evolved Publications and narrating the occasional audiobook for Audible, Inc. His short fiction has appeared in twenty-three publications over the last eleven years. He has had three plays produced and a non-fiction book published.

Most of his works fall under the literary or horror umbrella. His style and reading preferences tends toward the psychological, as he enjoys stories that linger in the imagination long after he's closed the book on them.

He lives in Scottsdale, Arizona with his wife and son, and does his best work in coffee shops on a dated Alphasmart word processor.

Morgan Crooks grew up in a hamlet in Upstate New York and now teaches ancient history in Massachusetts. Links to his stories are available on the Ancient Logic website (www.ancientlogic.blogspot.com). He lives with his wife, Lauren, near Boston.

Blair Frison lives on the beautiful island of Cape Breton, in Nova Scotia. He is pursuing a degree in Business Management and spends most of his free time writing and watching an unhealthy amount of horror movies – often with his equally horror-obsessed daughter. He has a passion for music and animals, and hopes to one day get over his fear of flying.

He has written for various publications (both online and in print) such as Fossil Lake IV:SHARKASAURUS!, The Edge: Infinite Darkness, Deadman's Tome, Boxing 24/7, and Haunt of Horrors. Blair is currently working on a collection of short stories.

Edward Ahern resumed writing after forty odd years in foreign intelligence and international sales. He's had a hundred fifty stories and poems published so far. His collected fairy and folk tales, *The Witch Made Me Do It* was published by Gypsy Shadow Press. His novella *The Witches' Bane* was published by World Castle Publishing, and his collected fantasy and horror stories, *Capricious Visions* was published by Gnome on Pig Press. Ed's currently working on a paranormal/thriller novel tentatively titled *The Rule of Chaos.* He works the other side of writing at Bewildering Stories, where he sits on the review board and manages a posse of five review editors.

Derek Nason lives and writes in the New Brunswick, Canada. He holds degrees in Philosophy and Film Production.

Max D. Stanton is an academic and writer of weird tales who lives in Philadelphia with his great hound Bear and his imperious cat Tristan. You can find his work in publications including *World Unknown Review, Sanitarium Magazine, Disturbed Digest, Lovecraftiana* [forthcoming] and the *Under a Dark Sign* and *Candlesticks & Daggers* anthologies.

Kurt Newton's dark fiction has appeared in *Weird Tales, Weirdbook, Dark Discoveries,* and *Shroud.* He is the author of two novels, *The Wishnik* and *Powerlines.* He is a lifelong resident of the Connecticut woods.

Leigh Green is a tech lead and community manager in the gaming industry with over a decade of experience in the IT world. She is a sci-fi and fantasy writer and has had flash fiction previously published in the 'zine *Fissure.* Currently she is completing a BFA in

Creative Writing with Full Sail University. A fan of DIY, she loves to start new knitting projects, but rarely remembers to finish them. Leigh can be found online at **http://www.twitter.com/HeroicLeigh**.

Victor H. Rodriguez is a talent manager, novelist and short story writer. He's been a scriptwriter for HBO and published short fiction with Murder of Storytellers, Jaded Books and White Wolf. He also has short stories in the upcoming anthologies Tales of the Once and Future King from Superversive SF, and Hyperion and Theia from Radiant Crown.

Bethany C. Gotschall is a writer and illustrator based in Cleveland, Ohio. Her writing has appeared or is forthcoming in Front Porch Review, Gravel, Short Fiction Break, and Cleveland Art magazine. Trained as an art historian, she also has a background in museum education and interpretation. Find more of her work at **bcgotschall.com**.

Markus Egeler Jones graduated with Eastern Kentucky University's MFA. He is an Assistant Professor in the English Department at Chadron State College in western Nebraska. His first novel, *How the Butcher Bird Finds Her Voice*, will be published by Five Oaks Press in 2017. His short fiction appears in *Crab Fat Magazine, The Story Shack, The Windward Review, Temenos, The Wild Word, The New Mexico Review* among others. Currently he is working on *Postworld,* a post-apocalyptic novel set in the Gothic south.

Jeremy Megargee was still a child when he picked up his very first *Goosebumps* book by R.L. Stine, and he knew he had fallen head over heels in love with all things horror. It's a love affair that has only grown stronger over the years, a borderline obsession with stories that explore the darkest recesses of the human imagination. He guesses you could say he's like a twisted explorer in that way . . . always stalking down those special stories that have the ability to invoke a creepy-crawly feeling right down to the marrow of his bones.

Jeremy weaves his tales of personal terror from Martinsburg, West Virginia with his cat Lazarus acting as his muse/familiar.

Sergio Palumbo is an Italian public servant who graduated from Law School working in the public real estate branch. He has published a Fantasy Roleplaying illustrated Manual, *WarBlades*, of more than 700 pages. Some of his works and short stories have been published on *American Aphelion Webzine*, *WeirdYear*, *Quantum Muse*, *Antipodean SF*, *Schlock! Webzine*, *SQ Mag*, etc., and in print inside 32 American Horror/Sci-fi/Fantasy/Steampunk Anthologies, 52 British Horror/Sci-Fi Anthologies, 2 Urban Fantasy/Horror Canadian Anthologies and 1 Sci-Fi Australian Anthology by various publishers, and 16 more to follow in 2017/2018.

ABOUT THE EDITOR

C.P. Dunphey is an author, editor, Lovecraftian scholar, and the founder of Gehenna & Hinnom Books. He has edited thousands of stories for authors, novels, and collections, both mainstream and independent while also publishing work of his own. His science fiction/horror novel *Plane Walker* was published in 2016 and was met with critical and commercial success, going as far as being nominated for several awards. Dunphey is the editor-in-chief of Gehenna & Hinnom, helming both the anthologies released by the company and the bi-annual magazine *Hinnom Magazine*. When he isn't tirelessly steamrolling through editing, Dunphey can be found at his home in Hattiesburg, Mississippi with his beautiful pit-bull Ripley Ellen, a book and movie shelf that holds all his secrets, and an insatiable thirst for everything horrific and imaginative.

If you enjoyed the *Year's Best Transhuman SF 2017 Anthology*, make sure to leave a review on Amazon and follow us on social media!

Facebook:
www.facebook.com/gehennaandhinnombooks
Twitter: www.twitter.com/GehennaBooks
Website: www.gehennaandhinnom.wordpress.com

Look out for our new releases in 2017!

June 30th, 2017

Hinnom Magazine Issue 001

August 31st, 2017

Hinnom Magazine Issue 002

September 30th, 2017

Year's Best Body Horror 2017 Anthology

October 31st, 2017

Hinnom Magazine Issue 003

November 30th, 2017

Year's Best Transhuman SF 2017 Anthology

December 31st, 2017

Hinnom Magazine Issue 004